ALEBRIJES

ALEBRIJES

Donna Barba Higuera

LQ

LEVINE QUERIDO

MONTCLAIR | AMSTERDAM | HOBOKEN

This is an Arthur A. Levine book
Published by Levine Querido

LQ

www.levinequerido.com · info@levinequerido.com
Levine Querido is distributed by Chronicle Books, LLC
Text copyright © 2023 by Donna Barba Higuera
Illustrations copyright © 2023 by David Álvarez
Library of Congress Control Number: 2023931659
ISBN 978-1-64614-263-7
Printed and bound in China

Published in October 2023
FIRST PRINTING

For Mark

As long as we have each other's hands on this journey, a muddy bunker
would still hold all the magic and laughter in the world.

THE OUTLANDS

E **N** **S** **W**

POCATEL RIDGE

THE TRENCH

OLD-WORLD HIGHWAY

WYRMFIELD

EXILE TRAIL

THE MARKET

TRENCH BRIDGE

THE ORPHANAGE

OLD MINES

ORCHARD

THE DUNG HEAPS

THE POX

THE PAPA FIELDS

THE DEAD FOREST

THE TREE OF SOULS

POCATEL MAIN STREET

POCATEL

OLD MINES

THIS IS THE STORY AS IT WAS TOLD
TO ME BY LEANDRO THE MIGHTY.

I

...（...

A WYRM'S SHRIEK PIERCES THE AIR. SOON THEIR heads will break the earth's surface to hunt through the night. They will slither across Pocatel Valley stirring up dust and killer spores in their wake. A second screech answers the first. I wait for the echo to hit the valley and bounce back. *Uno . . . dos . . . tre*—Pinpricks run over my bald head. This wyrm is barely a thin candle's burn from the city's border. I make sure our pock door is cinched tight.

Tía Lula turns her head away. With her wrinkled hand, she slips one of the sharp metal wings out of her tool, slicing off a piece of the hongo. She slides it under her tongue. Her shoulders relax and she breathes deep. Gabi and I both take a deep breath too. Within minutes, the angry lines on her face grow smooth, and she lies down on her bedroll.

Lula's pock is filthy and stinks like a rotted mouse, but pickpocketing for her at the market keeps me and Gabi out of their orphanage. Lula might be cruel, but without her, we know what the Pocatelans do to Cascabel orphans like us. We might be missing a kidney or two. We choose Lula for now.

Eyes closed, Lula speaks softly to no one. "Aw, yes. Hermoso. It's good work, mija. You will make an excellent weaver. A talented Cascabel." And I know her mind has already gone to another place, another time.

Gabi leans toward Lula and carefully pushes the hongo under her bed to make sure it's hidden. Her snores start to rattle our pock like a desert thunderstorm. I pull Gabi back quickly. She'd get a beating from waking her, for sure. But not as bad as what would happen if the Pocatelan Regime found hongo in our home. When we first arrived to Pocatel, Tía Lula would push her long, gray hair in front of her face, trying to hide what she took before sleep. But less than a winter after we arrived, Pocatel's Directors ordered, "All Pox dwellers must shave their lice-infested heads." One more way to set us apart.

The wyrm shrieks again. *Uno, dos, tres, cuatro, cinco* . . .

With the echo moving farther away, I blow out the candle. I make sure the pock door is as tight as I can get it. We are far from the Trench that protects us from the wyrmfield, but our pocks are not much help against the airborne spores they create during their hunts.

I take Gabi's hand and begin to hum like our mother did for me.

"H*mmm, hmmm, hmmm, hmmmm.*"

Then, just like a real cascabel, I rattle my tongue. "*Tccch, tccch, tccch, tchhh.*"

Gabi closes her eyes, and the corners of her mouth turn up in a soft smile.

I smile too and continue humming softly, almost a whisper: "H*mmm, hmmm, hmmm, hmmm . . .*"

Gabi's breaths deepen. Now that she's asleep, I can too. I dream of the day—the day very soon—when we will escape from this place.

THE BELL ON the old church building chimes three times. Someone was exiled the night before. They only banish at night, when the wyrms are out hunting. I think of the monster's shrieks. Maybe whoever it was made it out of Pocatel Valley and over the ridge? The only reason the Cascabeles made it inside the city years ago was the sun above—and ignorance of the danger that lay under our feet as we passed through the valley. Even if we left by day, when the wyrms don't hunt, between the Pocatelan guards, the walled-in city, and the Trench . . . impossible. Still, one day soon.

Gabi and I sit up, but Tía Lula sleeps through the bell's final echo. She may be one of the elder Cascabel, but she's nothing like the elders we used to know. Wise, hard-working . . . we've lost so many of them these past few years. Because Gabi and I work, she will sleep as long as she likes and eat the food we return with.

Eyes half-closed, Gabi and I pull out our tooth scrapers to clean our teeth. We roll up our beds. Gabi stacks her bedroll on top of mine, as I clear the pock of any other sign of us. The less Tía Lula is reminded we exist, the better. I stand and hold out my hand to help Gabi up. She loses her balance. It's happening more and more lately. Normally after Tía Lula's made Gabi practice Serpientes de Cascabel much longer than usual. We have to earn more food today.

Gabi unties the door.

Tía Lula turns over and makes a gurgled cough. "Can't you cabritos be more quiet?" she yells, vibrating the air as I tiptoe past her bedroll.

Like ghosts, I see others are also exiting their pocks outside. Together we all walk toward the edge of the Pox toward the potato fields. Even with more exiles than usual, lately the Regime has been cutting the field workers' rations more and more. Yesterday, Gabi didn't earn a single papa, and Tía Lula ate most of the two I'd earned.

We exit the Pox onto the main street of Pocatel. In the distance to the south, I catch sight of the strips of cloth and hair tied to the Tree of Souls, fluttering like leaves in the wind. In the opposite direction, where the Patrol guards the north side of town, Pocatelans are leaving their homes for the day. Children in dark brown school robes walk toward a long brick building. Their mothers wave to them as they disappear inside.

A little boy with hair the color of corn screams at his mother. "I don't want to go!"

She grips his elbow and leads him *gently* toward the school, as others watch.

Gabi snickers. "Estúpido. Maybe he wants to trade places."

"Shhh," I say, trying not to laugh. I try to imagine any of those Pocatelan kids anywhere near the dung and potato fields.

The smell of burning charcoal and woodsmoke from a smelter begins to fill the air. The smoke's haze drifts across the main road of Pocatel. Soon, the *clink . . . clink . . . clink . . .* of hammering will echo through the valley all day long.

I stare down the center of town where they hold the markets. The women are already disappearing back inside clean homes made of stone and brick. I've heard they just weave cloth and knead potato bread until their husbands and children return. On the porch of one of the largest homes, two women sit in real chairs. Even from a distance, the deep pigment of their robes tells me these aren't the kind of Pocatelan women who knead bread or weave cloth. A man in a deep green robe walks from this home. The flash of a Director's badge reflects in the sun.

The man kisses one of the women on the cheek as he passes. She leans toward the other woman, saying something. Her laugh echoes down the street. I recognize it as the same laugh Tía Lula makes when she's pretending to make friends and be funny.

A guard walks slowly down the center of the street that divides our side of town from theirs. There is no wall. But the invisible barrier separating our side of town from the Pocatelans' homes may as well be a thick sheet of Pocatelan bronze. Apart from market days—when we are permitted to cross over for at least a little while—we would never dare enter into their section.

Gabi and I and the other Cascabeles walk in the opposite direction. As we near the fields, the smell of woodsmoke and baking bread is overtaken by the reek of dung.

I glance back. Maybe in a few generations, it will be different. Maybe our descendants will wear Pocatelan robes instead of tunics? They tell us to be grateful for the food their Regime gives us to survive. For saving us from certain death. But for now, Cascabeles are the ones who work the fields, to earn rotting scraps of what's left after they've eaten. So who relies on who? Who saves who?

We turn into the fields. I tell myself not to, but I'm close enough to see a long, rust-colored strip of cloth on the Tree of Souls that wasn't there before. It droops off a limb like the tail of a dead lizard. It must be the heavy fabric of someone rich's robe—not a strip of thin tunic.

The heavy fabric, we don't see as often. We aren't welcome in their death ceremonies, but tying the cloth for protection against unrested, angry souls has become our tradition here too. I've yet to see one of those wandering spirits in the trees beyond the Dead Forest. I'm either too far away, or, like the wyrms, they only come out when the sun goes down.

Gabi grabs my elbow just before I slam into one of the Patrol. "Cuidado, Leandro."

But the guard doesn't even look at me as he continues on his march along the edge of the fields. Once we're all lined in order at the ends of our rows—nearly a hundred Cascabel workers—the Patrol closes off the entrance to the papa fields, trapping us in for the day.

The Field Director oversees us all from his watch tower. His Director badge, a bronze dung beetle, gleams against his soil-brown robe. Every so often, the sun catches it, and it pierces my eyes.

The Field Director blows his whistle.

I pull my tunic up to my thighs and kneel, my knees sinking into the soil. The wilted leaves of the potato plants mean they're ready. I sink my arm up to my elbow in the soil and pull up the plant. One larger potato and several smaller ones tumble out. I place them in my bin and move to the next plant. I even dig where there are no longer plants, hoping to find one left behind.

Most work with their back to the sun. I face the other direction, so I can keep an eye on Gabi. Just like every day, I'm assigned to work beside Franco. One side of his upper lip lifts in a sneer and he spits on the ground between us. I look away. Behind Franco is Ari, a girl older than me who lives a few pocks from ours. She works a lot quicker since her parents died—I'm sure to stay out of the orphanage. I would do the same. Behind and half a row of unpulled plants after Ari, Gabi struggles to pull up a root.

Behind me in the final row is the oldest person in the Pox: Jo. Before we came to Pocatel, we never worked in fields like our ancestors—we foraged off the land, surviving off of what we could find. We worked hard . . . but it was a life. And there were three times our number. I was young and didn't know most of the people, but I do remember Jo. Even then he was ancient.

With his back to all of us, I'm not sure who Jo's speaking to. But just like every day, he begins: "Saben que, one hundred winters ago, my tatara-tatara-abuelo, a great Cascabel scout, discovered La Cuna?"

No one answers. We've all heard this story hundreds of times.

"He walked fifty-four moons with little food and water to bring our ancestors in San Joaquin the news of his great discovery. La Cuna with its river flowing through a cave, enough fish to eat, and water to grow food for all Cascabeles!"

Gabi stops what she's doing and tilts her head up to the sun, smiling. She sniffs the air, like La Cuna's river of fresh water could be just within reach. Even now, she hopes.

Who knows if the Cascabel scout was really Jo's great-great-great-grandfather. But the legend of the Cradle—La Cuna, an eighty-two-day walk to the east and north of San Joaquin—was what sent our ancestors, generations of hopeful people, searching for it.

Now Jo stops between plants and stares off. "Each night our people searched, a new bed by a new fire. We told our stories, we sang, and we danced." He smiles and dimples magically appear, like every time he tells a happy story.

Back in those days, I had this farting-lizard joke I even tried to perfect with some other people we walked with. Turns out farting lizards are only funny to me.

Jo's smile drops now. Without the deep pits in his cheeks, he instantly looks older. "But three winters ago, one bright morning while the wyrms slept, los Cascabeles crossed over a mountain ridge into a valley and found something we hadn't seen for centuries. Other humans." His shoulders hunch as he pushes his hand slowly back under the soil. "Before we knew what we'd done . . ."

His story trails off like it always does. I'm glad he doesn't say aloud the next part. How before we knew what we'd done, we were trapped. If a Patrol heard someone complain like this—or try to convince others to escape—it could get them exiled. They want us to be grateful that they keep us safe from dangers that lie outside Pocatel. We'd had a hard winter, we were starving, and we accepted their food. They say we should be grateful to pay off that debt. We might have made it inside the city by luck, but the chances now of surviving exile outside . . .

For hours more we dig, all the time Jo rambling in his slow, raspy voice. "Did you know there was once an animal, una rana, that could lie frozen, no breath, for an entire season? In the spring it would thaw and hop to life. It lived in a place called Ala . . . Alas . . ." He trails off.

Gabi stops digging for a moment and glares at him. "No, Jo! ¡Dónde! You can't leave it there. You've never told this story! Where did the rana live?"

I can't help laughing. Luckily, the guard for our field is at the opposite end.

Jo turns to Gabi and shrugs like he has no idea what she's talking about. "You seem angry, niña. I know what will help. Did you know our ancestors, the oilfield workers in San Joaquin, used rowboats to paddle through lakes of black oil when they discovered it?"

"That can't be true," Gabi scoffs, then digs her arms back into the ground. And we will never know if the ice frog was real, and if it was, where it lived in the Old-World.

"Long after the machines that required the black oil . . . new machines, airships, took men across the world in a day," Jo continues. "With a pail of water for energy!" He waves an arm in the air. "That one bucket . . . enough energy to travel to the moon."

"¡Tonterías!" Franco calls out. His wife, Naji, squeals out a laugh like a dying animal.

Jo's smile falls, and he lowers his arm back into the soil.

"You really think so?" I ask Jo softly.

"No miento." Jo shrugs, embarrassed. "It's as it was told to me."

As Ari passes him to dump her potatoes, she goes out of her way by many rows to pat his shoulder. "I believe you, Jo."

"¡Otro!" Gabi calls out to him.

Jo smiles. "Fine, fine." He clears his throat and raises his voice once more. "Once, people all over the world could speak to one another in an instant. You could look on a tiny glass"—he makes a small square with his hands—"and see the face, hear the voice of another, on the other side of the planet!"

Gabi and I exchange a smile. She shakes her head and rolls her eyes. Even we know some things just couldn't be real.

"Y como me lo contaron te lo cuento," Jo says.

I think of how our people barely survived living deep in the earth. How the first Pocatelans survived inside their abandoned copper mines. "Do you think they're still out there? People on the other side of the world?" I ask him.

But Jo doesn't answer this time, already back to picking papas, his mind now elsewhere. I see the guard start making his way back to us, and I go back to work.

When the sun is overhead, the others turn in the opposite direction, facing away from the sun. But I stay where I am, glare beating my face, to keep an eye on Gabi. Bin after bin, I dump potatoes into my pile at the end of the row. By the time the sun sets, hopefully I will have earned one or two to take home with us. The smallest potatoes with the most eyes go in a second pile. Each time I pull up the dead plant, I set in its place one of the seed potatoes and fill in the hole.

"Grow, grow, little semilla," I whisper, speaking life into each one, leaving the dead plant on top where it will feed its child and bring more papa plants soon.

On the far side of the field, I see some Pocatelans finally arriving to their work in the orchard. They climb ladders to pick the ripe, brightly colored fruit off trees. This food, only the

Directors and their families are allowed to eat. And those picking are the lowest of the Pocatelans—who hope that because of us, they'll never have to work on their knees in the papa fields again.

Behind the rare fruit trees, the dark entrances to the old mines of their ancestors dot the hillside.

The guards don't bother watching these Pocatelans working in the orchard, and I wonder if it's because those people have had a lifetime of knowing what would happen if they stole. Still, do they ever sneak to eat the fruit? Even a rotten piece?

A young woman in a brown dress, under a tree with yellow fruit, stares at us. I stare back, until a guard blocks my view. Does the Patrol circling the fields keep us away from the fruit trees? Or from the Pocatelans who work there? The next time I look up, the girl has her head down and she is being reprimanded by a man wearing a straw hat.

I laugh as behind them, two Pocetalan workers hold the base of the ladder in place while a man carefully climbs. I used to scale piñons with only my toes, ankles, and arms for anchors. I close my eyes and lift my head toward the setting sun, just like I did at the top of those trees, breathing in the smell of their needles. With warm sun on my face, and its glow through my eyelids, for just a moment, I'm back in the trees, foraging with my people. I'm on top of the world and I am free—

A dark shadow falls over the golden glow. I open my eyes.

The Field Director is standing over me.

2

· · · (· · ·

THE DIRECTOR LIFTS HIS HAT AND WIPES SWEAT OFF
his brow. His slow movements don't match the sharp, quick
words of his Pocatelan accent. "Leo, is it not?"

I quickly look down, pressing soil over a new planting. I nod
and don't correct him on my name.

When I glance up, he's scanning my row of replanting. He
bends down. Now, we're eye to eye. But he is not looking at me.
He is looking at my work.

I can't look away from his Director's badge: the beetle, symbol of Pocatel. The bronze body of his badge is round, its pincers short. The stag coins they use for trade at market are always faded and worn; this one hasn't lost a detail.

"You are a good worker," the Director says. "But, closed eyes lose sight."

Like most of the strange words the Pocatelans speak, this phrase makes no sense. A young guard with a pointed nose approaches and stands next to him, a smirk on his face.

"This work is in their genes." The Field Director waves his arm like the puppeteer does at market before a show, presenting his soulless performers made of wood and string. "It is what they were meant to do."

"Yes, sir. It is a great kindness that we give them work best suited for them." I see the young guard glance in Gabi's direction.

I can hear my own teeth gritting. Never mind she's just a little girl. Never mind we hunted and foraged across thousands of kilometers, for a hundred winters, carrying our people into the future. But yes, they know what's best for Cascabeles now.

"I am sure you agree, don't you, Leo?"

I don't look up and begin digging under the next plant. "Sí, señor."

The Director's boots don't move.

I continue digging. "Thank you . . . sir."

Finally, he moves down the row, but the younger guard remains.

Just like the Field Director, the young guard kneels. His forearm rests on his raised knee. His hand trembles, and he clenches it still. I recognize the scars lining the tops of his fingers of someone who once worked the fields. But he keeps his voice low enough, where only those around us can hear. "Daydreaming?" he hisses. Then he closes his eyes, mocking me. "Blind and sniffing at the air, just like a snake."

When I look up fully, he is staring me dead in the eye. But unlike the Field Director, there is something strange behind his look. Something I can't quite place. He knows I am flesh and blood. He just loathes us. Maybe . . . maybe we represent something he wants to forget.

Maybe he hopes his nice clothes and nonsense words will help him one day take the Director's job.

"Your people want to be serpents," he continues. "And look at you. So natural. You were meant to slither in the dirt, were you not, little boy? The eyes of snakes speak evil—best to keep them underfoot, where they cannot whisper to those who seek purity."

I know better than to look him in the eye now. It would be better if he thought I was made of wood and paint and string. My nostrils flare as I grit my teeth. I lift my eyes just enough to look behind him. Franco is snickering. Behind him, Ari shakes her head at me. Gabi stares, eyes wide.

I swallow and look back down. I set a small seed potato in my second pile. "Yes. Here you go." I force a smile and nod, lifting the biggest potato out to him, pretending I don't understand.

He scoffs and knocks it out of my hand, standing. Then he plants one heel down and turns, kicking soil back at me as he walks away.

I wipe dirt off my mouth and let out a breath. Ari and Gabi stare at me as we go back to work.

When the Old-World ended, our ancestors might've dug into San Joaquin's hills like snakes to survive. But the Pocatelan miners and their families crawled into their copper mines just like beetles in dung heaps. They're no better than us.

When I lift the next plant, strange black spots cover one leaf that's still green. "¿Eh?"

I must have hummed the word aloud, because Ari turns to look at me. I lift the plant up for her to see, and shrug. I saw some spotted leaves last week before the plants went limp. But this is the third plant with rotten potatoes today. Ari's eyes widen. She glances around to see if anyone is watching. She waits until a guard passes, then moves quickly without calling attention to herself.

"Give it to me," she whispers. "No digas nada. And make sure Gabi only has good ones too." She drops a healthy potato into my bin and scrambles back to her row, dropping the plant with its rot to the soil along the way.

I lift the next plant and luckily it's heavy with potatoes. One large one with no rot falls back into the hole. I hurry to reach down.

But Franco has seen and is already leaning into my row. He pushes his hand under the soil. His hand hits mine, and he yanks the potato away from me, along with two others.

I throw a fistful of dirt at him. "¡Oye!"

"¡Cállate!" he barks back. "Or I'll burn your pock tonight while you all sleep."

I fall back onto my knees and drop the dirt from my fist. He could easily do it. Pocks burn all the time. One candle too close to the shell: gone in seconds. No one would know what he'd done.

But if he's caught stealing, he'll be exiled on the spot. He knows I won't turn him in, though.

"Pendejo," I murmur.

Franco sucks his front tooth and lifts his chin. "That's all you got, chaparrito?" He laughs and stands. The sun is nearing the horizon, and now he has plenty to feed him and Naji. He leaves, dumping his final bin, and goes to wait in line for his rations.

I glance over at my pile and move to the next plant. I lean out to see Gabi's pile is again one of the smallest.

The sun hits the horizon. My heart speeds, and just like every day, I scramble to pull up a few more plants.

The guard's whistle pierces the air.

I'm not the only one who's grasping for a few last papas while the guards get busy handing out rations.

Ari stands to leave. She stares straight ahead as she drops three healthy papas into Gabi's bin as she passes. Gabi doesn't even notice. I do. It'll still be close.

As Ari dumps her remaining potatoes into a pile at the end of her row, she waits for a guard to approach. She might have enough for two, even three.

"Gabriela, ven acá," I whisper loudly, motioning for her to come over.

Gabi picks up her bin and hurries toward me, falling once on the way. "I don't feel so good again, Leandro. I did my best."

Her face is pale, and her lips are purple. If only she could eat a few from the bin she's holding. While the guard is inspecting Ari's pile, I search Gabi's bin and find two rotten papas near the bottom. I hurry to toss them out, like Ari said, and I dump half of my bin into Gabi's.

There are others worse off. I look around. Jo's hunched over, struggling to lift his bin that's barely half-full. A woman as thin as Gabi trips and her potatoes roll from the bin. A few help, but a young girl scoops up several and puts them in her own bin, handing only one back for show as a guard passes.

There's a kind of Cascabel who seems to get banished first. The weakest are the ones who suddenly commit a crime of exile, or so the Pocatelans say. And the Cascabeles who look to be near death anyway? They're the same people the Regime claims die from wyrmspore—not starvation.

Jo passes behind us and stops, turning with a smile. "Long ago mi papi had a wagon. He named his wagon Enrique, and just today he's given it to me."

I look over at Jo's pile. He has four rotten ones right on top. What is happening? My heart speeds, and I block him before he can leave.

I dump ten or so papas into his bin. I bend down and pretend to arrange them, plucking out the decomposing papas. So many more than I've ever seen. "Puedes llevar estas por mí, Jo. Estoy cansado." I don't even know if this will be enough to help him.

"Por supuesto," he says. "I am happy to carry them for you. I'm tired too, but I now have a wagon, so I will do you this favor, young man."

Jo shuffles away. Maybe with those healthy papas, he has a few more days.

"Leandro, you shouldn't do that," Gabi says. "What if we don't have enough—"

"I've earned at least one," I point to her bin. "And don't you see that others have done the same for you?"

Gabi lowers her head. I put my hand on her shoulder and squeeze. We walk to the end of our rows, and stop to drink from the trough. It's nearly empty. I cup my hand and lift the green water to my mouth.

A row beyond Gabi's is a pile of potatoes even smaller than hers, and I can see from here that many are rotted there too. The man with sunken cheeks dumps only a few more on top. Even if we gave him all we had, it still wouldn't get him the number he needs.

Jo is already at the edge of the fields, at the guard's recording table. The guard looks at the pile at the end of Jo's row, then in his basket. He marks a black hashmark on Jo's hand with a wood ember. Jo nods and walks toward the ration line.

He smiles back a toothless grin at us and yells as he leaves toward the Pox. He holds up one large potato. "Come see me, chaparrito! I will introduce you to Enrique!"

I sigh, but Gabi snickers. At least Franco's already gone, and didn't hear Jo call me the wrong name.

We wait for our turn in line with the others. The Director approaches, and the guard steps back and stands tall, making way for him.

"Cabeza en alto," I whisper to Gabi.

Gabi lifts her head, but her body still slumps. Next in line, we step up and set our bins on his table.

The Director stares down at Gabi's small pile. "How many in your family?"

Gabi holds up three fingers.

"Barely enough," he sighs. "Next time, work harder." He marks two black lines on her hand and motions for her to go to the ration line. She bites her lips together to hide her smile and stares at me with wide eyes.

The Director turns to me and his brow furrows. "Interesting. Your pile is not as large as I would have expected."

I shrug.

He stares at me, and I look away. I feel him pull the ember twice onto the top of my hand.

"Move along," he says.

I nod thanks and pull Gabi along with me.

As we walk away, Gabi looks up at me, her eyes filled with tears, and smiles. "Leandro, I got two!" she says.

But without what Ari gave her, she'd be walking back to the pock with one hand empty.

"Good job," I say, forcing a smile.

As we wait in line to receive our rations, we hear the Field Director's voice echoing across the field.

"You are nowhere near the quota." He holds up a papa that is nearly completely black and pitted. "What is this?" He tosses it onto the ground. "How many in your family?"

I look back; the man with the sunken cheeks stands in front of the Director and two Patrol. His knuckles are white as he grips the table to stay standing.

"Only me and a child. I was sure I'd picked enough."

I want to yell back to him. To tell him it's safer not to speak at all.

"Hold the line!" the Director calls toward the ration line. "Are you saying someone here stole?" He turns back to the man. "You must tell us immediately who this thief is."

This is where the man should try to walk away with nothing. He looks from side to side. He knows as well as we do "the price of stealing." He doesn't even look at those of us left standing in line to leave. "No, no. I did not say—"

"So, *you* are lying." The Director stares down at the man, who is now using both hands on the table to hold himself up. The Director must see what we all do. The man soon won't be able to work at all.

"I . . . I . . ." he says. "No one stole. And I did not—"

"Immorality is immorality is immorality," the Director says loudly. "Lying is also punishable by Banishment." He glances over at me, then looks outside the gate toward Jo, who's already nearing the Pox. Does he know what I did? But all he does is nod to the guards.

Within moments, the man is being dragged down the main street to the Center of Banishment. He will not be in the fields tomorrow. No one speaks.

We don't look up as a guard places two potatoes into my hands and two into Gabi's.

I link my elbow through Gabi's, and at last we walk away quickly, not looking back.

There will come a time when it's between Jo and me. When one of us will have the smallest pile. Will I give Jo papas then? Will someone help me?

EVEN WHEN WE'RE out of the fields, Gabi and I keep our elbows locked. My arms shake, feeling like I still hold the bin, but I won't let go until we're safe in our pock. I try to still my shaking, and I realize Gabi is trembling too.

The squawk of a Pocatelan child's flute echoes down the street, followed by laughter.

Even from this distance, I can see the lanternlight falling from inside their safe stone homes. Homes that survived the end, with thick walls and this valley to protect them. The houses lining the center of town belong to the wealthiest and most powerful: the Directors. But over three hundred more lie behind those, to the east and west. Light pours onto Pocatel's main street from the largest windows.

Even as we near the Pox, Gabi's shaking doesn't stop. So I nudge her with my elbow. "I heard a joke today," I say.

Gabi rolls her eyes. "No, you didn't."

"Yes, I did."

"Is it a farting lizard joke?"

"I'll try not to be hurt by that."

"Okay, who told you the joke?"

I bite my lip. "Uhh. It's a secret."

"You said we don't keep secrets."

"Shhh. I'm trying to tell you now." I clear my throat. "So, a Cascabel walks up to Pocatel's Field Director." I pretend to hold out a potato. "Here, señor, I have your papa."

Gabi leans over, looking at me, one side of her mouth turned up in a smile.

"Then the Director says"—I pull my chin in to make my voice deep—"what do you mean, kind sir? My father has been dead for two yeeears."

Gabi snorts. "That is the stupidest joke I've ever heard, Leandro."

She's right. It's stupid.

But we're no longer shaking.

Bitter smoke from campfires in the Pox starts to burn my eyes and hurt my nose as we walk in. Close to home, we slow. Gabi unlinks our arms and brushes the dirt off her potatoes. She holds one of them out to me and smiles. "They gave me two! This is a good one."

The smell of potatoes cooked over the fire makes my mouth water. But outside our pock ahead, there is no fire. I step in front of Gabi and set our papas on the ground. I lick my fingers and wipe off one of the black lines from her hand.

"Ewww," she says.

"Shhh." I pick our potatoes back up and hand her one. "Hurry," I say, taking Gabi's best potato. I approach the woman I've traded with before. She doesn't give any favors, but I also know she won't tell Lula. Within a moment, I've traded the large potato for one that's smaller but already cooked. She nods and tosses the uncooked potato onto the cinders. We walk away. It burns my fingers as I break it in half. Steam drifts upward, and I hurry to blow. I hand Gabi's piece to her.

"Pero, Leandro . . ."

I glance in the direction of our pock. "Don't talk. Hurry and eat."

She bites into it, sucking in air to cool it down. She chews quickly. When she's done, I hand her the other half.

"Gracias," she whispers. She stares up at me, her chin trembling. "This is the best papa I've ever eaten."

I tilt my head. "Really?"

"No," she laughs, and her face lights up. "I just wanted the potato to feel like I was *rooting* for it."

I sigh. "That was awful."

She laughs. "You aren't the only one with stupid potato jokes."

From somewhere on the far side of the Pox, the humming of the "Canción de los Cascabeles" begins with one small voice. Gabi and I smile at one another. It's been a while since we heard the song. We used to sing it on nights by the camp fire, out there in the world, but I'm not sure if she was old enough then to remember.

Hmmm, hmmm, hmmm, hmmmm.
Tccch, tccch, tccch, tchhh.

One voice joins, then another, until the words ring throughout.

Juntos buscamos La Cuna . . .

Hidden inside pocks, other voices join. We know the Pocatelans can't catch us all at once this way.

Por ahora, vivimos con la tierra,
un día muramos en la tierra.

Nuestros espíritus volarán con los ancestros
Convertiremos en el camino de las estrellas.

Hmmm, hmmm, hmmm, hmmm.
Tccch, tccch, tccch, tchhh.

Juntos buscamos La Cuna . . .

Por ahora las serpientes cavamos en la tierra,
Y traemos nueva vida al suelo.

¡Y luchar para traer vida nueva al mundo,
Las Serpientes de Cascabel volverán a triumfar!
Hmmm, hmmm, hmmm, hmmm.
Tccch, tccch, tccch, tchhh.

If they bothered to learn our language like we learned theirs, might they be more worried by this song of our people, and our resilience? Written so long ago, just after the world ended.

Hmmm, hmmm, hmmm, hmmm.
Tccch, tccch, tccch, tchhh.

By the time the song is over, every pock is lit, and most have already eaten and are resting inside. Gabi swallows the final bite, and we head towards Tía Lula again.

We pass by a pock. A woman weeps inside. Is she crying for a lost child? A partner? Maybe just remembering la familia perdío.

From high above, I think to myself that we must look like a cluster of stars. And if the song of our ancestors is true, one day, the Cascabeles will rise again, just like we did after the end of the world. The Pocatelans will no longer control us and be able to use us to help them survive.

But tomorrow, once again, Franco will call me names and steal my papas. And he will be right. Once again, I will be too small to fight back. Soon, what I pick won't be enough to save Gabi or Jo or myself.

Gabi's hand slips into mine. "What are you thinking?"

"Just of another great joke I will tell you later," I say, lying.

I won't let you have the smallest pile, Gabi. I'll find a way to get us out of this valley sooner than we planned, even if it means leaving our own people.

Soon, we will be free.

3

···❨···

TÍA LULA GLANCES AT OUR HANDS AS WE WALK IN, THEN
snatches the remaining three potatoes the second we enter the
pock. "Gaaah," she grunts. "If I could still work, I'd return with
three all by myself."

Gabi and I exchange a glance and duck outside, scouring the
ground outside to find Lula kindling. When we return, she
builds a small fire just outside the door and tosses the potatoes

on top, without waiting for embers. They'll be cooked, but scorched. We roll out our bedrolls and collapse.

I lean against an arched wooden beam of the pock and stretch out my legs. My feet still don't reach the furrow I carved in the dirt last season down the middle of our tiny home.

Gabi snickers. "You still haven't grown, Leandro."

I push out my toes further and Gabi laughs.

In the fading light, I stare out the pock's door toward the cage of mountains surrounding us. Its dry hillside is covered in the shadowed spines of dead trees. Pines. Each tree is the height of sixteen men. I know that green needles once covered their branches. Now, their thin, gray trunks lean on their neighbor's shoulder like they've fallen asleep. But for every fifty dead trees, one grows upward, green at its top. The dead world, trying to return to life.

I think of the open fields and pine trees in the world outside, before we got here. I was the only one small enough—and loco enough—to climb to the trees' tops to gather pinecones for nuts. Filling large pockets they'd stitched inside my tunic, I always pretended it was harder than it was to gather the small cones, so I could sit in the trees, hidden in the branches, dreaming of Old-World and sniffing green needles. The smell of pine so strong, it was the one thing in this world I had to myself. Dark sap clung under my nails. I'd scrape it out, my fingers sticking together. Alone, I'd stretch out my arms and stare up at the open sky, higher and taller than any human on the planet.

Now, in this new world of Pocatel, I'm too little to do any-thing. Like Franco said. Chaparrito. I can't even reach my feet halfway across a tiny pock. And my pockets contain only dirt.

Tía Lula turns away, but she can't hide the *pffft pffft* of her slicing hongo. So many of our people now downing it each night, "to kill the pesadillas." As bad as things may get, I hope I'll never use it. I see how it dulls the eyes.

Lula jams her knife under her bedroll and turns back to us. She sniffs the air like los ratas by the Trench.

Lula licks her finger and holds it out the door. "The air will be frío and thick tonight." She pulls the blackened potatoes off the fire and cinches the door shut. She lights a candle and tilts it toward her chin. Her face glows, and she squints, the right side of her mouth turning up. We know what comes next. She'll tell me and Gabi something to make us as afraid of the night as she is.

She lowers her voice to a whisper. "They say when the world broke, the monsters deep in its belly returned to the surface. The cold nights still remind them of their icy home, deep within the earth." She points her crooked finger at Gabi, then me. "Those are the nights they come to hunt for skinny cabritos," she cackles.

I nudge Gabi, and we jump back, widening our eyes and pre-tending to be scared. Gabi even adds a gasp. Tía Lula's not so dif-ferent from the Field Director. Knowing she has power over us is the only thing that will make her stop.

But we don't need her story to make the wyrms any scar-ier. Cold or hot, the wyrms still come, circling the Trench surrounding the city at night to hunt, and snatching the unlucky of the recently banished. We've heard too many tales of people who've seen wyrms devouring those exiled. The first season we arrived, the wyrms were so active, they stirred up enough spores to send the bodies of one of four Pox dwellers to the Dead Forest. Skin and bones, our peoples' bodies were carted out of the Pox south past the Tree of Souls. To me, it looked like they would have starved to death soon anyway.

Tía Lula kicks her bedroll and her hidden stash of stags clank together. She pulls out her pouch and narrows her eyes at us. She shakes the bag, checking its weight. She lifts a single bronze beetle out and kisses it.

Gabi nudges me when Lula's not looking, moving her arms and feet like a beetle and making a tiny scream.

Lula turns back and Gabi innocently pretends to tap her foot, smiling at Lula.

We shouldn't even know what their money looks like, let alone possess it. But thanks to Gabi and I, Lula probably has more than a few Pocatelans. But what Lula doesn't know is that just like the potato, we've kept some pickpocketed stags for ourselves over the past few years, hidden in a place she will never look.

Lula breathes deeply and is overtaken by a drum of wet coughs. When she speaks again, her words are strained. "One more good season at market, and I will leave this place."

"To where?" I ask, knowing better than to pat her back like I would for Gabi.

"Soon, I will buy a nice stone casita where I can grow my hair out and get me a new, thick robe—maybe a deep purple." Tía Lula pulls on her tunic. Her wrinkled, brown skin shows through the pale, shredded twine.

I shake my head. How can a Cascabel think of spending her days inside a stone house, living off the work of others? Like the rattlesnakes we are named for, Cascabeles were meant to live and survive in nature—for each other. Even someone so old has forgotten who we really are.

"Us too?" Gabi asks.

"Por supuesto," she answers. "You can live outside in my yard."

Gabi and I glance at each other. I roll my eyes and mouth, *Oh, gracias.*

Gabi bites back a smile. She spins her finger next to her head as Tía Lula stares away. "Loca," she whispers.

She's right. No way they'd let someone from San Joaquin buy or live in one of their houses. We might be the only others left in this world, and they aren't living better than we were outside Pocatel—just differently—but inside this valley, they control what we get, and put us inside these thin-skin pocks as some sort of punishment. But what they don't know is that all of us, including the Pocatelans, are trapped in here. They just don't see it. None of them has ever sat on the top of a pine.

Tía Lula pulls out our burnt rations. She crams most of the first half-cooked potato into her mouth, crunching down with the teeth she has left. As she slugs down water, it drips down her chin. She eats most of my potato and all of Gabi's. Then she tosses what's left to us. I break it in half, and Gabi and I shove it into our mouths. Gabi has to stop to catch her breath as she swallows.

"¿Ready, gusano?" Tía Lula says, before Gabi can finish her final bite. "Enough eating," she now barks. "Time to practice."

Gabi slumps. "Now?" she asks, her mouth still full. "We just did it last night."

"Your choice." Tía Lula smirks. "Market day is soon. Dance well and bring me stags, or take your chances and sleep outside tonight."

Gabi sighs and stands, closing her eyes. She rubs her hands over her stubbled head, then down her tattered tunic, like she's a Pocatelan Director dusting off a robe. I laugh and Gabi gives me a weak smile.

Tía Lula clears her throat, then makes a thumping noise from deep inside her gullet. It vibrates the air inside of our Pock. Gabi lifts her fists to her waist and slowly steps forward with one foot, clomping down hard, making her face angry. Dust puffs up in my face; I cough. Slowly, Gabi arcs her bare foot outward, her big toe drawing a line in the dirt in a symbolic C. Serpientes de Cascabel. She coils that first leg around the other. She repeats the move, then begins spinning, holding her tunic out, performing the Cascabel rattlesnake dance that has been handed down since the first tales of how our people survived.

Gabi bows down and waves her arms in front of her, pretending to dig like our people did just before Old-World ended. Instead of panicking like everyone else on the planet, the field workers in the San Joaquin Valley—and even some of the oilfield workers—dug into surrounding mountains and caves, and lived alongside the rattlesnake dens. Gabi flinches, pretending she's been bitten like some of those people were.

There's no way for her to act out the next part . . . the part most don't speak about. How bodies of the dead were eaten by both the snakes and people, after months inside the caves. Instead, she crouches down and shifts her lower half one way, and her upper half the other, pretending to crawl then slither out of the cave like the Cascabeles did. Only to find, the green fields of San Joaquin had turned to dust, all other humans missing or dead, and the rest of the world gone.

Gabi peeks over at me for approval, and I smile and nod to her.

She continues, clomping and spinning like those first Cascabeles, celebrating their survival and saying goodbye to the dead.

Lula smiles too and pushes her tongue through her missing front tooth. "You're almost as good as Tía Lula was at your age."

Tía Lula's not really our aunt, of course. Que suerte for her, finding two orphans to pretend to take in when their mother died. One known for being good at climbing trees and gathering food, ensuring she wouldn't be left behind, by tethering herself to two kids who would do her share of the work. And Tía Lula doesn't really care about the dance—not in the way that we do. She only wants the money the dance will bring her.

I don't remember much about my mother, but I know that she danced the *Cascabel*. She would hold her tunic and spin, telling me it was not a dirty tunic, but to imagine a flowing white dress with ribbons of a rainbow. Or maybe my mind made it up. I no longer see her face. Or her eyes. But I know I would brush her long, wavy hair aside, to rub my finger over the raised rattlesnake heads of the five cascabeles carved up her neck as she sang me to sleep. One snake scar for my dead father. The four others, I will never know.

When the elders held me down to carve my second cascabel the night my mother died, I screamed. But I wasn't wailing from the knife's cuts. When they finished, I only stopped when my throat went raw. That was the day I began foraging, to keep Gabi and me alive.

Tía Lula's neck has so many carved rattlesnakes that she looks like she walked through a forest of thorny branches. I guess even she had parents, siblings, children. As she watches Gabi dance, she reaches up to her neck, rubbing her fingers over two small, intertwined rattlesnakes off to one side. She shakes her head like she needs to wake from a bad dream. These are the nights she takes more hongo than usual.

Gabi makes the rattling noise now, her tongue fluttering against her front teeth, just like Lula taught her. Tía Lula mostly takes and takes, but she's given Gabi one thing—Gabi's the best dancer in the Pox. As she nears the end of the dance, though, Gabi's face grows pale and she wobbles. She's probably burned up all the potato with this one performance. Do her lips seem even darker than normal? I should've given her my other half.

I take her hand and ease her toward her bedroll. "Sientate, Gabi. That's enough."

"But she is not done," Tía Lula growls.

I ignore her and pull Gabi down to rest.

Tía Lula skitters toward me so fast, I barely see her coming. She yanks Gabi away from me and I stand to challenge her. She shoves me back, and I fall on my hip against the wooden frame of the pock.

I don't move, lying there. I'm too small to even fight off an old woman. I glance at Gabi. Her eyes are filling with tears, and she stands back up, her lips definitely blue. She blocks me from Tía Lula's view. She rattles her tongue, picking up where she left off.

If I was bigger, I would fight the people who hurt us. Maybe even fight Franco, and steal some of his food for us. But I'm trapped in this body. We are trapped in here.

A loud wyrmscreech pierces the air. *Uno, d—*

I clutch Gabi's hand and pull her close. I don't care what Lula does to me. But this time, she doesn't care either. We've never heard a wyrm this close. What if the Pocatelans aren't telling us everything? Could they ever jump the Trench?

Gabi freezes too, her stomps and rattles going silent. I realize the distant noises of Pocatel, and the voices, laughter, and the squeaky flute of the Pox, have stopped. Even the buzzing of the bugs outside stills.

The wall of our pock ripples.

"A wyrmstorm," Tía Lula whispers. They may have never broken through the Trench, but this brown fog of spores will take hours to die down.

My hands tremble as I check the pock's door. The wind is stronger than usual. But there's no way to secure the ties any tighter. I watch as dust blows in through the gaps. I glance at Gabi. She already looks like those who die of wyrmspore. I can't let her end up as another snake on my neck.

Tía Lula pulls something from beneath her bedroll. My eyes widen at the flash of color. She ties a blood-red scarf around her face twice. It shines in the candlelight, looking softer than any I've ever seen.

"Tía Lula!" Gabi gasps, reaching out to touch it. "Where did you get that?"

Lula swats her hand. "¡Cállate!"

I clench my teeth tight; pain shoots up my jaw. I can't hit her back.

Gabi and I just stare at each other again. Getting caught with Tía Lula and the bright, stolen cloth could get us banished immediately too. I can't help but scoff.

Lula narrows her eyes at us and points a gnarled brown finger. "Escúchenme, little gusanos. If word of this finds its way outside this pock, I'll throw you into the Trench myself."

She lifts her scarf and blows out the candle. Our pock goes dark. And through a tiny hole in the door, I watch as the lighted domes around us darken one by one, like golden stars snuffed out.

Even in the shadows, my scavenging eyes see Tía Lula reach for more hongo.

I curl up on my bedroll and close my eyes, winding my finger up my scars one at a time.

MY MIND DRIFTS from the quiet of the pock to my memories of the day. The Director and the guard stand over me. I reimagine it playing out with things I wish I *could* have said.

"You are right. I was meant to slither in the dirt!" I yell up at them. "I am proud to be a serpiente! If your insults mean we know how to work, you are right. And you could never be what we are."

The image erupts. I look down and I am holding Gabi's hand. But the Gabi in front of me in this memory is so young. We are marching over the Trench bridge into Pocatel. Gabi's hair blows over her worried face as we cross the windy bridge. "Está bien, Gabi. I have you. I have you."

Then my mind turns to an earlier time. A time long before.

A flash of my mother fills my mind: this time it is her long dark hair in the breeze. She is wearing a long white tunic, her hands at her waist, her belly swollen with a baby. I sit on the ground staring up at her. I feel proud of her, but I am so sad. Others surround us. Elders sit at either side of me. Together, they begin trilling their tongues. "Tccch. Tccch. Tccch." Then the older man on one side stops, creating a deep drumming from his throat. The elder nods for my mother to begin.

My mother sobs and places her fists at her waist. She looks down to her side, and I see him. A man lying motionless, next to a waiting grave. I know him. All these years later, I know I love him.

Even as she arcs her bare foot out—making a C in the dirt—she sobs. She stumbles as she curves one leg around the other.

The elder next to me stands and steadies my mother. He stops his drumming for a moment. "Tú puedes hacerlo," he says, releasing her elbow.

My mother takes a deep breath and stands tall. The elder sits back down, and the drumming and rattling continue. My mother begins spinning, her long hair fanning around her in a blur.

She finishes and collapses next to me. She pulls me into her arms crying softly. She slips one of her hands onto my cheek. "I have you. I have you," she says over and over. Why can't I see her face? My eyes begin to burn. I don't want this man to leave us. Is this real? I don't want to see this. *Stop!*

I open my eyes to see Gabi staring at me.

She pulls my hands from my scar and whispers. "Leandro . . . ?"

I hurry to wipe my face. "It's okay, Gabi. I'm fine. Just a sueño. Go to sleep."

I feel Gabi's hand brush my arm. "Maybe . . . maybe you can tell me about La Cuna?"

I'm not sure if she's asking to hear the story for herself, or if she thinks she is helping me. Tía Lula is breathing deeply now. She snores, the hongo already doing its job.

"Not now." I glare at Tía Lula. I will never let her make me feel small again. "But Gabi, it's time . . . we are leaving."

The whites of Gabi's eyes widen.

I lower my whisper even further. "We just need enough food and water, so we have energy. I think we have enough stags . . . we just need to get a few more. We can travel the wyrmfield by day while they sleep, and be out of Pocatel Valley by dark." Once over the mountains, I can forage again. We won't escape without food, water, or a plan. When we leave, we will be ready.

One sudden wyrmscreech is followed by a response, then they suddenly die away. I think of the man from the fields. The wyrms must've found their meal.

I whisper. "I won't let her hurt you ever again."

Gabi holds my gaze, and I reach out, slipping my hand under her cheek. I wonder what she's thinking. We've talked about escaping before, but she's never really said much.

She closes her eyes and turns away.

I tap her shoulder, but she doesn't turn. "Gabi, I promise you, our life will be better soon."

I turn toward the pock's shell and reach under my bedroll. I pull out my bundle of dry pine needles, slipping one out. It snaps in half when I fold it once, then again, and push it under my nose and breathe deeply.

4

··· ☾ ···

OUR POCK TREMBLES, SOMETHING THUMPING ON ITS
surface. Gabi jumps to my bedroll. The day's first sun pours
through a crack in the tied door.

An angry voice yells, "Open your door!"

Tía Lula sits up and blinks hard, her mouth wide. She unwraps
the red scarf from her face and shoves it under Gabi's bedroll.
My heart thuds like booming thunder in my chest. I try to pull
it out.

Tía Lula grabs my arm and yanks me to her side, pulling her knife from her belongings. She flicks out one of the tool's wing blades and pushes it into my neck, twisting in a circle. I flinch as it slices into my skin a little. My neck burns, and something warm drips onto my shoulder.

She glances at Gabi and whispers into my ear, "Say one word, gusano, I'll make sure you have another serpiente on your neck by the next moon."

I know she means it.

There are two kinds of people from San Joaquin, I know now. Those who remember how we used to live out there in the world, and mourn for what we've lost. And those like Tía Lula, who remember, but think our life in the Pox is temporary and they will get what the Pocatelans have instead—even if it means using their own people or hurting others.

"Cut it open!" the deep voice outside yells.

Tía Lula rubs her thumb up my neck and over the cut she just made. It stings. She lifts her thumb to her mouth and licks off my blood with a smile. "Coming, coming, señor! I am old and move slow."

She throws the knife under her bedroll and pushes her stag pouch deep under the dirt, packing the earth down tight. Then she stands and unties the opening.

Two Pocatelan men wearing the night-blue robes of the Patrol stand in the doorway. A smaller man with long black hair puffs out his chest and grips a gun made of wood and bronze. The entire gun fits in the palm of his hand, but its bronze bullets inside could still blow a hole through my body. He grips it tighter, like he just might.

One man is nearly a head taller than the other. Red slicked-back hair stands out against his dark robe, like a blood sun against the dark mountains. A Director's badge—the large bronze beetle with two huge pincers—sits on his shoulder, its legs hooked through the cloth. His eyes are dark and searching, just like a rat's. I always thought the Field Director was intimidating, but a shiver runs over my skin at this Director who holds no gun, only a long staff. The stained wooden bastón in his grip is covered in pits and gouges, down to raw wood. It's seen a lot of use.

Tía Lula glances at the beetle on the man's shoulder, her grin so fake and wide, I can see her tonsils through the hole of her missing front tooth. Her voice softens like she's talking to a baby: "Bienvenidos, Director. Welcome, welcome. How may I help you, sirs?"

"We are here to search your . . ." El Bastón stares down at the dirt floor, ". . . home."

Tía Lula straightens her back; her mood shifts slightly. "Whachu want with a kind old lady like me?"

El Bastón motions to the younger man.

The gaurd pushes past Tía Lula and moves toward my bedroll. He won't find anything there but dirt and maybe a few old pine needles. But I know Gabi's, with the stolen scarf, will be next. I would throw up if I had food in my stomach. I try to think of a way to distract the men, but I can't move.

The smaller man yanks on his glove and makes sure his hood covers his long hair. I think of the day all Cascabeles were forced to shave our heads. How we all avoided one another's eyes. I want to yell that they are the only lice around here now. He lifts my bedroll between his thumb and finger like it's covered in snot.

He finds nothing and looks up at me. His eyes flick to my bleeding neck. If I was truly a serpiente de cascabel, my tail would be rattling right now.

El Bastón faces Lula. "Is there anything in your dwelling that does not belong to you?"

Tía Lula holds her wrinkled hands at her waist and looks down. "No, señor."

"If so, now is the time to tell us."

I steer Gabi closer to the door. "Por si necesitamos huir," I whisper.

Tía Lula sucks on her front tooth. Fake bravado. I can tell that this time it's she who's scared mierda-less. She glances at the ground where the Patrol is looking, under her bedroll. But he's nowhere near where it's buried, in the exact spot her head lies at night. She narrows her eyes at me. I know what she's thinking. *Don't you say a word.*

The Patrol moves next to Gabi's bedroll. And in a sharp voice, I hear: "Director." He pulls out the red scarf.

Tía Lula gasps, rounding on Gabi. "You little delincuente! I give you everything I can, and this is how you repay me? Stealing!" She clicks her tongue, and turns back to the men. "Lo siento, señores. I took them in when their mother died." She folds her hands softly under her chin, her eyes and mouth drooping now. "They have been a burden to me, but one I cannot pass on to your Pocatelan kindness. I know you must banish all liars and thieves," she says, quoting their law. "I know the rules, so por favor, por favor, take them."

The Patrol holds his hand over his pistol and stands in front of Gabi, separating her from the rest of us. When he stands in front of her, his long black hair and dark blue robe block my view of her, like a massive shadow.

"Wait!" I yell. I take a few breaths and try to stiffen my words, so I sound more like them. "It is not true. Gabi did not steal the scarf!"

El Bastón turns toward me. He frowns, and deep wrinkles at the corners of his eyes fan outward.

"No lo hagas, gusano," Lula says.

I lean out to try and see Gabi. El Bastón holds the staff up to block me.

I can't let Gabi take the blame. My eyes flick to Tía Lula's bed.

El Bastón grins, and one of his front teeth is plated in bronze. He drops the staff. In one motion, he bends over and lifts Tía Lula's bedroll. Her wing knife lies beneath.

No one speaks.

Lula eases toward me slowly and places her arm around me. "An old woman must protect herself and these poor children from the dangerous people who live in the Pox."

I stiffen, the skin on my neck from the cut still on fire.

The Director pushes his robe to his back and kicks his boot over the ground; its pointed end sinks into the packed dirt. He kicks up, and Tía Lula's stash of stags jingles. Her bag of belongings lands next to the knife.

An even more pleased bronze-toothed smile covers his face as he hooks his arm around Tía Lula. She drops her arm from my shoulder. The other Patrol secures her hands behind her back. She juts her chin out, stretching her snake pit neck. "This is a mistake!"

He holds up the scarf. "Apparently not, woman." He leans in. "And you fit the exact description of a scarred Cascabel crone who Director Holand's wife saw near their clothesline."

I think of all of us in the Pox. Same shaved head and same torn tunics. Not much to set us apart. But I'm also wondering how or if he really knew he'd find stags. Could he know about my and Gabi's secret hiding place too? Pinpricks run up my neck, and I squeeze Gabi's hand. "¿Lista?"

She glances at me for a moment, then nods. The choice has been made for us.

Tía Lula's voice rises like a dying rat. "No, no, señor. That could not have been me. I found that scarf in the street near the Pox." She motions in the opposite direction of the Pocatelan homes. "It must have fallen and blown here in the wyrmstorm. I . . . I was going to return it on market day."

The Director holds up the small bag, shaking the stags. "And . . . ? Pox dwellers are restricted in the possession and trade of stags."

"Oh, those?" Her mouth turns up in a crooked grin and she waves her hand dismissively. "It is only my collection of trinkets, dropped by a careless marketgoers."

The Director tucks Tía Lula's stags inside his robe. Even under such pressure, that's the worst excuse I've ever heard. He picks up the bag with her hongo, candles, and flint. He looks inside, then tosses her things to the ground next to the knife like they're worthless.

Tía Lula's mouth drops open. In less than one sleep, she's gone from thinking she'd be living in one of their dwellings, to this.

I pull Gabi closer to the opposite side of the pock.

Lula lurches forward in their grasp, tripping over the mess they've made of our bedrolls and leaning into me. "This is your fault, gusano," she spits. "I will haunt your sueños the rest of your life."

I glance at the two small snakes on the far side of Lula's neck. Is it possible she once loved something? Did her dead haunt her?

It takes both of the men to yank her back and out of our dwelling.

"I will escort the children to Director Marguerite," El Bastón barks, as they go through the door.

Gabi squeezes my arm so tight it will leave a bruise. "Who is Director Marguerite?" she whispers.

Tía Lula kicks El Bastón in the knee outside, and he buckles to the ground. They can barely hold on to her. "Sir, we may need assistance with this one," the Patrol bites out as he wrestles Lula into submission.

El Bastón gets to his feet with a grunt. "No. We will not." Then he leans back in toward me and Gabi. I can't see beyond his bronze tooth. "You will remain here," he whispers icily.

I nod in response. He bends down and picks up the red scarf. Then he walks out and wraps it tightly over Tía Lula's head and eyes twice. She holds an arm out, trying to feel around, but it's too late. He grabs the back of her neck with one hand and grips her elbow with the other.

I overhear through the walls of our pock: "We will have the orphanage Director get them herself."

This is our chance. Gabi and I poke our heads around the door, watching as Tía Lula blindly kicks and hisses while she's led away. Maybe she will give us something in the end after all. And, if I'm certain of one thing: if she can find a way to haunt us, she will.

5

· · · ❨ · · ·

ICE RUNS UP MY BACK AS GABI GRABS MY ARM. I PULL
her inside and hurry to cinch the door shut. Word is probably
already spreading through the Pox of an empty dwelling with
only two kids to protect it. There are people in the Pox worse
than Franco and Naji who will come to scavenge soon. But, if I
stop to take our pock down for shelter, or collect our bedrolls,
the Patrol might return before I've finished.

"Run to the Dead Forest and wait for me," I say.

Gabi's eyes go wide. "But Leandro, the spirits will eat me."

"Gabi, ghosts don't have teeth." I've never seen one. Maybe they do. "Just don't go past the Tree of Souls."

She folds her arms over her chest. "No. I won't go without you."

I glare back at her, but we don't have time for a stare-off. I pick up Tía Lula's knife and slip out the longest wing blade. "If we get separated, hide." I place the knife's handle between Gabi's fingers, so the blade juts out. I try to slow my breathing. I have no idea what I'm doing. I've never hurt anyone. I wrap my hand around her tiny fist. "But if anyone tries to hurt you, you use it. Like this." I thrust the knife outward, trying to act confident.

Gabi nods and wipes her eyes with her arm. She scrunches her face, then lets out a breath and straightens her back.

I hurry to tuck Tía Lula's hongo and candles into the inner pocket of my tunic and try to cover the lump, hugging my arm over the top. "Vámanos."

I take Gabi's hand and we duck out, leaving the pock behind. We zigzag through the Pox toward Pocatel's main street. The sound of morning coughs and the smell of smoke from small fires follows us. A naked boy sits outside his dwelling near the entrance. One skinny arm rests on his swollen belly. With the other, he holds a small, speckled egg and sucks from a tiny hole at its end. Inside the pock, a woman lies, eyes closed, her breaths coming out in a dying rattle. Her arms and legs are thinner than the little boy's. I wonder how long they've been without food, unable to work in the fields. He sees us watching and hides the egg behind his back, crawling inside. Maybe someone scavenged it from a bird nest. A pity gift for a dying family. I hope he enjoys it. He'll be in the orphanage in days.

People are getting ready to leave for the fields. Ari watches from the door of her pock. She stares at the lump in my tunic and the knife in Gabi's hand. I think she knows we won't be in the fields today. She looks up at me, and her eyes and mouth turn down sadly. Even she cannot offer to hide us. But then she puts her hand up for us to stop. She digs quickly in the ground near her pock door, and lifts out a dirty potato. She tosses it to me and cinches the door again. We continue on. Others pretend not to see us at all. No one's loco enough to draw attention to themselves. Who knows what other Cascabeles hide inside their pocks.

We make it to the edge of the Pox. We turn south away from Pocatel's center and toward the fields.

The watch towers surrounding the fields are still empty, except for one sleeping guard. We pass by the papa fields. Soon, the rest of the guards will arrive to watch over the workers.

We sneak past, toward the dung heap. As we approach, the beetles scatter to hide beneath the heaps' surfaces. We know better than to steal any of them for food either.

It smells so bad no one ever comes this far, unless it's to dump waste or gather beetles for Pocatelan meals. We go to the backside of the heap. Gabi stands watch as I lift the black rock with the white stripe we use as our landmark. I cup my hand and dig. I wretch as I pull up the compost, thankful, for once, that my stomach is empty. One handful at a time, I lift out our hidden stags. I let the dirt sift through my fingers. The bronze beetles clink as one by one, I hand them to Gabi, until the hole's empty.

"So gross," she says, wiping the grime off their bodies until each stag shines. Some are missing legs and pincers, but nothing that won't give each full credit. "Uno, dos, tres," she counts until she reaches, ". . . catorce." But I could've told her exactly how many there are. "Is it enough?"

Eighteen stags will hopefully buy the supplies and silence of the Mongers we need to buy from. We only need four more. "I think we can do it," I answer. We just have to avoid the Patrol long enough to trade with the Mongers, then sneak out of Pocatel.

We walk out of the fields like we were meant to be there, in case the guard wakes up. We walk past the rows of plants we would have picked in a few hours and turn away from the city center toward the Dead Forest.

Ahead, the Tree of Souls waits. The fabric and strands of hair wave in the breeze. We approach slowly. We've never been this close. From here, I see most of the hundreds of dark braids are Cascabel—those who died the winter before the Pocatelans made us shave our heads. For some, it was the last piece of ourselves we had left.

Thin pieces of tunic cloth are more recent: thin strips from our dead's clothing, their families hoping their loved ones will protect them from the evil and angry ghosts who roam the forest graveyard beyond. Gabi and I have no one up in that tree to protect us. But we have no other choice. We hide behind the trunk, where no Pocatelan would dare to cross, and hope we won't be attacked by spirits from the other side for at least a little while.

In the base of the tree, in the shade, sits an unpicked circle of hongo. I crouch to forage the mushrooms and shove them in my pocket. Maybe they will dry in time for me to make a trade.

When I stand, Gabi is staring at me, her mouth sagging.

"It's okay," I say. "It's only this one time. These alone might get us a day's ration."

"Okay," she nods.

I take Gabi's fist and unclench the knife from her hand. Her fingers slowly get their color back.

We peek around the side of the tree. It's too far to see who, but three figures walk toward the Pox, one wearing a dark orange robe, the other two the dark blue of the Patrol. The thump of a stick hitting the ground with each step echoes across the town toward us. The three turn into the Pox.

"Do you think they're looking for us?" Gabi asks.

"Yes."

"Do you think they'll come look for us here?"

I look above at the hair and cloth blowing like ghosts, then behind to the forest. Dead tree branches weave across the forest's floor like shadowy arms and legs. "No," I answer.

By now, they'll be asking others if they've seen us. Even if Jo saw us, I'm not sure how he'd answer. He might try to tell El Bastón all about his father's wagon, Enrique. As we wait longer, I imagine El Bastón flinging open pock doors with his staff, scaring small children with his bronze tooth. I trust Ari won't talk, but Franco and Naji might sell us for a single papa.

The sun is cresting over the ridge when El Bastón and the orange-robed person exit the Pox onto the main road. They go in the opposite direction back toward the town's center, just like I hoped. They won't waste much time on us. They know we can't survive long on our own anyway.

The boy I'd seen earlier wanders out from the Pox, following them.

Like ants in the distance, Pocatelans are now beginning to leave their homes for the day. The kids in their matching brown robes walk toward the school building. Their mothers wave goodbye like always, and return to their homes. Closer to us, workers leave the Pox and walk slowly toward the fields. I can't smell it yet, but the woodsmoke from the smelters begins to drift through the city over the road.

Most of the Pocatelans pass by the naked boy, turning their heads the other way, but a woman in a pale blue robe stops. Looking around to make sure others are watching first, she bends down to wrap a scarf around his waist, then pats the kid's head with her gloved hand. Another hooded woman nods in approval, but keeps her distance.

The woman pushes the child back in the direction of the Pox. I think of Tía Lula being sent down the exile bridge. Will it be dark and windy tonight? I imagine her balancing on the swaying bridge, tiny coldpox covering her skin as she shivers in her tattered tunic. I shake my head to erase it from my mind.

Without me or Gabi to hold her steady, Tía Lula will be at the bottom of the Trench before she makes it halfway.

The exiles happen at night where no one sees. But Franco said he once heard a falling scream that lasted three seconds. I don't know which is better: a long freefall, or making it to the other side just for a wyrm to make a meal of you.

"Now what, Leandro?" Gabi asks, pulling me back to the now.

"Cállate," I whisper.

Her shoulders slump.

I don't want to hurt her feelings, but I need to think of how I'm going to keep us alive. "I'm sorry. I just don't want you to disrupt the spirits," I speak softly. "The Pocatelans won't come to search for us in the Pox after dark. We wait until the sun goes down, and sneak back for our bedrolls and our pock. Then we get ready for the market."

Gabi nods.

We squat against the backside of the tree. Gabi lays her head on my shoulder. After a while, we take turns sleeping.

Gabi lays with her arm dangling over a rock. With the tree above us, I'm reminded of how little we are. Suddenly, Gabi feels like a tiny baby again. I close my eyes and remember my mother sitting on the ground, legs crossed in front of her. Just like Gabi here, beneath the protection of the tree, my mother would tuck Gabi in the safety of her lap.

My mother's spine showing through her tunic.

"Mama, are you talking to the earth again?" I asked.

"Yes," she said quietly. "You should too."

I kick the dirt and stub my toe. "I don't know how."

"It is not difficult," she said. "Close your eyes. Steady your breath. And say thank you. Thank her for giving us what we have." My mother waves for me to join her.

"What good will it do? She has no mouth to talk back," I grumble.

"But she will hear. And it will help her to heal, just as we are. Come."

I sit next to her, crossing my legs, and close my eyes. As I take deep breaths, her hand slips into mine.

Just like then, I close my eyes and lean back into the tree. I breathe deeply and thank the Dead Forest. I thank the Tree of Souls. I hope the words will help them to heal.

I WAKE TO THE sound of someone yelling.

"I will bring my wagon tomorrow! Un regalo de mi papi. Se llama Enrique."

I arc around the tree to see a hunched-over figure, his dark shadow holding up a potato to the field Patrol. But they pay him no attention, and he walks on.

I watch as the last of the workers leave the fields not far from where we hide. The sun dips below the mountain to the west.

I let out a breath as Jo passes safely into the Pox for the night.

For once, luck has found Gabi and I. There's a market day tomorrow. Trading with the Mongers will be dangerous. But they're just as desperate to get stags as we are to give them—for different reasons. With enough stags, these men and women can buy their way back inside Pocatel. So, they brave the Outlands to find scrap that they trade for food, and what they have left over, they sell for stag. It's a messed-up system for them, but they might risk trading with two Cascabel kids who have enough stag.

As the Mongers leave, crossing over the Trench bridge at the end of the day, we'll hide in the undercarriage of one of their wagons before the bridge is drawn up again. As soon as the bridge is up, we'll jump from under the wagon with all we need. We'll run across the wyrmfield, before they begin to stir for the night. We won't have much time, but if we're fast, we can run up the ridge and leave Pocatel Valley, before the Patrol or wyrms can slither after us.

A wyrm calls out through the night air. Gabi grips my arm, her face pale.

"Lots of people to eat in between first," I say.

She snickers.

The wind blows, and a *whooooooo* whistles above our heads in the tree. Could Tía Lula already be at the bottom of the Trench? Her tortured soul on its way here to find us?

Gabi loosens her grip and whispers: "I wish we had something of our parents to put up in the tree. Someone to protect us—"

I set my jaw. "We'll protect ourselves."

I take one bite from the papa Ari gave us and hand the rest to her. The raw papa will make our stomachs twist, but it's better than no food at all.

We finish and I take Gabi's hand and pull her up. We step out from behind the tree and walk as quietly as we can toward town, staying on the far edge of the path. For once, I'm glad we don't have streetlamps on our side.

As we pass the fields, a chorus of slow singing flows out on the air from the Pox. Some of the words get lost in the wind, but when the click of rocks begins, Gabi and I can't help smiling a little at one another. Even without seeing the singers, my mind pictures them. They are sitting on the ground in a circle. Cascabeles used to play this game every night, for fun. It's been a while, but Gabi got to play once last season when there was a competition for extra food. That can't be the case now. Maybe someone wove some cloth? Or created a tool? The singing quickens.

Zango, zango.

Rocks click like drums between words, laughter between the singing.

Con su triqui, triqui tran.

The final hitting of the rock is louder than the rest.

"Oh, Leandro. Can't we go watch?" she begs.

I want to go as bad as she does. But it'll never be like before. This city has changed us. So many would turn us in now, for so little. Maybe not those singing, true . . . but we can't take the risk.

"Not tonight, Gabi."

But the truth is, after tonight, there won't another time. She knows it too.

I pat her shoulder. "I promise, you and I can play the game—"

"That's stupid. It doesn't work with only two of us. And you are slow and have no rhythm, Leandro. What fun is that?"

"Nice," I say.

"Hmmmph," she huffs, walking on.

As we get closer and closer, the rocks clicking on the ground gets faster and faster. The singing speeds. The words take form over the wind.

Acitrón de un
Fandango zango, zango
Sabaré que va pasando,
Con su triqui, triqui tran.

As the song begins again, more quickly this time, I hold my finger to my lips and we tiptoe back into the Pox.

Acitrón de un
Fandango zango, zango.

The game is too far to see, on the opposite side of the Pox, where they have time to break it up if the Patrol arrives.

Gabi and I weave through the night using the glow from flickering candlelight within each house. The pocks sparkle, bright and alive.

Sabaré que va pasando
Con su triqui, triqui tran.

The song starts over a third time, the pace quickening even more. But someone is offbeat.

"¡Ayyyy!" someone yells. A burst of laughter echoes as that person is eliminated. I imagine the circle growing even smaller. They may be laughing, but is this why they are playing? Do others sense what I do? One by one, our circle is growing smaller.

As the singing quickens, so does my heartbeat. Music that used to make me happy, in a time we were united, now makes me uneasy.

We approach our pock at last. My heart falls, and Gabi gasps. A few shreds of dirty fabric from El Bastón's cut are all that's left. Two pocks away, Naji is stitching by candlelight what looks like pieces of our old home. She's half done adding it to her own, a new room to its backside. Our bedrolls are gone too. Franco sits at her side. When he catches sight of us, he glares and stands. This could go badly for both of us. If he reports us, we go to the orphanage. If he calls for the Patrol, I could report theft. He could be exiled. Neither of us move.

Gabi elbows me and I turn to see a small figure ducking behind a pock in the distance, a bedroll tucked under their arm.

The pounding of the rocks feels louder in my ears, but the voices are fewer.

A desert wyrm's scream vibrates the air, much closer than the last. The music stops. The sound of scrambling and the shadows of people scattering is followed by doors cinching one after the other. Franco pulls Naji inside their new, larger pock.

Gabi's eyes are filled with panic. "Leandro, what now?"

All around us, one by one like dying stars, pocks darken and go silent.

I stare at Gabi's bare nose and mouth. The storm will be here soon. My stomach feels like I ate live beetles. I hurry to pick up two shreds from the ground. I knot them together and try to tie one over her nose, but the other isn't wide enough to cover her mouth. Then I remember the dying woman and the little boy. No one would dare take her pock so soon after her death—to risk the malvado of her spirit. And if she's still alive, she'll be too weak to kick us out. The boy is too young to tell. It feels wrong, but if we don't . . .

If we don't, we'll die out here.

I take Gabi's hand and we run for the dead woman's pock. "Hurry!"

The pock is dark, its door waving in the breeze. We enter and it's empty now, but it's filled with a terrible smell. Gabi squints one eye like she just ate a rotten potato.

Something crunches under my foot. Speckled bits of eggshell mix with dirt. I realize we're disturbing this home just like Franco and Naji did to ours.

A fog of dust moves outside among the pocks. I cinch the door tight. It should protect us for now.

I reach inside my tunic and take out Lula's bag. I dump out the sack holding her knife, flint, and candles. I light the candle and pull out our stags hidden in my other pocket. I hold the bronze beetles in my palm.

Gabi's eyes shift around the pock like she's waiting for Tía Lula to punish us for something.

"Gabi," I say, interrupting her thoughts. "We'll need thicker tunics, or even a Pocatelan robe for the winters to come." I push three stags into my opposite hand. "Pocatelan shoes if we can find a Monger who will sell them to us." I push out three more stags. "And enough food and water to get over the valley's east ridge and into the Outlands." I push the remaining stags into my other hand. "From there, we should be able to forage."

Gabi's stares back, with her pale skin, dark circles under her eyes, and purple lips. "Should?" She stares down at the stags in my hand, and bites her lip. "Leandro? Are you . . . are you sure this is the right thing to do?"

I hold her eyes for a moment, then look away. Am I sure?

I don't know. But I do know that she is growing weaker each day. And what little I remember of my mother . . . she wouldn't want this life for us.

"Without having to share what we earn with anyone else, we will have more than we've had in years." I put my hand on her shoulder. "Don't you want to go back to how it used to be?"

Gabi shrugs. "I don't remember it so well. I only know what you've told me. That . . . and the tales of La Cuna."

She might look doubtful now, but I've seen her face each time Jo tells the story. She still believes.

"If it's really there, we'll find it," I say. "And until we do, I will gather us a lot more food than we're used to here."

"Okay." She smiles. Then, hopefully: "Hey, maybe we can pay a Monger to smuggle us all the way past the wyrmfield."

"¿Neta, Gabi? I don't know. That could get them banned permanently."

But she could be right. The right Monger, for the right number of stag. Maybe they would smuggle us over the Trench bridge, even past the wyrmfield, for an extra fistful of bronze beetles. They'd probably think it was a good deal. Ten stags in one pocket, eight in another, and no one left alive to tell the Regime they'd done it.

"I suppose we could try the one-armed Monger if she's here. I've seen her staring at the orphanage," I reply. I always figured she must have left a child behind. It's said that some Mongers will kill and steal from the others to get what they want. Any bit of scrap, metal, clothing, food . . . . We'll just have to avoid those.

"We'll go to the one-armed monger when the market closes. But if my stomach goes sour, we stick to our original plan and hide under her wagon." Gabi nods. I continue: "We'll have to stay very still until we're across the Trench. No matter what, we cross the entire wyrmfield before sunset and hide up the ridgeline."

Gabi's smiling, but taking shallow breaths. I'm not even sure we can make it that far. But for now, I will let her dream.

I slip the stags back inside my tunic. "One more day, Gabi. And we leave Pocatel forever."

Gabi smiles wider, and her eyes fill with tears. She wipes her face on the inside of her arm. She lifts her head, and in an instant, her smile falls. Eyes wide, she stares behind me. I jump at a ripping noise. I whip around to see a knife slicing down the side of the dead woman's pock.

El Bastón grips his pitted stick above his head. "Do not make me use this."

6

· · · ☾ · · ·

MY LEGS FEEL NUMB AS EL BASTÓN MARCHES US DOWN
the center of Pocatel. I hold Gabi's hand and squeeze over and
over, hoping she understands I will do what I can to protect her.

The Director's staff hits the ground with each step as he leads
us right through the wyrmspore air. We walk under light cast
from the upper windows of the other Directors' homes. I try to
look inside the windows, but they're too high.

To our right, the black metal door at the back of the Center of Banishment leads to the rocky field. A well-worn footpath down the field's center leads toward the Trench. The path ends at the narrow exile footbridge. I can't see the metal footbridge in the dark against the blackness of the Trench it lies over. But I hear the wind whistle through the chasm below. The footbridge clinks in the wind as it shifts back and forth. We will not make it across if El Bastón exiles us now.

We walk past the Center of Banishment without entering. I let out a breath.

We continue down the main street of Pocatel. We pass the empty stalls of the market. Tomorrow those stalls will be full of the Mongers' goods. Four wagons lie alongside the stalls. They're pieced together with wood, metal, and Old-World salvage. A sheet of metal with a window at its top and a silver handle beneath is drilled onto the side of the wagon. Two of the wagons have perfect spots for two small humans to hide, in the undercarriage. I can only hope that one of them belongs to the one-armed woman.

One cart is heaped with metal scrap from the Outlands.

Ahead lies the drawbridge. The entrance to Pocatel is pulled up and secure. But what if El Bastón decides to just toss us over the side into the Trench?

I'm imagining the twisted metal scrap Franco says juts up from the bottom, and the scream he swears he heard, when El Bastón shoves us to the left. The stone orphanage sits in front of us. It is entirely surrounded by a black metal fence. Its windows are dark. At its entrance is an ancient carved rock sign. I sound out the letters like my mother taught me. *Pub* . . . *lic Lib* . . . *lib* . . . *rary*. *Public library*. A house for books.

El Bastón pounds on the door so hard it echoes down the street.

Footsteps thump from inside, and the approach of lamplight flickers through a small window at the top of the front door. The door swings open.

The large person in the dark orange robe I'd seen earlier with El Bastón answers the door. Now I see, part of what makes her tall is a frizzy bun, spiraled on the top of her head. A bronze stink bug beetle snags the fabric on the shoulder of her robe.

"Director Marguerite," El Bastón says.

Her voice is high, like one of the Pocatel's town bells. "Well, who do we have here?" Her nostrils flare, and dark hair pokes out from inside her nostrils, like spider legs. I can't tell if her nostrils are surprised or angry. "Looks as if you finally found the two you lost." She clicks her tongue. "Many are lost, but with penance, the path may clear." She motions for us to enter.

El Bastón glares at her and steps closer.

I think of the secret knife, flint, hongo, and stags I have hidden in my pockets, and how we'll need them to sell or survive. I quickly pull the bags out. The Director looks from side to side outdoors, then at the lid on a metal box on the wall marked *Book Return*. She coughs, and I toss it in. A few stags clink together, but the orphanage Director and El Bastón don't notice. Not until it's too late do I think we should've kept the knife.

El Bastón reaches around and pulls me by my shoulder, then pushes me inside. Gabi trails behind.

"Well, I suppose we are just fortunate you found them before one of their own harmed them," Director Marguerite says. I want to tell her my people only learned to harm one another from the Pocatelans. And that I'd take my chances in the Pox over here, despite it all. "I am just glad you were able to find them, for your Patrol's reputation." She grins now at El Bastón. Thin brown lines run between her teeth.

El Bastón prods me with his stick. "Well, we will see if you can keep them from getting lost any better than I," he answers tersely.

"I don't lose my charges." She goes to pat Gabi's head, then stops, staring down at her, "Uh yes, precious," she says. "Well, let us get you settled." She closes the door behind us, leaving El Bastón outside.

I see the top of his head through the window at the top of the door. The Director turns around, but stays where he is in the entranceway. He doesn't seem in much hurry to get out of the murky air stirred by the wyrms.

"Bridget!" Director Marguerite cups her hand to her mouth and tilts her head upward. "Two Pox!" She looks down at our feet. She scoffs. "Scour rags, please!" Then she sighs and motions for us to go up the stairs. "Clean bodies, clean minds."

I watch as this Director picks up a cup of dark liquid from a table. Steam rises from the top of the drink as she lifts it to her mouth, then sucks it through her teeth. "Go on," she says, motioning to the stairs again. "Do not be timid."

Gabi and I look at one another. I realize in a flash that we've never walked up stairs before. I take the first step, holding on to a piece of wood attached to the wall. Gabi locks her arm around my elbow. I feel her body trembling.

"It's okay," I say, even though I don't feel that way. We take the steps slowly together.

"Stop on the second floor at the bathroom," Director Marguerite calls. I turn to see her twisting a metal switch on the door, locking it shut. El Bastón is still there, just outside the window. Maybe he's waiting to see if we try to run?

By the time we're at the top, Gabi's out of breath. She turns to me and makes an awkward face, unsure of where to go. Is she thinking what I am? What's a *bath room?* We turn in a circle.

Director Marguerite's voice rings up. "There!" she barks, pointing to a room on the left. She follows us up the stairs. I'm sure I hear the words "foul" and "rancid" muttered from behind.

We approach the door, and I push it open. The walls and floor are all covered in shiny, sky-blue rectangle stones, unlike any I've seen before. In the center of the room is a round piece of silver metal. Holes are drilled through it, and water is pooled around its edge.

Gabi squeezes my elbow. "Leandro? What is this?"

A young woman nudges us out of the way, walking past. She is carrying a bucket in each hand. Tunics and square cloths are draped over the woman's shoulder. The edges of her mouth are turned downward, deep lines curving from their edge to her chin. She grunts, and I can't tell if she's angry or because the buckets are heavy.

One of the buckets is filled with bubbles, and gives off the smell of fresh grass.

"Soap!" Gabi squeals. We only saw it once on a market day when a Monger was washing his mule.

I take a step onto a cold floor, and Gabi follows.

Director Marguerite bustles past us too and takes the bubble bucket and cloths from the lady's hand. "Thank you, Bridget." She sets the bucket down and hands us each the square piece of rough fabric. "Use this to scrub your bodies and heads." She points to the metal circle with holes. "And please do not to forget to stand over the drain while you do it. We do not want to spend the next two hours cleaning this floor."

"We can use the soap?" Gabi says softly. She looks over at me, mouth ajar.

Director Marguerite ignores her and takes the other bucket from Bridget's hand, dropping it next to the first. "Use the clean water to rinse off when you are done."

Gabi and I bite back smiles. She's right to think we wouldn't know.

Two pale green tunics sit on a bench. They're a color I've never seen before on any of the Pocatelans. Not new, but they look clean.

Director Marguerite stomps out but Bridget waits with her back to us, facing the hallway. We laugh quietly. We know the Pocatalens aren't used to uncovered bodies. I wait for Bridget to give some strange saying about being naked, but she doesn't.

Gabi and I take our time to scrub. I flinch over a few spots and remember the cut on my neck Tía Lula gave me, as my hands brush over it. I find a long scrape over a red-and-black bruise from where she threw me against the pock too. I turn so Gabi can't see it. The second time I soap up my body, I close my eyes and allow myself to pretend for a moment that I'm back in the Outlands, picking grass to eat.

"Do you think they want us clean for when they steal our organs?" Gabi asks quietly, rinsing her feet.

I whisper: "Shhh. Our plan hasn't changed."

Gabi smiles and scrubs harder.

The bucket of fresh-grass soap water eventually turns brown. I scrub one more time and motion for Gabi to do the same.

I lower my whisper even more. "If we don't smell like humans, maybe the animals and wyrms won't know to hunt us."

Gabi nods and leans in. "Yeah, no monster wants to eat grass."

But I'm also not sure we'll ever see soap again. I shiver, and bumps cover my skin. I slip the green tunic over my head. They're the same size, and Gabi's is barely bigger on her than mine is on me. The fabric slips over my skin like the softest of feathers. I look at Gabi, her mouth wide open in surprise. I reach inside the tunic, looking for my pocket on instinct, but there isn't one.

So far, the orphanage isn't at all what Tía Lula warned us it would be.

When we're finished dressing, we walk to the door. Bridget peeks over her shoulder to make sure we're fully clothed.

"Well then," she says, turning to face us. I didn't think she could look angrier, but then she smiles, and the downward furrows in her face get even deeper. She reaches inside the bathroom door with her foot and kicks our old tunics into the corner, next to what I think is dung wipe. Gabi gasps, but I shake my head at her. We just got thicker tunics, without having to use any of our stags to pay for them. All we have to do is find our way to the market somehow tomorrow morning.

Bridget picks two clay bowls off a small table in the hallway. She sets one in each of our hands. A heap of white mush with gray lumps lies in its center. I touch the food, and it's cool. I narrow my eyes at Bridget and sniff it. Potato mash. Even with the gray lumps, it still smells better than most of the rotted food and raw papas we eat. I push my finger to a gray spot and realize it's not potato. The lump has legs of the same color.

"Gabi," I whisper. "Larvas." I point to the bowl. Gabi looks down. Her eyes widen, and a huge smile breaks across her face. She must see the grubs too.

Bridget rolls her eyes. "Eat up," she says, now sounding annoyed.

She stands in front of us holding up silver scoops.

Gabi and I stand by the table and cup our fingers into the bowls, shoveling the papas and larvas into our mouth. Bridget shakes her head. She holds one of the scoops and pretends her other hand is a bowl, then scoops imaginary mash out.

Gabi and I watch her and continue to scoop with our fingers and chew. Bridget's face starts to turn red. She slams the metal scoops to the table and hands us each a cup of water.

The cup is made of blue glass and Gabi holds it up to the light, spilling a few drops. "Que bonito," she says.

Bridget's lips are even thinner than before. "Tomorrow you will learn to eat, drink, and speak properly."

I swallow the rest of the water and turn to Gabi. Her cheeks are already darker than they've been in days. My own stomach is the fullest it's been in winters. I set my bowl down and wait for Gabi as she takes the final bites.

"Follow me." Bridget takes the first step up to the next floor.

At the top of the final step, we face a large square opening. In hallways to both sides are doorways. Bridget walks to the first and opens the door. She holds her lamp up into the room. "This will be your classroom."

The room is filled with chairs and tables. One entire wall is covered by a large black rectangle the chairs face. A ledge at the bottom of the square holds little white rocks. At its top, bronze letters are mounted to the wall's surface. S-a-c-r-i-f-i-c-e and P-r-e-s-e-r-v-a-t-i-o-n gleam in the lamplight. I can't know what they teach here, but I'm not sure I could sit still in a chair all day long.

Then Bridget points to the opposite side where there is an identical room. "The younger children are in that schoolroom."

"¿Escuela?" Gabi whispers. I shrug, wondering what else they would want to teach Cascabel children.

Bridget continues straight ahead through the large opening without a door. She hangs the lamp on a hook at its opening.

Inside is a room almost the entire size of the building. Another single dim lantern hangs on the opposite wall, and soft breathing fills the room. We step inside and the air of the room smells like the desert after rain.

Four rows of twelve beds line the room. So many! None of the beds lie on the floor like our bedrolls. Sitting on posts, the floating beds are all full. And from what I can tell, over half of those sleeping look like . . . Cascabeles. How are they all still alive?

A ceiling of windows lies overhead. Moonlight mixes with the glow of the lanterns. Empty shelves cover the walls from floor to ceiling. The house for books is now empty.

A few kids look up at us as we enter. But most sleep. With over two thousand people in Pocatel, and a few hundred in the Pox, I guess I expected there would be other kids without parents. I just didn't expect so many of them to be like us. All of the orphans are wearing the same green tunics we are.

A boy sits up and waves to us. I recognize him. He has a full head of hair, but for sure: it's Vincent. He lived near Jo. His father fell over one day in the fields and didn't get back up. Vincent lived and worked the fields alone for half a season before they figured it out.

I'm so surprised, I can't even wave back. He should be long gone. "You still have your kidneys?" I whisper.

He flinches back and tilts his head.

He shouldn't be alive. But there he is. I want to laugh for happiness.

Gabi waves to him and elbows me in the side. "Leandro, it's . . ."

"I know." We look at one another, confused. When the Patrol came for him, Tía Lula said he'd be dead within the week.

Most of the kids have lots of hair. They've been here long enough to grow it. Maybe they're taking longer to steal our organs, or . . . maybe what Tía Lula said was all a lie. Tía Lula never actually said why they wanted them. When I asked Jo, he just said, "Ah, yes. Kidneys. Very valuable." But why would they? We just believed Lula, and didn't disobey when she told us not to speak of it. We did whatever she said, because she made us afraid.

Bridget walks to the opposite end of the room. Two beds off to one side don't fall into any row. At the end of each is a real blanket.

"You will sleep here tonight," she whispers. "We will wake you for chores." She clears her throat. "I hope I don't need to remind you, but do not leave your beds until morning. It displeases Director Marguerite." She walks away finally, humming softly.

I push my fingers on the top of the floating bed. It doesn't sink to the floor. "The poles hold it up," I say, looking at Gabi.

Gabi squats to look beneath her own bed. "Maybe they're off the ground to leave room for another child on a bedroll below."

I shrug, and we lie on top like the other kids.

Gabi watches Bridget until she's out of the room, then scurries immediately over to my bed and crawls next to me, sticking her cold toes under my legs. "I'm scared," she whispers. "Why is it so cold here?"

I glance at the empty shelves, floor to the ceiling, surrounding us. "Because books lived here, not people. Books don't need fires to keep them warm."

"Do you think they still have books here?" she asks. "I'd like to read on paper one day . . ."

"I don't know, Gabi. We won't be here that long."

Someone from a few rows over shushes us.

Gabi pushes up to her elbows, scanning the room.

So far, we've gotten a bath, and more food than I could even scavenge. And the promise of school? I hope Gabi's not having second thoughts—even if I can't help myself having them too. It might seem like all we could want, but there must be more going on. Why keep us all alive? Why worry about us learning "their" ways and manners? Why classrooms for kids they never cared about educating before? There must be a reason they're holing all of us inside the stone orphanage walls.

"One day, Gabi, I will write you a story myself." I give her a squeeze. "I promise."

"I hope it's a good one," she says. "With no farting lizard jokes." Then she looks at me with the smallest of grins.

We giggle, and someone shushes us again.

I HAD A real book once, and I even knew all the words in it. It was my mother's. But Tía Lula burned it for kindling one cold night shortly after she died, saying it was worth more that way now. Even with the fire, it was the coldest night I can remember.

Gabi was too young then to remember. Later, I taught her all the numbers and letters and sounds I'd learned, using the soil of the fields.

But the first time I learned a letter it was in the bright sun, while the men were hunting. My mom pulled the book from our family's sack.

She sighs, and when she speaks, her voice is like a happy song. "It's time for you to learn." She sets it on the ground.

I brush my finger over the gold letters on the spine.

"The letters make sounds, the sounds make words, the words help us learn something we didn't know before. This *World Book* tells the stories of all things once in the world that begin with the letter J."

I rub my finger over the single letter that goes straight down, then curves small, like a sewing hook. "Where did it come from, this *World Book*?"

"This book was a gift from my father, and his mother carried it before him, and so many generations before." She points to the hook letter. "*Juh, juh, juh.*"

"*Juh,*" I repeat.

She opens the book close to the end, then points to the word at the top of the page. The edges of the pages are yellow and crackly. I place my finger on the first letter of the word. "*Juh,*" I say.

"Perfecto, Leandro."

I can hear the smile in her voice. But still, even in this memory, I can't see her face. I can't see the smile I know she has for me.

I look down and put my finger on the next letter. This letter is half the height of the J, and looks like a worm that was pulled straight down at its middle.

"*Yuuuu*," she says. "But it sounds like '*uhhhhh*.'" She points to each letter. "*Juh, uhhh*."

I run my finger over the remaining letters. "What's the whole word?"

"*Jungle*," she says.

"*Juh-uhhh-ngle*." I stare down at the picture next to it. Trees with huge leaves are wrapped with green vines. Water drips from the leaves. "Is this real?"

"It was, one time long ago."

I stare up at her. I think she's looking back into my eyes.

"See, Leandro. This book is magical. Now you know new letters and sounds, and something about the word they create, that you didn't know before." She nudges me with her elbow. "What do think of this word?"

I wonder what the *juh-uhhh-ngle*, with all its green and leaves and water, smelled like. Then I think for a moment. "I know it is a word of a place that I will never see."

"Look more closely." She leans into the page. "Do you also see that there was once a place the Creators of All Things made for us, in this world? It was so big and green. And the jungle was not all. There were many magical places. Most are gone now . . ." She cups my chin. "But when you see even the smallest bit of green, know that someone who has left the world before is sending us a bit of the Old-World back, reminding us we are still loved."

7

· · · ☾ · · ·

"GABI, YOU NEED TO GO TO YOUR OWN BED," I TELL HER,
after we lie there together a while more. "If that lady, Director
Marguerite, catches you—"

"Hmmph," Gabi huffs, shoving her foot further underneath
me and hooking it around my calf. I give up trying to fight her.
"I am not afraid of those ladies."

Moonlight shines on our legs through the clean windows

above our heads. The wind outside whistles. I pull the blanket up higher.

"Leandro, do you think Tía Lula will haunt us?" she asks quietly.

A small cough echoes from the other side of the room.

"Yes," I answer with the truth.

I look up through the glass, and the sky is full of thousands of bright stars. I've dreamed a thousand times of me and Gabi flying out into space and never coming back. The last time I saw so many stars, we were sleeping underneath them, before we came to Pocatel and a pock blocked our view. Back then, Gabi would sleep tucked under my armpit just like now.

And before she was under my arm, I was under my mother's. She may be foggy in my mind, but I still remember her story.

I point above. "Those are the ancestors," I whisper. "When the world died, the souls of the dead became stars. They shine down to let us know they're not so far away."

"How many people do you think died, Leandro?"

"Millions. Billions. We traveled a hundred winters and we never saw any other humans. So, everyone, I guess . . . everyone but the Pocatelans and Cascabeles."

But I do wonder if somewhere else in the world there are others. Trapped in a valley, or caves, or underground. Maybe they hid too and will one day emerge. Or maybe they have, and just live so far away we will never see each other, as long as we shall live.

"Will you tell me about the people in our family? Before the world ended."

I take a deep breath. The truth is, if I close my eyes, I know every word as it was spoken to me by my mother. Even if I can't see her face. The way she would look at me . . . at us. Maybe I am still too sad to remember.

I sigh again and straighten my tunic. "In the days before the wyrms, when the planet was green and blue, your tatara-tatara-tatara-tatara . . ." I start, repeating how I must have first heard it.

Gabi giggles, and the loudest "Shhh!" yet quiets us from across the room.

I lower my voice more, ". . . tatara-tatara-abuelo was a man named Francisco, who worked the fields of the San Joaquin Valley. He came from a land to the south, and he wanted nothing more than to have a home and a wife and children. But he had one small problem . . ."

"What was the problem?" Gabi asks, like she hasn't heard this a hundred times before.

"Pues, Francisco loved to gamble," I answer. "He lost the money he earned in the fields playing with cards and betting."

"Betting on what?" she asks.

This she's never asked before. On what, I don't know. I do know that Francisco died. He left his wife and child in the final days to drink and gamble. His young wife, Elena, was the one who was frightened but strong. She is the one who took her child to the mountain and helped dig, along with the other field workers and oilfield families, saving their lives. I should tell Gabi the truth. But, like always, I want her to hear something hopeful . . . so I will finish as I always have.

"It's not important what Francisco bet on. What is important is that he met a woman named Elena and they fell in love. They had a daughter, and when the end came, he left his old ways behind. He took his wife and child deep underground with others and the rattlesnakes."

"Do you think Francisco ate dead bodies?" Gabi whispers.

"No! Not our family," I reply. "Only Tía Lula's family did that sort of thing."

Gabi giggles, pulling the blanket over her mouth.

I finish with: "As you know, when the skies cleared, the workers of San Joaquin returned to the surface. The stars, which had been hidden for so long, returned. But now there were millions more than before."

I rub the snakes on my neck. And then . . . a flash of my mother's wavy, dark hair, and her hand tossing a rock into the fire. Sparks fly upward as she speaks: "*We were few, but Cascabeles came from the earth and survived by the earth, always with a thankful and sharing heart, as her gifts belong to us all—*"

Someone coughs, and it brings me back into the orphanage. My body makes a quick shiver, thinking I may forget her words one day like I have her face. I think of how beautiful they sound to me, but how strange they'd sound to the Pocatelans.

"We should sleep now," I get out, clearing my throat. "You'll need to dance the best you ever have tomorrow, Gabi. We only need to pick from a few people at market—one, if we're lucky—and we'll have the stag we need to leave."

She wiggles back and forth. "If we have a good day at the market ..." She lets out a hum. "I'll put my feet in a real river one day. I'll play with fish ..."

"Gabi, I don't think—"

"I'll eat fresh fruit, and in La Cuna, I'll dance, not because I have to, but because I want to. I'll sleep outside under the millions of stars watching over me, without worrying about restless spirits and wyrmstorms ..."

I won't ruin Gabi's dream, even though La Cuna and the dying scout has always felt too strange to be true to me. If it was real, wouldn't we have found it in all our years looking?

Even if it looks like the orphans here are treated well, and aren't getting their kidneys stolen, I decide to stay awake a while longer, just in case.

About now, Lula would be slicing her hongo for the night. Gabi and I would be whispering stories or talking of our day until we fell asleep. But tonight, Tía Lula must already be over the Trench.

Mumbles echo from below soon enough, followed by footsteps up the stairs.

Gabi slides out of my bed and crawls to hers, next to mine.

The door opens and Director Marguerite's annoyed voice no longer chimes like a bell. "Not sure why this one could not wait until morning?"

Director Marguerite walks in, holding the hand of a small, crying boy. He has a full head of curly blonde hair, and can be no older than five winters. He wears a brown Pocatelan school robe and looks like he doesn't need to wash with the buckets in the bath room.

The Director leads him in our direction. Gabi and I hurry to close our eyes, pretending to be asleep. I peek and see Gabi squinting too hard.

Bridget is with them, and she pulls a bed from the edge of the room next to ours. Director Marguerite plops the boy down on top. She pulls off his brown robe and slips a pale green tunic over his underclothes, making him lie down.

His crying is broken only by his hiccups.

Director Marguerite whispers, I'm not sure to who, "What we must do to preserve order." She huffs and pulls the blanket to his neck as he lies down. "What a waste. Who will take a boy whose mother has committed such atrocities?"

Bridget doesn't respond, but picks up his robe and walks out of the room, her footsteps clicking along the way.

The boy lifts the blanket to his mouth, his sobs and hiccups muffled.

Director Marguerite leans in, and I see that her teeth are gritted. "I said that's enough!" She leans over the boy until they are eye to eye. "Let this be a lesson: our Regime does not tolerate treachery. You have been given a great opportunity to wash yourself of your mother's ill deeds."

My Pocatelan isn't so great. But I know the little boy has no idea why she's so angry—or what her complicated words mean.

I was only a few winters older than him when my mother died. I know how the boy feels. One moment, he is standing in place, then the next someone slams into him from behind. He may be lying in that soft bed, but he feels like he's crashed onto a flat stone and is unable to breathe. He feels like he might never stand again. And now he's getting a stupid speech he doesn't understand.

"Stay in your bed and be grateful for all you have been given," Director Marguerite finishes, "or you can join your mother outside Pocatel." Then she stomps out, closing the door behind her.

The boy hiccups over and over, not catching his breath.

Gabi starts to slide off her bed toward him.

"Gabi! No!" I hiss. I put one finger to my lips and shoo her back.

The little boy hiccups again.

Gabi huffs and folds her arms over her chest. She takes deep breaths herself as the boy cries.

Finally, Gabi turns away from me and faces him again. "Niñito," she whispers.

He looks over, his face splotchy and quivering.

"It's okay. Would you like to say adiós to your mother?" she asks. "That might help you feel better."

He does not respond, but for a loud hiccup.

Gabi goes back to her bed and lies flat, lifting her arms into the air, then she makes fists, dropping them to her sides. Her tongue rattles on the back of her teeth. "Tccch, tccch, tccch." Still lying down, she points her toe high. He stares at her curiously as she arcs her foot to make the letter C in the air.

He glances over and over at her, his hiccups between her rattles and mouth-thumps sounding like part of the dance. I'm sure he doesn't know what she is doing. He has probably never been this close to one of us.

His face is covered in confusion at first as Gabi dances. Then he turns on one side toward her. He keeps staring, his mouth ajar. With each blink, tears fall from his eyes. He rubs his forearm over his splotchy face.

Gabi continues, until she has danced the entire Cascabel for him from her bed, sending his mother an honorable goodbye. It is the best I've seen her do.

By the time she wraps her coiled cascabel leg around the other in a final bow, his hiccups have stopped.

8

THE TOWN BELL CHIMES THREE TIMES. MAYBE TÍA
Lula? Maybe the little boy's mother? Would they exile a Pocatelan
and Cascabel together on the same night? I don't think there's
been enough time for it to be the boy's mother.

The day's first sunlight pours into the windows. No one is
up yet but me and Gabi. The Cascabel orphans have gotten too
used to these soft beds. No matter how late we work in the Pox,

we rise with the sun. The little blonde boy's arm and leg dangle over the side of the bed. Gabi covers him with the blanket.

I look down and can't believe how clean my feet are.

The town bell chimes once this time. The market will be starting soon.

A boy sits up and run fingers through his hair. A girl with longer hair begins weaving braids, while a few fold their blankets and lay them at the bottom of the bed like we found ours. Gabi and I hurry to do the same, then I motion toward the door. Suddenly, all are starting to move around the room. This is our chance.

We move slowly out and into the hall. Only now, in the light of day, I see that the two classrooms can easily hold every single orphan. We look over the railing downstairs but don't see Director Marguerite or Bridget. We tiptoe below to the bath room and find our old tunics.

As we walk out into the hallway, a young Cascabel girl with curly dark hair stands waiting. She smiles. "¿Terminados?"

I hide the tunics around my back and nod.

"Yes," Gabi says. "I . . . I only used one piece of dung wipe."

The girl tilts her head, and I elbow Gabi. She steps in and closes the door behind her.

"¿Neta, Gabi? That's all you could come up with?"

She shrugs.

Above our heads in the ceiling, the floor sounds like an entire flock of birds are pecking on the ground, as all the kids get ready for the day. No one could sleep in the noise they're making now.

We peek down to the first floor. Bridget's muffled humming echoes from downstairs. We just need to make it out the front door without anyone seeing. We hold on to the wooden beam as we walk down the final steps to the front door.

The metal lock is cold. I twist it in the opposite way Director Marguerite did, and it clicks. I lift the latch and the door squeaks open. We slip through the gap and close the front door carefully.

Smoke from the smelter drifts down the street. The steady *clink . . . clink . . . clink* tells me we'd already be in the fields by now, on a normal day. But it's market time. Outside the orphanage wall, people are already out, headed over.

I open the *Book Return* lid and let out a breath. The bag with our stags, flint, and knife still sits at the bottom of the box. I stand on my toes and push my arm as far as I can, grasping the bag, but it slips from my fingers. I try again, pushing my arm in further. I catch the bag's edge and hold on tightly, pulling it out, then shove it inside the roll of dirty tunics.

I crouch down under the window and Gabi does the same.

We peek through the bottom of the window, hearing Director Marguerite on the third story landing, calling, "Up, up, little bugs."

She might see our made beds and think it's weird that we caught on so quickly, but I hope she has more to worry about than two new orphans.

Hidden on the side of the building, I pull out our old tunics. These new pale green ones would get two kids straying from the orphanage gates picked up in an instant, I figure.

I pull off my new tunic and slip the old one over my head. The smell of our dirty pock fills the air. I hand Gabi hers. She pinches her nose.

"We got used to their soap and clean clothes too quickly."

Gabi holds the green tunic at her side. Her eyes sag. "Is it so bad here, Leandro? Maybe we could stay for a while. Eat delicious food like grubs. We can still leave when we're ready." When I don't answer, Gabi motions back toward the orphanage and whines. "The other kids had *hair*, Leandro."

The sun is already sitting over the valley's ridge. If all goes as planned, we'll be there before dark. "Gabi, you'll have hair again too. But we . . . we're not meant to live in this place." This time, she does not speak. "You saw the classrooms and saw the others . . ." I continue. "Something is not right. I just have a feeling. I can't trust them."

She stares to the south, in the direction of the Pox. "I know you're right." She pulls the new tunic off and slips the old one over her head. "I just liked being clean," she mumbles.

We gather our things and tie the tunics together to make a fake market bag. We peek our heads over the brick wall of the orphanage. Gabi might be on her toes, but even four winters younger, she's almost as tall as me.

The cart from the night before with all the scrap is empty. All the market stands are already set up, and the Mongers are starting to display their goods.

The Monger trading fruit today has dirty hair, held back by a loosely woven scarf. The same scarf secures a patch over his left eye. He sets his fruit in rows, turning the brown and bug-eaten spots underneath. He sets a single red apple top center. From here, it looks perfect.

I notice that he's arranged his fruits in perfect rows, his display tilted so that only he can touch or pick up the fruit from the very top without them toppling off. A clever way to secure his treasure.

The other three Mongers have mostly piled buckets of potatoes and wilted greens.

The Center of Banishment casts a shadow over the second Monger's stand. With one arm, the woman cradles a bin from her wagon. She wears the yellow robe of a weaver, but it's faded and frayed. It's the same Monger I was hoping would be here. She looks in our direction, and a cold sweat covers my face. She might've seen us; we shouldn't be out here alone. Then, I realize she's not looking at me and Gabi. Like always, she's staring at the orphanage behind us. I'm sorry for what she must've lost. But maybe she'll be more distracted today than the others? Her wagon with its undercarriage hidden in the shadows—it's one of those we need. She returns to her work, stacking two bins of potatoes, sorting the largest papas to the top.

Behind her stall sits the cracked-glass storefront of a tech store from Old-World, called Gadgettica. I can barely imagine what Old-World tech was like—to have a light we could turn on instantly when we were afraid of the dark? Or use a toothbrush that moved by itself to clean teeth, instead of a scraper? If the store's ruins weren't still there, I wouldn't believe any of that stuff had ever been real.

Three Cloaks come out of the black exile door of the Center of Banishment. Their faces are covered by hooded cloaks the color of fresh pine needles. I've only seen their kind a handful of times, but I know they hide their faces so no one can tell who they are. Bound to their work, they almost never leave that building—just like the orphans in the orphanage. Dust floats into the blue sky as the Cloaks sweep the path outside, erasing the single set of footprints leading to the exile bridge. The prints could be anyone's. A warning to all—any one of us could be exiled for breaking a rule. Marketgoers glance just long enough at the vanishing tracks to be glad they're not their own.

I know we are watching Tía Lula's footsteps drift into the air. My chest feels tight, though I don't know why. She was horrible to us.

Gabi and I watch the Cloaks finish. Their green robes flow in the breeze. The shortest Cloak then walks out toward the metal footbridge over the Trench. My hands sweat, and I squint my eyes. Did Tía Lula imagine falling before taking the first step? Did she look down as she crossed? Did she make it?

The short Cloak closes the gate leading over the Trench and returns inside the building, behind the others. Gabi moves her arms stiffly in front of her like they do. I bite my lips together, trying not to smile, despite it all.

The lowered drawbridge will stay down only a few more hours, until the last Mongers' wagons have crossed back over to return to the Outlands. They need a couple hours of additional daytime to make it across the wyrmfield before the monsters stir. Gabi and I will have to be in the undercarriage of the potato Monger's wagon before she leaves.

A few Cascabeles approach the edge of the market, not too close. They sit on the ground to watch the bartering that will begin soon, forbidden to participate. Some sit with their children in their laps near the puppet show stage, still a safe distance away. The Pocatelans may allow the Cascabeles a day off in the fields on market day, but I think it's only so they don't have to watch us. And so we can "watch" them. Everyone knows we aren't exactly welcome.

Apart from the food Mongers, two artisans sell stoneware and textiles. The potato seller sifts through her barrel and lifts out a potato. She holds it close, then quickly tucks it behind her back. I watch as she looks from side to side nervously and tosses it into her wagon. I can't help thinking she's seeing the strange rot we saw in the fields.

I face Gabi. "We pick one job, then meet next to the Monger's stall." I hold up the fake market bag. "Then we change into the new green tunics and tell her we need to buy potatoes for Director Marguerite."

Gabi nods.

"Once we have our food, we buy watercells from the textile Monger and say the same." I sigh. "Then we hide and wait. I've thought about it and I don't want to risk bartering with the Monger for passage. It won't be long after that when they'll cross back outside Pocatel." My insides turn just saying the words.

"Maybe we can hide the entire crossing at least?" Gabi says.

My gut is telling me it'll be better if we run for the ridge as soon as we're over the Trench, while it's still daylight. If the potato Monger loses a wheel, or decides to stop before, she might find us. "Maybe," I answer instead. "But if we're found, we run. She won't chase after."

Gabi closes her eyes and takes a big sniff. "I can smell the berries, Leandro. They must be so sweet." She tilts her chin down and her eyes widen. "Do you think we'll ever taste a strawberry?"

I look away and close my eyes. I doubt it, and I know how she feels. To be so close to them—but to risk death if caught. I'd hoped one day I'd know what a strawberry tasted like, too.

"Can we at least try to buy one before we leave . . . ?" she asks.

She knows better. This is not the time. I turn back. "You know if I could . . ."

"Leandro, we might never see fruit again in our entire lives."

"It won't matter if we get caught and exiled, Gabi. Dead people can't eat at all."

Gabi's shoulders sag, and she nods.

"Best of the best!" The fruit Monger rings a bell, interrupting us and announcing the start of the market. He holds the apple high in the air. "Half of my wagon's scrap was spent to acquire this one specimen for market. Beautiful fruit normally reserved for Directors and their families, but today it could belong to one lucky citizen!"

It's silent, even though a crowd of Pocatelans have gathered at this point. I know from our years of watching that a low bid, especially from a common Pocatelan, would be humiliating in front of so many.

The Monger continues: "And the metal treasure I discovered deep in the Outlands, in a location I shall take to my grave . . ." He laughs and points to his eye patch. ". . . and almost did!"

Marketgoers exchange awkward laughter and glances. I scan the crowd. No new robes. Mostly worn shoes. No jewelry or Director badges today. No one who looks like they'd have the stag we need.

A fake wyrm's screech echoes from the puppet stage down the street. It still makes me jump. The puppeteer holds a metal tube to his mouth and honks out a second screech. Kids cover their ears. Some pull hoods over their faces to hide. Some leave their parents to watch, while others drag them along. Even the kids from the Pox cling to their parents, but can't help watching over shoulders and through gapped fingers.

Gabi smiles and follows a small group of kids.

I run after and grab her elbow. "Don't, Gabi. It'll give you nightmares."

"I already have nightmares," she calls back, pointing at the Monger's stand and the people waiting to barter for the fruit and berries. "Why watch someone else get something we'll never be able to have?"

She's got a point. Until we find the right target, there's no point hanging around the fruit stand drawing attention to ourselves. We have to act natural. So, I follow her, and we stand near the other Pox dwellers.

The puppeteer raises his arms. Specks of different colored paint dot his robe and hands. A real feather pokes from a round cap on his head. His moustache curves up on each side like two scythes. "Welcome theater goers." His cap slips to one side, and he hurries to slide it back on his head. "Today, my young friends, I bring a tale of what lies outside the safety of Pocatel, in the Outlands." He clears his throat. "You need never meet a wyrm in your lifetime if you obey the laws of Pocatel, and remain grateful for all the Regime has given you. Do not *cheat*." He leans in and pulls his fingers up the scythe on one side of his moustache. "Do not *lie* to your parents and instructors." Kids exchange nervous glances. He grits his teeth and leftover flecks of beetle shell, from his last meal, stick to his front tooth. "Most of all, do not *steal*! Or you will be banished to the Outlands, where the mutant creatures and necrotizing sand pits await!"

He runs behind the stage, and another screech echoes as the curtain draws back.

Like a monster from my worst nightmare, the scaled gray head emerges first from the wooden earth of the stage. Daggered spines jut from down the center of its head to its back. Fangs flecked with red paint chomp at the air. It shrieks and thrashes, erupting from the stage. A wyrm.

The monster takes up half the puppeteer's stage, and it jumps with its bloody fangs toward the audience. Smoke pours out from behind the stage, sending a cloud of wyrm dust toward the crowd of kids.

Gabi screams with the rest. I take her arm and pull her away back toward the fruit stand. "I told you."

"I'm . . . I'm fine," she stammers. But her smile now is not a real one.

Last market, Gabi and I had picked three stags at market by this time and handed two over to Tía Lula once we were safely back in the Pox. I look back toward the stalls. Still no one who looks like a good target near the fruit stand. There's nothing we can do.

I watch as the fruit Monger shudders, finishing a story I couldn't hear the beginning of. ". . . stealing the egg of the protective mother wyrm."

I'm tempted to yell out "¡Tonterías!" like Franco would. Really, he stole a wyrm's egg?

The crowd's laughs are even more strained than before. Everyone knows Mongers risk their lives outside city walls, bringing in the metal scrap that helps keep Pocatel running. But this guy is working extra hard to make his stag today.

"Forty stags!" a woman's voice finally yells over the crowd. Gasps fill the air as a lady wearing a deep purple robe steps out. She holds up a sagging bag. I think of how heavy all those bronze beetles inside must be. How did I miss her? I should've spotted her early and picked her pocket before she drew attention. Knowing who to target, and how get out early, is how we've never been caught. Today of all days, I can't get distracted.

The Monger shakes his head for show. "I risk my life venturing into the lair of the desert wyrm, and you offer . . ." He sighs and holds up his four-fingered gloved hand, one finger missing. Hushed gasps weave through the crowd. He smiles at the crowd's response and places the apple in his four-fingered hand. "Shall we agree on forty-five?" He holds the thumb of his other hand next to the four fingers.

Most of the crowd snickers, but a few wince. The crowd parts, all eyes on the woman. Forty-five stags is more than most Pocatelans earn in a month. But backing down now would make her look small to the others. Her eyes shift nervously to those around her. She nods and pulls another five stags out of her pocket, walking up and dropping them in his palm.

If he really did lose an eye and finger to a desert wyrm, he should've charged more.

Now that the first deal is done, the stalls all start getting busier. Even the potato Monger has a few customers begin to line up. I nudge Gabi. "It's time."

The cloud of dust from the puppet show grows larger as the wyrm puppet disappears into a necrotizing sand pit, and boils cover its skin. Kids start running around the market in chaos. If I've learned one thing from picking at a Saturday market, it's to never waste a disaster.

A few paces away from us, a woman with a red scarf knotted around her neck walks away from the fruit stand, holding a second newly-traded apple in her hand. She slices off a piece of it and hands it to the little boy walking between her and what must be her husband. The boy shoves the entire piece into his mouth.

"Lucas!" She glances around and smiles at a passing couple, speaking to her son through her teeth. "The boy who bites off more than he can chew chokes on his own gluttony!"

Lucas spits half of the wedge, coated in saliva, back out into his hand. He bows his head.

The man walking with them laughs, sweat dripping off his chin. He wears a thick winter robe, but it has no bronze beetle Director's badge. The woman's scarf might not be as tightly woven and bright as the one Tía Lula stole, but the dye to make it had to cost more than the stags they'll be carrying in their pockets.

"¿Lista?" I nudge Gabi and motion to the family.

Gabi glances from one side to the other before she locks on the couple. The wings on a shiny bronze moth clip in the lady's hair catch the sun. I move my eyes to the bottom of their robes. They're wearing newer shoes, even the boy. Gabi's already skipping toward them.

I bite back my smile. I've taught her well. Gabi veers off, zigzagging ahead in the crowd until she's a little bit in front. I used to feel bad that she's always the one put up as bait, but without her, it would take us three times as long to get the stags we need.

My neck grows hot as she starts. Gabi lifts both arms in the air to get their attention. It works. The couple glances at one another with nervous smiles, but they stop and watch. We've found that a cute Cascabel child is more interesting than scary to people like them—more so than an adult would be. Gabi drops her arms, placing her fists at her waist. She rattles her tongue to her teeth.

"Oh," the woman says, pulling her son tightly to her side and placing her hand to her throat over her scarf. She tilts her head to one side, folds of skin forming at her neck.

Gabi smiles, knowing we've got them. She arcs her leg, drawing a lazy C in the street, then curls the leg around the other. She twists and twirls until she's directly in front of them. Even as she dances, the rapid, thudding drumbeats Tía Lula made when they practiced play in my mind. My own heart beats along.

The couple smiles. The boy peeks around his mother's skirt at Gabi. Just like every other time we're about to steal someone's stag, the man and woman are completely focused on the adorable bald kid dancing Serpientes de Cascabel. A few glance curiously as they walk by, but they pretend not to show much interest. We have to work fast. I search their clothing with my eyes, and sure enough, one pocket of the man's tunic is weighed down with stags even after the apple. I probably only need half of what's inside.

Even a single stag will get us banished if we're caught. I kneel to the ground and pick up a few rocks.

Gabi stomps her feet, twirling in a blur. She rattles her tongue. "Tccch, tcch, tcch, tcch . . ."

Now the lady's head is tilting back and forth, clapping her hands together softly. The little boy giggles. Gabi moves faster and faster as I inch forward.

I scoot closest to the man, making sure the little boy is safely on the opposite side, still clinging to his mother. I slip my hand into his pocket, my size good for this one thing at least. I drop my handful of rocks and wrap my fingers around the stags at the same time, their horns of tiny metal pincers and legs poking into my hand. There must be at least ten! I take as many as will fit in my fist, the man's pocket now weighted down with something else.

Like a puff of smoke, I've already disappeared back into the crowd and am back at the potato stall before the family is any wiser.

People are still jostling to get a better view of the first Monger's stand and watch the restricted fruits and vegetables selling. It seems like Pocatelans are buying even more than usual. Even the stoneware and textile Mongers leave their booths unattended to come watch.

Sweat drips down my face as I hunch down between the Gadgettica storefront and potato stall. I pull out the stags, counting them one by one until twenty-one *clink* into my pocket. I smile. This is definitely enough to get us everything we need, including two bedrolls.

I count again, but this time for Gabi to return. *Uno, dos, tres, cuatro, cinco* . . . Where is she? I wipe the sweat off my jaw. *Seis, siete, ocho, nueve* . . . Gabi's never more than eight seconds behind. I run back to peek around the edge of the stall. I see her. She's standing to the side of the fruit stand now, hiding, apart from the rest of the crowd. The family is nowhere to be seen. *Not part of our plan.*

Gabi glances quickly from one side to the other, like she's scoping another target. She crouches behind the panel of wood holding the fruit in, on the side of the Monger's stand. I can see that no one's watching her. She rises slowly. Her eyes lock on the strawberries. She pulls one hand from behind her back.

No!

Gabi reaches out toward the highest strawberry. Coldpox run up my neck. She stretches, on her tiptoes. A woman twice my size steps in front of me, and I lose sight of her. I push around the woman and see the Monger holding out four ears of corn to a man. I bump the man who's holding out a small pile of stags. One falls to the ground, and its bronze body disappears in the dirt, feet sticking up.

"Hey!" he yells. "Lice-infested mongrel—" But his voice is drowned out by the ringing of the Monger's alarm bell as red berries now tumble off his display, into the dirt.

The crowd scatters in an instant. People scramble to get as far away as they can from the theft. The chaos leaves a cloud of dirt surrounding the stand.

I push through the panicked people into the cloud. I find Gabi crouched along the side of the stand, where she'd been hiding. She looks up at me, eyes sagging, mouth ajar. Red juice drips from her fingers, her hand gripped on the strawberry.

The fruit Monger sets the bell down. The dust begins to clear. The Monger's eyes scan the front of his stand, looking for the thief. His eyes fall as he finally sees us at its side, the evidence on Gabi's hands. He knows he can't un-ring the bell. Even on a nine-winter-old girl.

I stand in front of her and face him. "Please," I say.

He shakes his head and grumbles, turning away. "Stupid Cascabeles." He throws the bell to the ground, moving to the opposite side of his stall.

I grab the mushed strawberry from Gabi's hand and wipe her fingers on the front of my dirty tunic, destroying the evidence. Her eyes are filled with tears. She opens her mouth to speak. I shush her, shaking my head.

The dark blue robe of a Patrol approaches, shoving market-goers aside. As he gets closer, I see it's the smaller one with the little gun who took Tía Lula. I hurry to push Gabi back behind the stall's curtain, next to the cracked glass storefront. I shove the market bag with the stags and the rest of our belongings into her hands.

She whimpers, "I'm sorry, Lean—"

I give her a quick hug, but I squeeze so hard. I know it will be our last. "Shhh. It's okay, Gabi." I put my hand out, telling her to stay there. And I run into the marketgoers, putting distance between us. I hold what's left of the strawberry up in my hand, where the Patrol will be able to see it. Juice runs down my elbow and my hand trembles.

My face burns and my head thrums with my heartbeat in my ears, like the "Cancíon de los Cascabeles" rattle.

A lady standing nearby, with narrow-set eyes and spiraled blonde hair, glances from me to where Gabi's bare feet jut out from beneath the stall's curtain. She takes a breath and straightens her back. She knows. She looks the type to stick her nose into someone else's business, too. Her mouth purses, and she steps forward.

"¡Oye!" I scream, and the woman stops.

Every last person in the market turns their eyes on me. The guard stops, a few paces away. I steady my hand and place the strawberry carefully between my fingers. No one moves. Not a single human, animal, or bug makes a noise. Only the sound of the cascabel rattle, beating in my head. I take another step forward and my legs shake beneath me. I swallow, and saliva runs over my dry throat like razor blades.

I place the strawberry at my lips and open my mouth, pushing it inside.

Gasps and pointed fingers all aim at me.

My mouth explodes with the most wonderful flavor I've ever tasted. I chew and swallow. There's no point in trying to run. People back away like I've got a disease.

The Patrol grips the gun at his waist and rushes forward, grabbing and clenching my elbow.

Stares follow us as he leads me away down the street. No one says anything further. A crowd of different-colored robes parts to let us pass. Now the only sound I can hear is the clinking metal of the exile bridge in the wind. Every Pocatelan stands by as a kid of thirteen winters is led away.

I pretend to trip as the guard walks me outside the market, glancing back to find Gabi as I stumble. A tiny eye watches from a gap in the stall's curtain. The Monger's already back to bartering, forgetting easily about the little Cascabel thieves whose dreams he just ruined with his bell. I shake my head in warning at her. If she confesses even after I'm gone, or is found here in the market by the orphanage Director, she'll get exiled just as if she'd been caught red-handed. This will be the last time we see each other. I feel my lips tremble even as I force a smile goodbye.

9

WHEN I TURN BACK, A DARK ORANGE CAPE IN A STORM of dust is stomping down the street toward us. Just like a bad dream, my feet want to run, but I'm frozen. In the time before we came to Pocatel, we once found a bloated opossum carcass on the side of a desert road. Director Marguerite's pink cheeks jut out from the top, puffed out just like it. She stops, facing me, hands on her hips. Blonde strands of hair escape from her bun, plastered to her sweaty forehead. She scans the crowd of the market, now a distance away, huffing. "Do you want to tell me where your *hermana* is?" she mocks, attempting a Cascabel accent.

I don't dare look back.

Farther down the street ahead at least four Patrol wait for us near the Center of Banishment. One points in our direction, and El Bastón appears from behind them, striding toward us.

He taps his stick casually with each step until he reaches us. He smiles at Director Marguerite. "Well, that didn't take long for you to lose one, did it?"

Her eyes flick from me toward the exile trail. "Some are incapable of repentance." She scans the market again, stained teeth clenched. I know she's looking for Gabi.

I don't speak. They just need someone to punish now. My footprints will be swept away by the Cloaks soon enough. But I won't go quietly after that. I will run for the ridge and find a way to return for Gabi.

Director Marguerite leans into me, nose to nose, and huffs right on me. The same smell from the steam of her cup of hot brown water fills my nostrils. I turn my face, pretending to be scared of her, just like I would with Tía Lula.

I look back toward the market now, but the crowd is too thick to see the fruit stand anymore. Then I see Gabi. She's scampering past crumbling storefronts, back toward the orphanage. I watch until she crosses the street and is inside the stone wall. Her dirty tunic flies over the wall and then my green-tunicked sister emerges, dashing inside the front door.

Director Marguerite must see her too. She makes a pleased, tooth-stained grin, then says quietly: "When the path of penitence closes for one, the path widens for another." She nods her head at El Bastón, and stomps away toward the orphanage. Her strange words send a chill through my body.

But at least, for now, Gabi will have clean clothes and food. I hope she doesn't feel bad about what's happened. She was just doing what we were taught . . . what I taught her.

El Bastón's dark rat eyes bore into me as the smaller Patrol ties my hands behind my back, then we're walking again. They begin dragging me toward the Center of Banishment. We pass a smelting hut, and molten slag hisses and spits at me as the metalsmith pours water over it.

Anyone not at the market turns away as we pass by.

I catch sight of a few Pox dwellers on the outskirts of the market, still looking at us. Among the Pocatelans, the dirt on our faces and tunics stands out even more. I see Ari. Her mouth goes slightly ajar, then she closes it, eyes welling with tears. Slowly, she pushes one leg out and carves a C in front of her. Heat burns behind my eyes, and I hold my head higher.

I stare past them to the end of town, where I can see the Tree of Souls in the distance. From here, the braids of hair and shreds of tunic really do look like leaves blowing in the wind. If I could break free and run past it into the haunted forest, I would. Getting eaten by ghosts seems better than what's ahead of me.

We turn at last into the Center of Banishment. El Bastón pulls out a key tied to his waistband and unlocks the front door.

He smiles and holds it open for me, like he's welcoming me inside his home.

I step inside. Icy pinpricks hit the bottom of my feet from the cold floor. El Bastón locks the door behind us. His shoes click on the hard floor. My footsteps are silent.

The thick smell of oil fills my nose. Lamps hang from hooks on both sides of the dark hall. Their flames flicker across the floor. On the end of the hall, a larger door waits. As we near the door, I see a carving of a blindfolded woman in a long robe holding a sword in one hand, hundreds of winters of cracks splintering through her wooden body like a corpse.

The tip of the wooden lady's sword hits the bottom of the door, like it might scrape the floor. In her other hand, she clutches a scale.

Just as we're nearing the door, the hall opens up even more, to the side. Sitting on a bench in a corner is a small woman and a guard. Like mine, the lady's hands are tied behind her back. The guard sitting next to her is slumped to the side of the bench, snoring.

El Bastón hits the guard's leg with his stick and he snorts awake.

"There is little distinction between the stillness of sleep and the stillness of death," El Bastón states.

"I am sorry, sir." The man straightens, like that actually means something.

The guard moves over, motioning me to sit to his side closest to the large door.

The blonde woman's sad eyes make a quick glance at me, but I think the look is for herself, not me. Her breath catches for just a second in a familiar hiccup. And I know in a split second. She is the little boy's mother.

It doesn't take long before El Bastón leaves us. The young guard, the woman, and I sit for hours. My tongue scrapes the roof of my mouth, so dry it feels like it might rub off sand, but what's the point of asking for water? Why give water to a doomed person? I watch as the sun crosses the sky through a window.

It's nearly dusk when the scream of a wyrm finally echoes from outside. The guard jolts awake and stands, mumbling something about the stillness of death. He walks across the room to secure the front door. Then returns to his spot on the bench, and within minutes, his head nods in jerks as he fights sleep again. Sleep wins.

Eventually, the sound of the main door squeaking open breaks the silence. The woman on the bench sits up tall. A set of quiet footsteps, then another, then many echo down the hall. Even in their numbers, they enter so quietly, the guard's breathing remains steady.

I'm frozen. Is this it? Are these Pocatelans, coming to watch our Banishment? One by one, though, the footsteps disappear. Only the murmur of voices remains. I lean out toward the hall we entered, to see. The hall should be full of people. But it's empty.

I crane my head further to look around the corner, just as a robe—the color of dried blood—disappears inside a door in the hall. As the door closes, the robe catches the door's edge. From the gap that's left, a strip of light falls across the stone entry hall.

Three large *pings* echo from inside the room. Voices all speak a sentence together at once, too muffled for me to hear.

I turn back and look at the woman sitting further down the bench from me, the guard in between us. Her nervous eyes meet mine, but her expression betrays nothing. I scoot to the edge and lean forward, pretending to stretch. I still can't hear what they're saying.

I glance at the sleeping guard again and stand. My butt and legs are numb. Blood slowly flows back into them. The lady's eyes widen then, and she shakes her head at me. "No," she whispers. "*Stay.*"

My bare feet make no noise as I walk softly to the door. As I near the door, I catch snatches of words like "snakes" and "Pox" and "drought" and "blight." As quietly as I can, I hurry to slide closer and closer until I'm near the crack. Unlike the carved wooden door, this one is so dark and blended to the wall, I might not have seen if it weren't a little ajar. The light hits my eye and I squint, staring through the gap. I'm breathing too hard, so I try to breathe through my nose.

I put my eye as close as I dare to the sliver of light.

Twelve men and women, each wearing dark, tightly woven robes, sit around a round table. The table fills the entire room. Bronze Director beetles sit perched on the shoulders of shades of red, green, gold, orange, blue. Words cast in bronze line the wall above their heads, just like the orphanage classroom. *Unity.*

Sacrifice. And words I've never heard before, like C-o-n-s-e-n-s-u-s. In between each one, a larger bronze *Preservation* is repeated over and over.

There are more Directors here than I've ever seen in one place. The Field Director. El Bastón. Director Marguerite. The puppeteer? He's changed his clothes and has a clean black robe, but it's him—his hands are still flecked with paint. And now he's wearing a bronze beetle on his chest.

Others I've never seen. But I know there are Directors for things I'll never know about, like Education, and Procreation, and Trade. One woman, with a smooth bun of red hair and a deep blue robe, I recognize as someone I picked two stags off of three markets ago.

Another woman with blonde hair and pale purple robe sits next to her. Her hands are hidden beneath the table. She doesn't look up like the others.

At the head of the table, a man's chair sits higher than the rest. He hovers like a cloud over the room. Even his hair is a mix of gray and black against his dried-blood robe, almost like a thunderstorm. The largest Director's badge I've ever seen sits on his shoulder. A horned bronze beetle, three times larger than the others, crouching with its pincers pointed angrily in attack to the sky. This man I've definitely never seen before, not in the fields, not at the market . . .

"Let our Directors' meeting begin," the man says. "It is with solemn hearts, but determined minds, that we proceed with the Thinning."

10

···(···

"THE WORDS OF OUR FIRST LEADERS. OUR CORNER-
stone," the man with the dried-blood robe speaks, in the steady
rhythm of a smelting hammer. He pauses before speaking the
final words slowly: "No war, no conflict, no starvation."

All but one answers in unison: "*Lest we not forget our
origins.*"

The blonde woman I noticed earlier lifts her head, and in a
soft voice, says, "May I humbly say, I believe our forefathers'

words were meant for all humans? What of those we welcomed—"

"Welcomed?" El Bastón leans in. "For hundreds of years we lived in secluded peace, without disruption from other humans. We had no choice! Leave them to wander—to return and destroy all we've created? We integrated them in a way that was best for us at the time, that is all."

All eyes fall on the woman, and she lowers her head.

The Field Director turns and glares at the woman. "Soon we will not be able to hide the blight from Pocatelan citizens. Our ancestors," he spits out, "said nothing of taking on the burden of outsiders in desperate times."

The man with the dried-blood robe clears his throat and speaks calmly. "Patience with imperception, Finneas."

The Field Director lowers his voice. "Yes, Imperator Wallace."

My blood freezes. *Imperator.* I've only heard whispers of this person . . . a sort of head Director. I didn't think them true.

The man—the Imperator—smiles at the woman, but she won't look at him. "We have not had such a trial as we have now for some time," he continues. "As Dolores knows, we care for as many as is sustainable." His voice grows stern now. "But we must remain in consensus, or our system fails. We must trust our forefathers' design will resolve this issue. There is a reason the duties of Directors are passed down within our families. We alone understand the secrecy needed to Preserve our ways. Our own offspring will be tasked with doing the same, in this very room, as our parents and grandparents before us. However . . .

arduous ... these choices we are forced to make may be to some."
His voice grows louder. "And that is why the words spoken in
this room remain sacred and secret, to protect our citizens. And
once we leave this world, those trained to replace us will do the
same, just as their ancestors before."

The blonde woman, Dolores, twists her hands under the
table. "But our people have never known a life without the terror
of the wyrmfields, or necrotizing sand pits, or the Outlands ..."

"Perhaps we should inquire with our Director of Truth," El
Bastón says, turning to the puppeteer. "Elias?"

"Fear is healthy," the puppeteer speaks, but it's like he's talking
through his nose. Nothing like his booming voice in the market.
"If our people are united in fear of something bigger, we will not
fear one another. We will not turn on one another." He pulls at one
curved blade of his moustache. "The frightened will not rebel."

"Perfectly spoken!" the Imperator answers, nodding.

The puppeteer bows his head. "Thank you, Imperator
Wallace."

"And we all know what happened when our ancestors devi-
ated ... when long ago, some in this room sought more beyond
the Pocatel Valley," the Imperator continues. "Greed wove its way
into the heart of our Regime." He slams his fist on the table suddenly, his pinky ring making a loud *ping*.

Murmurs fill the room. Then together they speak at once.
"*Remember the sin, lest we not forget.*"

The Imperator's eyes burrow into Dolores now. I see her
hands trembling under the table.

"No," he continues. "We will not speak of deviating from what has kept us alive all these centuries." He brushes his hair back with his hand. "Preservation above all. Preservation of our customs. Preservation of our resources. Even if that means sacrifice. *Especially* if it means sacrifice. That means I . . ." he clears his throat, ". . . *we* . . . will do whatever we must to preserve ourselves and our way of life. Just as the first of us survived by remaining safely in the mines." He speaks so softly now, it is even more frightening. "A sacrifice that starved some, to save many. That is why we act swiftly, to cut off the diseased limb of the body if one of us ever threatens to infect our beliefs. No one is above sacrifice. You know better than any, Dolores. No one is immune."

She glares at him now. "Yes, I do."

The Imperator straightens his back, scanning the rest of the Directors. "We will tell the citizens there has been an outbreak of lying, cheating, stealing. Dangerous, rebellious behavior that threatens the safety of our ways. One that requires unprecedented Banishments."

I let out a breath before I can catch it, but none hear.

This time, there is no objection. "If we are all of a consensus?" he asks.

El Bastón hits his staff on the ground, not waiting for an answer. "I believe we are. I can organize my Patrol so it begins quietly, without revolt of the snakes."

Goosebumps run up my arms.

"Still," Director Marguerite's voice rings out, "our food supplies are depleted like never before. Will Thinning the weakest
be enough?"

"We exile so many as it is," Dolores's voice trembles.

The woman with the dark blue robe speaks. "Yes," she agrees,
turning to Director Marguerite. "And with what we are propos-
ing, our own people would soon be back to working the fields.
Perhaps we should reconsider another way. I could revoke all
permits of procreation . . . ?"

"No. No. We should never sacrifice in favor of fewer
Pocatelans. We must . . . find a balance." Director Marguerite clears
her throat. "Today's account was forty-nine mouths. More than
ever."

El Bastón sneers, his upper lip higher on the side with the
bronze tooth. "Do you not mean forty-eight?"

Director Marguerite's eyes could spit venom. "Yes. Pardon the
correction. Forty-eight."

The Imperator turns casually to Director Marguerite. "Thank
you for the register."

Dolores leans over the table and scans the faces of the others.
"You cannot be serious? The orphans?"

The Imperator taps his pinky ring on the table. "Yes, yes.
Arduous decisions." He sighs and shakes his head. "But we've
planned for the usefulness of these orphans. They will soon
replace all the Cloaks and snakes. With Director Marguerite's
direction and reeducation. . . . Younger, stronger, faster, obedient

field workers, completely dedicated to service of the Pocatelan Regime, unlike those before them. We are creating a society where our principles will hold the descendants of the snakes in alignment."

Director Marguerite gazes off, a strange smile on her face. "Yes, but to help the balance . . . I can already see the promise of some, but others . . ." She clicks her tongue at the final words. "I will have an updated count of mouths of the most promising within the week."

I close my eyes and take breaths, focusing to keep from throwing up.

"I will sift through those less apt toward our needs, the most disobedient first," she finishes.

My entire body shivers. *Oh, Gabi.*

"And the Mongers?" the puppeteer asks. "I have trained many of them."

"We have succeeded in our system with them for hundreds of years this way," the Imperator says. "For now, they have their usefulness."

"Until they do not," Dolores says.

The Imperator turns slowly to face her. "Yes," he smiles. "Until they do not."

Director Marguerite claps her hands together. "Then it is decided. This week for the count. In the next, we begin. For now we continue as usual, which means . . ." she grins at the Imperator. "You have a few exiles to attend to?"

"I do." He nods. "Shall we proceed first? All in agreement?" The Imperator hits his ring three times on the table. Just as before, they speak as one, but this time I can hear the words. "For the Preservation of Pocatel . . ." Even Dolores, her face paler than before, speaks the three final words softly along with the others: "*Unity, Consensus, Sacrifice.*"

I can't help staring at her. Then she looks up.

As her eyes meet mine, they widen. She stands and quietly walks in my direction. I flatten my back to the wall, but it's too late. Her footsteps approach, the beam of light disappearing as she nears the door. But instead of yanking me inside to face instant punishment, the door shuts with a quiet click.

11

· · · ☾ · · ·

I WANT TO RUN BACK TO THE BENCH, BUT I TAKE TWO deep breaths and back away slowly from the room. The guard still sleeps. I slip back on to the bench. The woman is right where I left her, staring at me, her mouth agape.

There's no way she could've heard what I did from where she sits. How her son, and Gabi—the weak, the disobedient—are next. But I can't hide the pain on my face.

The click of footsteps and screech of chairs moving behind the door signal the end of the Directors' meeting. My stomach twists. Our time is up. I turn to the woman, but she's still looking at me. She squeezes her eyes and her chest moves up and down with quick breaths. Mine does too. A tear falls down her cheek. But I don't think she's crying for herself. She turns away.

"Pssst," I whisper.

She turns back. Her brow is wrinkled with worry and the sides of her mouth turn down.

Nothing I say could make this worse than it is. "Your hijo . . ." She tilts her head.

"Your son . . ." I repeat.

She wipes her face and leans toward me.

"He was sad," I say quietly, one eye on the guard. "But my sister, Gabriela, danced for him, and I think he will be okay now. She will watch out for him."

I can't know how long it will be true. But if I know Gabi, she will try to protect him for as long as she can, no matter what happens.

The Pocatelan woman stares at me for a moment, trying to make sense, I'm sure, of what I've said. Then she bites her lips together and makes a small nod. *Thank you,* she mouths.

I smile, and I think of how different this boy's mother and I are. But somehow, in this moment, we're also the same.

The door in the hall opens, and just as they all entered, the footsteps exit through the front entrance. One set of footsteps followed by the thump of a staff on the floor approaches us, but this time I don't lean out to see who it is.

We stare straight ahead. The guard jolts awake and wipes drool from his mouth and stands. He motions for us to stand. El Bastón waits in front of the door with the wood-carved lady. We stand behind him.

El Bastón pushes the door open, splitting the carved woman on its surface in half. Empty rows of wooden benches line each side of the room. Lamplight dances up wood-paneled walls.

El Bastón pulls the woman forward and points for me to sit on a long bench on one side of the room.

A raised desk sits in the center of the room. On its surface is real paper and a pen. To its side, I see a black metal door with the faded word Exit across it, where there were once Old-World letters. I recognize the black metal door as the same I'd seen from the outside in the market. The one leading to the trail of Banishment, and the exile bridge. El Bastón releases the lady's elbow when they're standing in the center of the room in front of the desk. El Bastón remains at her side. He doesn't need to guard her, though. She's paralyzed.

To my other side, the Imperator with his dried-blood robe enters. As he passes, a breeze the smell of woodfire floats by. He walks past the rows of benches inside the room and past El Bastón and the woman, who wait.

He sits and pulls a lamp closer in front of him. The lamp's fire dances on the silver in his hair. His dead eyes, the color of tarnished stags, stare down at her now. "I trust you know who I am?"

The woman nods, her voice trembles. "Yes, Imperator. I am sorry to pull you from your duties."

"As you know, sacrifice is at the heart of repentance." He clears his throat. "Then, we shall begin. Celia Stone, your charge is subversion. How plead you?"

Celia picks nervously at the fraying braid of the vine-tie holding her hands behind her back. "I . . . I did not think anyone heard, Imperator."

He pushes the lamp back to his side and glares at her. "But someone did. You shared with a fellow Pocatelan that you opposed the Regime's policy."

Celia looks away.

"Do you know why they call me Imperator?"

She doesn't move.

"I am the Director of Preservation. And to command preservation of Pocatel is above all." He grins widely, and suddenly. "You, Miss Stone, are in direct opposition to my duty to Pocatel, are you not?"

Celia says nothing in response.

He grins swiftly again. "I will take your silence as your answer." The Imperator writes on his paper. When he raises his head, his face has gone as still as stone. "Celia Stone, your sentence is Banishment. I gain no pleasure in this. For a lesser charge, you might have received passage to the Outlands, and a chance to return, as a Monger. But the hour is nigh."

Her head drops. "Please, Imperator. It was a careless comment, told to a friend in confidence. I did not intend . . ." She hiccups. "I only meant I disagreed with . . ." She takes three long breaths. "Sir, I have a son. He has no one else."

It's so quiet in the room, I hear the tear hit the floor after it drops from her chin.

But unlike Celia Stone, I won't cry. And I won't lower my eyes to anyone.

The Imperator removes his glasses and slowly folds the arms in. "Disagreement is a small step from opposition. Opposition is a small step from rebellion, which is one small step from the end of our society." He pinches his brow. "I truly do not take joy in my duties, Miss Stone. But because our ways establish unity, your son . . . could be a great Pocatelan one day. Even the sons and daughters of Directors are not immune from admonishment." He sighs and finishes, "Celia Stone, you are banished from Pocatel, to never return."

Celia lets out several shocked sobs.

The Imperator focuses downward, writing on the sheet of paper, paying her no heed. "Preservation above all."

El Bastón grips her elbow. This time it's good that he does. Celia's knees buckle, and El Bastón carries her like a bin of potatoes toward the exile door. He cuts the twine behind her back. She pulls her hands to the front of her body and rubs her wrists. The other guard hands her a watercell and a few day's rations. I'm not sure why.

Celia closes her eyes for a moment, then hands it all back. "Will you please give this to my son instead?"

The Imperator interrupts to respond, still not looking up from his desk: "He will have sufficient food in the orphanage. I suggest you take it."

I think of Gabi and hope I'm right—that she'll have the good food she wished for, at least until I can come back for her. How will I come back for her?

Celia doesn't move, still holding the rations out to the guard. I understand why. She has little chance of making it through the night, and everyone in this room knows it.

The Imperator finally nods and flicks his hand, motioning to the guard. She makes a small bow of thanks to the Imperator. But even if she gets past the wrymfield by some miracle, she's just guaranteed herself a quicker death sentence.

Knowing the reason Celia was banished and how we're in some ways the same, I still know better than to trust a desperate person. If we both make it over the bridge, I'll have to run in the opposite direction.

She glances back at me quickly before walking to the closed door. El Bastón follows, standing next to her. She stands very still, her forehead resting on the metal door. She takes a deep breath and pushes it open. A gust of wind and darkness greets her. Dust blows into the room and onto El Bastón's boots. Celia shivers and wraps her arms around her waist.

She takes a small step, then stops. She crosses her arms in front of her body and pulls her dress up at the waist and over her head.

El Bastón turns his head the other way, and the Imperator scoffs. Celia looks directly at El Bastón, even though he won't look at her. She hands the tightly woven clothing to him. "Please give this to my son also. He will need it more than I." Then she turns and straightens her back and steps out onto the trail of Banishment. Metal clinking of the swinging exile bridge calls her ahead.

Don't look down. Don't look down.

The heavy door closes behind her with a thud.

The room is washed in silence and the smell of lamp oil again. The guard tosses Celia's food back into the bin with the rest. I hear the door open behind me, but I don't turn to see.

El Bastón wipes the dust off his boots with her dress and throws it into the pile with the food. The Imperator stares down at his desk and returns to his writing.

I want to yell out that I saw what he just did; that I heard them in the room; that they're all liars. And that he is the worst of them. But El Bastón just comes and lifts me to my feet by my elbow, leading me to the center of the room.

We stand in silence, the only noise now a faint whistle through the Imperator's nostrils as he breathes.

"Your name?" he finally calls out, without looking up.

"Leandro Rivera," I answer. "Leandro Rivera Garcia Salgado Hernandez San Joaquin de los Cascabeles."

He writes on a paper and sighs. "Landro Rivera, you've been accused of . . . ?"

"Theft!" someone calls out. I turn my head to see it is the pointy-nosed field guard standing inside the door. The one who kicked dirt on me.

The Imperator glances up. "You witnessed it?"

The field guard sways back and forth. "I saw the little snake take the fruit from the Monger's stall myself."

Liar. I let out a deep breath and shake my head. I never stood a chance.

The Imperator nods at him. "I see." He looks back at his paper and continues to write. "Any arguments or pleas?"

"No," I answer.

"You don't deny stealing it?" he asks.

The field guard steps forward. "He doesn't speak Pocat—"

"No," I interrupt. "I stole it, then I ate it. And my Pocatelan is better than yours." I smile at the guard, and he steps back, his face red.

The Imperator squints at me. "You think this is funny?" He glances at his form. "Landro," he mispronounces.

"No," I answer, not bothering to correct him. "I just want you to know what happened."

"Then I have come to my decision," he says stiffly.

I think of Celia and how she must be to the metal walkway by now, staring into the depths of the Trench. I don't want to think of her naked body, lying in the jagged slag pit of its bottom. "Would you give my food to my family too if I asked?"

The Imperator peers over the desk with his tarnished golden eyes, and his sudden smile returns. He doesn't answer.

I want to answer back, I *will take your silence as your answer.* But at least this time he's not lying. So why even bother with a fake trial? Why not just dump me straight into the Trench? Inside

of this room, there are no eyes to witness these men's crimes—
and outside in the dark, no one can see.

The click of footsteps echoes from behind me in the room.
The blonde woman in the pale purple robe—Dolores—enters
and stands at the side of the room, her hands clasped at her waist.
Light reflects off her Director's badge.

"As a minor, your Banishment is a sentence of three years,"
the Imperator says.

My gaze turns quickly back to his. "*Pffft.* Why pretend? You
all expect me to die out there."

He continues, ignoring me. "After which time, Landro, you
will return."

I shake my head. I know what's next. I walk to the guard to
wait for rations just like Celia. But, unlike her, I won't give mine
back. I'll need it for when I make it to the ridge. My tunic may be
thin and dirty, but I won't give it to El Bastón to wipe off his
boots. I'll sprint to the east, where the mountains are closest. I'll
stay along the edge of the Trench as long as I can. If the wyrms
screech, I'll find boulders they can't burrow beneath to sit on,
until the sun comes up. I *will* get back to Gabi.

I look up at the guard, but he hasn't moved or come to cut
the twine holding my wrists. The guard looks from side to side.
"What?" he says. "Why are you staring at me.?"

The Imperator clears his throat. "Mr. Rivera?"

I turn back and he's pointing to Dolores. She has the smallest of smiles and is motioning for me to follow.

I furrow my brow. She has the same look I saw on Ari's face. Pity? Sadness? Something feels even more wrong than before.

The Imperator flicks his hand like he's shooing a fly. "Landro Rivera, go with the Physician."

Physician?

I don't move. What other punishment will they give me? Maybe Tía Lula wasn't lying after all and this Physician *is* here for my organs. She may not seem to agree with them, but she knows what they've done. She's part of it.

The Imperator sighs. "You should comply. I suspect when we reunite one day, you will find yourself grateful for the opportunity I give you today." He shakes his head. "How close you came . . ."

El Bastón flares his nostrils and steps in my direction, lifting his staff. But Dolores reaches me first and takes my elbow gently. She whispers, "Leandro. Come with me."

El Bastón turns his staff sideways and uses it to push me forward. Dolores pushes on one of the wood panels in the room, and it swings inward.

She slips through and El Bastón shoves me after. He crouches and turns sideways to fit through after me. The wood-paneled door clicks shut behind us.

My eyes adjust to the dark. A single lamp flickers over a shiny black floor.

"Where are you taking me?"

Dolores speaks softly. "To your Banishment."

I stop. "Then you're going the wrong way."

She glances at El Bastón, then stops to face me. "Like the Imperator said, Leandro. You are a minor." I think I see her eyes welling with tears, and she turns away. She doesn't look angry or even sad, though. Her voice trembles. "Your Banishment will be . . . different."

12

THE FLOOR IS THE BLACK OF A STARLESS SKY. I'VE
never felt stone so cold under my feet. As my eyes adjust, I see
that in the shadows of the far corner of the room, bars run from
floor to ceiling. A shiver runs up my back. Is this what will be
"different" about my Banishment? Forgotten in this cage with
its night-black floor, no footprints left behind on the trail outside for the Cloaks to sweep? Gabi will not even be able to see
the last sign of me drift into the sky. Just gone.

That is why the cage is empty now. Exiles like me just disappear—like they never existed. My breath catches in my throat just like Celia and her boy.

But then I feel a hand on my shoulder, and we pass through the room with the cage. My heartbeat slows. We enter a long hall.

On the floor ahead of us, ghosts of animals stare back at me. Their bodies are warped like I'm looking through water. Underneath faded colors, silver or gold peeks through. I jump back and my head hits El Bastón's chest. Completely still and silent, birds and other creatures I've never seen are watching us from another place and time.

I glance at the woman for an answer, but she doesn't slow. Can she not see them?

It can't be real. "Brujería," I whisper, bending down to try and touch them.

El Bastón pushes his staff out, holding it to my neck, and Dolores swats it back away from me.

She glares back at him as she kneels next to me. "It is just a reflection, Leandro." She points upward to each side of the hall.

I follow her finger and blow out a breath. Glass shelves above our heads line the sides of the walls. Metal animals of all sizes fill the shelves. I *think* I know what they are, but I can't believe it's real. Believing they're magic is easier.

She pulls me up, and we walk inside.

A furry four-legged creature with ears pointed into triangles leans down like he is stalking me. Golden-rimmed black eyes stare back at me. His fangs snarl. But he is motionless, his attack frozen in time.

Beneath the furry beast, a rabbit crouches. He must have crawled from the safety of his underground burrow. I want to stomp at him, to warn him so he's not the creature's meal.

A bird as small as my finger sits on a perch. Its beak, sharp like a sewing needle, is aimed at the center of . . . a flower? Behind him, an animal with a long tail extends a clawed paw toward the unaware bird.

On the opposite side of me, thousands of the same bird are lined like an army of flying warriors, along with tiny striped bugs with wings of their own, and other creatures just smaller than the needle-beaked birds, with stick-like legs, and large wings with swirling patterns.

Just as in the orphanage classroom and the wall over the Directors' room, words in bronze lie above the metal animals. *Remember the sin. Lest we not forget.* The same words the Directors spoke.

"These are called drones," the Physician says, standing. She motions for me to follow her. "Have you heard of them?"

"El Mundo Viejo," I whisper. "Old-World."

I've never seen so much real tech—hundreds of winters old—all in one place. Not a single one is broken. Their polished metal shines brighter than a Director's badge, and their black glass eyes glint like a snake's. If they weren't cast of metal, their beaks, claws, feathers, and fur could be those of a real animal. The Pocatelan smelters and casters could never make beetles and jewelry this beautiful.

I stand to follow her and stare up at the . . . drones . . . as we walk. Light glints off the talon of a bird and catches my eye. A sign beneath reads Hawk. The bird clenches what looks like a market bag. But this bag isn't made of cloth. It's shiny black. A gold arrow, piercing the center of three purple circles, decorates its side. The same arrow and purple circles are painted on the bird's body. Dark domed eyes stare out angrily. Another larger bird holding an even larger bag has piercing eyes and a hooked beak. It is labeled Eagle.

Dolores stops in front of these animals. "In the Old-World, the metal used to create these was mined in the hills surrounding Pocatel."

Below the army of the tiny flying animals and bugs is a sign with a word that is hard to sound out in my mind: Pollinators. Below that it says: Bees, Butterflies, and under the small birds with the long beaks, Hummingbirds.

We always thought the stories Jo told by the fire at night, before we arrived to Pocatel, had to be made-up. Most of them, at least. "En el mundo viejo, people even owned real animals as pets," Jo had said.

"Not meat?" I asked.

"No," he answered. "And, if your pet died, you could create one made of metal that would never die."

We'd laughed, and he just shrugged, saying he was only repeating what he'd been told.

But that was before Gabi found the alebrije along the path.

"TÍA LULA!" GABI squealed. "¡Mira!" She bent down to pick up a metal bird.

Tía Lula pulled us off the path and out of the way of the other Cascabeles. At this point in our journey, we were all struggling. I don't think we had eaten anything for two days.

"Ooooh!" I reached out to touch it. "Is it real?" Its silver eyelid was half-closed over little glass eyes. I brushed dirt off its eyes. Its rusted silver wings jutted out stiffly, like the fingers of the dead.

I'd seen a few crows—and even what I think was a hawk off in the distance once—but not much more than that.

Tía Lula's brow pinched in a V. "Un alebrije."

"¿Alebrijes?"

"Magical animals," she grumbled. "Animales fantasticos. Perritos with wings . . ."

I try to imagine a flying dog.

"Gatos that could swim. Fish that could walk. But don't hope to find them in this dead world." She sighed. "There is little magic left."

"But this can't be one of those. It's not alive." I looked down at the metal bird and tapped it with my fingernail. "So, why call it un alebrije?"

She shook her head. "Because . . . because just like alebrijes, it's one of those things that doesn't make sense. It is unnatural."

Gabi hid it behind her back. "Can I keep it?" she begged.

"Why keep it? How could this metal scrap do good? It can't feed people." Tía Lula stared off for a moment before holding out her palm as she smiled. "Lemee see it first."

Gabi took a small step back.

"Tchh. Just to make sure it's safe, niña." She pushed her hand forward.

Gabi's hopeful smile fell. "Okay," she hesitated, pulling it out slowly. She took a breath and laid it in Tía Lula's palm.

Metal plates across its wings were linked tightly to look like real feathers. Then, a black square fell out of its metal head into Tía Lula's hand. I'd heard of black glass rocks we had chipped to make cutting tools and arrows in San Joaquin. Its surface shone just like that.

"What is that?" I asked.

Tía Lula tilted her head and picked out the black cube, tossing it aside. She hocked up a glob of spit, letting it drip on the metal bird. She rubbed her thumb over it. She tilted it back and forth. Its bronze chest caught the sun and flashed in my eyes.

Gabi smiled. "It's so pretty."

A small group walked by, watching us as they passed. Tía Lula quickly hid the bird, making a small laugh and nodding at them. "Buenos días."

Only when they'd passed and no one else was near did she pull it back out.

I pointed to tiny letters carved into its belly. "It says something."

Before her eyes went bad—before life in Pocatel and the hongo took over, and before she burned our book—Tía Lula had even learned a few words with me out of my mother's book.

Tía Lula held the metal bird out further, squinting her eyes. "You read it, gusano," she said after a moment, looking around again to make sure no one was watching.

I reached out to take it, but she yanked the alebrije back. "Read with your eyes, not with your hands."

I sighed and leaned in. "It says . . ." The letters were so small. "The smal . . . smallest fffl-flap of w . . . wi..ngs can ch . . . chan-change the coo-cooourse of his . . . tory."

Tía Lula laughed so loud and deep, we jumped.

When she stopped, she slipped her finger over its glass eyes. Then she ran her thumb along its wing. "Tssch!" She quickly pulled her hand back, blood dripping from her finger. "¡Basura!"

In one quick move, Tía Lula bent the bird's head to one side, snapping it off.

Gabi gasped and started to cry. "Why did you do that, Lula?"

Tía Lula narrowed her eyes and hissed at Gabi, "¡Cállate!" She looked from side to side. "And it's Tía Lula to you." Then, one by one, she plucked the feathers off the metal bird's wing. "It was too dangerous. It's more useful to me this way." She put the bird's body and its head in her pocket. She sucked on her finger, hocking pink spit to the ground, and finally walked on after the others.

Gabi stared after Tía Lula like she'd just seen her snap the head off a real bird.

"She killed it, Leandro."

I stared from Tía Lula to the ground, and at the black square that came from its head. "It was already dead."

Gabi squatted on the ground next to what was left as more of the others passed us. She dug a hole in the dirt and set the black square inside. "Do you think they were real?" she whimpered, looking up at me. "The alebrijes?"

I thought of all the things people said existed long ago, that some swore could not have been not real. Whales. Milk from animals, in boxes to drink. I tried to imagine the bird with its golden wings, high in the sky. And other metal alebrijes—crawling, soaring, and swimming.

There was so much ugly in the world. I wanted Gabi to be able to imagine something beautiful. "You saw the proof. They were real, Gabi." I pushed dirt over the top.

She patted the ground over the grave and stacked pebbles in a tower, just like we did for every Cascabel when they died. She sprinkled dirt over the grave like we'd seen. She closed her eyes and cleared her throat. Then she drew a C in the ground around its grave on both sides, enclosing it in a blessing. "Watch over this little alebrije bird, ancestors . . ."

Gabi cracked an eye open to look at me. I sighed and carved a second set of Cs, protecting it even more. "Corazones puros y espíritus fuertes son quienes heredarán la tierra," we whispered together, repeating words we didn't understand, but had heard each time one of us passed. Words we'd been hearing more lately.

But even with the engraved words on its body—*The smallest flap of wings can change the course of history*—Tía Lula had pulled the bird apart like it was nothing. We could be pure of heart, and strong of spirit, but in that moment, I knew the two of us were too small and powerless to change anything. We'd never inherit anything.

I don't even know why, but tears filled my eyes that day. I turned to where Gabi couldn't see and wiped my face with the front of my tunic.

Tía Lula was right. I stared down at the mound of dirt and tower of rocks covering all that was left of the alebrije. Not magical at all. And just like me, so small, and never powerful enough.

It was just a few days later that we came upon Pocatel.

I TILT MY head, confused at the shelves of metal animals people created once just because they could. Metal pets, on display? I thought all the Old-World tech was gone. We were told anything that couldn't be smelted into bronze was now a protective jumble of rusty metal at the bottom of the Trench, a collection over three hundred winters long.

But now I see there might still be bits out there. Not just the little bird Gabi and I found on the trail. But even that didn't survive long in this world.

We continue walking through the room of alebrijes. I'm sad thinking of what were once real animals, almost all now extinct. But I wonder about them like I do about humans: if somewhere on this world, there's a pocket of these animals that survived there.

One bird we pass looks more . . . square than the others. I slow down to stare. Metal triangles sit on top of its head. Ears? The sign beneath says *Great Horned Raptor 206*. Maybe the metal triangles are horns. This animal might've been one of my favorites. But its dark glass eyes stare down on me without expression, like the Imperator.

As we near the end of the hall, an entire wall is filled with what are labeled as *Cats: Felis Catus Electronicis* and *Dogs: Canis Lupus Familiaris Electronicis*. The cats look bored. But the dogs come in all shapes and sizes. There are far more of the smallest drones labeled *Puppies*. I lean in and see one labeled *Shelter Mutt*. It is the most beautiful. Tiny golden strands of metal coat his body like real fur.

The glass shelves finish with a *Wolf: Canis Electronicis*, *Fox A50-Trickster*, and *Crow B20 Scavenger*. They are set up to look like they're stalking one another, ending with the crow stalking the rabbit. *Meta-Hopper X 2050 (Production 2040–2042)*. This rabbit looks different than those I know with long black ears and black tails. We used to hunt them, just like the metal fox and crow are doing with the little, fat rabbit here. I want to tell whoever made this that crows would never hunt a living rabbit.

I'm staring at the hunt when I feel a sharp baton jab in my back. I fall forward into Dolores.

We both turn to see El Bastón lowering his stick. He stands with it held in front of him. He stares at Dolores, no emotion on his face, like he's challenging her.

Dolores steps around me and faces El Bastón. "You and your Patrol can do what you want outside this building. But here, you will keep your weapon to yourself."

She grabs my elbow and pulls me ahead, around a corner to the right.

I stare up at her. My mouth goes dry thinking what the man might do to me now. No one in Pocatel has ever defended me. Dolores's arm shakes as we walk quickly ahead. But I hear the steady footsteps of El Bastón as he follows behind.

I hear a noise in the opposite direction and turn my head to see the pine-needle green robe of a Cloak disappear down a sloped tunnel.

We continue walking in the opposite direction of the Cloak. Ahead, the smell in the air burns my nose; it smells like the solution the Regime uses to spray the Pox after virus outbreaks. I follow Dolores into a room. Next to a metal table, a gray chair with a silver footrest and black arms crouches like a monster. Dolores places her foot on a pedal, and the chair lowers. I squeeze my burning eyes shut.

"This is the preparation lab," she says.

My face numbs. I back away. So far, this building is full of secrets. Secrets I know even most Pocatelans don't know— and would never believe. The chair that lies ahead looks like the Imperator's badge. A horned beetle lying on its back, the arms of the chair its disjointed limbs, ready to grip around my body.

"Don't be nervous," Dolores says. "I will explain in a moment."

I feel my heartbeat in my throat. I stare at the metal beetle chair and think of Celia, naked, entering the pitch-black wyrm-field. I wish I was with her instead.

Dolores walks ahead to a cabinet and pulls out a glass container filled with water. While she's not looking, El Bastón comes from behind and shoves me further into the room, toward the chair. I stumble. He grabs one arm and cuts the tie off my wrists. I pull my hands to the front of my body and rub the scratches the twine left behind, just like Celia had. I sit down before he can force me. He straps me in and hovers over me. His knuckles whiten as he grips his staff. Dolores sets the glass water container on a metal table next to me. She steps in front of me to block him from my view.

"Leandro Rivera, you will be returned one day," she says stiffly, hands clenched at her waist. "And when you do, it will be with a more mature and appreciative mind. You can resume your life where your path went astray." She glances quickly over her shoulder twice while she's speaking. It feels like her words might be more for El Bastón than me. Finally, she turns to face him. "I can handle the proceeding from here."

"Are you sure?" he asks. "The boy is a thief."

Dolores rolls her eyes. "The sooner you leave, the sooner you can get back to protecting Pocatel from children who steal berries."

He remains in place.

"Perhaps I should discuss with the Imperator this delay in the preservation of his plan?"

He makes a bow to her but keeps eye contact. "Whatever you say, Physician." He steps out the door and uses his stick to thrust it closed behind him.

Dolores slips off her shoes. She walks softly to the door, placing her ear to the crack. I hear his footsteps too as they echo away. Slowly, she spins the lock to the room, and then suddenly, she rushes to a drawer beneath the metal table.

Dolores pulls out two small silver boxes. She hurries to push one next to the glass jar. The box hits the jar, and it clinks, water sloshing inside. Inside the drawer is also a tool—two knives connected with pointy ends. I let out a breath when she doesn't remove it.

"My name is Dolores," she whispers.

"I know."

She nods. "Of course, you do."

My heart pounds in my chest. "What are you going to do to me?"

She barely glances up at me. "I know what you must be thinking, but I am not a barbarian, Leandro."

"Tell that to those you and the other Directors are planning to Thin. And to Celia."

Dolores winces. "I could not help her. And I can't help what is coming." She stares back toward the direction we came in. "No matter what you have seen, Leandro, I promise I am not like them. But I am the last who can help you."

So far, what I've seen of her, she isn't entirely like them. But her Director's badge says the opposite, and makes my stomach twist.

As she fidgets to open one of the boxes, she looks up. "You overheard enough to know that things are in motion that I cannot stop. But, I am giving you a choice, one you would not normally have. Certainly not in a few days' time." She lifts out a small black cube from the box, holding it up. "This is called a Spark." She holds it near my eyes. "And I know how strange this may sound, but with this . . . only your mind will be banished, Leandro."

My hands and feet feel like ice. I recognize it as the same black cube inside the bird we found by the trail. The cube Tía Lula pulled off and chucked away, like a tick she plucked off her skin.

"You must be wondering how this is even possible." Dolores's fingers tremble as she pulls the cube apart into two pieces. "Each Physician passes down dying knowledge from Old-World, parent to child. I did not choose this path. It chose me." From one half of the cube, a *whoosh*, then tiny silver needles spring out. They come alive, wiggling like legs. "It's called a neural link," she says. "In the Old-World, they had started using it to connect people to machines when their bodies failed. This is yours."

I push myself back into the chair and squint. I close my eyes. When I open them, the legs of the neural link are still moving. I tilt my head, watching the legs move. This makes no sense. It has no blood or living body parts to make it act like a real bug.

She must see my confusion. She holds up half the black cube. "This will connect your mind"—her hand trembles as she lifts the other half—"to something else for your sentence."

My mind? How can she remove who I am from my body? Unless . . .

I grip the chair's black arms. My heart is pounding harder than the first time I heard a wyrm's scream. My head feels strange. I blink to keep my vision from blacking out. Cold sweat covers my face. My face tingles, and I close my eyes.

"Oh, no," she whispers, pushing my head against the chair and tilting the entire chair back, until I am lying almost flat.

If I could, I'd jump through the closed window behind her. My words get stuck in my throat. "You . . . you're going to remove my brain and put it in something else?"

She lays her hand on my arm. "No, no, Leandro. No one is going to hurt you." I flinch at her touch.

Why is my body acting this way? My body didn't react like this when I thought I'd die in the jaws of a wyrm, or when I thought it could be taken over by an evil spirit. But those are things I understand. Things I know are real.

Dolores places a glass of cold water to my lips. I drink half in seconds. It is the cleanest thing I've ever swallowed. My vision clears, and I don't feel as hot.

She sighs. "I need to explain this better. It is not what you're thinking. Your body will remain intact—here, with me—but your mind will leave."

I don't understand what she's saying. But I know better than to trust a Pocatelan.

I stare at the little square with its squirming legs. Whatever this is, in some way it's real. I see it with my own eyes. I need to calm down so I can really understand what she's saying. I take deep breaths, and this time, slowly, I nod.

Dolores clicks the two halves of the cube back together and the legs go still. She sets it on the table.

Dolores picks up the Spark up again.

"You are not the only one who's been given this choice. All have accepted, but none have returned. I need to know why." She hands me the cube. I cup it in my hand.

Pinpricks run up the back of my neck, but at least my vision isn't blacking out. "You are saying this black box . . . will put my mind in something? You can really do that?" I whisper, "Old-World magic."

"Yes, the black box . . . the Spark . . . will put your mind—"

Approaching footsteps, followed by a cough, sounds from outside the door. She freezes. El Bastón.

"I need more time," she calls out.

He doesn't respond, but we hear his footsteps walk away again.

"We must hasten. Leandro, the Regime wants me to confine your mind to a vault." She looks pointedly at the glass jar of water on the table beside me. "But I'm giving you a different choice."

I still don't understand exactly what she means. "You are say-ing I have the choice to have my mind put in that . . ." I look at the jar, then into her eyes, knowing it will be harder for her to lie to me. "Or something else? What is the something else?"

She grabs the Spark out of my hand and puts a finger to her lips. She walks softly to the metal table and reaches deep inside the secret drawer. The scrape of metal-on-metal echoes. She pulls something out with one hand. "If you agree to what I offer, instead of the vault . . . this will be your new body."

She turns around, holding a faded silver, purple, and blue metal hummingbird.

13

· · · (· · ·

DOLORES TIPS THE HUMMINGBIRD BACK AND FORTH IN her palm. Its metal feathers change from blue to purple, then back, as she rocks it. I know this bird is like the rusted gold alebrije Gabi found and Lula snapped apart. The little black square that shined like San Joaquin glass was a *Spark*. So if what Dolores says is true . . . beneath the grave of stacked rocks Gabi and I made . . . someone who was once real is buried.

My voice cracks. "You want to put my mind in that little bird?"

Dolores makes a tiny nod. "You will still be Leandro, only now, Leandro's body is a hummingbird drone."

The same sick feeling comes over me. How can I, a boy, become a drone? I lay my head back before my vision blacks out once more.

"These artifacts of functioning Old-World tech are a miracle," she continues, tilting my entire chair back. My head feels a bit better. "There is so little left of their old machines. And to have something that functions . . ." she says. "Centuries ago, some of the first Directors even insisted on having their own consciousness placed in them. They flew east, with the hope of searching out resources, better land, other humans . . ." Her voice trails off, and I wonder what they found—or if they came back. "But while they were gone, those who stayed behind, they did the unthinkable." She sighs. "They eliminated those who did not share their ideals."

"Eliminated?" I ask. But I know what she means. And I also what she means by "their ideals." If the Regime is the product of those people long ago, those who dared to seek more outside the safety of Pocatel would have been eliminated here and now too.

"I am here to protect you from that." She pats my arm.

I stare down, and she pulls her hand away. "And if something happens to you?" I ask.

She leans in. "That is why you must hurry. I know you heard at least part of what was said. No one will be safe, including me."

"A Thinning," I say.

She nods. "They will begin soon . . ." She clenches one of her fists. "With those they value the least. But it will not stop there. This I know."

"The vault is my only other choice?"

"Yes." She looks at the jar beside me, then behind her. I realize there are rows of more glass containers lining the shelves. The containers are filled with water, half a Spark floating inside each of them. But the top row holds only four containers; the lower row, many.

"The Regime would prefer you were right there. But you are still in danger on that shelf, I promise. Only there, you wouldn't know when it is coming, and you will have no control to change the outcome."

I stare up at the vaults, trying process what she's saying.

"They would have you trapped in that jar, Leandro—until, of course, your human body is the optimal worker for Pocatel. Until you can be removed and will comply with whatever they ask, so that you are never returned to that prison."

The Imperator's three-winter sentence makes sense now.

I look, and at the bottom of every single container, names are etched onto metal plates. The top row is too high to see, but the four plates are darkened, tarnished by time. The names on the lowest rows are Cascabel, but as I hurry to read, I see a few are Pocatelan too.

I flinch. What could a Pocatelan kid have done to be banished like a Cascabel?

Now that my hands are free, I remove the belt holding me and stand.

Dolores points to the highest row with its ancient nameplates and four containers with Sparks. "After they eliminated those first Directors, the ones left behind preserved the remaining drones, as a reminder of the sins of the past. Over two hundred years ago, Pocatel's Regime even implemented a drone Banishment program for rebellious youth. But when these four didn't return, it was halted."

I point to the top rows. "Are those four people . . . from hundreds of years ago . . . still alive out there?"

"I want to hope they are. When their human bodies died, the other halves of their Sparks remained safe here. Their minds could still be alive out there. But there is no way to know for sure." I think I see her give the smallest of smiles. "Still, I make sure their Sparks are maintained, just in case."

Seeing her with this hope, I decide not to tell her of the rusted bird. Whoever it was is probably up there.

"And these?" I point to the lower row, at least twenty.

"The Directors decided to reinstate a different Banishment program for youth three years ago. One with the vaults."

Three winters ago. Right when we Cascabeles arrived to Pocatel.

"You did that?" I ask.

"I wanted to give them some sort of freedom. The drones were the only way I could see." Her chin quivers. "I am not proud of it. But I must live with it. Allowing the Regime to believe the children are stored in a vault was a far better option than what was proposed otherwise."

"None of those Sparks are real? The real halves of those Sparks are off in drones somewhere?"

I turn to look at her, and she's biting her lower lip, holding out the hummingbird.

I realize Dolores is pulling a pickpocket rock switch on the Regime. So many times, I dropped rocks inside pockets to match the weight of the stags. Dolores is just a different kind of trickster. If she gets caught ...

On the table in front of me, a container filled with only water sits waiting, a shiny, uncarved plate attached to its base.

She pushes it toward me. "You ... your mind, could spend your sentence imprisoned in this vault just like the Imperator intends." She slides the hummingbird drone in front of me. "Or you could live free in this drone outside Pocatel, like the rest, and I will put you back in your body as soon as you return." I stare at the tiny metal bird where she expects me to live. "The Spark connects your mind to the drone's sensory inputs," she continues. "Whatever the drone feels, hears, sees, smells in the inputs, you will too. Instantly. You will be you, just in a new body."

I stand and walk to the vault, where I'd still be inside Pocatel—near Gabi—at least for a little while more. I run my finger over its surface.

She frowns. "The vault is nothingness, Leandro. A void. No external input at all." Her voice shudders. "The others couldn't get out of here fast enough," she goes on, scanning the lowest row. "But none have returned as they promised me they would. And when their sentences are up and I cannot produce the real halves of their real Sparks, the Imperator and the other Directors will know what I have done. After that, I cannot control what the Regime will do. I won't be able to protect them all any longer." She sets the Spark in my palm. "With this, you can be free and perhaps help them live. Do you not see? Now, with the coming Thinning . . ." She holds the hummingbird in front of me. "This *is* your opportunity to help your sister."

I don't see how I have any other choice. I lean in to get a closer look at the hummingbird. "It's small." I motion back toward the hall of dead drones. "Shouldn't I have something bigger—maybe one of the big birds back there?"

She shakes her head. "Delivery drones are too large now. We cannot risk the Regime or Imperator discovering what I am doing." She holds the hummingbird in front of me. "I promise you, *this* is safer."

I cross my arms on my chest, then drop them quickly to my sides, realizing I must look like Gabi. "So, how does this thing work if there is no Old-World power?"

"It's called fission," she answers. "A type of energy where you only need a drop or two of water each day." Turns out, Jo's story about the bucket of water and the flying ship may have been true.

She points to the little black box. "Its internal conductors will do the rest. You will locate a source, but until then . . ." She holds up a vial, a miniature rubber stopper with a pinpoint hole at the top. "This should last you at least a month. Two, if you are cautious." She clips the vial to the hummingbird leg, where its beak can easily reach the hole.

"And if I run out of water?"

She closes her eyes and lets out a slow breath. Her voice is flat. "The Spark will give out. Its other half here would fail also."

"So, my body would die?"

"A single drop," her voice rises. "That's all you need."

A drop of water I can find. I was born to live from the land. But . . . "And what if my body dies here?"

She looks down, suddenly not meeting my eyes. "As long as I preserve the other half of the Spark, like I have with those"—she glances at the highest shelf—"your *mind* will live on for as long as the drone does. Perhaps hundreds of years."

I lean down, forcing her to meet her eyes. Something a Cascabel would normally never do. But this is not normal. "Hundreds of winters? As a drone!"

Her voice is suddenly hard like Tía Lula's. "I trust you will return sooner . . . much sooner. You heard what the Directors said. You know of the danger your sister is in."

If Tía Lula taught me one thing, it was not to trust those who offer something in exchange for nothing. I squint. "Why are you doing this? There's more you aren't telling me."

Dolores's eyebrows pinch together. "I told you. Time is running out. I need someone to return." She glances from side to side. Then she glances to the door and whispers: "Leandro, when there is absolute control, the payment for freedom is an absolute price. And no one is immune from the Thinning."

She's definitely Pocatelan. But even if the words make no sense, I'm pretty sure it all means: if Dolores dies, I die.

She twists her hands together. "Someone I care about is out there, Leandro. Once the Regime discovers what I am doing . . . The Imperator will not hesitate to destroy all this. And any chance for the banished to return to their bodies would be gone." Her forehead wrinkles, and a deep V forms again between her brow.

"I'm leaving my sister behind here. But you won't even tell me *who* you want me to risk our lives for?"

Her voice trembles. "Her name . . . her name is Selah. She is my daughter."

Shocked, I take a step back. I glance at her Director's badge. I always thought the Directors were untouchable. What could have gone wrong?

She sighs. "I was sure Selah and the others would return. When they didn't . . ." Dolores straightens her back. "They might be . . . different now."

"Different?"

She turns away. "There is no way to know what they might have become out there. I hope that whatever she is now—wherever she is—will be good."

If the drones have been fighting for survival in the Outlands, maybe they have become monsters too. Pinpricks run up my neck. Could I become something . . . different?

"I promise you. If you return with Selah, I will reunite you with your sister and help you escape Pocatel. But Leandro, if you stay here in a vault, I will not be able to protect your sister. And I assure you, she will be . . ." She takes a deep breath. "She will be gone."

Ice runs through my veins. I heard what Director Marguerite said. But this woman I don't even know is bartering for our lives like the Mongers barter fruit and stag.

But she's not only helping me return to Gabi. She's offering what we've always wanted. Escape.

"If you return quickly, I promise to keep her safe—"

From outside the door, El Bastón coughs again. Dolores closes her eyes, and I think she's stopped breathing. "You must decide, Leandro."

I swallow, and my throat is dry. I can't protect Gabi from inside a container. Dolores is offering us something I've never hand much of. Hope. I know what I have to do.

I look at the shelf full of vaults. So many are out there—but she only wants her daughter. "What about the rest?" I ask. "If I get you what you want, even if you help me and my sister get out . . . what about all the others out there?"

"They had a chance to return and escape Pocatel for good," she says. "Just like I'm giving you. I will do whatever I can to help return them to their bodies, but . . . I will barely be able to get you and your sister out, along with me and my daughter."

Why didn't they return? Maybe she's right, and they changed in some way. Maybe they didn't have someone to return to.

Maybe they just decided to take their chances with the Spark they left behind. I won't stay out there long enough to become whatever they have.

"Okay. Where do I start looking?"

"East?" she says, biting her lower lip.

"You don't know for sure?" The strawberry feels like a rock in my stomach.

Dolores steps to the open drawer. She lifts the inner base. Hidden beneath is another compartment. From inside, she pulls out a yellowing sheet of paper. In its center is a smudged ember drawing with tiny squares for buildings, a dark finger-wide line labeled Trench, and a forest of spiny trees next to Dead Forest. When I stand back, I see the word Pocatel beneath the entire drawing, just like the evil that crawls around the real city. The valley beyond the Trench shows the spikes of a dragon emerging from the earth in the Wyrmfield. Along peaks of small triangles to the east is the label Pocatel Ridge. Beyond Pocatel Ridge, the paper is covered in scribbles of more triangles, but also blank areas with no markings, labeled Outlands. On the very edge of the paper, marked with an E: a winding path like a snake, labeled River Valley. The drawing is so simple, Gabi could've drawn it. Still, I stare up at her, eyes wide. "Is this real?"

"This is all I have," she says, quickly slipping the map back in its hiding place.

"Where'd you get—"

She shushes me. "Study it quickly."

I look down at the map and memorize it. How can she make these promises to me? She can't know for sure we will survive. But I have no choice. If I don't, Gabi is dead for sure. I know the map, but I continue staring at it so she can't see my eyes. "Her name is Gabriela Rivera." My voice catches. "Gabi."

I glance up and Dolores nods. "I'll make sure Gabi is still here when you return. It is a benefit of being a Director . . . for now. But you must hurry and get back before the Thinning worsens." She slips the map back in the drawer and puts the tool with the pincers on the end inside the secret compartment too, securing it and closing the drawer.

I hurry to wipe my eyes, forcing them not to tear, and I'm ashamed. I sit back down in the chair. "Okay." I nod. "Before I change my mind."

"I promise, Leandro, you won't feel anything," she says, turning back.

She pulls the black cube apart and its silver legs poke out from one half, beginning to squirm. She places a drop of water in a tiny opening on the Spark and it spirals down inside. I'm sure I hear a small hum. She opens the top of the hummingbird's head and places that half of the Spark inside its metal skull. It clicks into place, and she closes its head, setting the bird drone on the metal table. She hands me the other half. The six needle legs make tiny clicking noises.

My heart pounds, and I lie back as my vision blacks out again. I close my eyes and whisper, "Sana, sana, colita de rana. Si no sanas hoy, sanarás mañana."

Dolores coils cotton around the end of a thin stick. "What was that, what you just said?"

I shrug and lie. "It's a powerful spell from San Joaquin. If someone is lying to you, it curses them for eternity."

She smiles and leans in, twirling the stick inside my left nostril.

I don't even know what all the words mean. Cascabel parents say it to children when they get hurt. Something about a frog's tail. But when I said it to Gabi, it always seemed to work.

Whatever's on the cotton swab tingles as Dolores pushes it farther up my nose. My eyes begin to water. I think she might poke my brain. Suddenly, that side of my face goes numb.

"Like this." She nods at my half of the Spark and pretends to hold her own below her nostril. "It knows what to do." She gives a small nod, motioning for me to do the same.

I set it beneath my nose just like she did. My hand trembles. My nose itches as the Spark breaks free from my fingers, crawling inside. The higher it crawls, the more it hurts. I grip the arms of the chair. I close my eyes and grit my teeth. White and blue stars flash in my vision before everything goes black.

14

··· (···

I'VE BEEN HUNGRY FOR SO LONG. MY STOMACH'S NOR-
mally cramping each morning. But in an instant, the knots in
my stomach are gone. I usually wake up wishing I could go
right back to sleep. But now, I feel like I could dance Serpientes
de Cascabel circles around Gabi. The smell of disinfectant is so
strong—she must have put the bottle to my nose. I open my
eyes. A gong like the town bell echoes inside my head, and then

the soft voice of a woman with a strange accent speaks: "*Com Connect.*" A red *100%* floats in the air in front of me.

"*Mobility Online.*" Even as I look from side to side, the red number follows. I jump back, the sound of clanking metal exploding in my ears.

"It is okay," Dolores says. "It takes a moment for your body to boot up. Much longer if your battery is drained."

I turn toward her voice, so loud it could be inside my head. Dolores stands over me like a giant. Her face is so clear the sweat on her chin stands out like raindrops on a pock after a storm. Her robe—pale purple a moment ago—is now a deeper violet. Behind her lies the shelves of vaults. Tiny bubbles I couldn't see before cover the shiny, black Sparks inside the water vaults. I jump back again, suddenly remembering where I am and what we were about to do. I fall to one side, and a clank rattles my entire body . . . my body?

In front of me in the prep chair, my own real body sits silently. I . . . I . . . My body is huge! I think I could throw up. Am I still alive? The eyes of my human body are open, and my chest moves up down as it . . . I breathe. Something is very wrong. I should be breathing air into my own lungs. Feeling my heartbeat. Instead, something speeds inside me like a ticking clock.

"Please remain calm, Leandro," Dolores whispers, picking me up and setting me upright. "Your internal processors react to your emotions. The drone body will move and respond with how you feel."

Right now, whatever's inside me vibrates so quickly I think I might explode.

The red 100% continues glowing like a red moon in front of my vision, but I can see through it, like it is a ghost. I lift my hand to touch it. The weight of my own arms, hands, legs . . . is gone. Instead, a tiny metal talon slices right through the number in the air easily. So stunned, a buzz runs from deep within me, outward. My feathers ruffle, making a rattle like a pocketful of stags. This is real. Dolores did it. Just like she said, everything this drone sees, hears, feels, senses . . . I see, hear, feel, and sense too.

I stare upward and see each dust mote floating between Dolores and me. I hear her quick shallow breaths. I feel the cold metal on the bottom of my feet.

I *am* the hummingbird drone. Dolores lifts me up in the palm of her hand. I'm not even a human anymore. What have I done?

I try to move, just like I'd lift my hand to wave, or move my legs to walk. I am weightless. It feels like I could . . . fly.

A loud buzz vibrates the air. I fall over, startled by the fluttering. Fluttering of my own . . . *wings*?

"Leandro?" Dolores whispers. "Are you okay?"

No! I want to fly away and hide. How can I get back? Will I ever get back? Am I still a person?

I still have my thoughts, so am I still me? Is this what it feels like to die and become a spirit? To no longer have a body with blood, and muscles, and arms, and legs, but to have my thoughts?

I force myself to hold completely still for a moment. This is really happening. I lift my right wing, and just like with my human arm, it obeys my mind's command.

I nod to Dolores. The vibration inside me slows a bit.

She presses her lips together. "I should have warned you. Apparently the sensory inputs are . . . intense."

I face the chair. My human body does not move at all, my face blank. I turn quickly back to her.

She smiles, keeping her voice low. "I promise, you are fine. And don't worry." She motions to my body. "I make sure you—I mean, not just you, but . . . all the bodies left behind—are safe here."

I lift one of my feet—talons—and tip over in her hand.

"Careful." Dolores sets me upright and places me gently on the window's ledge.

A knock on the door breaks the quiet. "Physician?" El Bastón calls out.

"Just a moment. Nearly completed." Dolores holds a finger to her lips and whispers even softer. "Flying should come naturally to you." She grips the bottom of the window and lifts. It squeaks open. We both stare at the door. "You have to go now." Her eyes well with tears. "Please find her. Tell Selah to come back, please."

Leaving Pocatel's the right decision. So, why does it feel so wrong?

I poke my head just out the window. Clouds in the night sky hide the stars, but the moon is so bright that downtown Pocatel glows. The distant screech of a wyrm echoes, as ever, but now the squeal vibrates my body. *Too loud!* Instantly, the sound lowers, softening in my head to my thought. How is this real? A body that can change to hear what I want it to hear. Will it do the same with seeing and smelling and touching? How different our lives could be if we had bodies that could turn off the things we dislike and turn on the ones we love.

The doorknob rattles. "Physician, unlock the door."

Our eyes meet, and Dolores picks me up. "Do not stop until you're well outside the walls. If you're seen, it's over."

I nod.

"Return soon, Leandro." She tosses me up and out the window.

I soar for second, then gravity takes hold and I topple suddenly downward to the ground below. I hurry to flutter my wings, tipping to one side then the other. I concentrate to use both wings equally, and my body straightens just before I hit the ground. I'm hovering. I rise up and up, until I'm at the window, then higher until the roof of the Center of Banishment comes into view.

I forget to flutter for a moment and I plummet again. This time, I catch myself much quicker than before. I rock from side to side. I struggle to hover back up to the window and remain in one spot. I stare at Dolores, who's still at the window. She makes a shooing motion and turns her back to me.

"Physician, open the door! Now."

She lifts her hand over her shoulder in a silent goodbye.

"Just a second!" she says, slipping her shoes back on before hurrying toward the glass vaults. She speaks far more loudly, and I know once again, the words are not for me. "And now, Leandro Rivera, one final thing before your Banishment." She pulls apart the second fake Spark and places half inside the water vault. "The body serves the sentence, but the solitude of your mind will bring you back to us with a fresh appreciation for the Preservation of Pocatelan society."

The door flies open. El Bastón grips his wood staff, his knuckles white. Dolores's fingers tremble as she holds a metal tool, carving the words *Leandro Rivera* into the metal nameplate. Half the fake Spark floats in the container of water, its tiny silver legs rippling.

Projected in front of me is the number *1095*. The soft voice speaks in my mind again. "*You have one thousand and ninety-five days remaining in your sentence.*" The voice might sound like a beautiful song, but with the words she speaks, it jolts my mind like the Field Director's whistle.

I hover higher and higher into the night sky. I need to get over the Trench before anyone sees me. No one ever really saw kids like Gabi and me in the Pox. I have the feeling no one will notice one tiny bird either.

Then again, I thought Gabi and I were invisible in the market.

"*Navigation On,*" the strange voice says. A see-through, four-sided star appears in front of the moon. The star's point at the top has an E. To the left, an N; to the right, an S; and the bottom point is a W. As I shift, the arrow does too. I turn right, and it rotates from E to S.

Since I am close, I cross the street and fly over the Pox.

Hundreds of Cascabel pocks lie directly below me now. I wonder for a moment if they'll hear my buzz and come out to see what is in the sky. No—they're all too busy trying to survive, looking down, scouring the earth for what is in front of them.

From here, the domes candlelit from inside really do look like stars. If only los Cascabeles could see what I see. If only they could know how the gods must see us: that we still look like a constellation of beautiful lights.

I turn and fly toward the main street. I pass back over the Center of Banishment and see El Bastón and Dolores exit the building. Dolores does not look up.

Darkness has fallen over the main street. A lamplighter walks from one lamp to the next, lifting his wick. The street basks in the golden glow of the lamps and light from the Directors' windows. The market stalls have all been packed away, leaving only the empty street. The Mongers have all safely left the valley by now.

The four-sided star symbol with N, S, E, and W projected in front of me shifts to one side. *120 meters* flashes in its place, then quickly disappears. I rise further, and it flashes *130 meters*.

By the time I'm over the orphanage, everything below has become miniature. Gabi is probably in there right this very moment. I won't cry. Can I cry?

I swoop down, and through the ceiling of glass, in the room of beds lit with one lamp, I see Director Marguerite pacing between the rows. I fly directly over her head. I wish drone birds could poop on command. I look for Gabi but can't tell which kid she is. I want so badly to find her—to say goodbye in some way. But if she saw me like this, she'd shove me into her pocket as a pet. She would have no way of knowing it was me.

If I'm caught, it would be over for Dolores—for all of us. The Directors and the Imperator would know all those Sparks in Dolores's vault aren't real. To "preserve" what they have, we could be stuck as drones forever, or even die, and it would be my fault.

My reading drops suddenly from *50 meters* to *40 meters*.

I steady my wings and continue until I'm over the Trench. I hover and stare down at the crater Celia and Tía Lula had to walk over. My wings quiver. Below, hundreds of winters of collected jagged metal jut up from the bottom. Then I see it. A long shred of tunic flaps in the wind off a jagged rock. The wind catches it, and it twists and twirls like a writhing ghost snake. For just a moment I close my eyes and look away.

Tía Lula flashes in front of me, her body mangled and bloody: *This was your fault, gusano!*

I open my eyes and she's gone, but I am frozen. What is happening? I stare down at the tunic and know she lies somewhere far below. I hover in place, staring at her ghost-snake tunic too long. I do not close my eyes again, though. I need to do what Dolores said and get out of here quickly.

I snap out of it and fly past the Trench, and in an instant, I am out of the cage that has trapped us inside the past three winters.

I follow the Banishment trail below until I'm over the wyrmfield.

Moonlight falls over the valley below. Then, the dark speck of a tiny shadow catches my eye. It's running through the valley below, too fast to be Tía Lula. Celia?

I want to yell at her to turn toward the ridge. But why would she think like Gabi and me? She hasn't planned escape for winters like us.

All I can see below is her lone figure. There don't seem to be any wyrms out now, only the earth mound trails of previous hunts. Maybe she has a chance.

A yellow triangle projects like a ghost in front of me. Just like the navigation symbols, it must be old tech I don't entirely understand.

But what I see below is not some image. The woman is real. And if she can run fast enough . . . if her footsteps are light enough where the wyrms can't hear . . .

Safe passage, Celia.

The yellow triangle in front of me grows more solid, and a ticking noise fills my head.

I turn in the direction I sense it, toward the see-through E. But just as I do, a deep rumble echoes from below. The earth heaves upward like the lined mounds we create for potato plants. But this mound is moving. Fast. It makes a turn, heading directly at the tiny shadow of the running figure. It gains speed.

Even if Celia runs toward the ridge, I realize it's too late. I hover in place. I can't move forward or back.

It gets closer. And closer. And closer, until . . .

I can only watch in panic as the moving mound breaks open. Earth pours over the person below as she stumbles to the ground. The wyrm's spiked head rises, twisting, from the earth's surface.

There is no scream from Celia at the sight of the monster writhing above her. No yells of terror. She stands with arms at her sides, not even trying to run, as if she's accepted her fate.

A screech vibrates the air around us. The metal of my body buzzes like lightning on the air.

Then the shadow hoists farther into the air, the tiny speck in front now doused by the darkness of its body. And, finally, its mouth gapes and crashes downward. A plume of dust spirals upward, clouding the air.

For a moment, all is silent. The storm of dust settles.

The wyrm dives back through the opening, its tail slithering back underground.

Celia is gone.

15

. . . (. . .

I DO NOT KNOW HOW LONG I STAY AND WATCH. THE
yellow triangle in front of me fades as the wyrm's rumble grows
faint. All that's left behind is a fresh mound of dirt among a few
others where the wyrm disappeared.

I'm left only with my horror and the quiet of the moonlit sky.
The hiccupping boy is now truly alone. There was nothing I
could do for her. "Bless Celia, ancestors," I pray. "Corazones puros
y espíritus fuertes son quienes heredarán la tierra."

But she doesn't need my prayers to send her peacefully into the stars. She was pure of heart and strong of spirit. One of the bravest I've ever seen.

I stare back into the darkness of Pocatel to where the orphanage lies, where both Gabi and Celia's little boy sleep. There are no real tears. But there's a pain worse than anything I've ever felt as I turn away.

A dust devil grows near Pocatel's Trench. Maybe the same wyrm. To actually see one was far worse than anything I imagined.

I force myself to fly ahead over the valley. I put my gaze to the moon in the east. I dip my right wing and wobble over Pocatel's ridge, the one I've dreamed of crossing for so long. The one I had planned to be crossing right now. Just not like this. Not alone.

Halfway over the ridge, a crumbling Old-World road comes into view. A lamp sways in the darkness. I swoop lower to see. I fly over the road to see the fruit Monger in his wagon. It's pulled by a mule. I hover over him. The Monger stops for a moment, searching for something in his bag. I hope the pendejo doesn't find it. I hope he searches for the rest of his life and never finds anything he's searching for.

If he'd just stopped before ringing the bell, Gabi and I would be somewhere down there right now. But the sooner I find Dolores's daughter, Selah, the sooner I can get back to Gabi, and she and I will leave Pocatel behind for good. Together.

On both sides of the cracked road below lie skeletons of trees. Some still stand. But most topple over one another like cornstalks after a strong storm. Jo says hundreds of winters ago, trees in this part of the world were a blanket of green next to a glowing highway. I'd hoped that when I finally saw it, some of that would remain. Instead, only small, splintered parts of the road show beneath the sand.

I think of all those dead pines below and imagine climbing to the top of them. Now, if I find any living pines, I'll *fly* to their highest branches, and smell the needles just like I used to.

But this is not how I dreamed freedom would feel. The weight of what I have to do, and what's at risk if I don't, makes it feel more like a prison.

Once over the ridge, tracks from wagon wheels lead off the old highway. Some tracks veer off to the east, but the deepest-rutted trail leads north. That must be where the Mongers live. Maybe an old city where they find scrap to trade for food. Where they can survive without being crushed or eaten in the night.

As I fly east into the night, the fallen trees thin out. The mountain peaks flatten to hills, then flats, and the windy, crumbling road straightens. I shift up and down, cool air flowing over my body. I travel so far and fast through the clouds. When I dreamed of flying away from the Pox, as I stared at the stars, I thought it would feel like floating. It does not. I am soaring, and I am not sure I'll ever want to walk again.

The outlines of large squares cover the earth below. They are the same markings I saw on areas we used to forage through. It was said, the same outlines covered most of the land of our ancestors in San Joaquin. Dust blows over their surface in the moonlight.

At least in this body, I do not need to forage for survival in that danger below. It is just me, soaring through the air.

For half the night, the only thing below is the wagon trail. So, I follow it. Then I see something in the moonlight. But these squares below now are not fields. Cement and stone outlines of buildings and homes are all that's left of a city. Everything else is gone. No roofs. No candlelight. No people. Nothing growing at all. The Old-World city's body lies picked over by scavengers, time, and the Mongers who yanked out its metal bones.

From so high, I see a road weaving up a hill. Partway up the hill, half the hillside is missing, boulders and dirt concealing the path. But on the other side of the blockade, the road continues, ending at a camouflaged half-standing building. The clank of metal on metal, like the smelter's hut, echoes on the wind. Could it be? I fly closer to the noise in the direction of the building.

A metal chain hits against a steel pole. The Mongers could never have seen this. That chain, and even the pole, are far too valuable just as they are. I sit on the chain as the wind pushes it back and forth. I stare ahead at a metal ladder. It is turned on its side and propped up in the air by poles on each side. I fly to it and jump from rung to rung, trying to figure out how it was used.

From the top of the ladder, I look down at what's left of a building. Near its entrance is a stone sign, half of it missing. The letters left make no sense.

dridge

entary

I fly over the remains. On a cement wall, in faded color, is a painted rainbow with words beneath, one stacked on top of the other. I land and stare down at the words. *You are amazing. You are brave. You are strong.*

I tilt my head. What kind of place was this?

Next to what looks like the white bowl in the orphanage's bath room is a sign. Carved into a rusty piece of metal: *Did you wash your hands?*

This strange place with its odd words is a mystery. I have the weird thought that Gabi would like it here, but lingering won't get me back to her any sooner.

I fly back into the night sky and stare west. It would've taken me ten days on foot to cover the distance I've traveled in a single night of flying. But as far I can see, there is no plateau or river like the old map Dolores showed me.

Two hours later, the shadow of a solitary tree catches my eye and grows bigger below. Bare branches jut out like the arms of a skeleton. In the dark, its trunk looks hunched over, like Jo after a long day digging for papas.

The ghostly red number showing my charge reads 23%. I don't know %, but the number gets smaller and smaller. Something tells me I should keep going, and not risk stopping. The last thing I need is to crash in the dark and end any chance of finding Dolores's daughter. But I also can't risk running out of power completely. I glance at the vial on my leg. It's close enough to drink, but I'm still barely good enough to fly in a straight line. Landing seems like the best plan.

I wobble downward toward the tree.

The ground surrounding the tree shows no sign of anything green or living. But high in its branches, a nest lies, holding one tiny spotted egg. I can't tell how old it is; the nest looks like it's been there forever. The egg probably didn't hatch and was abandoned by its mother.

I think of landing in the branches, but an opening halfway up the tree stares up at me like an eye. Anything could live inside its hollow. I hover in front of the hole, expecting something to pop out at me. It's drier and hotter here in the Outlands. Maybe some creature lives inside the hollow of trees to keep from cooking in the sun. I turn in a circle.

A warm wind blows, and Tía Lula's voice feels like it is right next to me.

¡Gusano!

Her ghost could not travel so far from the Dead Forest. This is only my mind playing tricks.

I close my eyes and she's there holding a candle to her face, light falling through her missing tooth onto her tongue. I open my eyes, and she's gone. Only the tree with its hollow stands in front of me.

It's just some sort of memory. Maybe this is the way a drone shows us fear or doubt—or the past. I'm not sure which.

I close my eyes, and we're all back in the pock: me, Lula, and Gabi. Tía Lula nods like she'd heard the Pocatelan's stories her whole life. "You are the perfect size for a baby wyrm to eat in one bite." She looks right at me, then Gabi, and points to the gap in our pock's door. "That is all that separates you from death. I can no longer protect you out there."

I want to tell her she *never* protected us. Without her, I've made it to the Outlands. Why couldn't she have told us stories of brave Cascabeles instead, those who survived and found a better life?

Gabi's voice shakes. "How do they kill people, Tía Lula?"

"With machete talons." She slashes the air with a rigid hand, looking from me to the imaginary Gabi.

Gabi swallows hard.

Tía Lula rubs her shriveled hands over both her arms. "You can smell their breath, death on the wind, much sooner."

I sniff deeply, hoping Lula doesn't see. "Why does their breath smell like death?" I ask.

Her brow wrinkles, and she clicks her tongue. "Why do you think, gusano? Their breath rattles over flesh and the splintered bones of dead bodies in their throats."

Gabi pulls her dirty tunic over her eyes. My entire body shakes with fear. I open my eyes, and Tía Lula and Gabi are gone.

I can't move now, hovering in one spot.

Here in front of the tree in the dark, my body buzzes just as it had when I saw the real wyrm. Maybe whatever might lie inside the tree will devour me at any moment. But I don't smell rotting bodies, or hear rattled breathing. I circle the tree, flying to the other side. Nothing is there.

I return to the opening. It is only a tree. *Sé fuerte, Leandro. Sé valiente.* I quickly fly inside, then back out. *Sé valiente.* Then in again. Strange. The words actually work. After the third time, when nothing tries to eat me, I land on the splintered ledge and peek downward inside the tree. Maybe Outlands monsters only eat humans.

The buzz of my wings echoes in the hollow tree.

I spin to look around inside a little. A tiny dark dot crawls directly in front of me. I jerk backward.

How am I supposed to see in the dark!

Instantly as I think it, my vision shifts, and the dot turns red, orange, and yellow. I fall back in surprise, crashing against the inside of the tree. Everything surrounding the moving color is black and green. There is so much about Old-World and its machines I don't understand. But now, I see that the moving dot in the dark is an ant. If the ant notices me, it doesn't let on. It crawls, then stops, in no rush. I'm happy to have something—anything—living around.

But the ant can crawl deep underground to places I can't. If only I could ask it to stay with me a little while. The ant creeps downward until its glowing green body disappears underground. I can't believe I'm wishing I were even smaller.

How long could I live in the Outlands without seeing another soul? For a moment with the ant, I was no longer by myself in this world. In the blackness of the hollow, I'm reminded of how alone I am.

I spring up to the ledge of the opening. I *want to see the stars.* My vision shifts back instantly. Except for the stars, the sky is black. I lean against the opening.

I check my charge. 17%. I look down at the vial on my leg. I've seen no water on my way here. Without it, I'd never make it back to Pocatel for more water in time.

The little metal bird Gabi and I buried suddenly makes more sense now. Knowing now that they were . . . what I am now . . . I wish we'd spent more time paying respect. My feathers bristle, thinking of how the bird's feathers ended up as knives in Tía Lula's hongo tool. I hurry to aim my beak into the stopper.

But just as I'm about to take a drink, I'm sure I hear the distant flap of wings. I turn toward the noise. A dark speck in the distance grows closer and larger.

My vision shifts even as I think it, and the black speck now glows bright against the sky. I recognize the body, the flap of the wings, and the beak of a crow. I have not seen one in so long. I can't help but stare. It would be a meal of a lifetime for someone in Pocatel.

The crow lowers its course and points its sharp beak in my direction. Maybe it saw the tree just like I had and needs a branch to rest.

I straighten my feathers and bolt up into the air to its height, just to see what it does. The crow shifts its aim again toward me. I dive quickly. It follows.

The nest. Now I know whose egg it is.

I change my direction, but the crow's still right behind me. I make another steep dive. She dives too.

How can I escape when I'm still awful at flying? She's big and powerful, and I'm so small.

The sky can't protect me, and I can't think of anywhere else to go. I dive back inside the hollow tree and fly to the very bottom, where the ant disappeared. I stay completely still. The flap of the crow's wings is now as loud as our pock flapping in the wind. She's landed on the lip of the hollow. She only needs to look down.

The crow's "CAAAW!" inside the empty tree pierces my hearing like a wyrm howl on a still night.

I'm frozen. The crow speaks in little clicks, and her voice sounds like Tía Lula's:

"*How dare you come near my home and child! Come out, gusano. Come, so I can pick at your eyes and eat your guts. Don't worry. I will make it quick.*"

I need to be ready to fly far and fast as soon as she leaves. I focus on the vial and move my beak slowly to reach for the stopper.

"CAAAAW!" explodes right above. A beak pecks my head. Over and over, it jabs until my vision goes in and out of blackness. In the storm of dark wings and a sharp beak, she pins me down with her talon and rears back to strike, aimed at my eye. As hard as I can, I push my wings outward. Even the crow seems surprised by my strength. I zip up, but not before her talon snags one of the feather plates on my wing. I spin out of control, bouncing on the edge of the hole, but into the night air. The vial of water pops off my leg.

I reach out, but I'm not fast enough. The vial hits a tree root. The stopper pops off, and water scatters across dirt, sinking below the surface.

Another "CAAAAW!" echoes from the opening of the hollow. The image of a metal hummingbird in pieces flashes in my mind. Just like Dolores said would happen, the metal panels of this body tremble like my old body. A drop of water won't matter if the crow kills me first.

I zoom away as fast as possible and don't dare look back. The crow's shrieks grow faint behind me.

I speed toward the east. The sky shifts from dark blue to purple. 11%.

After a few more hours, the 4 % in front of me isn't as bright against the rising sun.

No mountains, just flatlands. A human couldn't survive long here. Not even a Cascabel. I've seen nothing to forage for what would've taken thirteen days to walk. I was wrong. Gabi and I would not have survived out here. I would have taken her over the ridge, and we still would have died. I can't believe I'm happy our plan didn't work. Now I know we will need to go in the opposite direction. Maybe even return to the land of our ancestors.

I must be at the far edge of the Outlands. I fly higher, hoping to find any sign of the river valley I'd seen on the map. Any sign of water at all or something green. I only need one drop. But there is nothing.

Because I had to be curious about the tree, I might've ruined our chances all by myself. The charge's ghostly 3% is almost lost in the rising sun.

In the distance, the dark face of a mountain finally comes into view.

I force my wings out into a glide, to save my energy. As I approach the mountain, I see its plateau, but no river. A small building comes into view. It's mostly buried in sand, but it hasn't been scavenged like the city. For a moment, I hope. Maybe beneath its metal roof it holds a drop or two of water. I tuck my wings and dive.

A sign dangles from a rusted nail on the front of the tilting building.

White Sulphur Springs. Float the river! Permit required!

A river! It was here at one point. From the collapsed building's side, long arced pieces of cracked wood stick out; they come to points at each end, but the centers are hollowed out. At least five of them line up next to one another. They don't have metal engines like the *jet boats* in the letter J encyclopedia. But if this was a river, these could have been real boats? Chips of red paint are still visible on its surface. The words *Kayakabunga* are carved into its side and *Shake Your Buoy* on another, but they are barely visible. I don't know what the words mean, but I know they won't help me find water.

I stare down and want to give up. Just like Dolores's map, a winding dry riverbed lies between two rock faces. There's no sign of anything alive. No sign of any others like me.

2%.

I scan from side to side. How is it I can be so thirsty for a drop of water without feeling thirsty? I fly up quickly, as high as I can, then back down again, over and over.

Dolores knew how desperate I was to protect Gabi, and she used me to search for her daughter. How many before me ended up as metal scrap? Maybe every fake vault on her shelf. I probably flew over most of them on my way to this dump.

A lightning bolt blinks in front of me. 1%. The lightning bolt grows a deeper and deeper red.

Swirling clouds twist above me. I right myself and fall back into a dive. *Caution. Rapid descent.*

No one will even know what happened to me but Dolores. How soon before she walks into her lab and finds my dead human body? Will she let Gabi believe I've fallen into the Trench, or been eaten by a wyrm? Or will she tell her I ended up like the ancient bird drone, buried in the sand for hundreds of years?

I can no longer fly straight. I think of my mother, her belly swollen, her foot arcing out and her tongue rattling, saying goodbye to my father lying on the ground next to me.

I fly as fast as I can. I feel myself speed toward something I can't find, like I'm running out of breath.

Small caves dot the cliff faces on each side. If this is where I have to end, let me lie down somewhere that people might think I'd been carefully placed. Maybe they'll think I had value to someone.

I hit one side of the canyon and veer downward. I inch one of my wings back out and flutter my feathers on the other, until I level out. Locking both wings, I glide above the dry riverbed. My vision blacks in and out. Then, one by one, flashing yellow triangles pop on my screen.

Invitation to connect.

I reach out with my mind to the echoes of clicks, that speed like rocks tapping on the ground, in a song around the fire. Is this what dying is like for a machine?

I bounce like a rock on a flat surface, screeching to a complete stop.

Powering down.

I think as hard as I can and yell toward Pocatel with my mind. *Lo siento, Gabi. I tried!*

I can't move. My vision goes black. I see Gabi in my mind. She wears a long white dress, with brightly colored ribbon woven across the front. She raises her arms above a rainbow of feathers fanned above her head. In the middle of a desert, in front of the one-eyed skeleton tree, she twirls. Fists at her side, she smiles at me, rattling her tongue. She holds her dress up and carves a C in the sand to say goodbye.

16

I CRACK OPEN MY EYES. I CAN'T MOVE. I'M UPSIDE
down midair, my foot clamped in the beak of something large.
Water drips over my head and eyes.

100%.

My compass flickers back on. The world shifts from my view
of a sandy riverbed, to the bright sky, to a rocky plateau. I swing
helplessly back and forth. Not knowing what's clenching me in
its mouth makes it worse. I've seen scavengers gut animals in

seconds. How long will this thing take to shred my panels off and scatter my feathers? Shutting down would have been easier.

We drop straight down, and in an instant, we move from sunlight into complete darkness. The fresh air becomes musty, like water on dirt. Water?

"You have one thousand and ninety-four days remaining in your sentence."

My captor's wings whistle through the air until we're inside a rocky cave. I catch glimpses of rocks and . . . lamps? My body clatters as it drags across the ground, then is finally dropped. I can only wait, staring ahead at a wall. The animal hovers over me from behind. Completely silent.

Then, its footsteps click on the hard floor one after the other, leaving the way we came.

I try over and over to flail my wings or scramble away. But my body won't respond. Could I actually explode from fright, leaving only bits of metal behind?

The air vibrates, and the sound of something—*somethings*—scraping against rock gets closer and closer, until they are in the cave with me. Then, as suddenly as the noises approach, they stop.

Shadows ripple in the flickering light of the cave. Whatever they are, they're right behind me.

The first night I heard about Pocatel's wyrmfield, I had a nightmare. The wyrm sunk its fangs into my chest, its venom paralyzing me. My own blood dripped from its teeth onto my face, flowing into my nose and mouth. I woke up gasping.

Play dead, I say to myself. *If they think you're dead, they won't kill you.*

But *Com Connect* projects in front of me just like it had in Dolores's lab, though the voice is gone now. And the tiny yellow triangles I'd seen earlier are back. At least twelve. One by one, they turn solid.

Drones?

There are too many. I wasn't ready for this. Like Dolores said, no one knows what they've become.

I want to stand. To fly. At least face them bravely. But I can't move. I can only hear them moving. I smell dirt after the rain. How can such a peaceful smell feel so unsettling?

A raspy voice, the words stiff like a Pocatelan, speaks in my head: "I did not think we would see another."

Another voice speaks, this time with the slow pattern of someone from San Joaquin: "Que suerte. When I found it, it didn't even have any water."

"Is it dead?" the raspy voice asks.

I've never heard Cascabel and Pocatelan voices have a conversation like this. Like we're equal. If I'm dead, the ancestors have a strange sense of humor.

"Nah," the Cascabel voice answers. "You're awake, aren't you, colibrí? It'll take it a minute to reboot with how drained it was."

"What is that word?" the Pocatelan asks.

"¿Colibrí? It means hummingbird."

Gabi and I used to pretend to be asleep when Tía Lula would wake up in the middle of the night, trying to throw us out of the pock, her mind twisted from hongo. I hurry to close my eyes. For a moment, it's silent. Something hard flicks my belly. I open my eyes.

A strange metal lizard, eyes set on the side of its head, sits in front of me. It pulls its long, rolled tongue back inside its mouth. It moves closer and with a *tic, tic, tic,* lifting its foot to my body. As it touches me, its dusty silver body shifts like a rising dust storm to the identical gold color of my chest. Then it moves its hand to the top of my body, and, like witchcraft, the gold disappears, now becoming the same blue as my head. The lizard looks up. It licks dust off one eye with its metal tongue, like a razor on glass. In an instant, its body coils into a spiral and rolls away, disappearing behind me.

The same deep, tapping footsteps of the drone that carried me in returns. It stares down at me. Except for a deep gouge along its side, I see now it's identical to the *Great Horned Raptor 206* drone I'd found in the lab.

The great horned raptor nudges me with its beak. My body spins around slowly. One by one, they all come into view. I'm surrounded by metal animals. Many I recognize only from the hall of drones back in Pocatel—like the *Meta-Hopper X 2050,* two eagles . . . even a wolf, cat, and three puppies. I want to jump back, but my body still won't move.

The eagles here are larger than the drone I'd seen in the gallery. The same symbol—purple circles with a gold arrow—is coated in dust across their dark chests. I can't help staring.

The ground vibrates next to me with a heavy footstep. *Boom!* Then another. *Boom!* A layer of dust coats my eyes. A clawed metal foot, even bigger than those of the eagle drones, comes within an inch of my face. The foot lifts and passes by my head. Frozen, I can only stare as it gently smooths my crooked metal feathers back like they're soft as . . . feathers. I'm instantly back on the trail with Tía Lula when Gabi found the bird drone. *"Magical animals . . . metal . . . one of those things that doesn't make sense . . . unnatural."*

"Alebrijes," I whisper to myself.

"What did it say?" one of the eagles asks.

The great horned raptor stands next to the clawed foot. His judging eyes stare down. "It said, 'Alebrijes,'" he answers, pronouncing it perfectly with a rolled R.

"Where'd you find it?"

"Right outside," he answers. "Like I said. Por suerte I heard something."

Each toe on the clawed metal foot of the largest drone is bigger than me. I look up very slowly, to see the foot attached to . . . a monster bigger than a man. Metal fur covers its body. It's on all fours and has teeth bigger than me. I think of what Dolores said about not knowing what they'd become.

My mind tells my body to fight. I thrash out and . . . my wing moves.

The monster steps back. Someone giggles. "Looks like it's coming around." The creature leans in, until we're eye to eye. Except her eye is as big as my entire body. She moves slower than the others. "What's your name?"

I pull myself up with my wing. I stare up, suddenly back in the papa fields where the guard is demanding an answer. "*You were meant to slither in the dirt, were you not, little boy?*"

But she's not the guard. Still, I don't speak. Why am I hesitating?

"You don't have to say. Most of us make up our own. I go by Oso."

I'd heard of this animal. An extinct one. Oso. It lived in forests. Ate honey and even humans who got too close. It was one I was sure was made up.

If they're all changing their names, finding Selah might be harder than I thought. I think of answering, "Colibrí," but being a hummingbird isn't as cool as being named something tough like Oso. "Leandro," I finally answer.

Oso lumbers back and squats by the entrance.

One of the eagles flies and lands in front of me. "You were lucky you found us." His quick, short speech gives him away. "Leandro."

There are no shaved heads, clean robes, dirty tunics, or stags in pockets to tell me who's in control here. But my San Joaquin name's a dead giveaway.

"Leo," I say quickly. I don't even know why I say it. I want to unsay the name the Field Director gave me immediately.

The eagle steps even closer. He towers over me now, glaring down.

Don't show fear. Don't show fear.

I fall backward.

The great horned raptor tries to step past the other eagle, who blocks its way. "Ezra, stop," he says.

But the eagle pushes out his wing, shoving the raptor back.

Ezra lowers his head to mine until his needle-sharp beak touches my head. It makes no sound, but the vibration of metal-on-metal rings inside my head. I hold completely still.

"You are here. So, someone is still trying to find us," Ezra says.

The other eagle flies in between us and faces him. "The hummingbird did nothing, Ezra. And Mother said that actions made in anger lead to an exile trail of regret."

"Maybe if Mother had been more angry, Rose"—he lifts his head—"we would not have been exiled at all." He nudges her aside and turns slowly, flying out.

Rose lowers her talon and clips on to my wing. She gently lifts me back to my feet, but says nothing more, flying out after him.

No one else moves or speaks. I have no way of knowing who agrees with Ezra. I can feel and hear my feathers still shaking. I just hope they can't tell.

Oso's footsteps thud out. A cat slinks after.

The rest follow. One by one, their signals disconnect from mine. Why didn't Dolores tell me Selah's drone form? I've only heard two Pocatelan accents, and it sounds like Ezra and Rose are brother and sister. The sooner I can find her and get out of here—

The great horned raptor stops at the door. "I did think you were dead, Leandro. If you hadn't yelled out, I would have never found you."

Maybe they don't all want to see me dead. I try to remember the last thing I'd said. *Lo siento, Gabi.* I *tried!* "Oh." I look down. If he's the one who found me, I haven't thanked him yet for saving my life.

"For now," he says, "all you need to know is that you found us."

I might have found *them*, but I only *need* one of them. But if Dolores gave them all the same chance, I can't just ask where Selah is. They'll know what I'm doing.

"Uh, thanks, uh . . ."

"My name's Jovi," he calls back.

I've never heard of an extinct flying animal called a Jovi, so it must be his real name. I fly to the entrance and see the great horned raptor's shadow disappear down a torchlit hallway. "Thank you, Jovi!" I call, but his signal is already gone.

I fall to the ground. When I left in search for Selah, a hidden cave full of the banished drones is not what I expected to find. No one even asked what crime I committed to be here.

I glance around. I have no other choice but to follow him.

As I move slowly down the center of the cave, it widens, and a rumbling noise in the distance builds and the smell of wet dirt grows stronger. Sunlight falls on the ground from an opening ahead, and dirt stirs up in a breeze. I flash on El Bastón opening the door for Celia, at the Center of Banishment, and even here I can see her standing naked, walking onto the exile trail to her death. I slow. Something feels too familiar. What will I find?

I fly into the light.

17

· · · ☾ · · ·

WARM AIR HITS ME. SUN BEAMS THROUGH AN OPEN ceiling into a closed-in, cavernous room that could fit three of Pocatel's entire downtown. Vines and ferns run up walls ten stories high, covering them in a green blanket. Openings lie behind the vines. Doors? Lamplight twinkles through the leaves like stars in a dark sky, broken ladders woven between each floor. The smell of soil, and water, and growing plants hits me all at once.

I wobble and barely catch myself, hovering just before I hit the ground.

Rows after row of plants cover the ground. A square section of plants like green broom handles lie on the distant side. Leaves longer than the rabbit's ears dangle from their long stems. Both the soil and plants are darker than Pocatel's fields. Vines wrap around wooden stakes on one section of a field. In the distance, trees with brown trunks stand tall, not bleached and hunched over like the skeleton tree. Red, green, and yellow fruit lies scattered on the ground beneath the trees.

A river winds like a snake through the fields. Water splashes out onto the ground surrounding it. Something jumps from the water's surface, arching midair before falling back in. A *real fish*.

I can't believe water can make so much noise. Enough to last our entire lives, and every Cascabel and Pocatelan for twenty generations.

Jo's tatara-tatara-abuelo, the Pocatelan scout, didn't come even close to how magical this is. My feathers quiver.

La Cuna.

"It's real." This time when I fall to the ground, I bounce hard and push myself back up on my own. I don't see Jovi until he's at my side.

"Yo sé. It's a lot at first."

In the center of the massive space stands a pine tree twenty times higher than the tallest piñon I've ever climbed. The tree watches over La Cuna like a protective mother. I lift my chin, aiming at its highest branch, and breathe deeply. With the smell of fresh pine, for a moment, I'm free again.

"¿Qué esta pasando?" the lizard's voice asks, and I know others must be watching.

"Shhh," Jovi shushes. "Give him a minute."

I lower my head and pretend I was just trying to get a closer look around.

"I felt the same," Jovi says. "I'd tell you that you get used to it, but I haven't."

The lizard walks slowly in front of us, one eye aimed on me.

"That's Charlie," Jovi says.

Charlie looks at me for a second more, then curls into a ball and spins off like a speeding wagon wheel across the fields.

"Just so you know," Jovi continues, "if you see one of our signals, we can see and hear you too."

I think of the yellow triangles and how I can sense some now. Charlie rolls farther away until his signal disappears.

The hum of unafraid voices inside this place is nothing like the hushed fields we work in Pocatel.

I'm glad I'm not alone, but not sure how I feel about someone in my head. "So, you can hear my thoughts?"

"Only if you're close enough to connect. And only if you think you're talking, like before. Not your thoughts. ¿Comprendes?"

I don't know exactly what he means, but I nod anyway, understanding it's how Jovi found me.

I look around to see where everyone else has gone and what they're doing. High above, one on each edge of the opening in the ceiling, Ezra and Rose stare outward. The wolf paces the edge of the fields just like the Patrol in the papa fields. A *Shelter Mutt* dog, followed by the three puppies, trails after.

The cat disappears down a tunnel, then reappears. I'm not so interesting that it stops what it's doing.

I'm thankful Jovi didn't leave me alone.

"My name's Leandro," I say. "Not Leo."

He nods. "I know."

He steps in front of me. He towers over me too, but I'm not scared anymore.

"I need to explain some things," Jovi says. "Just like you, we all ended up here for a reason. Some of us traveled the Outlands longer than others. But now that we're here . . ." He turns back, staring out at the fields. "We get to start over."

I picture myself and Gabi working the fields, but not for someone else. I wouldn't have to face into the sun all day just to keep an eye on her. We wouldn't have to rush at the sight of sunset, hoping for a single papa. In a way, we would be living at one with the earth again.

One of the eagles—Rose, I think—swoops across the fields.

"I hope one day—" Jovi starts, then stops as Rose gets closer, her signal growing stronger. She nears the opposite end of the cave and the signal fades. Then she circles higher and higher until she is in the sky above.

"We don't agree on everything," he continues. "But we do all agree that we have to protect La Cuna."

I understand a bit better. I just have to figure out if by "protecting," they mean like the Patrol protects the fields with guns, or "protect," like I make sure our pock is secure at night. One could get me killed; the other is as easy as squeezing through a gap.

"You said some of you were in the Outlands longer than others. So, is your sentence almost over?"

Jovi nods but doesn't speak. Drones don't have facial expressions, so his silence isn't helpful.

"¿Por qué no regresa? ¿Qué hay de su familia?" I ask.

At the mention of his family, Jovi looks up. "Sí, tengo familia."

I see that Ezra is no longer alone. A golden hawk Alebrije, one I hadn't seen when I arrived, now sits at his side. It's half his size, but it somehow looks more powerful. The same marking is painted on the hawk as all the other. They're so far away, I don't sense their signals, but I'm sure the hawk turns its head in my direction.

"I . . . We planned to . . ." Jovi continues, his glare locked on Ezra and the hawk. "Like I said, we don't agree on all things." He lifts to a hover. "I'll come find you later. Quédate cerca." He hovers for a moment, then flies away quickly; within seconds, his signal is gone too.

La Cuna is far better than Gabi and I dreamt or Jo described, but it may as well be a dung field if I can't get back to her before the Thinning. I've waited long enough. I need to find Dolores's daughter.

I hover upward for a better look. Then higher. No one seems to be concerned at all with me anymore. I fly down each row of plants, so fast the plants become a green blur. Every so often a streak of dark silver from the wolf, or a blue and green lizard, whizzes by out of the corner of my vision. Someone laughs . . . I think, maybe at me . . . but I don't care. I can't imagine any of the other drones are as fast as me. I zip up and down, stopping just before I plunge into the river. I land and dip my beak in to test it, and my charge fills instantly.

I fly along and through the vines running up the walls. Many stories high, now I can see that the lights I'd seen shine from openings lead to empty rooms. The ancient ladders make sense. But who lived here? And where'd they go?

I make a second loop, and by the time I finish, I can soar all the way to the ceiling in an instant and fly across a field bigger than all of Pocatel in seconds. And I can do it without crashing. I'm more Colibrí than Leandro. This place, La Cuna, and being able to fly . . . it's all magic.

Then I'm going too fast. A loud squeal goes off inside me and something takes over, stopping me instantly—like a mother grabbing a toddler's arm, just before I crash into the great pine.

I can't help how long I hover and stare. Someone giggles again. Again, I don't care. I've never seen a tree like this. It's four times as wide as any of the dead pines near Pocatel. I hover around its trunk that's wider than our pock. I circle upward until I near the top. As I weave through branches, the smell of its needles swirl in the air around me. Without even crushing them between fingers, the aroma is sweeter than the piñons from my past. They must be part of the same family; this one, the elder of the pines.

Near the top, I can see the sky. Jovi warned to stay close, but I see nothing stopping me. And who could? With my charge full, if I leave now and don't stop, I could make it back to Pocatel easily. I could tell Dolores where they all are, but only after she helps Gabi and me escape.

I fly higher and higher and breach the ceiling's edge. I spin in a circle, but still no one is watching. I dart up higher. Then higher. From here, I stare to the west where the sun is beginning to set. I could be back before the next sun.

In an instant, a yellow triangle pops up in front of me, just before a shadow blocks the sun. I'm hit so hard from above, I plummet downward. I topple over and over again and can't regain my balance. Far below, the ground waits.

My wings correct the fall after a moment and I fall into a spiral, but I still can't control myself. I hit the very top branches of the tree. It slows me enough where I can splay my wings and clutch the edge of a branch.

The needles tremble as I cling to the branch, shivering. I stare down at the ground that was a few seconds away from being my grave.

The signal approaches again, and the shadow falls over me. Rose lands softly next to me, pointing her beak to my face. "What do you think you were doing?"

"I . . . I . . . was just—"

"There is no acceptable answer," she interrupts. "I should not have given you that warning," she says, scanning the room.

"*That* was a warning?"

She hovers off the branch. "And it will be your last, Leo. Next time I will not protect you." She scans around once more before zooming away.

I got off easy.

I don't dare move. I remain on the branch as the sun passes directly overhead, then disappears. The afternoon sun turns to dusk. I'm going to have to rethink my plan. I move closer to the tree's trunk.

Deep, dark furrows wind like rivers up its red skin. I think of what the world must've been like before. How many were there? Did trees like this one make those people feel small too? I'm not sure I would've been brave enough to climb so high. I tuck inside the safety of one of the splits in the bark. If it were only me, I'd never leave this spot.

I close my eyes. I see a quick flash of Jovi pouring water over my beak and face. It really happened.

When I open my eyes, I'm back at the top of the pine. I shiver, thinking of what almost happened to me—twice—and in one day.

I close my eyes. This time, the flash is different. My mother holds water to my mouth. "*Drink this, Leandro,*" she says.

Why can I still not see her eyes? But for the first time . . . I can see her lips are dry and cracked. I hold her hand as it shakes, holding the water for me. Her fingers burn with fever. "*We will feel better soon."* Why is she giving me her own water? Is this memory real? Are those really her lips?

I feel the same sadness as when I saw her carve the Cascabel C into the dirt for the dying man.

I hurry to open my eyes and stare down at the river. I shake my head. She is gone. The rush of water sounds like a strong wind through the high branches of a piñon. Plants blow in the breeze. The first souls of the night begin to twinkle in the sky above.

If this was our world . . . La Cuna . . . would we finally be free of all that hurts and frightens us? Would I remember? I'm not sure I even want to anymore.

I close my eyes again, but Jovi does not come to give me water. My sick mother doesn't return. Instead Tía Lula lunges at me now, spit flying through her tooth gap as if she were right in front of my eyes. *"Gusano, blow out the candle or I'll use it to burn off the stubble hair your niñito chin is trying to grow!"*

"Go away," I mumble. "Can't you see I'm happy here?"

"Sorry, am I bothering you?" a slow Pocatelan voice asks.

I flinch and open my eyes. Next to me sits the hawk. I hadn't even sensed its approach.

"No," I say. "You aren't bothering me. I'm just . . ." I don't know *what* I am—or what I'm feeling—so I don't finish.

"Thinking," the hawk says. "You were probably just thinking. We were not allowed to do much of that for ourselves in Pocatel. Here . . . you can think all you want." The words seem strange coming from this hawk. I didn't think Pocatelans ever had these kinds of thoughts about Pocatel.

But I saw the way Jovi glared at this Alebrije. And the hawk is friends with Ezra, who definitely hates me. The hawk takes a step closer, and I nearly topple off the branch. The arrow on its side is bigger than me.

Once again, a small movement from this creature could kill me.

Suddenly, I see the pattern. The more powerful flight drones—Ezra, Rose, and this hawk—are all Pocatelan kids.

But I'm not going to hide my San Joaquin name to this hawk.

"Leandro," I say, holding my cabeza alta and sitting up on the branch. "My name's Leandro. And I was just thinking of how much I like it up here." I'm telling the truth.

The hawk doesn't react at all to my name.

"Me too. I like it here too," it replies.

We sit in silence. It seems impossible, but this Pocatelan hawk and I have at least one thing in common.

"Once you are rested and recovered from your reboot, we will find work for you. I think I know just the job."

Ezra flies in so fast, I don't even feel his signal until he's almost on top of us.

I'm almost startled right off the branch, but the hawk doesn't budge.

"Time to go," Ezra says. "Rose saw something."

In the distance, Rose hovers just above the ceiling's opening, facing north, her eyes fixed on something in the night.

"I should leave you to yourself now anyway." The hawk jumps to the edge of the branch. This time I clutch on tight. "I do not think you need me to convince you of how lucky we are to live here."

I don't disagree. They don't need food. There's water for lifetimes. No one calls me gusano. No one threatens anyone with Banishment. I could spend my entire life right here on top of this tree. If it weren't for Gabi . . .

"You will need for nothing here. You are free to think whatever you would like without fear of betrayal or exile," it says. "You are safe here, Leandro."

As the hawk flies away after Ezra and Rose, its signal fades. But then it makes a sudden spin, and returns. It hovers for a moment in front of me before speaking again. "There is just one rule. And we will dismantle you if you disobey."

The word *dismantle* isn't familiar. But I get its meaning. Maybe they are just the Pocatelan Regime in new bodies. I try to stay steady on the branch. What could I do that they would "dismantle" me? I grip the branch tighter. "What is it?"

The hawk flies closer until the hum of its wings vibrates my body. "No one leaves."

Yeah, I got that.

But if Rose's reaction was just a "warning" . . . .

I understand why none have returned to Pocatel. The others might not be as afraid to speak. They might not be hungry. But just like we were trapped in Pocatel, they're trapped inside La Cuna.

Still, not Rose, and definitely not this bossy hawk, is going to stop me.

The feathers at my neck ruffle in fear. "Bueno," I say quickly, then realize it may not understand.

The hawk flies off, but calls back, "It was good to meet you, Leandro. My name is Selah."

18

···(···

SELAH DISAPPEARS INTO THE NIGHT SKY AFTER EZRA.

I look below at La Cuna and all the trapped Alebrijes, then back up into the starry sky where Selah just flew. Convincing her to return to Pocatel with me feels impossible. But she doesn't know what's happening there—though if she'd even care, I don't know. I just hope Gabi doesn't do anything stupid until I can return. My feathers shudder, imagining her sneaking away from the orphanage to the Dead Forest or over the Trench.

I should go to Jovi now. Tell him about the Thinning. He has a family too. He'll understand why I didn't tell them right away. But my best chance just flew out into the night sky. I push off from the branch and follow the direction of Selah. I land on the lip of the opening. The air is clear and cold. I spin in each direction, but don't see Selah, Ezra, or Rose, or sense their signals. They might not be real scavengers, but they could attack me like Rose did before I knew they were on top of me. Selah said, "*No one leaves.*" But *they* just did. Still, I shudder looking just above my head at the spot where Rose hit me.

I look west toward the Outlands, but I see nothing in the dark. Then, a light catches the corner of my vision to the north. *15.7 kilometers.* It sways back and forth in the dark. It's much too far to be Selah and the others. It would be a half-day journey on foot, but with how fast I am now . . .

Suddenly another light appears. The second light is brighter and steady. The swaying light approaches the other until they are so close, they could touch.

I could be there and back before anyone notices me missing.

I lower my signal as far as I can. I hover for a second, and when there are no other signals, I speed to the north. The lights grow brighter and brighter. In the dark, my vision shifts. The heat of the light glows just like the ant inside the tree. The shape of a—could it be? Yes: the shape of a person lights up orange and red in the darkness. But there's more. Something else gives off heat too. Something far larger sits next to the person. It's too far to see, but I will be there in . . . just . . . a . . . minute . . .

Then in an instant, they both disappear.

I fly low to the ground. A cloud of dust surrounds me and clouds my vision. I spin to look in all directions. But there's no sign of what left the dust behind.

I know what I saw. Next time, I'll have to be faster—if I'm lucky.

The last of the dust settles. Suddenly I'm reminded of Celia. Very slowly, I lift higher and higher. What if I'm hovering right over a wyrm? What if he devoured the person and burrowed beneath, like he'd done with her?

Spores can't hurt me anymore. But one leap upward from a hungry wyrm and I disappear, never to be found. When I'm so high I'm sure the wyrm could never reach me, I stop.

Maybe it was my imagination.

I turn back toward La Cuna. This time I know exactly where I'm going.

As I approach the mountain, beside the old building, the rocky plateau and dry river valley don't look special at all. Every cave opening has been blocked or buried by rocks and earth, hidden by the Alebrijes. I fly above the open ceiling and see the fields and underground river of La Cuna. No one would ever know it was here, unless they grew wings. My people could've searched and searched in the Outlands for years. Maybe never have found it.

Far below, Wolf still paces along the walls and fields, trailed by Shelter Mutt and puppies. Oso sits facing the largest cave tunnel, her body blocking the entire entrance. Cat steps right on top of Oso, walking directly across her back. Just like it has over and over, the cat goes down the next tunnel, then returns. They can't be happy doing this all the time.

I turn back to where I'd seen the strange lights and swear another flicker dances, casting a shadow over something large and dark. Then, just like before, the light disappears in an instant. I don't know what's real anymore. There are things San Joaquin elders swear were real long ago, but which I still can't believe. People eating until their stomachs told them to stop. Throwing clothes away when they didn't like them anymore. Taking showers with one soap for your body, another for your hair, and whenever you wanted. But just today I learned fish are real.

As I stare down at the river, signals of other Alebrijes pop up. I fly quickly back inside La Cuna and land at the water's edge. I search, but Selah, Rose, and Ezra's are none of those signals. I'm safe.

I stare into the rippling surface. Fish huddle together, their green bodies—dotted with black spots—waving smoothly back and forth like a dance. They've been corralled in by a wall of rocks. The rocks are covered in algae; whoever built the trap did it long before the Alebrijes. They swim against its flow and somehow remain in one spot. But one has jumped the trap and left the group. It swims just beneath the surface on the river's edge. I hop closer to the edge and poke my beak near the water. It moves its tail suddenly and water splashes over me.

I laugh and jump back, bumping into Jovi, who's landed next to me. His talons sink into the soggy ground under his weight.

I speak first. "You could sell a few of these fish for all the stags in Pocatel." I turn toward the fields. "Or just one row of vegetables."

Jovi turns to face the fields with me. "That's why we have to protect it from their Regime." He pauses. "Even protect it from some of our own people."

I flinch just a little at his words. But I think for a moment, and realize I can't imagine the damage someone like Tía Lula could do to a place like this, in just a short amount of time.

"You left," he says.

"Yeah . . . uh . . . I didn't go far," I say. "And I came right back."

"Mira, Leandro. Not everyone dreamt of La Cuna for generations the way Cascabeles did. It means something different to Selah, Ezra, and Rose than it does to us," he says. "They're serious about what they'll do to you."

Yeah, I found out.

I can't even think of what to say. The river and fields in front of us are everything our people searched a hundred winters for.

"¿Qué hay de nuestras familias?" I ask.

He tilts his head, like he's wondering if he can trust me. "We haven't forgotten our families, Leandro." His voice seems softer, and I wonder if he's whispering. "But it has to be in the right time."

If what he says means waiting, I can't. Dying in Pocatel together is better than Gabi dying alone, or me living in La Cuna without her.

"But when we do go back for them," Jovi continues, his voice firmer, "we return to La Cuna with only our own families. No one else."

I turn toward him and hop onto a rock. Now he sounds like Tía Lula, wanting a Pocatelan house all to herself.

"What are you talking about?" I exclaim. "The Cascabel scout traveled until he dropped dead to bring the news of La Cuna for all Cascabeles. That's not what he died for. For only a few Cascabeles to hoard so much for themselves? That would make us no better than the Pocatelans, Jovi. We are better than this."

He turns away, and I can tell I'm speaking to someone who's already thought of this a thousand times.

But if I accept what Dolores has offered me, for just me and Gabi, aren't I doing the same? If what Dolores says is true, the others were given the same choice. Now they're the ones keeping La Cuna for themselves, while Cascabeles fight for rotten potatoes and bitter water back in Pocatel.

Jovi nearly sinks in the mud as he takes off. "Follow me." He flies over the river, then along the edge of the fields, passing Wolf and veering onto a ladder next to the vine-covered wall.

Collapsed and splintered, the ladder's held up only by vines.
I land next to Jovi on one of the rungs.

"How many in your family?" he asks quietly.

I hesitate. For a second I wonder, will their rules for orphans
be different here? We don't have Tía Lula anymore.

"It's okay," he says. "I only need to know if your room will be
big enough for you and your family."

I think of Jo. I doubt he'll make his count without me. But if
I get back in time . . .

"Three . . ." I say. "Mi abuelo, Jo, y mi hermana, Gabi."

"Solo tres," he says. "Un abuelo . . . I will give you a room on
the main floor, then, for him."

I suddenly remember Celia and the hiccupping boy. He has
no one. I don't even know his name. "I mean four. A primo. He's
small though. He won't take up much room." I'll have to shave
his head, put a dirty tunic on him, and hope for the best. What
if they won't let them in? But I have to try. He did say family only.
"And . . . I have otra prima, Ari."

He leans in. "So many cousins, Leandro." I wish I knew
if his face was smiling or angry. "You sure that's all? Do you
have the only living great tío in the Pox you forgot about too?
Even with your tiny cousin . . . we might need to find a bigger
room."

He for sure knows I'm lying.

"No, no. Whatever it is will be fine for all of us."

Jovi pulls more vines aside. And behind . . . a hidden door,
open. It's dusty and hard to see, but the room beyond doesn't look

like the rest of La Cuna. A jacket made of animal hide hangs on a metal hook. Stones are pasted with clay onto the wall, the fingerprints of those who placed them still visible.

I gasp. This is better than I imagined! And there is plenty of room for all of us.

I think of the people who made those fingerprints—hundreds of winters ago, just after the world ended, maybe before even—and what they must've felt.

Jovi motions to a dark passageway in the corner. "There are two more rooms back there."

"More rooms than this?!"

"Since there are a few of you, you might want to split up for privacy."

"Privacy?" I laugh. I can't imagine living in a space where someone else doesn't know every time I sneeze, cough, or fart.

I look back toward Jovi. Behind him, the lower half of the great pine lies beyond the door.

"What do you think this place was?"

"No one knows," he answers. "But whatever it was and whoever lived here, disappeared. Not sure if they died out or just left. But they left all we needed to start over."

"La Cuna," I whisper.

"Yeah," he says. "Just like our ancestors in San Joaquin dug into the mountains, and the Pocatelans' ancestors hid in their mines . . . someone survived in this cradle."

I know it takes a certain number of people to carry on. Maybe that's what happened to these people. There weren't enough of them. With so many Cascabeles now dead, and a coming Thinning . . .

"Jovi, La Cuna has to be shared with more people than just our own families, if anyone is going to call us ancestors one day."

He doesn't answer at first. Then, he turns to face me. "You're old enough to remember before."

"Remember what?"

"How we used to be. Before we came to Pocatel." He holds out his wing toward the main room. "We're still learning not to be so suspicious of one another here. But it's taking us time, in bodies that can survive on their own, without being manipulated with hunger and humiliation." He drops his wing. "Some of us have lost too much. Pocatel still rules their minds."

"We're going to have to trust one another."

"Yes," he says.

I haven't relied on anyone to tell me the truth or be kind, besides Gabi, for so long. "Then I will try to trust you, Jovi."

He nods before flying from the room. I follow but glance back. Do I dare hope to imagine people and laughter inside of it?

I catch up and land next to Jovi on the edge of the fields. We stare out, and I breathe in. I smell how much richer it is than the dusty soil of Pocatel.

"So, why'd you plant all this, if you never planned to use them?"

"We did plan to use them." He glances toward the sky. "Things changed. When the time is right, we will—"

"Jovi, if we all leave now, together, we won't be here for Selah, Rose, and Ezra to dismantle us. When we come back with our families, what could they—"

"Don't you think we've thought of that? *They* know we've thought of that. We'd come back to nothing. They'd destroy it all. We'd bring your family here to starve to death."

But we can't wait for a "right time." And I'm not the only one who has someone to lose. "I need to tell you something. About our families—"

Jovi puts his wing out just before I sense her too. Selah's body whistles as she lands on the ground in front of us. She pulls her wings back and straightens her posture, towering over me. "You went outside," she says tersely.

I don't know if Rose told her what I'd done earlier, or if Selah saw me just a bit ago. "I . . . I didn't leave," I lie. "I just wanted to look around."

Jovi steps with a thump between Selah and me, his body clinking on hers. "You need to back off, Selah."

She pushes Jovi back, in a standoff. "Go back to your perch, pet. I won't let him lead some Monger straight to us." Selah leans down to glare at me, eye to eye. "Do you think the Mongers would hesitate to turn you into a tooth scraper, if it paid off even the smallest part of their debt?"

I've never seen a metal tooth scraper, but I shudder thinking of my tiny feathers rubbing over Director Marguerite's stained brown teeth.

"I warned you, Leandro. Of what we would do." She looks at me for a second longer, then turns to leave.

Jovi is still in front of her, and she stops. At least when humans breathe there's noise. Two breathless drones in a stare down is frightening.

Selah finally flies up and shreds leaves off a plant with her talon on her way. I sigh. She'll never agree to go back with me willingly.

After she's a fair distance, Jovi speaks. "So . . . you were about to tell me something?"

I let out an awkward laugh. "Yes, and it's important."

In an instant, Jovi's eyes widen, and he goes completely rigid. Beams of light shoot from his eyes. Purple. Then orange. Then blue. Then green. His wings clank, flapping up and down. "Wakey wakey eggs and bakey. Whoooooo needs to wake up? Davis needs to get up, that's whooooo!"

I jerk back in surprise. I'm about to get help, when Jovi feathers ruffle to a puffy ball, and his face is instantly as calm as a moment ago.

I hover up to his eye. "¿Estás bien?"

He pushes me away with his wing. "Pffff. I'm fine." He makes a loud sigh. "I should've warned you. Goes off twice a day." Even though no one is near, there is no way they didn't hear that. They must all be used to it, because when I search the room, no one seems to notice or sync to communicate.

"What was that?"

"*That* was why Selah called me a pet."

"You were someone's pet drone?"

"This body was a pet drone." He sounds offended. "At some point, the pollinator body you're in probably fed hundreds of people, but that wasn't you."

It's been a long time since I felt like I was part of anything. These past few years, some Cascabeles would have slit my throat for a week's rations. But that's not who we are. We've just forgotten to protect one another. Maybe this place and the Alebrijes really *are* a chance for something different. If he and I are going to trust each other, I have to tell him everything—beginning with who I really am.

"I'm here because I'm a thief," I blurt out. "That's who I am. A thief." ·

He turns back. "What?"

My words come out shaky. "My sister and I . . ." I lower my head. "I made her pickpocket too, at market, so we could escape Pocatel."

When I look up, his raptor eyes do not look like they're judging me at all. "Most of us did what we had to do to survive, Leandro. We all had dreams of escaping." He stops for a moment. Then, "I was caught inside a Director's home."

I move closer. "What!" I think of the guts he must've had to break into a Director's home to steal.

"I was caught right away."

"Not such a good thief, then."

His brows click into a deep metal V. "I wasn't there to steal, Leandro." His brow relaxes. "I saw a boy at the market. He made eye contact with me. He motioned for me to follow." He closes his eyes. "I wanted a friend. Maybe someone outside the Pox and fields. An escape." He knocks himself on the head. "I was only thirteen winters and stupid."

"Hey!" I say. "I'm thirteen."

We both laugh.

"So, what happened?" I ask.

"I got lost."

I snicker. "Lost?"

"A Director was coming up the walk. Probably his dad. I panicked. I thought I was leaving through the back of their house, but I ended up in a room for cooking."

I think of the orphanage and its three floors and the bathroom, and how some of the Directors' homes are bigger than the old home for books.

"Can you believe I thought the Pocatelan kid would defend me?" He motions outward with his wing, like there's an imaginary exile door in front of us. "He just watched as they led me out of his house toward the Center of Banishment, my abuela crying after me the whole way." Jovi sighs and continues. "Anyway, even here, we haven't exactly made friends with them. As you can probably tell."

"Jovi, there's more I really need to say now." I'm not sure if his abuela is still alive. But I have to tell him before I lose my nerve. I just hope he understands why I didn't tell him right away. I haven't trusted anyone in three winters—not even Ari. It might've been selfish, that I was only going to save me and Gabi... "Before I left, I made an agreement with Selah's mother."

He waves it off. "Oh, we all did."

I jump in front of him and stare up. "So what happened? Why didn't any return?"

He sighs. "Selah shut them all down. Don't worry though. We have a plan. It will take some time to get everything in place, but—"

"Jovi, stop," I say.

His head turns quickly. "What?"

I say the words quickly: "The Regime is going to begin a Thinning."

"A Thinn . . ." Jovi takes a step back, staring ahead, and once again, I can't read what he's thinking. "¿Estás seguro?" he asks.

I don't answer. He knows I wouldn't say it if I wasn't sure. "Soon," I say. "They're running out of food. And you know who'll be first to go. We can't bring our people at all if my sister . . . your abuela . . . are dead."

"I can't believe they would—"

"Really?" I say. "More Cascabeles have died since arriving to Pocatel than our worst days foraging. They exile us for a simple lie, if it means providing for themselves before us. Whose mouths will they eliminate first?"

He doesn't respond for a moment, then turns back to me, giving a small scoff. "My father and older brother were exiled for stealing beetles, you know? They were just trying to feed me and my grandmother. Imagine, dying for a few bugs." Now if Jovi's face shows anything, it's determination. "I guess we need to finish what we started before Selah, Rose, and Ezrah stopped us."

Now I am at a loss for words. "I . . . I don't understand. Finish how?"

"As soon as the fields are prepared, we go back for our bodies and families. I saw you. I saw how quick you are. We thought it would take weeks to pollinate the fields, so we could bring our families back. But you could pollinate the entire field in a day and they wouldn't even notice."

"Wait," I say. "You think I can do all that?" I stare out at the endless fields.

"If all you say is true, we don't have time to waste."

"Yeah, but . . . I've barely learned to fly," I reply. "Tambien, Ezra might pull me apart metal feather by metal feather if I'm caught!"

"The rest of us are too big and too slow." Jovi puts his wing out toward the fields. "You're quiet and fast and can work while Selah, Ezra, and Rose are out on their flight. We could do it tonight. They won't know."

He doesn't know about me. Too small to help my own mother. I couldn't even help Gabi and me escape Tía Lula or Pocatel. I'd probably just screw this up too.

"So?" Jovi asks.

"I'm . . . I'm not sure."

He leans in, and even in these bodies, I can feel his urgency. "Some of us have been waiting winters to get back to our families, Leandro."

I imagine Gabi dancing in the fields. No longer just a distraction so we can steal, but like she hoped, because she is happy.

"What about Selah, Ezra, and Rose? They aren't just going to let us leave. Didn't you just say they'd destroy it all?"

"Yes. But . . . they can't destroy it if they're trapped."

In the distance, a puppy trips over a stone and face-plants. Oso sits at the cave entrance, poking vines with a claw.

"Really?" I ask. "And who here's strong enough to do that?"

He motions for me to follow, and he flies back into my new room. He disappears behind the vines. I fly in also to find him waiting. Any noise, and all signals, are gone. "A few things we Cascabeles know how to do are forage . . . and hunt," he says. "I told you, we've been working on a plan. We've talked about trapping them. We knew it would come to that, eventually. Now we don't have the choice or time to figure out exactly how. But we still have to try."

I shake my head.

"¡Carajo! I need to tell the others. Pero Leandro, no matter if you decide to help us, we will have to move ahead with our plan. For our families. We will leave with the next sun." He flies toward the door and through the vines. Between the leaves I see the great pine. In a flash, I imagine myself sitting high in the branches.

"Jovi," I call after.

He hasn't gone far. He's back through the vines almost as soon as I call his name.

"Just tell me where to start."

19

BY THE TIME I'M OUT OF THE ROOM, JOVI HAS OSO,
who connects and calls Wolf, who calls Shelter Mutt and the
puppies, who call to the cat, who's the last to skulk out of a
tunnel. They fly, run, and clomp toward us until everyone but
Oso is in a group. Charlie whirls around us over and over. Jovi
whips out his wing, and Charlie crashes against it with a clank.
"Leandro needs to tell us all something."

Oso is still walking step-by-step toward us slowly, but I've connected with her signal. I hover higher until everyone is looking toward me. "I'm sorry. I should have spoken right away. But I wasn't sure I could—" I want to say the word. *Trust.* But I don't think I do trust anyone, even now.

We do have one thing in common, though. We are Cascabel.

They look at one another confused. I carry on.

"The Regime . . . the Directors . . . are beginning a Thinning."

"Thinning?" Wolf asks.

"It is just as it sounds," I say. "Like we do with crops. But this is with our people."

Angry words and gasps come in all at once, colliding in my mind.

"How do you know?" Cat hisses.

"I heard them talking myself." I reply. "It's true. I promise."

A mix of voices fills my head.

"Mentiroso."

"What do we do?"

"I'm leaving now."

"He's full of mierda."

Now I'm wondering if Jovi acted too fast. Maybe not all of them feel how he does.

"I understand you had a plan of when you'd return for your families. But I can tell you, there's no time for planning any longer."

Jovi flies next to me. "He's right. We can't wait. And as soon as Leandro gets the fields pollinated, he and I leave. By the time we get our own bodies back and return, there should be enough food for all of us, including our families."

I notice he still doesn't include *all* Cascabeles.

"The Directors think we're all up in those vaults. So, they won't be looking for two drones sneaking into Pocatel. Leandro and I will go."

"That is not a plan," Cat says. "How are the two of you supposed to get my mother and sister out? I'm coming—"

"The rest of you have to stay here!" Jovi yells. "It would take too long." He sighs and shakes his head. "No, this is the only way."

Just as he says it, Oso finally shuffles up to the group.

"It's not perfect," I say, facing Cat. She turns and flicks her tail at me. "But I can tell you, Dolores is desperate to find Selah. She won't have any choice but to help us. All of us."

Instinctively, everyone looks up. But there's no sign of Selah and the others.

I think I'm clearing my throat, but it comes out as a series of clicks. "We should say some things out loud. Some of us—some of our people—might die. Whether it's the Regime's Patrol, or the wyrms . . . but they can't kill us all. We can overpower enough and try to leave at dawn."

Someone scoffs.

"Whatever happens," I go on, "it's better to die trying to reunite, than letting the Pocatelans decide when, how, and who of us goes."

It's silent for a long time. Cat turns back around. "Bueno," she says.

The puppy steps forward, and the deep voice who said I was full of *"mierda"* speaks. "Fine, I agree to help too."

"We'll need the names of your family members," Jovi says.

Jovi and I might be building our trust, but there's no way I'm leaving Pocatel without getting out as many Pock dwellers as I can. I won't say it now. But in a way, just like we all competed for food, and forgot who we were, now we are competing to find our families—even if it means sacrificing others. I get it, but it makes me sad.

I look past them toward the rows and rows of plants. La Cuna's fields are four times the size as those in Pocatel. "And what about Selah, Rose and Ezra? How long do I have?"

"Lately, they've been gone all night," Charlie says.

Each field could take an hour or more—if I'm fast. I might be able to finish within a day or—

"Or they could return any minute," Jovi responds.

Charlie's tail unrolls, and a wave of gray washes over his bright scales.

"So, what if we're caught?" I ask. "There might be more of us, but they're stronger."

I can't help glancing up at Oso. Her big shadow covers me like a blanket. She takes a thudding step back. "I know what you're thinking. But I was an entertainment drone."

Wolf steps out. It's the first I've heard him speak. "It's in their nature to go after the weak. We'll trap them as soon as they return. Charlie, Hopper, Oso," he says, "you know what to do. Just like we practiced."

Hopper glances toward the restricted tunnel leading outside, his whiskers trembling. Charlie nods.

"But how is it in their nature? They're not real scavengers," I reply. "They're drones."

"I didn't mean *that* nature," Wolf says. "I meant their nature as Pocatelans." The way Wolf says it is filled with venom. We all have been harmed by the Regime; some of us probably more than others.

"Oh." I glance up at the opening Selah left through. "But how will we know when they return from all the way down here?"

Jovi stands in front of me. He puffs out his chest. "Don't worry. I'll give a sign. You just go back to the tree when you see me and pretend to be thinking again."

"Very funny," I say. "What will the sign be?"

Jovi launches upward before answering. He flies higher and higher until he glides through the gap, a lot smoother than usual. Then he perches on the edge of the hole, moonlight reflecting off his body.

This is it. The sooner I finish, the sooner I get back to Gabi.

I speed to the closest row of plants. The Field Director would not be happy. Even Gabi could've done a better job. For now, though, they don't need to look straight. They just need to grow food.

Besides Charlie and me, the others spread around the room to keep watch.

In the first row, every meter, a new cluster of thick vines runs along the ground. Yellow horn-shaped flowers are wide open, with plenty of room for me.

Charlie rolls to the row next to me. He extends his leg and touches the pollen, then brushes his foot off exactly where a butterfly or bee or hummingbird would land.

I fly to the first flower in my row and sit on its petal. The petal collapses beneath me, and I plummet headfirst into the dirt. I push myself up and shake the soil off. I look toward the others and see Wolf watching as he circles the fields. He pretends not to see and nudges one of the puppies, who's staring. But I can see Cat, and she is shaking her head in annoyance.

I can see why the others can't help with this. Besides Charlie and me, the others are too big and clunky for this job. If Selah, Ezra, and Rose came back without warning, they'd all be scattered throughout a field so wide, and not fast enough to hide. We wouldn't be able to trap them. We'd all be caught for sure.

I try again, and this time I'm careful not to drop my weight onto the yellow petal. My body glides over the inside of the tube that's as smooth as soft skin. I push my beak along its center. My sensors feel grains of pollen coat my feet and underbelly. My wings hum, and even more pollen coats my body. I fly quickly to the next plant and brush the pollen off inside.

By the fourth plant, I pick up speed. When all the pollen drops are gone, I pick up more.

Charlie rolls alongside in the next row. His entire leg extends out with a *click, click, click* as he sprinkles the yellow grains on the wide golden flower; then, his leg retracts back until it's the same length as the other. At first I think it's my imagination, but after a little while . . . I hear humming.

Moments later, a whispered song . . .

Acitrón, de un
Fandango zango, zango
Sabaré que va pasando.

I look up and Charlie is tapping his paw between plants.

"*Con su triqui, triqui tran,*" I finish.

Someone giggles. Other voices join in from the outskirts of the field. This time, the song grows louder and faster, and as some click their metal paws on the ground or rocks, Charlie pats the flower gently to the beat. While it feels a bit strange to be singing at a time like this, it also feels perfect.

Acitrón, de un
Fandango zango, zango
Sabare que va pasando
Con su triqui, triqui tran.

Oso immediately loses the beat, and the laughter is so loud it startles me.

We start over. The pace quickens.

Con su triqui, triqui tran.

Now Charlie is up to nearly one plant for every two of mine. Between the singing and laughing, I lose track of time.

I scan the room and see that while the others are still walking the tunnels or perimeter of the field, as always, they are also watching us protectively. Charlie and I finish row by row by row, as he explains the big yellow flowered plants are something called squash and zucchini. The stalks with ears are corn. Without speaking, we skip past the rows of potatoes we both know don't need pollination.

By the time there are only a few of us left in the song, we've pollinated enough to feed our families far better than the scraps they get in Pocatel.

We continue working through the night, with still no sign of Selah or the others. I've already pollinated nearly all the fields. But Jovi was wrong. Maybe this *is* who I am in some way. As the song and the beat ring out over and over, I think maybe, in some small way, our group of Alebrijes has found a part of who our people were again. I'm no longer so scared.

I look up to see Jovi's dark form still sitting on the ledge, keeping lookout. Hopper waits by the tunnel opening, hopping nervously back and forth.

When we have one more row to finish, Charlie spins toward me in the opposite direction. He stops at the next plant. As we pass, I lift my wing and wave. Charlie waves a tiny foot back. I think of how from high above, no one would even see Charlie and me tucked inside this huge field. Such small creatures . . . but in one night, we've brought life back to La Cuna and the world that has probably not been seen in centuries.

I'm partway down the final row of white flowered vines when a shrill, "Wakey, wakey, eggs and bakey. Whoooooo needs to wake up? Davis needs to get up, that's whooooo!" booms throughout the Cradle. Beams of different-colored lights shoot high above from Jovi's eyes as he dives.

Charlie spins by me toward the tunnel, throwing up dirt like a tiny storm.

For a moment I'm frozen. This is it. *That was the signal.*

20

JOVI'S ALREADY LANDED, AND HE GLARES OVER AT ME. "Go!" he exclaims.

I shoot straight up into the pine. I'm flying too fast, and overshoot the lowest branches by a lot.

It's too late. Selah and the others are already in the air overhead.

I land on the top of the pine.

I stare down at the fields. It's done. Now, Wolf, Charlie, Hopper, and Oso just need to trap them, and we can leave.

Charlie spins back and forth down the opening in a whir.

Hopper bounces around, to draw attention. Oso sits to one side, ready to follow and block them in with her body.

Charlie and Hopper start moving even faster.

Selah, Rose, and Ezra don't seem to notice at all, though, and each fly to different areas of the room. Hopper bravely darts out farther from his usual assigned post. They must see him. He even tries bolting down the restricted tunnel, but still, Ezra, Selah, and Rose don't take the bait. Selah sits on a crumbling ladder, while Ezra and Rose sit together on the ledge. Their signals are weak, but even from here I can tell they're distracted, squabbling just like me and Gabi.

Movement in the room stills. The normal chatter and hum of talk is gone. Jovi sits motionless on the rung of a ladder. Not a single Alebrije speaks. We will have to lure them another way. Or . . . confront them.

I close my eyes.

A gloved Pocatelan woman stands in front of me. I sit on a stool outside my pock. Her soft robe brushes against my skin, and I reach out to touch it. She yanks it back.

"Hold still, little girl," she says, pulling my hair into a bundle. I want to tell her I'm a boy, but the Pocatelans have strange rules for who can look like who, and I don't think she cares. The sound of her scissors slicing through my dreads is the same as when we butcher a rabbit.

Gabi's eyes beg as she stares at me. "Por favor, Leandro. Ayudame. Diga ella . . ." She turns to the lady. "I will be good, señora."

"Yes, you are a good girl," she says, picking Gabi up and setting her on the stool.

I stand in front of Gabi to block her. "Señora, please. No tiene piojos." I say. "My sister has no bugs."

The lady calls out, "Director!"

I feel something grip hard under my armpit. A man pulls me away. He turns me around to face him. I see the reflection of my bald head in the giant horned beetle sitting on his chest. The grays in his hair streak downward like meteor trails, ending at his dark robe. "It is for your own good. In humility, you will lead a life of service. Fortunate are those with purpose. And for now, you have no purpose."

"Thank you, Imperator," the woman whispers and grips her scissors. "Shall we try this again?"

Tears fall down Gabi's cheeks as the woman gathers her hair and cuts.

Gabi's long black hair falls in a pile on the ground on top of mine. She stares up at me, her eyes begging me to help. But I'm too small to do a thing.

I OPEN MY eyes to make the scene go away. How had I not remembered that? Had I met the Imperator before? Or is the drone putting him in this memory?

But the disappointment I felt then feels the same as I feel right now. Once again, I'm not protecting Gabi. I feel sick. We have to come up with another plan.

A whoosh of wind blows over me, and Selah sits in front of me. I speak calmly, even though I'm not. "You're back." If I were a human, she'd know what I'd been doing. I'd be sweating, out of breath, and have dirt on my face.

"That's the good thing about being a delivery drone," she says. "We travel three times faster than other flight drones and can see a heat signal within fifty kilometers."

I know from the trip from Pocatel that I can see at least sixty kilometers away. What I still don't know, though, is what Selah and the others are looking for out there.

"They taught us that Old-World drones like me we were for one purpose, but I don't think so," she continues.

"I came here to sort through my thoughts," I blurt out, even though she didn't ask.

"I have been thinking too," she replies. "I should not be so hard on you. You and I . . . we have something most of the others don't." She leans in. "Speed, flight, and stealth."

She's right. I do have something the other drones don't. But she has no idea what I've just done with that. Something that even she, Ezra, and Rose couldn't do. I try not to look at the pollinated crops.

"You could be of help to us," she continues. "There are things in the Outlands we don't understand. Dangerous things."

I think of the necrotizing sand pits, Monger pirates, and mutant wyrms. What else could possibly be waiting out there?

I'm afraid to ask. "How can I help you?"

"Do you ever wonder about what is unspoken?"

I shake my head, confused. "I don't know what you mean."

"Do you wonder what is real? And what could be a lie? For example . . . the Mongers."

I don't know what the word *example* is. But an image of the fruit Monger with his eye patch flashes in front of me. He rings his bell. "*Best of the best!*" He lifts the apple above his head. "*Half of my wagon's scrap was spent to acquire this one specimen for market. Beautiful fruit normally reserved for Directors and their families, but today it could belong to one lucky citizen!*"

When he rings his bell next, Gabi holds a squished strawberry in her hand.

My feathers bristle. "Mongers are real."

"I am not saying they are not real. I am saying they might not be what we are told. And that there is more I think the Regime lies about."

I heard their meeting. Selah may be right. I've also seen things that don't make sense, like the lights in the Outlands, and what must've been a Monger and the figure of something else . . . something very large. "Why make it up, though?"

She scoots closer. "Why do you think I am here, Leandro?"

I feel like the question might be a trap. "You must have lied, cheated, or stole." I hesitate. "And you are Pocatelan. So it must've been bad."

She scoffs. "No. I am here because I challenged the Imperator. I threatened to tell others of my suspicions."

I flinch back. Who would be crazy enough to do that? "Why would you—"

"I was not the first to question," she says. "And I know it begins somewhere out here. The Mongers are not what they seem. And the Regime is hiding something." Selah drops her head. "I just don't know what it is yet. I cannot go back until I know what it is they are hiding. But when I do, I will expose them."

Celia died for less than this. And I'm so afraid to see the truth, I can't even see my own mother's face. Selah wants the truth so badly she will fight until she gets it.

"So, in the time you've been here, you haven't figured it out?"

She stares at me silently, and I think I asked the wrong question.

"Each time I get close . . ." She makes a sound that's something like a grunt. "We're not fast enough."

"We? You mean you, Rose, and Ezra?"

She looks away. "They do not exactly care to find out like I do. They help me patrol, but . . . they prefer to remain in the dark, if it means we stay hidden. I need to know."

I stare out at the fields. Then back at her. I need to move more quickly. "Why not just tell the others all this? And what about your family?"

Selah stares toward the wall. "I do not have a family."

There's no point pretending. She has to know how I got here. *Don't be a coward. Don't be a coward.*

I pull my wings tight against my body. "Dolores wants me to bring you back."

Selah bends down, getting a little too close. "Finally. We are being honest." She pauses. "Then you should know. *She* is the one who put me in this drone."

"But I don't believe she—"

"You were not there! My mother chose to put me in this drone instead of standing against them with me," she hisses.

"But now she . . ."

She glares at me, and I don't dare say another word. For a long time, we don't speak.

"Selah, if I don't go back, my little sister will die. All of our families will die."

She turns to me. This time she's calm. "I am sorry, Leandro. What the Regime does is unforgivable. But until I find the truth so I can expose them once and for all, I cannot—"

I'm thrown back by a breeze as Ezra swoops in between us. "Why is your signal so low, Selah?"

"We were talking," Selah says.

Ezra turns his back to me, blocking my view. "We heard something again," he continues. "It moves slowly, but it is getting ready to pass us for the eastern Outlands. It's not far."

Selah leans out past Ezra to look at me. "So, are you ready to help, Leandro?"

"What?" Ezra screeches.

"Uh . . . now?" I ask.

"He's small and fast," Selah says.

Ezra puts his beak to hers. "The fool who rushes may as well leap into the Trench."

It's not the time to laugh. I turn my head away.

"I am only suggesting he trail us for now," she argues. "By the next season, he may be able to reach what we seek faster than us."

I glance down at the fields. I can't do anymore there. I raise my signal as high as I can for Jovi. "How long would we be gone?"

"What does it matter, pollinator? As long as it takes to make sure whatever it is comes nowhere near here," Ezra answers abruptly.

Selah side-eyes me. "Right."

He might be trying to keep it away, but I realize maybe Selah hasn't told Ezra and Rose the whole story: that she's searching for more.

As I hover toward the center of the cavern, I see Jovi, Oso, Hopper, and the others staring up. Charlie has one eye pointed at me. Jovi's head is swiveled entirely backward and tilted toward us. I can't stop to tell them what's going on. I hope they heard me and trust I'm on their side.

Selah disappears through the open ceiling into the night sky. I follow.

Selah and Ezra's dark shapes against the starry sky could be real birds. With three predators leading the way, the night doesn't feel as terrifying as when I was alone. I dare that crow to come after me now. We fly for a few minutes before they land on the rock ridge, above the river valley. I touch down next to Selah. She looks down at me and nods, but Ezra scoffs.

Rose nudges me and motions to the east. "Do you hear it?" she whispers.

With no walls and nothing but empty sky, I hear the buzz of some sort of signal. It's nowhere close enough to connect. But it's definitely out there somewhere.

"What do you think it is?" I ask.

"I do not know," Selah says, aiming her beak toward it like she could strike. Her eyes narrow in suspicion.

If Selah needs answers, and those answers will get her back to Pocatel so we can save our families . . .

I may not get another chance to get her the proof she needs. I fly into the night as fast as I can toward the signal, knowing I am even too fast for them to catch. "I'll be right back," I call behind me.

Selah yells after me. "Stop!"

Ezra huffs. "Idiot."

I barely hear Selah call: "Turn off your signals."

"How are we supposed to communicate with him?" Rose asks faintly.

"We do not." Then, Selah's signal disappears along with the others.

I aim toward the signal in the distance. It grows stronger and stronger. But as the sun rises, the signal begins to fade.

"*You have one thousand and ninety-three days remaining in your sentence.*"

I can't go back to Selah empty-handed.

In minutes, I close in to the exact spot the signal was coming from. There is nothing. I spin in a circle, scanning the area. *Again?* Sunlight falls over the dirt and rocks below. I see no sign of any human at all, or anything else that could've given off the signal. This time I know it wasn't my imagination. The others heard it too.

When I spin back around, my feathers smooth, I can still see the plateau of La Cuna.

And that's when I see it. Below, a trail of repeating tracks. The crescent-shaped tracks stretch for over a mile to the north. I've seen tracks before: lizard, snake, even a coyote. But never any like this.

I follow the trail until it disappears near a creosote bush. I fly lower and too fast. Overconfident, I skip a wing on the ground, tumbling across one of the prints. I stand up inside the pit. It takes me three hops to cross a single footprint. No sand has blown inside, so it's fresh. I hop along the tracks until they end abruptly in a dark opening, disappearing inside. Maybe it's winters of the puppeteer's Outlands stories, but I swear I see a dark shape moving down in the hole.

It moves again. Whatever's down there doesn't growl or jump out at me.

I work up my courage. It's rare to find anything alive out here. I've gone most of my life barely seeing any animals, and I might not get so many chances.

· 240 ·

I move closer.

Carefully, I stay near the entrance hovering just above the ground, ready to fly out if it attacks.

The glint of two eyes peeks from the shadows. Slowly it moves forward.

I move back and wait.

The metal head of a tortoise drone emerges from the hole.

21

···☾···

I HURRY TO TURN ON MY SIGNAL AND SEND AN INVITA-
tion to connect, but they don't respond.

With a *click, click, click,* the tortoise pulls their head into its
body.

All they have to do is think the acceptance. Maybe tortoise
drones are slow to respond by design.

I try again. I wait.

Finally, the yellow triangle appears on my display, but it's set so low. This can't be what Rose heard. Their head moves out slowly until their glassy eyes look toward me.

"Hello," I say.

The tortoise's head pulls into their shell, followed by their feet. I land and hold still, afraid to startle them more than I have.

"I'm Leandro."

Slowly their feet emerge, followed by their head. The edges of their body are rusted. "Well, hello." They laugh softly. They stare at me a while longer. "I am . . . I am . . . I cannot remember the last time I spoke with someone." They tilt their head. "I do not think I have ever spoken to anyone but the ants and beetles. And they do not speak back."

How would a drone talk to an ant?

The tortoise pushes a rock from the hole's entrance, as if I'm just a small distraction. I watch as they finish their work without saying another word. When they're done, they turn in a circle and disappears back into the darkness of their hole.

I follow behind them, feeling unwelcome in some way. I wasn't invited inside, but I have to know what an Alebrije is doing out here, in the middle of the Outlands.

The deeper into the burrow I hop, the darker it gets, until my vision shifts and the turtle glows a warm red. They continue down a passageway that ends in a large dugout. Then they sit in the center and close their eyes like they're resting. I know Alebrijes don't sleep. Still, I wait.

"Umm," I say quietly after a minute. "Why . . . why are you out here?" I hop in a circle, but I see that nothing else in the burrow glows with heat. "Alone?"

They open their eyes, then lower their mouth to a bit of mud. A tiny tongue projects from their mouth, and they pull in a tiny drop of water. "It seemed like the best spot," they finally answer.

"You're welcome to stay. It's cool here."

They're right. It's much cooler here than in the heat outside.

"I should be getting back to La Cuna."

"Is that your home?" they ask.

"You must have heard of La Cuna . . . the Cradle?"

They push dirt toward a tiny nook. "No, just the burrow."

I can tell by their speech that they're Pocatelan. I think of the vaults in Dolores's lab and wonder if maybe Selah or Ezra would know them. Maybe they won't be so mad if I can bring back news of someone else.

"What's your name?" I ask.

"Tortoise."

"Just . . . Tortoise? I mean, what is your real name?"

"Tortoise the Skillful," they say, continuing to scrape dirt.

I hop around the pile, putting myself in Tortoise's line of site. "If you come with me, we hope to go back to our families. We'll have plenty of food and water."

"Oh, I cannot leave."

"Why not?"

Tortoise the Skillful motions to a small stack of round rocks in the hollowed niche they've been filling. "Who will watch over my eggs?"

I laugh.

But they don't.

Humans aren't meant to live alone. Even if our consciousness is in drone form. This is exactly what I worried about if I were placed in the glass vault for three winters. Losing my mind. Forgetting who I was. Forgetting Gabi. I fly to their eggs and hover over a perfect mound of round rocks, covered in dirt. "Tortoise the Skillful, how long have you lived here in your burrow by yourself?"

"Not long. I arrived and began building this burrow nearly one hundred and eighty winters ago."

I fall to the ground and dirt flies up.

"Oh, yes, of course. Have a seat. What kind of host am I?" Tortoise the Skillful goes on. "You are not a predator and of no threat to my children, so you are welcome to stay. I can dig you your own burrow if you'd like. You will not take much room now, will you?"

I think of what Dolores said and of all those in the earliest drone program who never returned. The four uppermost vaults from so long ago, still filled with water and containing the other half of Sparks. Even if Tortoise's human body died two hundred years ago, Dolores said that they could live out here hundreds of winters more until their drones failed.

"Oh, why create what already exists?" Tortoise laughs. "This way," they say, and crawl slowly toward a tunnel next to their rock eggs.

I follow Tortoise the Skillful down the passageway. Every so often another tunnel sprouts from another. "No, not this one. Too cold in the winter for a little bird." I follow Tortoise throughout their den, passing through a maze of chiseled passages. They stop at each. "This one is quite deep, and a nasty snake makes it his home when the weather shifts." Tortoise juts their neck toward me and whispers. "He tries to eat my eggs, and has even tried to bite me."

I wonder if it's true. If it is, that snake got a nice surprise of metal to his teeth.

We walk through more tunnels until we end up back at an entrance to Tortoise's burrow, with the eggs. "I know the answer of where to put you."

"It must've taken decades to build this," I speak softly, almost to myself. "I could never do this."

Tortoise stops. I bump into them. I wait as they rotate slowly in the dugout, making a perfect turn without hitting the sides.

When Tortoise is facing me, they speak. "Surely you can do things others cannot. Ants may be able to reach what you cannot, but you can reach places I cannot."

How could Tortoise know how I felt about the ant back in the hollow tree, unless they, too, felt that way at some time?

Tortoise pulls in their legs, lowering to my height. "And I, Tortoise the Skillful, am just as valuable in my own way. You and the ant are too small to cover and guard my eggs."

One hundred and eighty winters of digging a gigantic tunnel system, and battles with snakes, and who knows what else, have left Tortoise with tiny scratches all over their metal shell.

"It is what you accomplish in the form you've been given that makes you powerful." Tortoise stands and turns, walking toward their clutch of eggs. "Here we go," they say, and place their clawed foot inside a small dugout next to their imaginary children. Tortoise pulls out a bit more dirt. "This is perfect for you. I know you are a visitor, but you are always welcome here. And I sense something more of you. These may not be your children. But you have a watchful spirit. A protector of others. Yes, I can tell. You are Leandro the Mighty." Tortoise's head lowers to mine. Their metal nose nudges my tiny head. "Small, but capable of great things."

22

· · · ☾ · · ·

I EXIT THE BURROW AND WATCH AS THE GLINT OF
Tortoise the Skillful's eyes disappears inside.

I call out, "Goodbye!" but Tortoise has already lowered their
signal, back inside the burrow with their rock eggs.

I'm not sure what the right thing is to do. Should I try harder
to convince Tortoise to return with me? They've already been out
here nearly two hundred of winters.

The moon is high in the sky. I've already been gone too long.

I have no choice. I turn back toward La Cuna. But as I pick up speed, ahead along the Old-World road, I see that something approaches. It measures fifty-five kilometers away, in the direction of Pocatel. I fly closer until I make out a wagon. A lamp swings back and forth from its side. It slows to a stop, and the man steps off.

When I'm directly overhead, I see the Monger's wagon is empty.

As the man pulls the lantern down, I circle around to the back of the wagon and stop. With his eye patch, missing finger, and scarred face, I recognize him immediately. My feathers tremble uncontrollably.

I remember the look in this fruit Monger's eyes when he realized Gabi had taken the strawberry; when he knew he'd just rung his alarm bell on a couple of kids. But the bell didn't get me exiled. The Monger standing by and doing nothing for us did. Me losing Gabi is all his fault. My neck feathers ruffle, and I force them straight. I want to peck out the Monger's other eye, but what good would that do?

22% flashes in front of me. At least I can use him to get a drop of water and return. I hover closer, behind him. Then I wonder, how'd he get so far so fast?

The Monger pulls out a small tube and holds it up to his eye, scanning the horizon in a circle. "Not a soul out there," he says; I'm close enough to hear even his mutter. "This looks like a safe place to stay for the night."

I near the front of the wagon and the mule brays.

"What is it, Ingot?" The Monger turns in my direction.

I fly to the opposite side and its undercarriage, where he can't see me. Hidden in a shelf built between the wheel wells are enough stacked watercells and supplies to last the Monger for months. There's no way his fruit stall earned that many stags. This can't be right! Did he pirate this from another Monger here? Maybe more than one! All of this feels wrong.

Ingot brays again.

The Monger's so close, I can see the threads on his bootlaces blowing in the wind.

"Shhh," he shushes his mule.

I fly forward and peck on the nearest watercell. My metal beak easily indents the case. One drop, and I'm gone.

I push my beak through the bag. Instantly: 100%.

"Gotcha!" the Monger yells.

My wings clank against something hard. I look up to see a metal lid enclosing me inside a jar. I flutter harder, and my body echoes against glass, like a mallet pounding a drum.

"What do we have here?" He peers at me with his one good eye.

My mind explodes like a lightning storm in panic. I have no idea what a Monger might do with a real drone. I quickly play dead. He wraps his bony fingers around the jar, and I lie completely still, hoping I'm not worth the effort for scrap. He holds me up to the lamp and burps.

"Hmmm." He lifts me to his eye. "What are you doing all the way out here?" He wipes one hand down his stubbled, dirty chin.

His eye narrows suspiciously, like Tía Lula's when she inspected our hands for ember marks after bringing a single papa back from the fields. He grits his teeth and leans in even more. "I know of you."

My mind freezes. What does that mean? Maybe he'd heard of drones in school? I keep holding still. He twists the glass lid tight, then tips the jar back and forth as I clank from one side to the other. Then he sets me down on the ground. "I know just the person you need to meet." Still, I don't move, even though my insides want to explode.

The Monger sighs and reaches into his bag. I stare at him, wondering what he plans to do with me. He lifts out a golden-brown loaf as big as his head. I can't believe I'm seeing an entire loaf of potato bread in real life. He untethers the mule and ties him up next to me. Ingot drops his head and sniffs the jar. Steam clouds its surface.

Through the fog, I see the Monger pull an apple, too, out of his supply bag. It's identical to the one the lady paid her month's wages for. There's no way the Regime would give him all this. And if he stole from another Monger, they shouldn't have this kind of treasure either. Surely someone died for what I'm seeing here.

"Eat up, Ingot. Long night ahead of us. And just your luck— no more outposts for another fresh mule. You have the honor of getting me the rest of the way back."

Now I understand how he made it this far. He had help. But I saw no outposts on my way from Pocatel.

The mule crunches his teeth down on the shiny apple, half of it disappearing down his throat.

It's hard watching a mule eat something most Cascabeles could never hope to taste, even once in their lives. Who did the Monger take this from? Where did that person get it? Selah's questions are making me wonder too. What is going on?

The Monger dumps water into a bowl. He drinks first, then holds it out for Ingot, who shlorps the rest down.

I scan the sky. Nothing but the stars. Any hope that Selah might be searching for me fades.

The Monger pulls out a bedroll. He unties it and unrolls it onto the ground under the wagon. What is he doing? Would he at least not want the protection of the wagon from a desert wyrm? He lies down and makes a deep sigh. Then picks up my jar and holds it out, just like he had with the apple at the market. I rattle back and forth inside, but I don't move a feather. He shakes his head. "It must have been my imagination."

He drops the jar to the ground, and I roll around clinking on the glass. "I suppose we are a safe enough distance."

He reaches up and slips his fingers under the scarf holding his eye patch, pulling it off. I close my eyes, afraid of what I might see—but when I open them to look, the Monger has two perfectly good eyes. I start a little in the jar in surprise, but he doesn't notice. He rubs his eyelid, then rubs a line left on his face from the strap. With the scarf, he wipes over his scar. When he pulls the scarf away, the scar is gone. No blood—not even a scratch—lies beneath.

I think of what all the Pocatelans at the market thought of him ... what I thought of him.

He sets the jar on its side and pulls it close to him. Now his hairy, full belly is all I can see.

"Get a few hours of shut-eye, Ingot. We will be home to a warm bed in no time." He slips his hat over his face and mumbles under it. "I think I did a good job this time. Between my performance, and what I have to share with the Imperator ..." He makes a long slow grunt. "I might just be back inside Pocatel within the week."

In minutes, the Monger is snoring. I hop toward the lid and try pushing up. It doesn't budge. I could remain sealed inside and forgotten forever. It reminds me of the vault back in Dolores's lab, and now I understand why she was so upset that I might choose it for my exile. But inside this jail, without water, I will die within hours. It hasn't been long at all, and I'm already panicking.

I try pushing my beak through the lid, but it's too hard.

Then I see a rock lying not far away. If I slam against the jar hard enough maybe the glass will break.

I walk along the curve of the glass, and it rolls. I stop, then begin to run. I roll quicker toward the rock. I run faster until the jar clanks against the rock.

I freeze. But the Monger's snores continue, broken up by one loud fart.

There's only a tiny chip out of the glass. I need to hit it harder.

I walk back slowly along the jar, rolling the other way until I near the Monger's belly. This time, I get a running start and even flap my wings as hard as I can. I'm moving fast. I can't stop now. I close my eyes. I clatter against the rock. A long crack runs up its side.

The Monger jumps up, banging his head on the undercarriage. He rolls out from under the wagon and spins in a circle, stirring up dust. He's hunched over, legs bent, arms arched out like he's going to wrestle someone. His chest moves up and down with each breath.

His words are slurred. "Who is there?" he yells into the Outlands.

But the desert doesn't speak back. I hope the Monger thinks it's the crackle of a necrotizing sand pit he's accidentally set his camp on. He spins slower now, his breaths rattling in and out.

He narrows his eyes at me. I'm nowhere near where he left me. He moves closer. Dirt fills deep furrows on his cheeks.

He lunges out, wrapping his dirty fingers around the jar like he's catching a fly. "Old-World dysfunctional trash." He grabs his scarf and ties it around the jar, dropping me into his bag, and turning my world black.

23

THE MONGER'S SNORES ARE NOW LOUDER THAN Ingot's. I can't see anything beyond the scarf.

My signal is as high as it can be. I yell as loud as I can. "Selah! Ezra! ¡Quién sea! I need help!" But there is only silence, and snoring. I don't even know how far I followed the Monger.

I hover toward the lid of the jar and knock my head on it over and over, but the metal doesn't even dent. I fall to the bottom of the glass and wait, imagining the stars passing overhead throughout the night. Finally . . .

"You have one thousand and ninety-two days remaining in your sentence."

It's been half a day, and I haven't picked up any other signals. No one's coming.

The Monger's morning noises are worse than Tía Lula's. I'm glad I have the glass jar to hide the smells.

A shadow falls over the jar as the Monger's thick hand lifts me out of the bag. He unties the scarf and holds me up to the sun. He clears his throat. "You do not look so old."

I hope he might open the top, just to get a closer look. I could fly away so fast and leave him with a cut as a reminder that what he saw was real. Instead, he sets me on the seat of the wagon.

The Monger walks to the front, holding another apple in his palm. Ingot's white-muzzled mouth wraps around the red fruit, his huge teeth sinking in. "This will have to tide you over."

Tide him over? How long? My charge flashes: 44%.

As the wagon begins to roll ahead, I turn and stare back at the ghostly four-sided star pointing to the W. La Cuna and Gabi grow farther and farther away.

Sunlight beats on the jar. The temperature rises. I can't turn my back to this sun. But just like in the fields, it climbs to the top of the sky until the day is half over. Suddenly, I swear I hear a signal. It's faint, but my body hums with excitement.

I call out, "Help!" but no one responds. I know, though, somewhere close, there's something that can communicate with me.

The wagon slows to a halt. I see a hooked tube the same color as the sand jutting from the earth in front of us.

A *boom* vibrates the earth. I rattle inside the jar. My body vibrates from both fear and the jolt of the bang. The entire wagon shudders, and Ingot whinnies, then squeals, "Heeeee! Haaaaw!" The Monger stares ahead, a smile on his face as the sand in front of us begins to rise in a massive heap.

¡Dioses míos! A *desert wyrm!* I jump back and clank against the jar. The trembling of my feathers is deafening inside the jar.

Why isn't the Monger running?

Because it's not a wyrm, I realize; a metal dome rises from the ground. Sand pours off its surface until it is level with the earth. A rectangular door on the front of the dome building lowers to become a ramp. The opening is just wide enough for a wagon.

We enter through a fog of dust into the opening. The signal I heard earlier grows even louder. A yellow triangle pops up.

"Hello? I need help!" I try again. But still no answer.

The door closes behind us, sealing us inside. As the dust settles, the wedge-shaped room we are in becomes clearer. How is this possible? I've never seen a home like this, one that rises from the earth. And what here is sending a signal?

The Monger pulls off his gloves, and his four-fingered hand has five fingers, two stacked on top of each other inside the glove. He sets his eye patch and four-fingered glove on a shelf.

He unties Ingot and leads him into a small stable filled with dry grass. "Good work, sir." The Monger is latching the stable door tight when a small girl clutching a doll runs out from a room on the opposite side of the building.

"Daddy!"

She leaps, trusting the Monger to catch her.

I can't even believe what I'm seeing. How is a family living hidden underground the Outlands? None of this makes sense.

The Monger barely snags the girl under her armpits and spins her around. Long golden braids swing through the air.

"How is my niblet?" he asks.

The little girl laughs and tucks her head into his neck. "You smell bad, Daddy." She puts a finger in the air. "An unclean body leads to an unclean life."

"Spoken like a true Pocatelan," he says, laughing.

A woman holding a baby enters and runs to him. She leans in. "Evelyn is right. You stink."

They laugh and he kisses the woman's forehead, then the baby's.

The woman squeezes his hand. "How was your journey?"

"Too long." He smiles again and lifts me from the wagon seat, holding my jar out to the little girl.

The Monger's daughter—Evelyn—grabs the jar and holds it up, her bright blue eye close to the glass. "For me?" she squeals.

"Yep." He unscrews lid and opens the glass top.

For a moment I think of making a dash for it, but there's no way out now. He tips the jar, and I tumble wing over wing until I land in her soft hand. Evelyn gasps.

"When we get back to Pocatel, we can replace it with new toys," he says.

His wife leans into him and speaks quietly. "You should not get her hopes up, Nathaniel."

Nathaniel?

He lays his grimy hand on his wife's cheek. "We will go back. And it might be a lot sooner than you think."

His wife's eyes widen hopefully and fill with tears. "Did something happen?"

He holds a finger to his lips. "We cannot know if they are listening."

She nods, and her voice shakes. "I will get lunch started. What did you bring us?" She lights a second lantern on the wall, filling the room with light.

The Monger closes the door to the room holding Ingot, the wagon, and the way out behind us. He presses a button on the wall and the entire house jolts, lowering. "Less than before. There is . . . change happening in Pocatel." He moves closer to his wife and whispers, "But with what I discovered, I can protect us from what is coming."

They disappear from view as Evelyn carries me into a large round room. Three arched openings lie around the room's edge.

Besides wooden stools, a small table, and a desk in the corner, the dirt-floor room is empty. The signal I'd heard outside is much stronger now, but I don't see anything that could explain it. The Monger and his wife come back in, but then she disappears through one of three archways. The clank of pots follows moments after.

Evelyn squeezes me in her hand and carries me toward the desk. She pulls her doll from under her arm and lays it on a miniature bed. "Go to sleep." She lifts me up to her mouth, and for a second, I think she might bite me. Instead, she gives me a slobbery kiss on my head and sets me alongside her doll. She covers me using the doll's dress as a blanket, tucking me in. "You are a pretty bird. Time for a night-night song."

She begins singing a song of six little birds. Then five little birds. Then four. She flaps her "wings" and uses her fingers to make "feathers on her back." If I close my eyes and forget her blonde hair, freckles, and light skin, her voice could be Gabi's at five-winters-old.

She sings the song over and over and over again, each time starting over again with six little birds. After a while, I want to beg her to stop. But then I see the corners of the Monger's mouth turn up in a small smile, and he makes a happy sigh. He slouches in a chair watching Evelyn like it's the most beautiful performance he's ever heard. He's not the same man here he was a few hours ago.

"Daddy, look at the bird's skin," Evelyn says. "It's the same as—"

"No!" The Monger rushes toward her. "Evelyn, we have discussed this. Once we return to Pocatel, you cannot speak of such things. If you do, the Imperator will send us straight back. Do you understand?" he asks firmly. "A closed mouth cannot a wyrm-spore catch."

"Yes, sir," Evelyn answers. But now she stops singing, her lips pinched together tightly as she hums the tune instead.

The Monger's sighs grow a little longer, and less happy. He rubs his eyes over and over.

"Come eat," the woman's voice calls from the next room.

Evelyn covers my head with the dress and jumps up. Her footsteps fade in the direction of her mother. The Monger's footsteps follow.

As soon as they're out of the room, I push the doll's dusty dress off my head and fly from the bed. I circle around the room. The soft hum of the signal I'd heard is so close. I search for any sort of opening, but the home is completely sealed. They have to get air somehow. Then I remember the tube I saw outside when we approached. If I can find where it ends, maybe it will lead to a way out. I fly as quietly as I can along the ceiling. A breeze of fresh outside air flows over my wings near a small circular opening. A metal grid covers the opening. I try to cut it with my beak. Whatever the metal is, it's stronger than my beak.

From where I am, I can see the Monger with his family in the next room. They each sit on a chair at a table, the baby on the mother's lap. The woman uses the tool that Bridget from the orphanage tried to make us use. She scoops potato mash into their bowls.

The baby smacks its hands into the bowls, and food splatters off onto the floor.

I fly closer along the ceiling but find no other openings. Maybe there will be one in another room. I move toward the next room. I lower to the archway.

The glint of two huge eyes stares back. My body trembles. I fly as fast as I can to the opposite side of the room—as far away as I can get. The Monger and his family walked right by whatever's hidden in the dark. I move closer, but still the eyes don't move. The creature itself doesn't move. Halfway through the archway, I freeze.

The animal lies coiled, its body taking up the entire room. The head is attached to a body big enough to fit the Monger's entire family in its gut. It can be only one thing. Now that I've seen it, all I can do is stare and hope it won't eat me. I scan the room for the hole it must have burrowed in through, but see nothing. The Monger and his family will surely be its meal the moment they walk out of their kitchen.

But this wyrm doesn't move. It's either fast asleep, waiting to strike, or dead. But . . . there's no smell of death.

I move closer, but what I see doesn't register either. Just like the wyrm that killed Celia, this wyrm is a wingless dragon. But the smooth scales I expected—what it uses to sneak up on its prey, and sink in saw-toothed teeth—are not smooth. Instead, uneven panels of metal cover the body of the entire creature. Its head is covered in tiny scales of different colors, just like Charlie's body when it shifts.

I fly closer. Words like Hopper X-2050 and B-20 *Scavenger* and *The Grizz*-PNW are carved into pieced-together edges. The spikes lining its head are the same as Oso's claws.

The entire wyrm, a sad mix of different drones.

I fly right up to it, and the signal from earlier is even stronger. Maybe it's shy. Just like I had with Tortoise, I whisper, "Hello."

But it doesn't move at all. It doesn't speak back like Tortoise. There's just a blank signal; a drone without a Spark. Still, I push my signal up all the way up and link to the wyrm drone. *Com Connect—Remote Control* flashes.

Suddenly, I see two views: my own and the wyrm's.

I remain perfectly still. Yes, I'm sure. I'm seeing through the eyes of both myself and . . . the wyrm drone?

Impossible.

I think about blinking. A metallic screech breaks the silence. I freeze.

A chair scrapes across the floor in the next room. "Did you hear something?" the Monger asks. "Were you sure to shut it down?"

"I . . . I do not know," his wife whispers. "I ran its weekly check, and its controls were functioning as always. I even cleaned the reaper," she mumbles. "I am not sure why we still have to check it all the way out here."

The Monger's bootsteps approach.

I disconnect from the wyrm and fly quickly back to the doll bed. I've barely pulled the doll's dress over my body when the Monger bursts through the doorway, still holding a fork, mouth full. He passes by and pokes his head in the room where the wyrm drone lies. He looks from side to side.

I lie in shock. Did I actually do that? Make the wyrm move? The signal with this drone was . . . different than what I have with Alebrijes. How did I, a Cascabel kid who digs in soil and dung to survive, make an Old-World technology linking two machines work? A season ago, I would not have dreamt any of this possible.

After one long exhale, he whispers. "Too much time out here. Even for you, old fella." He returns to the kitchen.

I poke my head out from under the doll's dress and return to the wyrm. I fly along its body: a collection of Old-World drones, with no Spark. It's not worth trying again.

The chair scrapes again in the next room. "I need to contact the Imperator tonight," the Monger says.

The woman clears her throat. "Finish your meal, Evelyn." She lowers her voice. "Truly, Nathaniel. The Imperator? Do you trust—"

"I will explain after. But I promise, it is good news."

I barely have enough time to crash back onto the doll's bed.

The Monger walks in slowly with a glass of water and stands in front of the empty desk in the corner. He runs his hand through his grimy hair and lets out a deep breath before sitting. He places one hand on the desk in front of him and opens a drawer, pulling out a black box. He unclips a latch on the box, and a small table drops. He dips his finger into his water glass and places it over a small opening. A drop falls inside. A tiny light on the box glows orange.

Fission.

Evelyn's laughs, followed by the baby's giggles, come from the next room.

The Monger presses on the orange light. There's a moment of silence and then a long beep. He taps his foot on the floor as he waits for something. Only the noises of his taps, a low buzz from the box, and the sound of his daughter playing in the next room continue.

Suddenly, a man's voice comes through the box like magic: "This is Imperator Wallace. Speak."

24

· · · ◖ · · ·

THE IMPERATOR'S FLAT VOICE COMES THROUGH AS clear as if he was in the room with us. Both the Monger and I jump. My entire body heats. "No one has used these lines for quite some time," the Imperator says. "Are you wasting my time, Nathaniel Barrett? You know the cost of false communication."

"No, Imperator Wallace," the Monger says. "That is to say, I am not wasting your time. And yes, I know the cost of a false report." He tilts his head to each side, cracking his neck. What the Monger cannot see is his wife behind him, snooping by the door.

"How are the accommodations for your family out there? I hear the Outlands are lovely this time of year."

The Monger closes his eyes, brushing his boot on the dirt floor, his nostrils flaring as he breathes in slowly.

The Imperator's voice gets louder. "Let us get to the point, shall we?"

"I would not have initiated contact if I were not sure, Imperator." The Monger swallows deeply. "As I was leaving Pocatel, just nearing the old highway, my radio caught a signal."

"A signal." A long sigh comes from the box. "RF signals can be anomalies."

I'm finding it hard to keep still. I'd seen the Monger stop below on the road on his way out of Pocatel just days ago. Now I know why. If the Monger only knew *my* signal was his mistake.

The Monger sits taller, even though there's no one in the room to impress. "I knew it was unusual, so I created a wyrmstorm to distract attention in case it was . . . more than an anomaly, sir."

The winters of terror I've felt over wyrms and plague storms have all disappeared in less than a day. I'm questioning all that I thought to be true. The fear I had of the Regime now feels like a different level of awfulness.

"Thank you for this report." He clears his throat. "I must leave now—"

"Imperator Wallace, there's more," the Monger speaks quickly. "When I neared my outpost . . ." The Monger taps his fingers harder on the desk. "I picked up another signal. The same. Too strong, too . . . intelligent to be an anomaly."

Even I can hear the mocking in the Imperator's voice. "I understand how badly you must want to return to Pocatel, but you occupy the farthest outpost for a reason, Nathaniel. Do I need to remind you what that is?"

The Monger fumbles with his shirt pocket and pulls out a device the size of his finger. He holds it in his quivering hand and places a drop of water to turn it on. "I know Preservation above all is our mission. The second time, sir, I was ready."

A sound like light rain on a pock fills the room. Beneath the whooshing noise, tiny clicks grow stronger and faster. A signal—an Alebrije's signal. Mine. Selah, Ezra, and Rose were right to be protective.

"Play it again," the Imperator commands.

The recording finishes once more. Besides the murmurs and giggles of the Monger's wife and daughter in the next room, all is silent.

"I questioned what it may be," the Monger says. "I even found a spent Old-World drone. A hummingbird."

"Our forefathers never used a . . ." The Imperator pauses. "You are sure? Where is it? This hummingbird."

The Monger turns to the doll bed. "I have it right here."

I grow warm, and I hurry to smooth my feathers. He picks me up and rolls me over. "Here, it says something." He lifts my wing and squints. "'The smallest flap of wings can change the course of history.'"

Once again, the room grows quiet.

The Monger leans in. "Hello? Sir?"

The Imperator whispers: "Dolores." I hear the familiar *ping* from him slamming his pinky ring on the table.

I grow even hotter, and I tremble. He knows. And it's my fault.

"Sir, should my family and I return now?" the Monger asks, his own voice trembling. "I ... I hoped this might be enough to end my service. For my wife and daughters."

From the box comes a pounding noise.

The Monger puts his head on the desk, his hands woven through his hair. "Please, please," he whispers, almost to himself. "Evelyn has never been to school."

Finally the noise from the other end stops, and the Imperator's voice comes through clearly. "Nathaniel Barrett, your service is over."

The Monger lifts his head and lets out a cry of joy. "Thank you, sir! I will never tarnish the bronze of Pocatel again! I am appreciative of the chance you've given—"

"For what I must do, I am terribly sorry," the Imperator interrupts. "But you were never going to return. Preservation above all. You've served well. I thank you for your watch."

The buzz from the black box goes silent.

Nathaniel sits back. He places me on the desk. His forehead wrinkles. "Sir?" He presses the orange light frantically over and over. He places another drop of water on the plate. "Sir?"

Within seconds, a flood of new signals flood my sensors. But none are like anything I've sensed with the Alebrijes so far, or the wyrm drone.

The whoosh of fresh air into the room stops. Nathaniel's smile falls completely. The dirt on his face grows darker as his skin pales. He calls out in a whisper, "Lilith." Then, in a panicked yell: "Lilith!"

The building jolts, and I bounce on the desk as the room begin to lower.

The metal grid falls from the tube inside the building with a clank. The entire home shudders.

Sand trickles through the hole, slowly at first, then pouring in. From the next room, Evelyn screams and the baby starts to cry.

No.

Nathaniel stands and runs toward his family.

I panic, flying toward the vent. I push through the sand, but it's pouring down with such force now, I hurl over and over toward the floor.

From the stables, Ingot brays.

"Lilith! Evelyn!" Nathaniel screams. His wife, Lilith, stands in the archway, eyes wide. At first she doesn't move. Then, the desk topples over as the sand shoves it against the wall.

Lilith runs back, Evelyn hoisted under one arm and the crying baby cradled in the other. Nathaniel dashes toward the wagon room. He presses the same button he used to lower the home, but nothing happens. He pushes on the door, but it's weighted shut with sand.

I hover as high as I can near the ceiling. Nathaniel scans the room desperately. He sees me. His eyes are locked on me in disbelief.

I try to connect with the other signals. Maybe I can stop this. But these signals are nothing like any I've sensed. It's too late.

Nathaniel climbs the mountain of sand. He grasps for a hold, but his legs and arms sink further. He slides down to Lilith. He takes Evelyn from Lilith, and they both hoist their children high above their heads. The sand rises past their waists, and the air fills with the fog of dirt. Kicks echo from inside the stable, followed by squealing brays. Then the kicks stop. Then the brays.

The room suddenly grows as silent as the Pox just after the one-second echo of a wyrm scream.

"I am sorry," Nathaniel says softly, as the sand rises to Lilith's chest. "My pride did this—"

"Stop." Lilith coughs and wipes sand from the baby's nose. "You did not do this. He did." She kisses her baby's head and whimpers. I feel her pain. Soon my signal will drown in the sand just as her baby's breath. Without water, I will die with Nathaniel and his family, just a little later. If only I were the wyrm drone. I could burrow us out . . .

I zip past their heads and Lilith gasps. I clutch to a ceiling beam as close as I can to the room where the wyrm lies. Its signal is a whisper. I focus to connect.

At first, it's like trying to grab a handful of water. The harder I try, the more it slips away. But finally: *Com Connect—Remote Control.*

I see only darkness through the wyrm's view. I raise his monster head, and it's no more difficult than it is to lift my tiny hummingbird head. As I lift it above the sand, the darkness disappears. I lower its head again and focus to thrash as hard as I can.

At first, with my own eyes, I can see the sand near the room stirring as I sway the wyrm's body in each direction. The sand shifts back and forth into the main room. Each time I slither in one direction, then the other, I rise higher and higher. I burst through the surface of the sand and suddenly, I have two views again. I see Nathaniel's family slogging up a hill of dirt in front of me; behind them, a metal hummingbird hovers near the gushing vent.

Evelyn and Lilith scream.

Through my hummingbird eyes, I see Nathaniel staring at the wyrm, then at me. I command the wyrm to lunge upward over and over into the ceiling. Unlike my tiny, useless head hitting the lid of the glass jar, my wyrm head bashes the ceiling like a metalsmith's hammer. My tail thrashes, leaving dents in the walls.

Just like the pock's frame, if I can break one beam, the home will collapse—and, with luck, leave an opening. I wedge the wyrm's body between one of the archways and the ceiling and push as hard as I can. The walls squeal like a dying animal.

The sand rises above Lilith's mouth. She spits out dirt and coughs.

"Daddy, Daddy, Daddy," Evelyn calls.

The creaking whines louder. *Buuuuhhhhmmm!* The dome breaks at one joint. The wyrm bursts through. I fly after as fast as I can, sand pouring over me. I burst upward into the open sky. Fresh air flows over my plates, washing away the dust. I soar higher, buzzing my wings, until all the grains fall from between my feathers. I stare around me. The sun is directly overhead, and the desert surrounding us is completely silent.

I stare down. The only sign below of the chaos—or that there was ever anything below—is a few pieces of metal scrap, and half the wyrm's upper body jutting up out of the sand. But no sight of Nathaniel, Lilith, Evelyn, or the baby. Aside from the buzzing of my wings and the desert breeze, I'm alone. I can't let this be their end. I send the wyrm back, diving under the sand. My wyrm view goes dark again.

Just like I know instantly how high I am above ground in the hummingbird, the wyrm has a way of telling exactly how far I need to dive underground. Like a giant spade, I use it to thrash then lift sand away from the spot where the house was. Each time the wyrm's head appears, the hole widens.

Finally its head finds the splintered dome of the house. I see the hole I escaped from and bite the panels. They fall inside the wyrm, into his body. Part of me feels horror, knowing this is where Celia ended up after she was crushed.

Careful to place the wyrm's spiked side up, I brush sand with the tail, hoping to see anything.

I'm too late. I want to scream. I fly lower, knowing if I were in my human body, I could help dig.

I'm just about to give up when a tiny hand erupts from the sand. I plunge the tail next to the hand, and she grasps on tight as I pull her out. Dirty blonde curls emerge from the sand. Evelyn claws her way out of the opening, coughing.

Carefully, I push the tail down farther. I sense something else grab hold, and as I emerge, arms thrust the baby upward. The baby makes no noise. Evelyn grabs the baby, and, finally, it wails.

I feel something let loose inside of me.

Evelyn lays the now screaming baby away from the hole and runs back. Lilith's face gasps for air as she reaches an arm upward. Evelyn pulls on her mother's arm. She reaches out her other arm and claws at the sand, scrambling free as what remains of the opening disappears.

"Nathaniel!" she screams out.

I pierce the wyrm's tail into the sand from where Lilith just emerged. I make the wyrm slither back and forth until I feel the tail hit something solid. Once again, I surface. This time, I see a hairy hand grabbing onto a metal spike on the wyrm's tail.

Nathaniel gags up a mouthful of wet sand and potato mash.

I send the wyrm back down near the stall over and over. But there is no sign of Ingot. After a while, I give up.

Nathaniel and his family huddle together crying, their belongings scattered about. Lilith runs her hands over her children, checking their eyes and noses. Water sprays from damaged watercells the thrashing wyrm unearthed. I fly through the spray in my hummingbird body, refilling my charge.

Nathaniel sees me and stands, taking a step toward me. I zip back away. But this time, he doesn't try to catch me. He just stares. He glances at the wyrm, now motionless, then back at me.

I should fly away, but I'm stunned too.

Nathaniel turns to what's left of their home and possessions. He walks slowly back and bends down. He stands back up, holding Evelyn's doll—one leg missing—and returns it to her. He glances to the southwest where Pocatel lies, then turns to his family, struggling to speak between coughs. "We need to leave. Now. The closest post is a half day away." He shakes his head. "Though we know not who to trust."

He unclips his robe and lays it on the ground. They begin gathering food and water and place it in a pile on top. I hover above two half-buried watercells. I buzz twice to Nathaniel's face, then back, until he sees them.

He's part of the reason I'm out here. This Monger rang the bell on Gabi. How could I go from hating him to caring if he lives or dies? I glance at Evelyn.

He might've tried to kidnap me and keep me as a pet, but it was my signal that drew his attention. And now it's my fault the Imperator knows the Alebrijes are out there.

I have to warn them. I turn to leave.

"Hey!"

I spin back and Nathaniel is staring directly at me. Lilith follows his gaze and sees me. Nathaniel Barrett nods. We watch one another for a moment, before he takes Lilith's hand. Lilith stares at me wide-eyed as he pulls her along. He hoists their supplies over his shoulder, and they begin walking to the west. All that's left of the Monger's outpost is scattered rubble and one wyrm drone. Even though Nathaniel and his family didn't disappear beneath the sand, like the Imperator hoped, I know they'll likely die out here.

But if I don't get back to La Cuna and warn the others what the Imperator knows, so many more will die soon. There's nothing more I can do for Nathaniel.

How can I prove to the Alebrijes everything I've found?

SUN REFLECTS OFF the wyrm as it slithers below me, knocking aside every dead tree and large boulder in its path. I can see how I mistook it for a real monster. But once everyone sees it in the light of day, they'll understand. How much we've been tricked. How the stories we are told have the power to deceive and damage.

"*You have one thousand and ninety-one days remaining in your sentence.*"

I spent too much time trapped inside Nathaniel's bag. The cracked road guides me back to the far edge of the Outlands and La Cuna. Nathaniel said they lived in the farthest outpost, but I wonder how many other Mongers are hidden beneath the sands of the Outlands. Or are most near the wyrmfield of Pocatel, where they control the drones that do the most damage? Close enough to see Pocatel, but trapped by the Imperator. Whatever their crime, this is worse. They are willing to deceive and frighten others—to kill—just to buy their way back. But with a few words, the Imperator will bury any proof they ever existed. All to hide the Regime's deception.

The screech of the wyrm's metal panels scraping over rocks pierces the air, just like the false puppeteer at market. Some lies do hold a bit of truth.

When I'm about halfway back to La Cuna, I spot a single heat signal ahead. My insides soar as the source comes into view. Ingot is galloping in the same direction. As the wyrm nears the mule, I see him kick his hind legs out at me and veer to the west.

The wyrm and I travel with the rising sun on our back.

My charge flashes 38%. That doesn't make sense. I should have twice that. Even as I glance down at the wyrm, it drops to 37%. I realize suddenly that if I don't leave it behind, I might not make it back to La Cuna at all.

I fly toward an outcropping of rocks. I spot a mound of sand next to the rocks and send the wyrm inside. As his tail disappears beneath, the yellow triangle and the ticking signal fades. A mound of dirt like a huge dung pile is left behind where the wyrm burrowed in. I take one last look at the rock formation. I note my location, so I know where to find him.

With the wyrm safely hidden, I speed south again toward La Cuna. Without the wyrm, they will have only my story of what happened. But maybe what I tell them will shock Selah, Ezrah, and Rose into helping us.

In the distance, La Cuna's plateau comes into view. One by one, yellow triangles pop into my screen, and the *tick, tick, tick* quickens as Alebrijes' signals connect with mine.

Something's off. Conversations should be filling my mind. But all I can hear is shouting.

25

I CAN'T FLY ANY FASTER, BUT I'M TOO AFRAID TO call out.

When I near the opening of the plateau, the smell of fresh soil is too strong.

Below, the rows of fields are no longer rows. I stop where I am. Selah and Ezra dive-bomb over and over, gripping the plants with their talons and pulling them from the earth. Rose hovers in place above, her talons filthy, staring down.

My entire body shakes. Nearly every plant has been uprooted. Leaves lie scattered like shreds of cloth across the ground. Rows of our pollinated vines lay in ruins. Only the trees along the edge still stand tall.

Selah snatches a root that won't come free.

Charlie spins around her in circles, jumping out at her, swiping with his paw. "No!"

Selah bats him down like he's a gnat.

Oso stomps toward Ezra each time Ezra dive-bombs a plant, swiping at him with her paw. But by the time Oso's clawed foot reaches the eagle, he's already flown off again. Within seconds, Ezra snatches another plant.

Oso falls to the ground. "Please!" she calls.

The puppies and Shelter Mutt yap as Wolf snarls, his fangs bared, trying to reach Ezra. Hopper hops in a blur around the fields in a nervous loop.

I scream louder than I ever have. "Stop!"

They all do, and stare up at me as I dive downward toward the fields.

"I told you this was wrong." Rose flies past me and lands high above on the rim of La Cuna.

"¡Mira! You didn't have to do this!" Jovi yells. "He's back!"

I land directly in front of Selah. My body trembling in anger.

"We should never have continued to grow them. Now we have nothing to worry about." Ezra flies after Rose.

Selah and I lock eyes. She holds her head high like she's challenging me. After a minute, she breaks our gaze and turns toward the group. "It is for the good of all of us here."

There is no arguing. As long as we ache for our families, and they don't, we will never agree.

Before I can respond or tell her what's happened, Selah's launched herself in the air and flown away in the same direction as Ezra and Rose. I need to tell her what I've discovered, but I don't think I can speak.

Jovi, Oso, Hopper, Charlie, and I sit at the edge of the fields, motionless. Someone's signal rises, then lowers, then rises again. I know whoever it is—whoever is missing—is crying. I don't see Cat anywhere. Wolf disappears down a tunnel. Oso sighs, over and over.

I collapse to the ground. All their work—all our hope for a future away from Pocatel—has been torn out by the roots. In time, we could rebuild. But now . . . the Imperator knows what Dolores has done. We have to return immediately to save who we can, even if only some of us make it . . . and even if it means we are bringing our people back to ruin.

Jovi tosses forward a plant from his talon. "Where were you?"

My screen flashes 32%. I dip my beak to the muddy sludge and recharge. How am I going to explain it all? I stare up at the pine for a long time.

Charlie rolls over to me and pats my head. "Don't worry, we don't blame you."

Oso raises her head and speaks quietly: "Shut up, Charlie."

"What do we do now?" Hopper asks. "If we start over, they'll just destroy it again."

Oso takes a booming step toward Hopper. "We're not giving up."

"Stop." I fly to the center of the room, where I know everyone—including Ezra, Rose, and Selah—can hear. "You all need to listen. The stories like La Cuna, the ones that we thought were too good to be true? They might've turned out to be real. But Selah was right to be suspicious of the Regime." I pause. "Other things that we thought were real, like the wyrms, the Mongers, and probably even necrotizing sand . . . ?" I pause again. "*They* are not real. They are all lies. The wyrms—they are just drones. Like us."

Oso approaches me slowly. "Are you okay?"

Charlie spins over to me and reaches out his front foot toward my head. I swipe it away with my beak.

I glance up to see Selah, Rose, and Ezra's shadows perched against the night sky in the opening above. "They know about us, Selah. Imperator Wallace knows what your mother did. The Imperator plans—"

"Rose!" Selah screams out.

One of their dark forms plummets off the edge. Rose moves straight toward us. I'm too afraid to move. Is she attacking? She's moving too quickly. Why doesn't she slow herself?

Then, I realize she's not attacking. She has no signal at all. She's falling.

Ezra dives after her, but there's no way he'll be able to reach her in time. We jump to one side just before Rose slams into the ground with a clatter. Soil flies up around her in a cloud. Her wing has snapped off, and her leg is turned in the wrong direction. No one speaks; the only sound, I realize, is the rush of the river. We gather around, unsure of what to do. Ezra lands next to her. He shifts from one foot to another. He nudges her softly with his beak. "Rose?"

Rose doesn't respond, her eyes dead. Her signal gone.

Selah lands too and steps softly next to Ezra and Rose. "He did it," she whispers.

I'm unsure who she's talking to, and who she's talking about. But I saw it. Rose wasn't pushed; she fell.

Ezra looks at us, his eyes and slumped body defeated. He turns to Selah. "We were never going to be safe here." Then I understand.

The Imperator.

Ezra scoops Rose's body and lays it gently at the base of the great tree.

He flies away into the night sky.

26

· · · ☾ · · ·

OSO DIGS A GRAVE WITH HER CLAWED FOOT. WOLF
nudges Rose's body to the edge of the hole, and Selah lifts her,
lowering her down. We work together to push the dirt inside
and gather around.

Charlie and Hopper leave and return, each time with a
smaller rock that they stack on top of the last at the head of the
grave.

Cat emerges from where she was hiding. She sits atop Rose's grave. Her eyes are closed. In the softest of purrs, she begins.

"*Tccch, tccch, tccch* . . ."

She arcs her clawed paw, carving a C into the dirt in front of her grave. And then she walks away, disappearing again.

The rest of us form a circle around the grave.

"Esperen," Wolf says. He walks behind us where Selah sits alone. He nudges her forward until she joins our circle.

The voices of all speak together: "Corazones puros y espíritus s son quienes heredarán la tierra."

Selah lies on the ground, wings tucked. She looks so small. She whimpers softly.

It's so quiet, but somewhere in the distance, someone is humming the song of the Cascabeles.

JOVI, SELAH, AND I fly to the center of the fields for privacy, and to hopefully mend some damage.

"If we want to save our families"—I turn to Selah—"and save ourselves, we have to go back. We need to lead our people out of Pocatel and back here."

"I know that now," Selah says. "I will return with you. To ensure my mother helps you, and that all of your people leave."

"She said the deal was only for me—"

I know she's not angry with me, but Selah rounds on me and speaks sternly. "I do not care what she told you. You will *all* leave with your families. All Cascabeles."

I didn't think anything could make me feel better. But knowing Selah is returning with us makes me feel braver. "And then what?" I ask. "Will you return to La Cuna with us?"

"I . . . I thought I belonged here. And I do—in this body." She pauses. "But I do not know who I will be once I return to Pocatel, once I am back in my old body. I am different here than I was there."

I can't understand. I am Leandro both here and in my hummingbird drone body. I am who I am in my mind.

"When this is over, you should return here with us, Selah," Jovi says.

"Yeah," I say. "Maybe we can be something new here. We don't have to be entirely Pocatelan or Cascabel. Together, in La Cuna, we are Alebrijes."

The words feel a little funny as I say them. But Selah stares toward Rose's grave for a long time. Then she turns back to me and nods.

And now I am wondering, does it matter what body I choose to live in, to still be Leandro? I did so much good in the tiny drone. I could do so much more.

Selah moves to face both of us. "But here is what you do not know. If we do not leave now and try to stop the Imperator, he will keep killing everyone here until I return."

"You?" Jovi asks. "How do you know that he's looking for you?"

Selah grips a vine, attempting to shove it back under the soil. "He was willing to store me away in a jar when I dared question why the Directors alone made decisions for all Pocatelans."

"You were brave to ask—"

"No. I only asked because I deserved to know what was expected of me, and why." Selah shakes her head when the root comes loose from the soil. "Most who even begin to question are exiled before the questions can grow. My mother just placed me in a drone instead of a jar. Either way—even *she* got rid of me."

She hands the wilting plant to Jovi.

He places it in the soil and tries to pack it down.

I want to tell her that is not how Dolores viewed what she was doing. She thought she was giving all of us a small piece of freedom.

"You were to be the next Physician," I say, thinking of the meeting and what I overheard. A small, secret group of families, passing their duties to those next in line.

"No." Selah takes a step back. "I was to be the Imperator."

Jovi and I turn to one another in confusion. I feel my body temperature rise.

"I know what the Imperator will do, and why he is so dangerous, because . . . he is my father."

Jovi and I both freeze. Neither of us speak. So many of our people, exiled because of him. Her own father . . . why didn't Dolores tell us? Or Selah?

Selah's voice shakes. "We cannot choose our lineage. I cannot make right the things my father and the Regime have done to your people . . . to my own people. But I can try to make right the harm I have done." Selah drops her head, and her voice grows firmer. "And I will stop my father from hurting any more of us and make him pay for what he did to Rose."

"How can you stop him?" I ask. "The Regime is still in control of the Pocatelans—they have the Patrol and the Mongers! Selah, you should have told us!"

She bows her head even lower. "I know. I am sorry. I wanted to keep what we built here for myself. It was selfish."

Jovi and I exchange a look. People like us aren't used to receiving apologies, especially from a Pocatelan. But even if Cascabeles aren't ones to hold grudges, I can't help still being angry with her.

She lifts her eyes slowly. "The Imperator may have all the power now, but not for long. Our people are engrained with certain principles. I do not think they will tolerate deceit, even from Directors. There will be chaos," she replies. I want to believe her. "And I will make sure the Mongers know how they've been used—how they, too, can easily be betrayed."

"And the Patrol?" Jovi asks.

This time she does not sound so confident. "Not all will defend the Regime. But there are fewer Patrol than citizens, and the people will insist my father and the other Directors pay for centuries of deceit." I'm not so sure. But just as I start to protest, Selah launches swiftly into the sky. "With or without Ezra, we must leave soon. My father didn't kill Rose as a warning. He did it to call me back. Be ready!" And her voice fades as she passes out of La Cuna into the night.

I watch her leave and try to process what I've heard. I might not entirely understand Selah, but I see none of the man she says is her father within her. I think of the lessons she must have learned from him. The lessons I learned from my own mother. Selah made horrible mistakes. She should have shared what she knew with us. But I know—just like Selah is discovering—that we get to choose who we become in the end.

I watch Charlie replant the same vine that's toppled over three times a few rows away. He carefully arranges its roots this time, then packs soil around its base. Jovi and I don't say the obvious. Charlie's vines might not regrow, but even more likely: we won't survive to see them, even if they do.

Jovi lowers his signal so the others can't hear us. "Now the stories Cascabeles told of our ancestors seem too magical to be real. Do you think our own people lied to us too? About San Joaquin, and what it was?"

I understand why Jovi would doubt, with all we've just found out. We spent so many winters trapped, believing stories of monsters, mongers, and other horrors that were all lies. Lies to frighten and control.

"I think that legends can be magical and give us hope, but the stories we are told can also have the power to kill that hope just as easily," I respond. "The stories of the Cascabeles, even those that were difficult to hear, will be the stories I believe in from now on."

"Maybe you're right." He shakes his head, and swipes soil over the base of a plant with his wing. "The Pocatelan Regime had us convinced a forty-foot wingless dragon was real."

"We weren't the only ones who believed it. Pocatelans believed it too. But soon all that will change. Selah will tell her people the truth. All the Cascabeles will leave Pocatel. You'll have your grandmother back. I'll have Gabi. And we'll decide what's real and what's not from now on." I help separate the roots of two tangled plants so he can replant this one too. "Hey, Jovi?"

"Yeah?"

I scrape my foot nervously in the soil. "If something goes wrong . . . mi family, mi hermana, Gabi?"

He stops. I know this is too much to ask of him. Keeping ourselves alive is hard enough. "So, only one sister after all?" he smiles.

"Well, the others I told you about too? If you can?"

"Only if you agree to watch out for my abuela," he says. "If something goes wrong."

I nod.

"I have to warn you, my abuela's bossy," he continues.

I think instantly of Gabi and snicker. If I die, he's going to regret agreeing to that deal.

Oso, Hopper, and Charlie approach. Wolf and the others are behind them.

"We aren't sure how to help," Hopper says.

"Yeah, it took me two winters just to walk this far," Oso says.

"Getting everything ready for us for when we return with our families is just as important," I say.

"It'll be ready," Wolf replies. "We'll have at least as much as we had in Pocatel by the time you get back."

"That's good," Jovi responds. "When we return with our families, we're going to be hungry."

We say the words hopefully. But no one says what most of us are thinking. We may never return. And if we don't return, it means their end could come here in La Cuna, just like Rose.

We finish our goodbyes, and within a few minutes I know Hopper has a mother named Milena who was sick when he left, but lived in the second-to-last pock in the south end. Oso has a father. Charlie was alone, his mom and dad banished at the same time he was exiled.

Oso and I stare out at Charlie, who's now spiraling between the rows. Wolf still walks guard along the edge of the fields, every other loop circling Rose's grave. I think he doesn't know what else to do.

"Do you think we can save them?" I ask Oso quietly.

Soil flings out to either side of Charlie, making perfect rows. Even with no family of his own, he has barely stopped working since we buried Rose. Hopper follows, dropping new seeds into the rows of plants that have wilted beyond recovery.

"Some will survive," Oso says. "I wish I could be of more help."

I'm not sure if we're talking about our families, the Alebrijes, or the plants. But I know Oso feels like she's too big to help in the fields and too slow to help us in Pocatel.

"Oso, can I ask you a huge favor?"

Oso clomps closer toward me. "Of course. What is it?"

I lower my signal, and she does too. Before I can finish explaining, Oso is already walking away out the secret entrance. This time, no one cares to stop her.

Selah's signal approaches quickly and she lands next to us with a soft thump. "Ready?"

"He won't come?" Jovi asks.

"He . . . he is not himself right now. But if what they did to Rose doesn't change his mind, nothing can. He's agreed to leave the fields alone. We must go," Selah says. "If he decides to help, he'll know where to find us."

Everyone else stops what they're doing to watch us leave. No one speaks. What can they say? Jovi and Selah fly out. I take a final look at La Cuna and breathe in the smell of its pine. Charlie stops spinning in the field and raises his foot to me in goodbye.

27

· · · ◟ · · ·

AS WE FLY TOWARD POCATEL TO THE WEST, I SEE OSO IN
the Outlands below. She takes one slow step after the other
toward Tortoise's den. A deep set of footprints lie behind her
in the sand behind her. She doesn't even look up, focused on
her own mission. A bear in the desert might have some luck
reminding Tortoise that they are not what they thought they
were. But really, I know Oso's patience will give her the best

chance at convincing Tortoise to leave the den and join us after one hundred and eighty winters.

Then again, Tortoise may not want to. Who am I to say? But I want them to have the choice.

Selah turns to the west, and the rising sun shimmers over her body.

"*You have one thousand and ninety days remaining in your sentence.*"

Jovi and I follow close behind.

We continue on silently for hours. We pass over the skeleton tree. Then we pass over the ruins of the building with the strange words. I repeat them to myself over and over.

Sé fuerte. Sé valiente. Sé fuerte. Sé valiente. Sé fuerte. Sé valiente.

"Did you say something?" Jovi asks.

I hadn't thought I was thinking of them aloud. "Nothing."

We continue on for the rest of the day, until sixty kilometers ahead, Pocatel Ridge comes into view.

When I see the mountain range, Selah heads straight toward the ridge that overlooks Pocatel and the Dead Forest, instead of following the Old-World highway.

"Selah?" I call ahead.

"This will be quicker," she says abruptly, climbing higher and higher. "You two can take the other way if you're too scared."

We don't answer. If the wyrms aren't real, maybe the ghosts in the Dead Forest aren't real either? Wyrms may not be real, but our souls don't just end. And there are plenty of people who would be just as scary dead as alive. Jovi and I fly side by side, struggling to keep up.

Selah's right. Soon we're over the mountains and in half the time it took me using the Old-World road to La Cuna. Pocatel comes into view in the distance.

Below in the Dead Forest lie nothing but skeleton trees. In the shadows of the setting sun, I search for wandering souls, but maybe drones can't see spirits. Farther up ahead, strips of cloth and hair wave in the breeze off the Tree of Souls as ever.

Just like a constellation, the Pox are lit for the night. "Mira," I whisper to Jovi.

For a moment, I'm happy.

"Mi abuela is down there somewhere," he says.

"We will find—"

"Do you hear that?" he asks.

It is not a signal. It's footsteps in unison. Then voices. Singing.

Hmmm, hmmm, hmmm, hmmmm.
Tccch, tccch, tccch, tchhh.
Juntos buscamos La Cuna . . .

But the words and beat are half the speed as usual; the pride in the words is missing.

In the fading light between the Pox, I see people are being led to its entrance in a row. Their arms are linked in a human chain. Close to a hundred Cascabeles. Almost half of our people.

The shadow of a hunched over figure is near the front. I'd know him anywhere. Jo.

He walks more slowly than the long days in the fields. And I notice something else. Those who walk alongside him are the oldest, the youngest, the weakest workers . . . those the Pocatelans value least.

Por ahora, vivimos con la tierra,
un día muramos en la tierra.

Nuestros espíritus volarán con los ancestros
Convertiremos en el camino de las estrellas

Guards walk on either side. The group halts at the front entrance of the Pox, waiting. But for what? Darkness?

Hmmm, hmmm, hmmm, hmmm.
Tccch, tccch, tccch, tchhh.

"What do we do?" Jovi asks.

"We cannot help them like this. If we have any chance, we have to keep to the original plan," Selah says. She looks towards the Center of Banishment. "We find my mother."

Jovi and I exchange a look.

We continue over the center of Pocatel. At the other end, outside the Trench, we can see the wyrmfield. It's not so scary anymore. Until we get closer . . .

Mounds of dirt dot its surface. They are identical to the hill of earth I left when I stored the wyrm near the rock formation in the Outlands. The same that were left behind when the monster killed Celia. But tonight there are so many more.

"They are fresh."

I think of how desperate the Monger was to get home. He would have done anything to get Lilith and his children back inside Pocatel—including leaving no sign of those exiled, aside from a mound of earth.

All those Mongers helping the Imperator create his lies and deceptions still don't know they're no safer than us. Just like Nathaniel, they can be next.

No one even asks where we should go. We stay on the east of town and land on the eaves of the Center of Banishment. We each drink from the trough surrounding the roof and recharge our batteries. I look down the road toward the orphanage. A rug hangs over a clothesline. The front door is shut tight.

Below on the main street, I can tell there's already been another market. But the normal crowds are gone. In the fading sunlight, the vendor carts are quiet. Only the one-armed Monger remains, her bins still full of half-rotted potatoes.

Even the Director of Truth—the lying puppeteer—has almost no one today.

His voice echoes down the street. "And for those naughty children who stray beyond the city limits, beware the desert wrym!"

From our perch on the eves, I see the puppeteer's wife throw a fistful of sand out, distracting the tiny audience, who hold their hands up to block their faces. Children scream. Some run.

Cascabeles drums echo in my mind like the rattle of the snake. A wave of nervousness hits me. This is the point where Gabi and I used the chaos to move in on our target and she'd begin to dance.

"Should we turn off our signals?" Jovi asks. "In case the Regime have a way to detect us?"

"What's the point?" Selah answers. "He knows I'm coming."

The puppeteer's wife raises an Outland mutant wyrm, with mop-strand wings woven over metal wire. The puppeteer runs behind his wife and lights wood shavings on fire. He blows onto the stage, creating the necrotizing sandstorm, then he blows smoke toward those watching. I remember the first time I saw it, jumping back in terror, sure the smoke would blister my skin. Now I want to fly through the curtain and pull it away, to prove to the kids watching that it's all fake.

Soon it will be dark. Dust mixes with the smoke of the extinguished smelters as the Cloaks sweep a single set of footprints away. The footpath over the Trench is empty. Maybe we can help whoever it was before too much time goes by.

We fly to a lower eave closer to the exile door.

Selah whispers, even though no one can hear us. "We should try her lab first. Maybe . . ."

The six Cloaks finish their work and head in a single line toward the back side of the building, directly beneath us, the shortest in front.

"This is our chance," Jovi says.

We're so close. If we can get in, we can find Dolores.

The first Cloak in the line reaches out his small hand for the door's handle. But it doesn't make sense. It's not the white hand of a Pocatelan. I hold perfectly still. As he raises his head to grasp the door, I nearly fall out of the air. The face looking out from the shadows of the shortest Cloak is me.

28

MAYBE GHOSTS ARE REAL. BUT THE CLOAK WITH MY face who's pushing the door open is as solid as I am. The Cloak *is* me. I imagined all our bodies would be stored safely somewhere near Dolores's lab until our sentences were over. But I watch as five other Cloaks and I enter through the door.

Then it hits me. The words of Tortoise whisper in my mind, like they're right with me: "*Ants may be able to reach what you cannot, but you can reach places I cannot.*

Before Selah can stop me, I fly to the opening and wedge my body into the gap before it can close.

Selah pushes her wing out and pulls it open. Jovi and I fly through, followed by Selah. The door clicks shut behind us.

The smell of lamp oil hits me. Golden firelight flickers on the black floor like glass. I'm filled with anger and fear inside the last place I was human. This is where they took me away from Gabi—took all of us from our families—and sentenced Celia and hundreds of others to death. Besides the Cloaks, it's empty. But voices approach from the double doors leading to the main entrance. We follow behind the Cloaks, along the wall in the shadows of their robes, until they disappear through the secret panel in the wall.

We fly in before it can shut. The hall is as cold as it was when I was led through with Dolores and El Bastón.

We enter the hall of drones. I think of the first time I saw the animal drones, their ghostly reflections cast on the shiny black floor. But the reflections are gone now.

Instead, metal pieces of drones are strewn about.

The *Great Horned Raptor 206* lies scattered like one of its own kills, its head on the opposite side of the display from its body.

I shiver. "Jovi, it looks just like—"

He nudges me with his wing. "Está bien. I'm right here."

The *Fox A50-Trickster, Crow B20 Scavenger,* and *Meta-Hopper* X 2050, who'd been staged to look like a hunt between predators and prey, now all lie in a shared grave. The only drones I can still see in one piece are some of the bees, butterflies, and humming-birds . . . too tiny for all of them to be destroyed, I guess.

"We need to get out of here," Jovi says softly.

I know these drones aren't us. I know they don't have Sparks. But I can't help feeling like I'm seeing the dead bodies of friends.

I follow Jovi but have to turn back and buzz Selah out of her trance. We leave the room and come to the hall with the lab in one direction and a dark stone hallway in the other.

The hem of the last Cloak—me—fades into the shadows down the dark hallway.

"Did you know we were the Cloaks?" I ask Selah.

"¿Cómo?" Jovi asks, shocked. "We are the Cloaks?"

Selah doesn't answer, turning away.

"Oh, ella sabía," Jovi says. "I guess we know where to find ourselves now." He sighs and motions in the opposite direction. "Dolores's lab is this way."

We fly in the opposite direction as the Cloaks. Within seconds, I smell the lab. The closer I get, the more my body trembles. When we approach Dolores's door, it's wide open.

Shards of glass cover the ground and a pool of water trickles out into the hall.

"I'll go first," I say.

I don't wait for them to answer. I zip inside. The glass cabinet is shattered, and the decoy Sparks are snapped in pieces and spread across metal table.

The only real Sparks in this room—those from a hundred years ago—are missing. The vaults, still filled with water, are now empty.

Selah moves around the corner slowly. I wonder if she smells what I do. Mixed in with all the antiseptic is Dolores's scent.

Selah lands on the table and brushes her wing on a broken Spark.

Jovi gasps, his voice shaking. "God. Are these all . . . ?"

"Decoys," I hurry to say. "Dolores placed them there to fool the Imperator and the Regime. So, when they destroyed these and the Cascabel Cloaks didn't die . . ."

". . . he decided to send me a message, and kill Rose," Selah finishes.

"Then we are all still in danger," Jovi says.

"Yes," Selah answers. "He's just waiting for me."

We may never know how they did it. Did they exile Rose's Cloak human body, to be killed by a wyrm drone? Did they remove the Spark from her head in the Cloak and destroy it?

"Where do you think Dolores would be?" Jovi asks.

Selah's words are shaky. "Maybe she escaped."

But none of us, including Selah, believe that. If Dolores has been exiled, all of our hopes and plans—as improbable as they were—may already be over.

"We need to search." I quickly fly out and back through the hall of drones. Commotion and voices come from the

Banishment room now—along with flickering lights, the smell of lamp oil, and the echo of two sets of footsteps approaching.

"Up here," Jovi says from behind me. He lands on a ceiling beam in a dark corner. Selah and I hurry to hide next to him.

El Bastón opens the door from the room a few seconds later and leads a hunched figure across the room, pushing them inside one of the empty cells. The clanking of metal-on-metal booms as he slams the cell door. The figure turns to face him. Blonde strands of hair plaster to her sweaty face. Her purple robe is wrinkled and dirty. Her eyes are now dark and sunken.

"Mom," Selah says, her voice so much smaller.

El Bastón reaches through the bars and grabs Dolores's hands. He holds a knife up where she can see.

Selah tips to one side, her wing scraping the wall. Dolores glances up. Her eyes widen, then she quickly looks down. Her voice shakes as she speaks, "Someone will need to instruct the new Physician of how the Sparks reconnect—"

"There will be no new Director for your program." El Bastón lifts her hands in front of her and cuts the ties. "Any sign that your secret project ever existed will soon be gone forever."

Dolores grips the bars. "You will all go to hell for what you are doing."

El Bastón slams his staff onto the bar next to her hand. His face cracks in a crooked grin. Even in the dim room, I can see the glint of his bronze tooth. "We are already in hell. Some of us just get to live here a little longer than others." Then he exits the room, a fresh gouge in his stick, tapping it on his way.

Selah arches her wings back and moves forward.

Jovi and I follow quietly.

Dolores crumples to the ground. "Selah?" Her eyes stare in disbelief. "Is it really you?" She sobs and reaches her hand out, placing it on the black floor. "You came home." Selah lands next to it and stares down.

Selah glances at Jovi and me. After a moment, she lays her head on Dolores's hand.

Dolores strokes across Selah's wing over and over. "I am so sorry, my precious one. I should have protected you. I thought I was protecting you."

"Why did you send me away?" Selah says, even though Dolores can't hear.

Dolores looks up at me. "Thank you."

But she doesn't know we're not back because of me, or our deal. She doesn't know we're trying to save all of us. Los Cascabeles . . . and everyone in La Cuna.

The Imperator's voice echoes from the Banishment room. "You have been accused of theft!"

The sound of his voice makes me sick. But I can't imagine how Selah feels.

Dolores glances toward the Banishment room. "You need to hurry. Food is running out. Even the Directors' families do not have enough. No one is safe. I cannot stop him." She whispers now, looking directly at me. "The oldest Sparks. Do you remember the secret compartment?"

I nod. I know the hidden drawer where she hid the map. I feel a relief for something I hadn't even thought about. Tortoise will be okay.

"I cannot tell you the horrible things the Regime has already done."

"We know," Selah says. "And if we don't hurry, we won't have a mouth or voice to tell the people of Pocatel."

Dolores's words are straggled. "Even with all they have done, it is about to get far worse."

"Do you have any arguments or pleas?" we hear the Imperator say.

A small voice answers, "Sí."

"Oh, no," I whisper. "Gabi!"

29

THIS IS NOT HOW AND WHERE I WANTED TO HEAR
Gabi's voice again. I thought when I found her, it would be
in the orphanage, and I would be giving her the news we were
leaving Pocatel. "*Really, Leandro? We are leaving?*"

"Eres estúpido," she says. "And I know I should not argue with
those kinds of people," she adds.

Jovi snickers.

"But you're wrong for starving us. You should be taking care of those younger before feeding yourselves."

The feelings of anger and fear are back, but this time it's even worse. My wings buzz as I turn toward the door. "Gabi. Stop talking!"

"Wait!" Jovi calls out.

But I'm already speeding toward the Banishment room. I stop when I see El Bastón just outside the doorway. I stare inside the room. Gabi stands barefoot and dirty in her green orphan tunic in front of the Imperator. Four other orphans stand against the wall, including the hiccupping boy. Gabi's chin juts out like she's talking back to Tía Lula. But here, she'll get more than a face slap.

The Imperator turns to a nearby Patrol. "Is it dark yet?" He peeks over the bench at Gabi's feet.

"Nearly, sir," El Bastón answers. "All parties are in place. Just Elias finishing to pack up his stage."

The Imperator lowers his voice. "Good. Not sure all of Pocatel is ready to see such young exiles."

El Bastón steps away from the door toward Gabi. He pulls the knife from his pocket, cutting the twine from her cinched hands.

"She's just a little kid," Jovi says next to me, angrily.

Selah speaks quietly: "Thinnings do not care if hungry mouths are old or young."

The Imperator peers over his glasses. His jowls shake. "Gabriela Rivera, you are sentenced to exile."

She rubs her wrists and takes the water from El Bastón's hand. "Bueno," she says to the Imperator. Then she holds her hand up, pushing all her fingers together in one spot to form a snake, making it strike at him. "My ghost will bite your head while you sleep, until the day you die. *Tccch, tccch, tccch.*" She rattles her tongue and strikes again with her hand.

Jovi laughs.

"Not funny," I say.

The Imperator doesn't respond. He doesn't even record Gabi's name on the paper like he did for me. El Bastón leads her to the exile door. I peek further through the gap in the door to the Banishment room.

"What do I do? I need to go after her."

"No. She will not know it's you," Selah says. "You will serve her best by staying. We will find her. But we cannot do it like this."

"Selah's right," Jovi says. "And something tells me su hermanita's stronger than we are."

But they didn't see Celia die.

Gabi pushes open the door but turns back to the Imperator, one hand on her hip. "Soy Cascabel—I can survive. I can walk far and forage, but you will stay here and starve and be ugly and miserable."

"I like her," Selah says. "Sounds like how I used to talk to him."

Gabi turns to the other orphans. "I will wait, and we will walk across together." Gabi exits, her first steps outside stirring up dirt in the last light of dusk.

All I've thought about since I was banished was finding a way to make sure we were together again. To make sure she was safe. And now I'm right here, and I can't do anything.

The exile door closes behind Gabi.

The Imperator sighs. "This is taking far too long. We must set protocol aside. Let us work them through in groups, shall we? We can Thin these last four mouths."

El Bastón passes by the crack in the door and motions the remaining green-robed orphans forward.

The Imperator calls out to a guard at the entrance door. "Lead down the seventy two from the Pox."

The guard nods and retreats from the room.

We hurry back to the shadows of the corner, then to Dolores.

"We need to move faster," I say to Jovi and Selah.

"I'm sorry. But I can't help you now," Dolores announces.

"We have to help her escape from this jail," Selah replies.

"And do not think of trying to help me," Dolores continues.

Selah scoffs. "How does she do that?"

Dolores turns to me. "The secret drawer?"

I nod again.

"Underneath the map you will find an instrument. It is how you reconnect the Spark to the one in your bodies. Once you eject your Spark, the impulse will remain in the drone's memory circuits for thirty seconds." Her eyes sag, but her voice grows stronger. "That is all. You do not have time beyond that. Once the drone's main Spark shuts down, its partner will cease to function, and shut down the human body."

Selah moves closer to Dolores, "And how are we supposed to do this on our own?"

"Leandro, you will have to go first. Use your beak to reinsert your Spark." Her hands tremble as she mimics placing the Spark up her nose.

"Again!" Selah squawks. "How does she know what I am thinking?"

"Once you are in your own body, it will be easy to bring back Selah and . . ." She stares at Jovi. "Your owl friend. I apologize, I . . ." She tilts her head and smiles. "Jovian Perez."

Selah sighs.

"Good memory," Jovi says.

The sound of footsteps approach.

I stare at the side door toward Dolores's lab. "We need to get out of here."

Selah glances back at Dolores as we fly back toward the lab.

"I love you," Dolores whispers after.

Besides the echo of footsteps from the hall the Cloaks went down, there's no sign of others. We enter the lab, fly to the secret drawer, and hover in front of the latch. I push in my thin beak, but it doesn't open. Selah hovers next to me and pushes one of her thick knife feathers onto the clasp. The drawer slides open.

I point to the base of the drawer. "Under there."

Selah pries it open, her feather nicking a piece of the old, faded map. Underneath in the secret compartment lies a water-filled tube containing four Sparks and the metal tool. At its tip are tiny metal pincers. The instrument is larger than I am.

Selah should be the one to pick it up, but Jovi's already lowering his talon. I know he wants to help, but . . .

Selah and I exchange a glance. Jovi lifts it up once and immediately drops it with a *clang* back into the drawer.

Selah and I both look toward the door, straining to hear any footsteps.

Jovi tries three more times before getting a grip. I want to cover my eyes as it dangles from his talon. "Now what?" he asks.

Selah stares down too. "We find the Cloaks."

THE STONE HALLWAY narrows and slopes downward. My head brushes the ceiling. "Careful," I call back.

The farther we go, the colder it gets. The sound of our flying grows louder as we leave the tunnel and enter a huge room, dug out of rock. Water trickles down the wall into a motionless pool of water taking up one corner of the room. I wonder if this is Pocatel's water source, and how they keep this underground well hidden. The water level is over a meter lower than the dried white waterline.

The opposite side of the room is filled with cots. There are twenty cots; on all but one lies a person in a dark green robe, most with brown Cascabel skin. I think of the thirteen of us that were in La Cuna and realize there must be some others surviving out there on their own.

On the cot closest to the door lies my body. I look no different than before. So much has happened since I was in that body.

But I realize—it's been only a few days. I look so small. Inside the hummingbird drone, I'm still me, but as I look down at my human body, it's hard to know which is where I truly belong.

Selah was right about some things. I haven't been hungry or thirsty as a drone. I haven't been hot or cold.

But I also don't have the feeling when my stomach hurts from laughing too hard while Gabi does something ridiculous. Or what it's like when it's flipping in excitement, as Jo tells a story I haven't heard yet. Or when it twists in pain when I eat a too-raw potato. Or aches, remembering our mother. That part hurt in a different way. But still . . . I want it back.

"This is me," I say.

"Que guapo." Jovi hovers next to me. "I can't believe I'm about to be back in my body after three winters. When I left, my voice was changing, and my abuela was weaving fabric to add to the bottom of my tunic." He laughs nervously. I see him glancing around the room, trying to find himself.

Selah motions to the door. "We must hurry."

I land on my own chest. Steam blows from my nostrils into the cold room. Dolores was clear: once my Spark is out of the hummingbird drone, I have thirty seconds to reconnect it with the Spark inside my body.

I think of Gabi outside alone out on the exile trail. I pop open my Spark's compartment. "¿Listos?" I ask. But I'm the one who's not ready. I count down to myself. "Tres, dos, uno."

The Spark releases from my head and bounces off the cot onto the floor.

It skitters toward the well. *Clink, clink, clink.*

Jovi panics and pushes me over on the bed. He falls over diving for it.

Selah swoops down smoothly, snagging the Spark in her talon just in time.

She flies back, setting it next to me on the cot, but we've lost five seconds already.

I hurry to place it under my human nose. We wait. Any second it should creep up to join its other half, just like when Dolores inserted it.

Nothing happens.

"What's wrong?"

I panic. I can't move. "I . . . I don't know. The other half crawled inside on its own before." Then I see: this one doesn't have tiny feet.

Jovi and Selah stare at one another.

"Hurry!" Jovi yells at Selah. "Do something."

I stare straight ahead. I was so sure. I can barely speak. "I . . . I don't know what to do."

"Leandro! You don't have time!" Selah cries out.

I think of the rod with the metal pincers lying on the bed next to us. Even if we could lift it, none of us would be able to operate it without fingers.

I can barely say the words. "We won't be able to do it."

"We need my mom," Selah cries.

"There's no time," Jovi barks. "Our time is almost up!"

Dolores said to use my beak. I pick the Spark up by the pointed tip and push it up my left nostril as high as I can. It trembles at the edge of my beak with a tiny vibration.

"Is it working?" Jovi asks.

"I . . . I can't get it high enough." I push as far as I can, but it stops at the top of the bone next to my eye.

I sit back and stare at the Spark. A tiny white light blinks a countdown. *Ten, nine, eight . . .*

I think of Gabi out there by herself. "Jovi?" I turn to him and can't say any more. I hope he remembers our deal. "¿Mi hermana?"

Jovi straightens his head and back. He looks strong, but his words glitch. "I'll find her." He hops closer.

What if he's not able to get to Gabi in time? What if she falls in the Trench, or the wyrms find her before Selah and Jovi get to her? What if they can't get back in their bodies?

"You only have a few seconds!" Selah yells.

The partner to the Spark is just next to my eye, behind the bone. It's. So. Close.

I pick up the tiny Spark in my beak and aim for the inner corner of my eye. My human body doesn't even flinch. My beak pierces the skin easily, then—*crack*—the thin bone.

Powering Down flashes red in front of my eyes as I feel the Spark sucked away from my beak's grasp.

Selah and Jovi's screaming voices disappear.

30

AN EXPLOSION OF LIGHT FLASHES IN FRONT OF MY vision and a sharp pain pierces my left eye. I lift my hand—

My hand? I look down, and I have . . . fingers. I cup a hand over my throbbing eye. Callouses scrape my face. "Ow!"

I sit up, and my bare feet hit the cold stone floor. A shiver runs up my back. I've been shivering for winters every night in the pock. How did I forgot what shivering felt like?

My eye pounds as I bend over. Blood and clear fluid drip through my fingers. I think of the Monger, and my hands shake as I hurry to rip a long strip off the bottom of my robe, wrapping it around my head. Just like before I was an Alebrije, my body aches. Did my stomach always knot from hunger, or is this something I'd just gotten used to? But the pain throbbing in my eye feels like I got stabbed with a hot knife. I look down and see the hummingbird, blood on its beak. I did get stabbed with a knife.

When I sit up, Selah and Jovi are staring at me.

I hear thudding footsteps. As I sit motionless, I realize the footsteps are my own heartbeat in my ears. My mouth has never been so dry. I rush to the well and scoop water, chugging several handfuls.

I stagger over and pick up Dolores's surgical tool from the cot and twist the top off. Inside is an opening for water, just like the Spark and the Monger's communication box. I bend back down to the well and place my hand in the water. Drops fall off my fingertips and funnel down the opening in the instrument. It hums to life.

"Which ones are you?" I call to Selah and Jovi.

They don't move. Jovi's beak is gaped open, and he hasn't stopped staring at my face.

"It's just an eye. Which ones are you?" I force myself to stay calm, even though my entire body shivers from the pain.

Jovi flies over the cots, stopping at each one, then doubles back to the final bed in the darkest corner of the room. He stares down, then lands next to the young man's face. Jovi opens his Spark compartment just beneath the metal triangle of his left ear.

I lift Jovi in my hands. I hold him closer to steady my shaking. It feels so strange to hold the small metal owl that towered over me for as long as I've known him.

"Don't worry," I say. "I've done this before." I wink with my good eye.

Jovi's feathers ruffle.

Unable to connect anymore, I can't hear his panic or the bad words he must be saying.

Heat runs up the back of my neck. "Please work," I say to the tool.

His talons poke into my arm.

"I mean, it *will* work." I think of Dolores's clean lab. In the Cloaks' room, algae and mud cover the walls, and dirt is jammed under my nails.

I place Jovi on his side. I smile and my voice trembles. "See you in a minute."

I count down for him: "Tres, dos, uno . . ."

The Spark pops out, and I have to focus with my good eye to catch it midair. My fingers quiver as I hurry to wedge the Spark between the two tiny prongs on the tool's end. I slip my fingers around the other end.

I let out a deep breath and place it deep inside Jovi's nose. His body doesn't move at all, but my hand is shaking so hard I nearly drop the tool. I don't know if my trembling is from pain or nervousness or both. I force my hand steady with the other. Still, it doesn't work. I flip the device the other way so the curved end faces his eye socket. It begins to vibrate in my hand. I hear a small click.

I glance at Jovi—my Jovi, the drone. There is no spark of life in him at all. Now both Jovis lie completely still. Finally, the human in front of me opens his eyes. They are green.

"I did it," I whisper.

He takes a deep breath and wraps his arm around his stomach. Jovi's body is thin, but the fullness of his cheeks are of someone who looks happy without smiling. For someone so young, the lines across his forehead tell of a hard life of worry. He smiles for real, and his eyes well up. "You sound like a Cascabel."

"You do too." I lean over and pull him into a hug. "We did it!"

He hugs me back, then backs up and winces. "Your eye, Leandro."

"I'll live," I say.

He holds out his arms, staring at them. "I thought . . . I thought I was seeing the ghost of my older brother at first." He turns away and wipes his eyes. "I've grown." He rubs his hand down over his chin. "And gotten hairier." He hurries to the well and scoops water too, guzzling down handfuls.

Selah flies over and starts pecking at my leg.

"¡Eh!" I say. "I didn't forget about you."

She flies across the room and lands next to a girl with the same long blonde hair and soft face as Dolores. Unlike all the others, this girl's face and hands are clean, her hair braided.

Jovi sniffs his armpit. "Ooof. Guess you have to know some-one around here."

I help Jovi up, and we sit on either side of Selah's body.

"You ready?" I ask.

Selah falls to one side and pops open her Spark compartment.

"Just so you know," Jovi says, "it didn't hurt, Selah." He turns to me, pointing to my eye. "Sorry."

The piercing pain in my eye is no worse, but my shivering has lessened. For now, I can't think of the pain. "Okay." I place my hand near the open compartment on her head. "Now."

The Spark pops out, and it lands in my hand.

I motion for the tool. "Jovi, hurry!" I click one half of the Spark into place and insert the tool up her nose. This time, the tool barely begins to vibrate in my hand when the two halves of the Spark click together.

Selah's eyes blink to life, just as bright and blue as Dolores's. Tiny freckles dot over the bridge of her nose, making her look younger than she probably is. She groans. Jovi tries to help her sit up, but she shrugs him off and rolls over.

"I am fine." She grabs her throat like she's shocked to hear her own voice. Even I'm surprised. Her voice is a lot gentler than it sounded as a hawk. In any other situation, hearing Selah's soft features and kind voice would have made me laugh. She holds out her hands and stares. Then, just like Jovi, she rushes to drink from the well.

When she's done, Selah stares down at her hawk drone. She picks it up and rubs her hand over the purple circles and the arrow on its side. "Goodbye, friend. I thought we'd be together a very long time." She sighs and hides it under the empty cot. Jovi does the same.

I pick up the hummingbird drone, and a feeling hits me that's something completely different than the first time Dolores placed it in my hand. I rub my hand over the scratches and dents I've gotten in the past days. A lump forms in my throat, and I slip it into my robe pocket, along with the Spark tool.

I pretend to fix my bandage, but underneath, my eye still pulses with a deep throb at every heartbeat. The water in the pool is still again, but I'm afraid to look at my reflection.

The three of us stand in the doorway and look back at the Cloaks.

"How do we protect them?" I ask.

Selah steps closer. "Stay here," she says to the Cloaks.

Jovi pulls at her elbow. "I don't think they plan to go anywhere."

We run back toward Dolores. I stop at the lab and grab the tube containing Tortoise and the other Sparks from long ago. I drop it into my pocket too.

The stomps of our feet echo like drums. My legs feel like I have a basket of papas tied to them with each step. When we come to the door of the cell room, we tiptoe back in.

Dolores stands, her eyes fixed on Selah. She sobs, and her knees give way. She grips the bars, pulling herself up. "You did it," she whispers.

Selah yanks on the latch and it doesn't budge. She sighs. "I do not know how to get you out."

"Do not fret, my strong child." Dolores reaches through the bars and slips her hand over Selah's.

Selah closes her eyes and pulls her hand away. Jovi and I pretend not to see.

Dolores takes a deep breath. "That is understandable."

I speak as quietly as I can. "How do we free you?"

Dolores turns to me; her eyes widen, staring at my wounded socket. "You must disinfect that as soon as you can."

Just thinking about cleaning the wound makes me sick. "Uh, I think I'll let you do it."

"No," she says. "You must leave me here."

Deep furrows cross Selah's brow. "What?"

Her brow has the exact same furrows as Selah's. "You know what they are doing out there." She lets out a soft breath. "They will leave nothing to chance with me. I know too much. We will not have the time together I had hoped for."

Selah shakes her head. "That is not acceptable." She turns to Jovi and me. "The Directors do not know La Cuna, or believe such a Cradle could exist. While our lies become legends, they have made your legends lies."

"It *is* real?" Dolores whispers, almost to herself.

"We will get you over the bridge," Selah continues, "and you can take all those they have already Thinned and escape with as many that can make it past the Wyrmfield to the ridge."

"What about the others?" Jovi motions toward where the Cloaks lie.

"We are not leaving them." I can't help the anger in my voice. "And what of the rest of our people? Those they are leading here now to exile?"

Selah nods. "You are right. I was too hasty. We stay with the original plan."

"Stop." Dolores's voice grows higher. "Be realistic. It is nearly dark. Your chances lessen with each minute. You must run with as many as you can now and hope for the best."

Even as she speaks, a commotion of frightened people being led into the next room erupts, much louder than before. I try to shake the image of the wyrm mounds from my mind. I want to think they would not do such a thing to so many children and elders. But even as I think it, wailing echoes from next door.

Selah grits her teeth. "You were part of that!"

Dolores turns away. "I did what I did to protect you."

Selah leans away.

"But you are right," Dolores says. "Just as my father before me, I watched while the Regime terrified our people into compliance. I even carried a child, mandated by the tradition of those before me." Tears fall from Dolores's eyes. "But Selah, you are still the best thing I've ever done. I thought smuggling children in drones was better than doing nothing at all." Dolores slumps to the floor. "I should have told all of Pocatel what I knew, even if

it meant my own life. Even if it meant I could not have you back."
Dolores's fingers tremble against the bars. "Leave now. They cannot stop all of you."

Selah looks toward the Banishment room. "No. Everyone should have a chance to leave. I *will* tell the Pocatelans how the Regime has deceived them. I have to believe there will be bedlam, and the Regime will lose focus on the Cascabeles. We will all have time to get enough food and water for the trip." She smiles at me and Jovi. "I will be back for you, Mother, and you and I are going to leave this place together."

I smile back. "What's *bedlam*?" I ask.

Jovi shakes his head. "No se."

"No!" Dolores calls as Selah turns.

But Selah's stomps toward the Banishment room. I run, beating her to the door. I hold it shut. "Wait. We should think about—"

I notice Selah's hand trembling as she reaches for the door yanking it open. The smell of lamp oil floods toward us. As I follow her inside, its smell is only drowned out by the reek of so many people in one place.

Starving Cascabeles are packed into the room, sitting on benches and lined up in rows along the wood-paneled walls. I look down at my own wrist and see that I'm just as thin as they are. Their hollow, hunger-dulled eyes widen as they all turn and stare at us. Among them, Franco and Naji hold hands waiting. Naji elbows Franco, and they both stare at me with mouths open.

"Su espíritu ha venido por nosotros," Naji says.

"Nah," Franco smirks. "He's alive," he whispers.

"Leandro! Where have you been?" Jo calls out waving, and I can't believe he remembered my name.

I take note of those I see. The old, like Jo. The weak, like small children. The disobedient, like Franco.

Only two guards were here for my trial, but half the entire Patrol is here now, all with guns. I try to pull Selah back.

The Imperator looks up, his eyes wide in confusion. He drops his book with a thud. "Selah?""

Selah steps forward. She tucks her trembling hand behind her back.

"Hello, Father."

31

MURMURS RISE FROM THE GUARDS AND THOSE WAIT-
ing to be Thinned. The Imperator's nostrils flare. There is no
love in his eyes like Dolores's.

El Bastón slides toward us, confused at what he should
do. Selah pushes me aside, wasting no time. She screams to
the Patrol: "The Imperator and the Regime have lied to us
all! The wyrms are not dragons. They are Old-World drones!
There are no monsters, or diseases, or killer sand to fear in the

Outlands." The Imperator slams his fist on the table and leaps to his feet, but Selah continues, glaring at him. "The Directors are false leaders and fake protectors. They use your fear to control you . . . all of you!"

Selah turns to the Cascabeles, now staring at her wide-eyed. "They have no power over you. The creatures beyond the Trench are machines. Ones they control."

"Es verdad," I say, stepping forward, seeing their confused faces. "Everything she says. Cuando puedan, vayan para sus familias y corran a las montañas."

The crying has stopped. The Cascabeles exchange glances. "Could it be true?" someone asks.

"We are leaving, Papi!" a little boy calls out.

Some of the guards even begin whispering to one another.

The Imperator screams, spit flying from his mouth. He nervously scans the faces of the people around him, Patrol and Cascabel alike.

"That is enough, Selah! Stop speaking at once!" He walks slowly from his desk to stand in front of her. His teeth are clenched together now. "So much like your mother." The Imperator turns to me. "Landro, isn't it? It has been barely a week." He inspects my bandaged eye. "It looks like the Physician was busier than we even thought." He nods at El Bastón, who walks back through the secret doorway toward where Dolores and Jovi wait.

Seconds later, he and a couple stone-faced guards walk back in with Dolores.

The Imperator turns in a circle, making eye contact with each of the guards. Their whispering ceases. "Today presents an opportunity for you all," he says, quietly at first. "You need only obey my command, without question, and I assure you . . . you and your families will be rewarded." He stops at his desk and taps his ring once on its surface. "Or, you may leave and return to your families now. Speak of none of this. And I assure you too, no harm will come to you or them."

A guard who looks as young as Jovi fidgets. His eyes dart to the others, but he remains.

Not a single guard moves. But I know it is not out of loyalty.

The Imperator smiles. "Excellent. Then we shall proceed."

"Imperator, please!" Dolores calls out.

He faces her and takes a breath, way too calm now. "Lock the door."

One of the guards walks toward the double door with the carved woman.

"Not that door," the Imperator barks, glancing toward the exile trail. "We will no longer be using that path to remove the disease from Pocatel."

The guard runs to the back exit door and bolts it closed. Jovi, Dolores, Selah, and I are pushed toward the Cascabeles.

The Imperator walks back to his desk. He lifts out a shiny bronze beetle, and closes his eyes for a moment, before pinning it next to the one on his right shoulder. I know this beetle. The matavenado—or deer killer—that crushes its prey in its jaws.

The leader of the Pocatelan Regime turns to face us, speaking as calmly as if he were telling a bedtime story. "As a boy, I watched as my father was bitten by a rattlesnake near the old mines. He ordered his own leg taken off above the knee, so the poison could not spread to the entire body." The Imperator's face becomes stone. "You have forced a different type of Banishment from Pocatel. One that will remove every last bit of poison once and for all."

32

···〔···

THE BRONZE DEER KILLER GLEAMS IN THE MOON-
light.

The Imperator approaches El Bastón and leans in at his side
as we are led out of the Center of Banishment, saying something
in his ear. I watch as the puppeteer runs from down the street
to join the two other Directors—a gathering I think even most
Pocatelans would question.

El Bastón releases Dolores and shoves her toward us. She takes careful steps toward Selah. They stand in front of one another for a moment. Finally, Selah falls into Dolores's chest. "I am still angry with you," she gets out, her sobbed words muffled by her mother's now-soiled Director robe.

"I know you are." Dolores kisses the top of Selah's head.

The street is quiet. Not a single lamp burns along the street. Faces of Pocatelans, including Directors, watch through the lighted windows of their homes. Guards block us in on each side.

The Imperator turns to lead our procession. As one large group, the Patrol surround us, and we move as one. The Imperator's robe blows in the wind as we are led to the center of Pocatel. I grip the hummingbird in my pocket, praying I can be as strong as I was when I was inside of it.

Eyes stare curiously as we are led away from the Center of Banishment. The Imperator, El Bastón, and the Director of Truth walk alongside. Once we're at the center of town, the Imperator speaks to El Bastón. "The entire leg."

El Bastón nods like it makes perfect sense. The Imperator turns to leave with the puppeteer.

"Father!" Selah calls after. "Let us go free, and we will leave peacefully, along with anyone who wants to follow us. You would still preserve all else inside the walls of Pocatel. You will not have to waste your resources Thinning any more." This Selah is not the one I know. If she were asking this for herself, I know she would not beg. But she does this for us.

"You have forced this." The Imperator's nostrils flare. "We cannot leave you to spread your vitriol. Do you know what Pocatel represents? It represents *all humanity*." He stands tall, the two beetles clinging to his dark red robe like scavengers on a carcass. "We alone carry civility into this new world, my daughter. We alone will determine what humanity will be going forward! Those before us warned of what happens when humans are left without rules."

He glances at me. "What our Regime does here, will affect humanity for thousands of years to come. Abundant fruit comes from pruning the desiccated." Now, he steps in front of Selah and takes her braid in his hand, inspecting it. "We must eliminate any pain, and . . . disappointment"—he sneers and tosses her hair onto her shoulder like it's putrid—"from our past." He sighs. "And unfortunately, you have chosen to be part of the rot."

Selah lets out a breath and turns to me. Her body slumps, her face defeated.

For these beliefs, even their own children will lose. Our ancestors and families were willing to—and did—give their own lives, so that we could survive. This Regime curses their children by taking the lives of others. We have so much already back in La Cuna. Charlie has probably replanted most of the field himself. These people could never share it the way it's meant to be shared. They would keep it themselves, deciding who gets more of what.

The Imperator turns to El Bastón, then glances at the Patrol, making a shooing motion. El Bastón sends his guards just out of hearing distance.

"If the girl or Physician try to speak to any Pocatelans," the Imperator says, glancing back at Selah, "have your Patrol kill them both immediately."

El Bastón nods, smiling at Dolores.

The Imperator turns and places his hand on Selah's cheek. Dolores slaps it away. El Bastón yanks her back.

This time, the Imperator lays his pinky ring on Selah's jaw. "You share your great-grandmother's name, but none of her greatness." He sighs. "Do not fret, Selah, your suffering will end soon." He scrapes his ring down her chin, leaving a pink mark. And calls out, "What is that saying you have about fear, Elias?"

The Director of Truth—the puppeteer—clears his throat calmly. "Fear is healthy, Imperator. The frightened will not rebel."

"Ah, yes. That is it." He steps away and turns his back on Selah. "Call for your Mongers now. We shall say the wyrms gathered to hunt like nothing we have seen. There was simply no time to draw the bridge before every last one of them were killed."

"But Imperator," the puppeteer responds. "Will the people not see—"

"We have laid the work of this for centuries, Elias. Their minds will see what we have planted within them, not their eyes." He turns to El Bastón, "Guard the neighborhoods and ensure our citizens remain a distance away, where their minds can imagine the worst."

"And if they do not comply?" El Bastón asks.

"Bring them to the snake pit."

The puppeteer twists one blade of his moustache nervously, looking at the guards just out of earshot. "And what of the guards and Mongers?"

"When all is over, gather and bring them all to me." The Imperator closes his eyes and whispers, "*Sacrifice for Preservation*." And he leaves, walking back toward the Center of Banishment, his robe trailing behind him.

Selah's chin is trembling, and she turns, wiping a tear from her marked cheek. The guard releases Dolores and she runs to Selah.

The puppeteer and El Bastón exchange a glance. The puppeteer follows the Imperator, while El Bastón splits his Patrol. A quarter of them surround those of us they've huddled in the center of town. He sends half into the neighborhoods, where they march between rows of Pocatelan homes.

Just as the lines of guards disappear into the city, we watch as El Bastón orders half the remaining guards to surround us, and dispatches the rest to gather along the edge of the Pox. One by one, they ignite torches. Moments later, they march forward, disappearing down the perimeter of the Pox. I see the light from their torches glowing in the night sky, moving until they are at the deepest edge of the Pox. A deep yell echoes, and in an instant, golden sparks begin flying in the air from the farthest homes.

33

SCREAMS CRY OUT AS THE SPARKS MOVE CLOSER AND closer. In a cloud of smoke, Cascabeles run from within out into the street and in our direction. The thin fabric of the pocks closest to the street burns in an instant, the sparks spiraling upward like a swarm of midges into the night sky.

Jovi runs toward the people who run toward us. "Abuelita!" he calls.

The guards with the torches follow the fleeing Cascabeles, encircling them until they are merged with our group.

I see Ari, tears flowing down her grimy cheeks. She is coughing when she sees me, and begins walking slowly toward me. She stares in shock. "Leandro," she sobs. She hugs me and it's the first person besides Gabi to do this since my mom.

Cascabeles panic, searching for their families. We lose Jovi in the chaos.

Dolores pulls Selah and me aside. I pull Ari with us. Just as we huddle, metallic shrieks pierce the air. *Un* . . . There is barely a one second echo.

The screams of wyrms so near the exposed city now start to drive panicked Pocatelans out of their homes. They walk to the edge of their yards holding up lamps. Even in the dark of night, they must see what we do. The Trench bridge is still down. The wyrms could enter the city any minute.

Most of the guards leave us, running toward the Pocatelan homes of stone and brick. They order the people back inside, but some don't listen. Entire Pocatelan families are pushed toward us screaming. I know what *bedlam* is now.

I turn to Ari and Selah, "I have to look for my sister."

Ari nods and tries to push past a guard who struggles with her. Selah joins her, causing a bigger commotion. While she's distracting him, I sprint past and toward the exile trail where I last saw Gabi.

The Field Director is on his front porch across from the Center of Banishment. His young wife pulls against him as he tries to coax her inside their home. He yells something at her, and she stops fighting and stares at him, looking stunned. He picks up their kid and they walk back in. They close the shutters and turn off the lights.

Those outside the Directors' houses—the ones with the biggest lights—scurry inside like beetles hiding under the dung pile. The windows go dark, and only the streetlamps of downtown Pocatel remain.

Other Pocatelans, sacks full of belongings hoisted over their shoulders, run toward the Dead Forest. I look north and see the monstrous spirals of dirt swelling on the opposite side of the Trench bridge. For most, I know that this many dirt devils can only spell a certain death. I look back to see that some fleeing Pocatelans, caught by guards, are being led to join the Cascabeles.

I stare again toward the approaching haze and catch sight of some movement: exiled Cascabeles, racing back into Pocatel over the lowered Trench bridge. I can only hope Gabi did as we had always planned and ran toward the ridge—hopefully out of the valley—before the Imperator summoned the wyrms. But I have to be sure. I run down the street toward the bridge.

When I near the orphanage, I crouch outside its wall to wait. I peek over the wall to see Director Marguerite standing in the doorway of the orphanage. She stares down the city's center at those fleeing toward the Dead Forest. She steps calmly onto the orphanage porch as another screech rings out. "I see we have begun," she says to herself. She leans against the brick pillar and sips her hot brown water from her mug. Children stand behind her in the doorway, looking out.

Director Marguerite points into the orphanage and yells something through gritted teeth. Moments later, Bridget runs out, sprinting off down the street and yelling something about her elderly mother, home alone. Director Marguerite barely glances back before strolling in the opposite direction toward the Center of Banishment, mug still in hand, leaving the orphanage door and gate wide open.

Another Cascabel child staggers over the bridge back into town. When it's not Gabi, at first, I'm happy, thinking she's made it over the ridge before the wyrms were summoned. Through the dust and smoke, more orphans enter, linked together, holding hands.

The dirty air clouds an approaching small figure that pulls another child along. The bigger Cascabel coughs, covering their face with their elbow. The dust clears.

"Gabi!" I call over a wyrm screech.

Gabi stops, jerking the hiccupping boy to a halt. She drops his hand and stares at me. She puts her hand to her mouth and runs barreling into me. It takes me a second to catch my breath. I feel her shaking as I wrap my arms around her. Her head is buried in my neck, sobbing. Tears, and I'm pretty sure snot, dribble down my neck. "You're alive."

"I have you," I whisper. I push her back from me. She doesn't look hurt. "You didn't run up the ridge, Gabi."

She looks at the little boy, wiping across her nose with her arm. "I couldn't."

I nod. "Bueno," I say. "You did the right thing."

The little boy approaches nervously. Gabi wipes her eyes and face on my tunic. Her words are mumbled. "Director Marguerite said you were dead," she sniffs. "And that it was my fault."

"It's okay, Gabi. I'll never leave you again."

Her eyes dart back and forth between my good eye and the bandage.

"Just a scratch," I lie.

Gabi's eyes widen, and she pulls away from me, running toward the orphanage.

"Hey!" I run after.

She stands on her tiptoes and reaches into the book drop, grabbing a handful of our stags.

By the time I reach her, she's shoving a second handful into her pocket. Bronze beetles fall from her stuffed hand and clank on the porch. She bends down to grab them, and I pull her up.

"We don't need those anymore."

She turns to face me. Tiny lines squiggle over her trembling chin. "We don't?"

Without Director Marguerite watching, several orphans are now wandering in the street in front of the building, with the wyrms just outside the city. They should be inside. But I realize, they won't ever be safe if I leave them here either. If they have any chance at all, they must come with us.

I see Vincent, who we used to know from the fields and the Pox.

"We are leaving Pocatel now. Together."

He looks as surprised as I did the first day I saw him at the orphanage, alive, and with both his kidneys. His eyes widen.

He looks at the open door and gate just as another wyrm screech rings out. Then another. I have never seen more than two spirals before. But behind the two now approaching the bridge there are at least another five others behind them. I don't have time to explain what the wyrms really are. It doesn't matter. Monster or machine, they can still kill.

"Our only chance to survive is together," I yell out. Vincent starts gathering the kids and pulling them into the yard.

Gabi pulls the little boy in front of me. "Leandro, this is Andrew. And we're keeping him." She puts her arm around him and juts out her chin.

I let out a deep sigh. "He's not a pet, Gabi."

The boy's eyes well up with tears. I see him grip her pale green tunic with his tiny hand. I think of his mother, shivering naked, walking into the cold night without food or water, just trying to buy him more time. I will find a way to tell him just how brave Celia was.

"I remember you, Andrew." I pat his shoulder. "I just meant . . ."

Now *his* chin is trembling.

"I meant you're not a pet," I say. "But yeah, we're keeping you."

A tear drops down his face and he hiccups.

"It's okay. You have us now. You don't have to be sad anymore."
I ruffle his hair. "Unless you need to."

He takes a deep breath and lifts his chin. One final, tiny hiccup sneaks out.

Just then, the first spiral within the wyrmstorm finally stops at the bridge. The dust clears, the wind blowing it north, until the moon reflects on a monstrous metallic head. And then the body. And then, behind it, a line of shadowed giants writhing forward, one after the other, until an army of wyrms lie behind the leader.

The Imperator was right. In the dark of night, no one will know what they truly are. With a screech of metal, the first wyrm moves slowly forward. Then the scream of metal on wood pierces our ears as its body slides over the bridge. Just like the wyrm in the Monger's home, its dead black eyes glisten. Its tail thrashes back and forth, pushing it over the bridge and onto Pocatel's main street. The moon casts shadows from its spikes in our direction. More than ten wyrms move inside the city—then at once, they all go completely still.

I take Gabi's and Andrew's hands and we race down the street toward Selah, Jovi, Ari and the others.

I look back as the Trench bridge rises behind the final wyrms, sealing us in. Some of the wyrms have already turned to the east. Some to the west. Just like the fish trap made of rocks in La Cuna's river, I realize they have used the wyrms to gather us into one spot. My spine freezes. The air hums with the unmistakable squeal of the wyrms as they slither slowly now along the edges of Pocatel. The rasp of their bodies, scraping the surface of the streets, hisses like a whisper in my ears. *We are coming.*

As we approach the group of Cascabeles waiting to be Thinned, the guards don't stop us from joining. I hurry to find Selah, Dolores, Ari, and Jovi. A tiny old woman stands with Jovi. She holds his hand and pats his face over and over, like she's making sure he's real.

Along with the addition of the orphans are more Pocatelans. The Pocatelans look bewildered at all that's happening and how they came to be clumped together with us. Most just stare now at the shadowy masses at the opposite end of the main street.

"Why have they stopped?" Jovi asks.

"Because they no longer need to rush," I say. "There's nowhere for us to go. We're trapped."

A flash of the Monger's home disappearing into the sand enters my mind. But we don't lie over a sinking pit. How will they make so many of us disappear at once?

A wyrm drone now blocks the entrance to the Dead Forest behind us. We can't escape that way.

In the other direction lies only . . . the Trench. Suddenly I understand.

Once again, I feel powerless to do anything. We are going to lose everything because we are too small and weak to fight. I squeeze the hummingbird in my pocket. And then, like a flash through my mind . . .

"*The smallest flap of wings can change the course of history.*"

Suddenly, the words make perfect sense.

I pull the hummingbird drone and the Spark tool out of my pocket. "I have to go back," I say.

34

SELAH'S HANDS SHAKE AS SHE LIGHTS A CANDLE. SHE glances to where Ari is talking to Gabi, keeping her distracted.

A full moon shines down on Pocatel through a veil of smoke and dust. It's so quiet. We crouch on the ground, others crowded around where the guards can't see. "Hurry, please," I beg.

Dolores lifts the surgical tool from my hand. Her blue eyes glisten with tears. "Leandro..."

I lay my hummingbird drone on the ground next to her. "Please."

Jovi has never sounded this angry. "You should've told me, Leandro." He points toward the Center of Banishment. "I left myself under the cot in that room!"

"You wouldn't have fit in my pocket," I mumble.

Jovi says a word Tía Lula would've slapped me for saying, and storms out of the pock.

Dolores shakes her head, looking at the end of the surgical instrument. "I cannot say I agree with this." She holds the instrument at the base of my nose. She slides it up, and I already feel the Spark moving. My eye throbs. I grit my teeth and squeeze my fist, trying not to move.

A warm hand lays over my fist, and I look up to see Selah.

Maybe I screwed up. I may not be enough on my own . . .

I grab Dolores's wrist with my other hand. "Wait!"

I turn to Selah. This may be our only chance. "Remember what you said about us . . . speed and stealth?"

She tilts her head. "Yeah, but that was—"

"I need you to do something for me."

JUST LIKE BEFORE, lights flash and the world goes black. The pain in my eye is gone. My stomach no longer cramps from hunger.

Gabi stares down, nostrils flared at my lifeless human body. Then she stares at me, her eyes wide.

I hover to meet her gaze. "I'm fine," I say. "Please don't worry." But she can't hear a single word. How can I explain that I'm still me?

Gabi points to me as I hover in front of her. "He's in there?"

"He can understand what you say, but cannot talk back," Dolores tells her.

A tear streaks down Gabi's dusty face. Her words come out choked between breaths. "You promised you wouldn't leave again."

Gabi glares at me. Selah hooks her arm over her shoulders.

"That *is* Leandro. He didn't leave you. He's right here. He just needs to do something very important."

She smiles at Gabi, and Gabi narrows her eyes. "Where? How long?"

"He will be right back," Selah says. "That is the amazing thing about us now. We can be both." She leans in whispering in Gabi's ear. "And this Leandro is going on a mission. The sooner he gets back, the sooner we can go."

Gabi falls into Selah, hugging her. Selah flinches back at first, then makes a shooing motion at me. *Go*, she mouths.

I do a quick loop, hovering next to Gabi, and flutter my wings gently on her cheek. I do the same to Selah and she swats at me. I take off and glance back. Gabi doesn't look happy, but the tears have stopped.

I hover above the center of Pocatel. From here I see eight wyrms lined up in two rows at the Trench. One at the entrance to the Dead Forest and a few more around the edges of town.

The wyrms near the bridge begin to move forward down the center of the main street. One at a time, they split off disappearing down side streets. I fly over them until I near the Trench.

Wind rushes in gusts, blowing my tiny body from side to side. I fly higher to get above solid ground where the air is calmer. But in the darkness below is the open Trench and its gorge of jagged metal. The group of Cascabeles, orphans, and unlucky Pocatelans are still where I left them in the center of town. I don't want to imagine what I know the Imperator has planned.

It's near the market stands where I finally see them: the Mongers. There are at least as many of them as there are wyrms. They are hidden in the shadows of the stalls and between buildings where the Pocatelan people won't see them. They hold the same black control boxes I saw in Nathaniel's home. I fly into a stall where one Monger hides. He glances back at me, but quickly shakes his head and turns back to his box.

I fly between two buildings and land on a broken brick.

A woman points in my direction. "Did you see that?" she calls out.

Another Monger leans out. "Just a flying beetle."

I hold completely still.

"Then why is it not leaving?" she says, aiming the gun at me. This gun is far larger than the field guard's gun. The Monger has to hold it with her two hands. "There!"

The man next to her pushes the barrel down.

"What are you doing? You do not know how to use—"

I zip out of their line of sight. From high above I study the scene. From the narrow window of Dolores's lab, a small figure leaps, then darts away. She did what I asked! But wait . . . it's too small to be Selah. Who then?

I move toward it to see Gabi running from the building back toward the Pox, Dolores's surgical tool in her hand. What is she doing?!

Seconds later, a yellow triangle and a familiar *tick, tick, tick* grows stronger, just before a whoosh and hawk drone swoops next to me. "Hey," Selah says.

"What was that?" I hope she senses the anger in my voice. "Why would you send my little sister in there! I only asked you to—"

"I did what you asked. And I know how to get around this city unnoticed. Besides, Gabi and I made a deal." She flies closer. "We thought you could use the help."

I back away from her. Selah's body must be back inside the room where we left her drone, with the rest of the Cloaks, and now she's in even more danger. "You should go back to your mom."

"I do this to make sure I can go back to her—and get you back to your sister."

Gabi waves at us as she runs back into the Pox.

"So, you told me part of your plan. But how are we going to stop the wyrms?" she asks.

It's no use fighting her. "There." I push a wing toward two Mongers holding black control boxes. "If we can take the

Mongers out, they won't be able to control the wyrms." I nod toward the open Trench. "And I think I know what they plan to do."

Selah tilts her head at me. "*That* is the plan?" She sighs. "I suppose it is better than doing nothing." Just like when we saw the strange lights in the Outlands, Selah aims her beak toward the Mongers. Just as if I were at the market, I scout below for another target.

Selah doesn't even give me time to lock on to one. She tips her wing and dives like an arrow. She swoops so close to the two of them I'm sure they feel the wind on their faces. Confused, the Mongers place their backs to one another.

Selah is already diving again.

The Monger points her weapon at Selah. "*That* was definitely not a flying beetle." She pulls the trigger, the *boom* vibrating my body, pellets sizzling through the air around us. Selah soars upward. I see the man train his weapon directly at her this time. *Boom.*

In the confusion, I lose track of Selah. I fly toward the orphanage and take cover under the porch. When the shooting stops, I search for her signal, then call out, "Selah!"

"Up here," she calls back.

I look up and see her shadow in the crook of a dead oak tree's branches.

"Are you hurt?" I ask.

"No," Selah says. "But this is going to be harder than I thought. How's your plan?"

I desperately search for any other help, but there is only her.

The Imperator storms out of the Center of Banishment, the Director of Truth behind.

"What are you doing!" the Imperator yells out, staring at the Monger whose gun still points upward. "Stop shooting! You will call attention to—" He stares down the darkened street at the crowd of people, then into the sky, searching.

He places his hand on the Director of Truth's shoulder. "You trained the Mongers, yes?"

He nods.

"So, they are under your watch?"

"Yes, Imperator."

"Then get them under control, and begin the next phase."

"Now? But—"

"Yes! Now." He continues to scan the sky as he turns to walk away. "Make it swift. And no more shooting without my order!" He looks from side to side at the windows of the Pocatelan homes. "We cannot afford attention."

Like he's puppeteering at market, the Director of Truth darts into the shadows where the Mongers are hidden with the control boxes. Within moments, the wyrms come to life. From the opposite side of town, there is a mix of metallic screeches, clouds of dusts, and . . . the screams of Cascabeles.

"Bring out the Cloaks," the Imperator calls out to the Patrol. Several guards quickly dash into the Center of Banishment.

I imagine the guards passing over the black floor of the hall of drones, crunching over the bodies of the smashed drones, down the dark hallway, until they find the human bodies of Wolf, Charlie, Oso, Hopper, even Selah . . .

I feel as sick as when I watched Gabi steal the strawberry.

"What do we do?" Selah asks. "I don't think the two of us are enough."

This may not work, but if Selah did what I actually asked . . .

I try to reach out, but find nothing. "Are you sure you were you able to—"

"Yes!" she yells. "I did it, Leandro."

"Then if it works, soon we will be enough."

"But why is it taking so long?" she asks. "Maybe they're too far away."

And like sand pouring over my hand, it begins. I catch only one grain at first. "I've got one!" I yell.

I hurry to connect with the other hummingbird drone. Its view inside the hall of drones becomes my view. I control the new body to speed out of the Center of Banishment toward the street to join me. Another signal flashes up—this one a bee. With it I do the same. In seconds, thousands of familiar yellow triangles appear, all invitations to connect. I collect the grains of sand, one by one.

Like with the wyrm, I am myself—and them—at the same time. All of them. Even more thousands of signals appear, and I connect to all, countless pollinator views coming to life. Like a wall of thousands of eyes, we rise.

35

· · · ☾ · · ·

CLOUDS OF POLLINATOR DRONES SWARM THE NIGHT
sky in my hummingbird's view. In others, I am the swarm.

The door to the Center of Banishment opens. The Cloaks
emerge, followed by as many guards who herd them toward
the Trench. Within the group of Cloaks, I see Selah's human
body.

"Leandro!" Selah yells.

The guards lead the Cloaks closer and closer until they stand near the edge of the Thinning abyss. The green robes of the Cloaks blow in the Trench's wind gusts. One wrong step . . .

The Imperator walks toward the guards, handing them each one the end of a rope. "We must bind the impediments which bind us," he calls out.

The guards, each holding one end of the ropes, walk to either side of the road. The Imperator nods at them, and they all take a step toward the Trench, pulling the Cloaks closer to the edge with the ropes. The Cloaks don't resist at all.

Selah lunges forward. "What are they doing?"

The Imperator might speak the strange words of a Pocatelan, but even I know what's happening.

"Again!" the Imperator yells.

Some of the guards, faces ashen, take hesitant steps.

I hear panic in Selah's voice for the first time. "Leandro! Hurry!"

"Almost there . . ." I whisper.

A few of the guards glance at one another, their eyes tormented as they walk the Cloaks closer. I think of what he said to them all. "*You need only obey my command without question, and I assure you, you and your families will be rewarded.*" I can tell by their faces they know what they're doing is wrong. Are the other guards, herding their own people with the Cascabeles, feeling the same? What about those guarding those Cascabeles and orphans? The panicked screams from the direction of the center of town continue.

I pull every last drone I can to join us. The night sky masks the pollinators' approach, but the air vibrates with the hum of the incoming swarm.

Gathering a swarm of bees, I fly in. I form a protective fence around the Cloaks. The guards stop, staring at the buzz of drones they now face. I move the drones against the Cloaks bodies, pushing them all, including Selah, away from the Trench's ledge. 82% flashes in front of me.

The Imperator runs toward them but I block him, sending bees directly at his stag-bronze eyes.

One of the guards thrusts his hand toward the Cloaks, and he's greeted with hundreds of metal stingers to his hands and face. Tiny pinpoints of blood dot his skin. He flails his arms, dropping the rope. His eyes widen as he stumbles, falling into the Trench. Barely a strangled yelp escapes his lips.

The remaining Patrol watch in horror. Most drop their ropes and sprint away back into neighborhoods. The Imperator screams after, but they don't turn back. I send a few of my army to follow so they don't return. One guard runs into the Center of Banishment. I track as he runs through the building, into the Banishment room and out its back door. He runs over the exile trail and its metal walkway to escape Pocatel. The remaining guards see it too, and follow after.

The Imperator rushes out. "Cowards!" he yells. He approaches the Cloaks, arms extended. I send the hummingbirds after him. Beaks jab his hands and face. He throws his robe over his face for protection. But I continue.

With my army of bees, I ease the Cloaks far from the Trench, toward the Center of Banishment. I don't stop until they are safely in their room, a solid wall of buzzing protection sealing them in at the door.

Like a spreading infestation, the screeches of wyrms from all directions of the city is followed by the screams of people. Within seconds, I send thousands more bees to where the Mongers are hidden in market stalls. I attack over and over. The Mongers scatter in all direction, some dropping their controls. The screams of the people in the city lessen. When the Mongers try to pick the controllers back up, I sting their faces. Now they are the ones screaming, cowering on the ground, and covering their heads with their arms. One by one, the confused Mongers stumble to their feet and run. Two escape inside the Center of Banishment just like the guards, and when they reappear from the back of the building at the black exile door, they follow the same path the guards had, over the rickety metal footbridge and out of Pocatel. The wind blows one man off balance. He clings to the edge as the other Monger behind him balances on the swaying walkway. The balancing Monger barely makes it across, then helps hoist the man up on the other side.

The three Mongers left stare up at the swarms, still working their controls determinedly, huddling together in stalls. The Imperator tries to emerge, flinging his cloak to bat down the hummingbirds, but I don't let up in my attack on him.

The Director of Truth emerges from the Center of Banishment and darts into a stall, snatching the gun of a Monger. The approaching black cloud of drones grows larger and darker. Selah joins my swarm above him. "I see you," the puppeteer yells up at the sky. "You think your facade can work on someone like me?" With a thousand views, I watch as he takes aim directly at us.

I split the swarm outward where he aims, leaving only empty sky. Selah soars toward him and he runs.

I send a few hummingbirds to attack his face. Stumbling out of the shadows, he sprints down the street, Selah and the hummingbirds pelting his head as he goes. They all disappear into the dark.

In the distance, El Bastón emerges onto the main street. He hits his staff sharply with each step. Only four Patrol flank each side. Selah returns to circle over their heads like she is hunting prey. The Patrol who'd been guarding the Cascabeles run to join them.

I regroup the bees and hummingbirds I have left to surround these remaining guards of the Patrol. Any earlier commands now forgotten, they shoot wildly into the swarm. With each shot, dozens of hummingbird and bee drones plummet to the ground.

Each time a shot hits one of the drones, the blast jolts me as if it was myself. Thousands of times, I spiral downward, then black out. I disconnect from each as they fail. I'm forced to pull the other hummingbirds off the Imperator.

I strike El Bastón's Patrol as hard as I can with each one, stabbing with beaks and clawing with feet. I slice wings across their faces. In the second wave, the bees sting arms, cheeks, and eyes. 67%.

Finally, the butterflies and moths approach slowly from the Center of Banishment. They flutter around, harder to connect with than the other drones. A bunch stray off like a toddler at the market. I disconnect from them to conserve my charge.

The Imperator gawks at the sky with bewilderment as the guards keep firing.

Screams grow louder from down the street. A writhing line of three remaining wyrms finally push the Cascabeles, orphans, and the Pocatelans who now know the truth down the center of Pocatel, toward the Trench.

Losing my fastest drones, I'm forced to reconnect to the flood of moths and butterflies and direct them down onto those left holding guns, hoping to mask their lines of sight. I aim for their eyes, but a few of them miss the target and flutter down the barrels. I'm frustrated until I see one guard struggling to unjam his weapon. I watch as a single moth disappears down another. The guard pulls the trigger and the barrel ruptures, the gun exploding in his hands. He screams and clutches his face. I hurry to get ahold of every last moth and butterfly, aiming them into the guns. One after the other, the weapons explode, and the remaining Patrol run away injured and confused.

Any guards who haven't run or crawled away now lie motionless in the street.

El Bastón stares down the street at the Imperator, then at his own Patrol lying around him. He shakes his head, and lowers his gun. Then he walks slowly down the street alone. He turns into one of the largest homes, its windows now dark.

Hundreds of signals suddenly disappear from my sync, and I see a group of hummingbirds rallying around Selah.

"You did it!" I yell, but Selah doesn't respond, collecting her troops to attack the final Mongers as the crowd of people pushed by the wyrms grows closer and closer to the Trench. She pelts their heads over and over. Two Mongers drop their controls, and their wyrms squeal to a halt. These Mongers flee back into the shadows between the buildings.

The remaining Monger presses frantically on his controller as an errant moth flies inside his gaped mouth. He releases the controller, his hand in his mouth, trying to retrieve the moth. The wyrm halts. The people stop, confused. A few try to run past. The Monger gags, gasping for air, spitting metal wings out of his mouth. The Imperator appears suddenly, grabbing the black box from the man and shoving him aside, regaining control.

As the Imperator takes control, the wyrm drone rears its head and makes a squeal so loud, the silence that follows is even more frightening. Its neck rises just as the wyrm's had with Celia. People run ahead as its gaping maw slams into the earth— for now, its reaper empty. With a vibrating *clink, clink, clink*, it shifts back and forth, driving the people once again toward the Trench.

The Imperator yells at the retreating Monger. "Fight with me today, and tomorrow I will make you a Director!"

The Monger smiles a greedy grin and runs back to pick up an abandoned controller. Within seconds, one of the dormant wyrms screeches back to life, making two.

The Monger rejoins the Imperator, standing at his side. His greed clouds the obvious—I know the Imperator has no intention of letting him live, when he might brag of what he's done here today. But for now, the two remaining wyrms thrash down the center of Pocatel, sending the Cascabeles and trapped Pocatelans fleeing in the direction of the Trench once more. A Pocatelan family splinters from the group, and one of their wyrms follows, herding them back.

Selah divebombs the Monger over and over, but his desire is too strong. Blood trickles off his chin.

The Imperator slams on his controller, and the largest wyrm disappears under the earth.

I attack his gloved hands, hundreds of bees piercing through the leather, then his face, but he doesn't even flinch.

24%. I can't stop for water now.

The rushing mound of earth barrels down the center of town. Ahead, the Trench waits for them, and I can do nothing to stop it.

The heaving ground suddenly stills, and the rumble grows quieter. The crowd stops. The ground under them rumbles as the wyrm passes beneath.

Selah and I gather all we have left for a group attack.

"Steady!" the Imperator calls out.

The Monger widens his stance.

"Now!" Selah calls, and we dive toward the two men.

The Imperator makes a harsh movement with his controller.

Just as we approach, the Imperator's wyrm erupts from the ground, lunging upward with a shriek. I bolt straight up to safety, but Selah barely darts to one side, spiraling out of control as its jaw hits her wing. Mouth open, the wyrm crashes through the swarm, taking out half the drones we have left. The Monger shields his heads from a hail of dead drones falling from the sky. The wyrm lands with a crash. Dirt explodes into the sky. Windows from the closest building shatter. Selah's hawk body spirals down, regaining control just before she hits the ground.

The Monger's wyrm disappears too, and barrels just below the surface, chasing the screaming crowd faster ahead. Pathways and widows crack. The main street of Pocatel is destroyed in seconds.

Selah and I struggle to regain control of any remaining drones.

Even from here, I see the fear on the faces of both Cascabeles and Pocatelans. The wyrms have done exactly what they were designed to do for all these years: make them afraid.

Then I realize, *The wyrms aren't our enemies.* Why am I fighting them? I search desperately for their signals in the confusion, and I find them too.

Just like with Nathaniel's wyrm, it's like trying to collect water with an open hand. I focus harder and one connects, only to slip away again. I try again and grasp one, then the next . . .

17% flashes in front of me.

I halt the Imperator's wyrm and then turn the Monger's slowly, pulling it back above the surface. I wait and let the shocked Cascabeles and others who were trapped run away from the danger. Now in control of everything, I combine the wyrm, the bees, and the hummingbirds to form a solid wall. As one, we move together down the street. With the view of thousands, I see the confused Monger push on a wyrm control that no longer responds. He runs away, controller in hand, leaving the Imperator alone.

The Imperator drops his controller and lets out an unearthly growl. He stomps on the black box, fists clenched at his side. His slicked-back hair is in strands over his sweaty face now, his dried-blood robe covered in pale dust.

I use my wall of drones like a giant hand to shove the Imperator. He sneers, but is forced to step back. I continue until he is trapped at the Trench's edge.

13%.

In all the chaos, I still don't release my wall of bees guarding the Cloaks inside their room. So many drones tied to my signal is draining the life from me, and there's no time for water.

"Selah!" I call out.

The Imperator punches at the drones around him. With each strike, they fly away before his fist makes contact. After six failed punches, he stops. He drops his hands to his sides and flexes his fingers outward over and over. He lets his head fall backward. This is it. We won.

I disconnect from all of my remaining drones but one. I approach the Imperator with only my hummingbird body and his wyrm, until he can reach out and touch it. The mound of earth it creates is so close, he must smell it. But he doesn't run like his Mongers, or the guards, or even the fellow Directors.

I fly closer and closer, until I know he can see me.

9%.

The Imperator limps forward, smiling. "Defiant to the last, Mr. Rivera. Yes, I knew it must have been you who Nathaniel found." His smile drops and his voice is a growl. "Serpents like you were meant to live beneath our feet," he hisses at me. "And we were meant to Preserve what our forefathers intended for this world. If you will not stay down, so that we may one day set that in motion, even now we shall show your people the way back underground." He smiles, and dirt coats his teeth. "What will you do, little bird?" He's still flexing his hands at his side.

I fly closer. He can say whatever he wants. My insides are soaring in triumph. "I will give you a reminder of how the smallest united to defeat you," I reply. I am so close I can hear the wheezing through his nostrils. I flick his cheek with my wing, leaving a tiny scratch and a trail of blood.

I am already zipping away, but in an instant, his hand is gripped around me. My body quivers inside his clenched and trembling fist. I frantically push the wyrm toward him . . . toward myself. But I realize I have no choice: I can't let him escape and hurt anyone else. The Imperator teeters on the edge of the Trench. His eyes stare at me wildly. He lifts me in front of him and wraps one hand on my body, the other on my head.

He smiles, bending my head to one side. I lose connection with the wyrm.

This is it. Soon Gabi will hear I've broken my promise. I'm not coming back.

The Imperator takes a step away from the edge and laughs.

I hope Gabi will understand I did what I could to protect her and my people. Some may be able to escape now. There is no way he can hide this commotion—this . . . bedlam—from all his people. Selah was right.

I hear the metal in my neck begin to crack. A flash of Tía Lula breaking off the head of that first Alebrije flashes in my mind.

A whistle so loud it vibrates my body shoots past me. Like an arrow, a dark streak—with a delivery-hawk emblem on its side—pierces the night, crashing into the Imperator's chest. He releases me, throwing his arms out to his sides in an attempt to catch his balance. His wide eyes stare at me in disbelief as he stumbles backward into the Trench. I fall with him, then buzz upward.

I stare in shock as dust flies off his robe and the Imperator disappears in the darkness.

Something small and black soars through the air past him.

I search the sky above, and hurry to reconnect. "*Selah!*" I call out. But there are only fluttering moths and butterflies— no hawk.

I use every drone view to search. The group of Cascabeles, orphans, and Pocatelans are still partway down the street, next to the dormant wyrm. The streets are littered with fallen drones, a few motionless Mongers, guards, and their weapons. Then, as I hover above, with my own eyes, I spot a dark hobbling figure with a vivid red stripe down its tail. The delivery drone symbol of the black arrow pierces the purple circle on its body. Selah hobbles toward me and I fly toward her as fast as I can. As I approach, I see that her right wing is twisted. But that isn't what terrifies me.

Her Spark compartment is open and it's empty.

36

"... THIRTY SECONDS. THAT IS ALL. YOU DO NOT HAVE TIME *beyond that,*" Dolores had said.

"Noooo!" I scream, flying over the Trench. I shift from side to side in the wind, staring down into darkness, desperately searching for Selah's missing Spark.

Thirty seconds. Thirty seconds.

"Leandro, it is too late," Selah calls.

In barely a second, I've flown thirty meters below. But Selah's right: I'll never find it in the pitch black, twisted mass of metal at the bottom of the Trench. Even the Imperator's body has already been swallowed by the abyss. It would take me winters to find her Spark, and I have only seconds left with her.

I fly back through a cloud of dust and land beneath Selah. Her powerful body is twisted and broken from saving us . . . from saving me.

My voice is small. Too small for how strong I should be in this moment. "Selah?"

For once, her voice sounds happy . . . hopeful, even. "You did it, Leandro. You saved everyone," she says.

"We did it," I reply.

"Yeah . . . we."

Footsteps approach, and we both turn to see a woman in a purple robe running frantically in our direction. She stops, seeing Selah's human body standing with the other Cloaks.

"Oh no," Selah says, her voice shaky.

She has to know she only has seconds. She watches as Dolores walks slowly toward her Cloak.

Selah stares at Dolores and speaks calmly. "Please . . . please tell her that I do love her, and I am so sorry I did not return when I should have. Tell her . . . tell her she was right to send me away. I was still myself. I was as alive and happy in this body as my human body." Selah lets out a contented sigh. "She had hope we would find family we could trust in this life." Selah turns her gaze to me. "Leandro, tell her I did find—"

Selah's Alebrije eyes flicker off as her Spark fades forever.

"Selah?" I tap her with my beak. "Selah . . . !" I search for her signal, but there is nothing.

An anguished cry fills the air behind me. I turn to see Dolores holding Selah's collapsed body in her arms. She kneels on the ground, rocking the lifeless Cloak, blonde curls spilling over her green robe like the rumbling water of the river in La Cuna.

Gabi and I always muffled our crying so no one would know our pain. Even from Gabi, I hid my tears in our pock. But here, where no one can hear me, I don't have to.

Dolores struggles to draw breaths through her wails. She screams, staring at me, her face pale.

As Dolores rocks the human girl, I lay on the only Selah I've ever known, and rest my metal head on her chest.

37

··· ☽ ···

UNDER A MASK OF DARKNESS, NOT A SINGLE LAMP IS
lit inside the city. Jovi pushes a vial of water onto my beak. I
peck him, drawing blood. He forces me to drink.

"I'm sorry," he says.

Gabi wraps Selah in a tunic and cradles the metal hawk in
her arms.

Jovi walks cautiously to Dolores and takes Selah's human body
from her. He holds her in his arms, carrying her toward the Pox.

I turn to see Gabi's mouth is ajar. "Leandro?"

I back up. I understand now why Ezra needed to be alone.

"Leandro!" Gabi calls after me as I speed toward the Dead Forest.

I think of flying back to La Cuna right now. I wouldn't have the pain of my human body. But I can't escape this kind of pain in either one.

I am Leandro, no matter if I'm human or drone. And like Selah found out too late, I can't leave behind those I love. The pain will follow me no matter where I go. No matter how hard my mind tries to forget.

I sit atop the Tree of Souls. There is no smell of pine.

JUST AS THE first rays of dawn break over the ridge, Jovi finds me. A tiny clot of blood dots his thumb where my beak entered. Still, he gives me a small smile. "Ready to come back?"

"*You have one thousand and eighty-nine days remaining in your sentence.*"

I nod, and he nods back, like nothing happened. We find Ari and the two of them put me back in my human body.

Near the Tree of Souls, we all meet again. Jovi lowers Selah's drone next to her human body. I've never seen him so steady. Dolores ties a strand of Selah's hair and a strip of brown cloth from what must have been her school robe to the tree. "Protect us, little hawk," she whispers.

Gabi arcs her foot out in a Cascabel C. "*Tccch, tccch, tccch.*" She lifts her arms, and Ari steps forward, doing the same, arcing her foot in a C on the other side of the grave. We enclose Selah in a circle of blessing. Even Jo and other Cascabeles who'd never met her join to say goodbye to the Alebrije who helped save them.

We bury three Pocatelans and four Cascabeles more, crushed alongside one another in the chaos, and send them all off with a blessing too.

Wind blows through the forest. Just like the others tethered above in the tree, the reminders of Selah blow in the breeze like the leaves that once covered this tree. It's beautiful.

38

WITH THE POX IN ASHES, THE CASCABELES HAVE NOTH-
ing left.

Having gathered and buried our dead, we find the controllers and send all but one wyrm into the Trench, along with
every weapon we can find.

The Cascabeles gather in the fields, collecting papas and fruit,
beetles and larvas for our journey. Already, whispers of La Cuna

are spreading amongst the people in the fields faster than the fire had in the Pox.

Jovi, Ari, and I sit in a circle planning our departure. A few other Cascabeles join us. And then four of the Pocatelan families who were trapped with us in the night approach the edges of the Pox nervously.

A man with the rough-woven robe of a metalsmith speaks first. "Forgive the interruption." He pulls a child closer to him. "Some of us have decided we cannot stay in Pocatel with what we have seen . . . what we now know. . . . It is said you will leave soon for a new settlement." He clears his throat, and looks back to the others with him. "We are not strangers to hard work, and we ask humbly if you would allow us to travel with you on your journey."

Just like that, we gain eighteen more.

Most of the Pocatelans who were hiding in the Dead Forest return. A few are exiting their homes. They look confused, staring at the destruction. Others remain inside their homes, shutters latched and doors bolted and locked.

Mongers have begun reentering Pocatel and retaking homes that were once theirs. Even with the role they played, I don't really blame them. I think of what they endured and wonder what promises the Regime made them.

Jovi points down the street. "Mira."

In the chaos, the puppeteer and his wife zigzag through the crowds into the Center of Banishment. He holds the door open as two more Directors and their families follow inside.

On the porch of his home, El Bastón strikes a Monger trying to get in with his stick. She's joined by others, and they rip the staff from his hand, pushing him out of his house and into the streets. The Pocatelan Regime will receive what they created, I think. Soon, maybe all the Directors' deceptions will be uncovered. They are the ones who've trained their citizens to have no mercy for lies.

Jovi and I lead a group to the Center of Banishment to collect the Cloaks and gather water for our trip. Jovi pries open the front door with a broken gun barrel.

We are met with darkness, cool air, and the smell of lamp oil, though not a single lamp in the main hall is lit.

The hidden door in the hallway clicks shut just as we enter. I nudge Jovi and point to it. We tiptoe closer. I place my ear to the door and hear whispers from within, but the Directors hiding inside don't dare come out and try to stop us.

I imagine the conversation inside as the "Director of Truth" tries desperately to plan how they'll explain the lifeless metal wyrm left near the Trench, and the drones spread across Pocatel: "We will say that we have been fooled! Old-World technology lives and must be stopped! All Pocatelan citizens must unite against this outside force that would destroy us . . . Preservation above all!"

But the puppeteer's lies won't be able to move quicker than the truth that now flies through the streets of Pocatel.

Quickly and quietly, we move the remaining sixteen Cloaks to the safety of our group first. Walking in and out of the building, we fill enough watercells to last every one of us a month. Jovi exits with the last of the watercells and his great horned raptor drone under his arm. "Just in case," he says under his breath.

In less than two hours, Cascabeles have dug enough healthy potatoes and gathered enough grubs and other food for our journey. The four Pocatelan families have returned from their own homes where they've gathered more supplies.

When Dolores is done examining the last of the Cloaks—a thin Cascabel with freckles, who won't stop wandering off—she leads me to a wall stacked with medical supplies. Her face is puffy and blotched.

"Leandro, you kept your promise to me, and gave me my daughter back." Her eyes fill with tears. "Thank you."

I want to yell at this woman. I want to tell her that she should've guarded her daughter more carefully this time. I want to yell that I brought her back to her, and she just let her sneak away to fight. But I know it's not her fault. I want to yell at myself too. I am the one who asked Selah to spray water over the pollinators and bring them back to life. If I hadn't asked her to do that—

My chin starts to tremble like Gabi's does, and I turn my face.

"I am sorry it wasn't the way we hoped." She pulls a bottle from the tub. "I know she was your friend."

I don't know how to explain to her that I'm not even sure *what* I was to Selah. But we came to understand each other, and in the end, she said . . .

Dolores unties the green strip of cloth from my eye. She bites her lip and looks away.

I wince at the smell.

"Okay," she goes on, opening a bottle. "Let us make sure it doesn't get infected." She pulls out a clean white patch and places it over my eye. It stings, but I try not to flinch. I can see the panic on her face as she looks for something to secure the bandage with.

I pull out my strip of cloth and smile. "I got it," I say, tying it back around my head.

"I am sorry." Her hands tremble as she screws the lid back on the antiseptic. "I cannot save it."

I wink my other eye and try to smile. "I have another."

She doesn't smile back.

"Leandro," she says, her eyes filling with tears. "I am not going with you."

"What do you mean?" I ask.

"I mean, I am staying here."

I look up at her. "That's not what Selah died for. She would want you to have what we have."

Dolores shakes her head. "I have spent my whole life not helping those I should have. For what remains of it, I must stay to pay my penance. Confession and sorrow are insufficient. I do not expect you to understand." She puts her hand on my cheek and smiles. Her eyes fill with tears again. "I do not think one such as yourself, someone like Selah, could understand my misdeeds. I am glad my daughter found someone more like herself . . . the family she deserved."

. . .

ALL OF US Cascabeles walk down the center of Pocatel toward the Trench.

When we pass the Center of Banishment, a group of Pocatelans are entering the front entrance door. "None of the Directors are in their homes!"

"A dung beetle can hide, but his smell will expose his burrow," a man with a red face wearing a smelting bib yells. "Come out cowards!"

Just as we are a safe distance away, the familiar sound of the secret door opening is followed by screams and yelling.

We continue on, passing other Pocatelans who wander aimlessly in their destroyed town. They glance over, but don't stop us as we pass, even when they must see many of their own have joined our group.

Down the street near the Trench lies a large crowd of Pocatelans. Ari squeezes my arm and Jovi and I exchange a look, but continue on.

We approach the orphanage. Two children in green tunics peer over the fence of the enclosed yard. Director Marguerite stands at the front entrance, Bridget behind her. "Children, children. Come back inside," she begs. "As always, it is my duty to watch over you!" Her voice shakes as she stares down the street at the Directors being dragged from the Center of Banishment.

"Do not move from where you are," I call out to the children.

"We don't live there anymore!" Gabi yells, pulling open the gate. Kids, Cascabel and Pocatelan alike, run out of the orphanage enclosure to join us.

Franco and four other men lower the Trench bridge. The sun will be full in the sky in less than an hour, and we need to be as far away as possible, before every Pocatelan discovers how deep the deception has been. We can't know what will follow.

The Imperator's single lifeless wyrm drone still lies ahead. While others watch, a smith runs his hand over it, his head tilted in confusion. "It is indeed metal." He pulls a panel off its tail. He tries to bend it, then sets it in the road and hits it with his mallet over and over. The pitch is different than the usual *clink, clink*. "But this metal is an ancient one. One smelted in the Old-World of Pocatel."

The crowd surrounding the dormant wyrm is larger than the busiest day at the market. We are leaving behind just what Selah had hoped. And maybe something better will emerge.

Some stare at us here, but still no one speaks. Even the Pocatelans traveling with us don't interact with them. I imagine they must be doubting all of what they've known. Who they can trust.

I take the first step over the windswept bridge holding tight to Gabi on one side, Andrew on the other. Ari locks arms with Jo behind us.

We walk down the center of the Trench bridge. *Don't look down. Don't look down.* But I can't help but glance at the spot where the Imperator fell. Where his body disappeared, I see nothing but darkness.

I take the final step off the bridge onto the other side. In what we once thought was the wyrmfield, we start loading the abandoned Mongers' wagons with enough food and water for the weeks of travel.

One more Monger's wagon approaches from across the wyrmfield. When the one-armed Monger arrives, she jumps from her wagon. "Abigail!" she screams.

A little girl with red spiraled curls, in a green tunic, rushes out and barrels into her.

A group of twenty or so Cascabel men are now gathered around the wagons, but instead of helping load, I see they still have their supplies in sacks strapped to their backs. The man doing all the talking is Franco.

"We can travel east faster on foot," Franco says. "We can be over the ridge in less than a day."

"Without enough food and water, you won't make it at all," I call to him. "You can't carry all you'll need. I know. I have—"

"Gracias for your concern," he replies, walking over to me, speaking loudly and looking so everyone can hear. "I don't know how to thank you for all you've done." Then Franco leans down and pushes his finger onto my forehead, lowering his voice. "But you still don't know when to shut up, chaparrito. We are Cascabel. We can forage and hunt."

Jovi steps between us. "You should listen. Leandro's been over the mountains most recently. There is nothing to forage. Your only hope is La Cuna." Jovi leans towards Franco. "Maybe *you're* the one who needs to shut up."

"I believe the boy!" Jo yells over them both. "I am following Leandro to La Cuna!"

"I will not follow him anywhere," Franco says. He turns around. "Who is with me?"

Many more gather around him than I would expect. I know I can't make them believe me. But still, I have to try.

"That is your pride talking, Franco," I say. "You can trust me. I tell the truth." I step closer to him. "If you come with us, we will still work the fields in La Cuna. But where we go, we will never steal from one another or fight for food again. We will return to how it was. How we were before we came to this place."

"*Pffft*," he replies, gathering what he can carry. As we watch, his large group follows him and Naji up the ridge. Maybe this is easier for Franco than admitting how he treated me. How he stole from me. Or maybe all those are so changed by Pocatel, they can't believe a place like La Cuna could be real anymore. Can't believe someone like me.

But the farther they walk into the Outlands, the less chance they all will have to survive.

I stand on the back of the wagon. Those of us left are not the biggest or the strongest. My voice shakes as I begin to speak.

"I am Leandro Rivera. And if you will trust me, I will lead you to La Cuna. The trip will not be easy." As I look at the crowd, I see that many of the Cascabeles wear half-burnt tunics. "There may be more hardships."

The people exchange looks. My legs are trembling, and I hope no one can tell. I slip my hand in my pocket and grip the hummingbird drone. Suddenly, I feel stronger.

"In this place . . . in Pocatel . . . I believe we forgot who we truly are."

I hear someone in the back hock a loogie and spit.

I ignore it and continue, "Just like our ancestors, none of us here are frightened by hard work. I think that will be true of our new family, too." I point to the Pocatelans, who smile nervously.

One of them steps forward. "Whatever you ask of our service, it is yours, Leandro Rivera."

Gabi laughs at my full name. I feel her fingers grip mine.

"Me too," Jovi yells. "I trust Leandro to lead us!"

Jo steps forward, his knees bloody. He smiles at me with his toothless grin. "I trust the small one too." He stands in front of me and turns to face the crowd. "*Tccch, tccch, tccch . . .*"

A few elders—the last few who still remain—step out from the crowd to join Jo, "*Tccch, tccch, tccch . . .*"

Then, one by one, the adults step forward too, each echoing their trill of confidence in me, "*Tccch, tccch, tccch . . .*"

Until in moments, the entire group, including the Pocatelans, have joined.

JO SITS HOLDING the reigns of one of the Monger's wagons. "I've found my father's wagon."

"¿Se llama Enrique, verdad?" I ask, looking around at all those finishing the prep of the wagons with us. Some make nervous glances back toward the city. But most are smiling and look excited.

"Yes," Jo responds, surprised. "You remembered. The wagon's name *is* Enrique."

"This is wonderful news, Jo," I say. "We are in need of this wagon to lead us to La Cuna."

Jo's face opens into a gaping toothless smile.

I continue, smiling. "And the tatara, tatara, tatara-nieto of the scout who first discovered it is just the right driver of this wagon."

"¡Por supuesto! I am an excellent driver," Jo answers, even though I'm pretty sure he's never driven one before.

Ari's agreed to ride with us. I will tell her of our new house soon, and hope she will be ready for a new family one day.

Jovi gives a thumbs-up and his wagon lurches forward, his abuelita at his side.

"This time, I am the scout," Gabi says to me as we climb in next to Jo. "Andrew, you are my assistant. I will need water and snacks."

Andrew nods, watercell in hand.

In a single line of wagons, we travel through the valley. I weave around the heaps of dirt left by the wyrms, trying not to think about what may lie beneath. I come to the mound I think might have been Celia's. I pull Andrew close to me and point away to the old highway. "That is where we are going."

He nods.

I don't know why I do it. I think I'm trying to protect him. Maybe sometimes the truth should stay hidden—and this mound of dirt is one of those truths. But one day, I will tell him of his mother's final moments in front of the Imperator. He will know how brave she was. He will know the truth.

Just as we reach the old highway, we're approached by three Pocatelan guards and five Mongers running from their city.

Gabi nudges me, her eyes wide. One of the Pocatelan guards breaks forward and nears Jovi and me at the front. The man lowers his head, but I recognize his pointed noise. He's the guard from the fields—the one who kicked dirt on me and called me a snake. The one who said we belonged in the dirt. The one who swore he saw me steal the strawberry.

He raises his head and looks me in the eye. Just as in the fields, I know he sees me. But now the field guard's eyes hold something other than hate and loathing.

His voice cracks as he addresses us. "My father was one of those killed," he says abruptly.

"I . . . I'm sorry." Jovi says.

An awkward silence follows.

The guard turns to me. "If you will allow it, we would like to come with you."

I let out a breath. Now he is the one looking up at me. And the taste of soil he kicked into my mouth is still fresh. The other guards and Mongers don't know of my history with the man speaking for them. They watch us, desperate.

The guard reaches up, rubbing his face with the scarred hand I remember. Damaged from working the fields. The same hand is now speckled with tiny bloody puncture wounds from the battle. He clears his throat. "Please."

If La Cuna really is going to be a place to start over . . .

I reach behind me and grab watercells, handing the first to him. I nod to him. I will never remind the field guard of the past. But, I think I won't have to. He and I will both remember.

He nods back. "The Patrol will take the rear," he says. "If anyone follows, we should be the ones to protect the group."

The guard holds a gun out to Jovi.

"Nah, man," Jovi says, pointing ahead. "We won't need that where we're going."

The guard tucks the gun back at his waist.

With over forty wagons, we travel thirteen days with the weight of one hundred and eighty-eight Cascabeles, forty-five orphans, and sixteen Cloaks. And twenty-six additional Pocatelans, including families, guards, and Mongers. I may not be flying back this time, but even carrying so much— including the three new snake scars on my neck, carved by Jo—my heart feels like it's soaring.

When the plateaus of the river valley come into view, and I know we're within a few hours of La Cuna, Gabi smacks my leg over and over. "Hey," she says. "Someone's out there."

Sure enough, in the middle of nowhere, three lone figures stand in front of a collapsing tent.

As we approach, the woman clutches the baby swaddled to her chest. The man stares at the line of wagons, eyes wide. I recognize Nathaniel and his family. And if we all know who he is, he must recognize us as Cascabeles. The gathering of people must make no sense to him.

The family stands frozen. I lift my hand for the others to stop.

"Stay here," I say to Gabi and Andrew as I step down.

Nathaniel and his family's limbs are skeletal, and I think about how long they've survived out here, with only what they had left from their home. I hand Evelyn water and it spills down her sunburnt cheeks as she drinks.

"We're . . . we're lost," the Monger whispers.

Evelyn hands him the watercell, and it trembles in his hand. He sees me watching, and he tucks it behind his back. What must he think? Cascabeles escaped from Pocatel? Maybe he thinks we took the others as prisoners? I imagine he is feeling the same fear we felt every day before.

"Hello, Nathaniel," I say, using his real name.

His gaunt eyes go wide, and his wife squeezes his arm.

"Don't be afraid. Would you like to come with us?" I ask.

He leans in, and his whispered words are shaky. "How do you know my name?"

I smile. "We're starting over . . . Monger. You're welcome to start over with us. We could use your help."

He stares at me with the same confusion that covered his face when the Imperator doomed him and his family. But I will take that man's twisted words and give them new meaning. Hope.

My voice shakes too as I speak the words: "Your exile is over."

39

IN A SLOW MARCH, WE ENTER LA CUNA. THE PAST FEW
years, we've kept our eyes to the ground beneath us for survival.
There has not been much time for joy. Now, Cascabel laughter
and happy sobs echo in our new home.

Gabi gasps. "Leandro . . ."

"Yo sé," I smile. "It's a lot at first." I wink at Jovi.

Gabi slumps to the floor and stares up at the pine tree. The
babbling of the river is even louder than the peoples' voices. "It's

real," she says breathlessly. Just like she had in the fields, she closes her eyes, tilting her head to the sky and sniffing the air. "It *is* real," she whispers again.

From now on, I will make sure Gabi can look to the sky as much as she looks to the earth.

While we've been gone, the other Alebrijes have replanted half of what was uprooted. Small plants have already started sprouting from Hopper and Charlie's work.

They all stand ahead of us in a group, like they did that first day I arrived. Even though I can't hear them, I can sense they are nervous. Charlie is tapping his foot back and forth between the ground, and Oso's paw is turning soil-brown, then copper, then brown again. Cat, Wolf, Shelter Mutt, and the puppies remain toward the back. Hopper hops back and forth, dirt flinging up behind him.

The people walking around start to stare at the Alebrijes, and the Alebrijes stare back. Even though Jovi and I tried to explain, the people fixate on them, holding on to one another with wide eyes.

Then suddenly, Oso breaks free from the Alebrijes and runs toward us excitedly. People scream as Oso singles out a Cascabel man and clomps after him. The terrified, yelping man runs away from her, around the fields of La Cuna, before I can stop Oso to explain she's scaring la cagada out of her father and he doesn't understand exactly who or what she is yet.

Oso's the first to follow me into the room where we've left the Cloaks. It turns out she's almost as short as me, with brown hair and dark skin.

"It's better if your father meets you again the way he remembers you. But now . . ." I smile. "We can return whenever we want. If you choose to be Oso again, you can." I pull Dolores's tools from my pocket, but leave my hummingbird body inside.

Oso turns her Alebrije eyes to a glass of water. Beside us, Ari slices cooked potato and squash and sets it on a plate.

"Getting used to your human body again is rough at first," I say. "You'll have to eat slowly."

Charlie tucks into a roll and spirals up my arm, crouching on my shoulder. Hopper watches from the door. The glint of Cat's and Wolf's eyes reflect from within the hallway outside.

Oso opens her Spark compartment.

"Ready?" I say, dropping water into the tool. I glance at Charlie with my good eye. "This is delicate work, so don't bump me."

Hopper's head turns abruptly, and I'm pretty sure Charlie just made a joke or rude comment.

"You're next," I say to Charlie. "Why don't you go find yourself for me." In a blur of blue and green, Charlie rolls over to the tall, thin Cloak with freckles who kept wandering off. I know that Charlie has no family waiting for him outside like Oso. He stares at his body for a minute, then spins off, passing Cat and Wolf in the hallway, leaving us behind.

"Should I go get him?" Ari asks.

"No," I swallow over a lump in my throat. Even though my heart hurts for him, I think he knows he has us, whether he's a boy or a chameleon drone. "It looks like he wants to stay as he is for now."

I SPOT EZRA camouflaged in the branches halfway up the great pine. But the Alebrijes say he's yet to connect with anyone. Jovi, Ari, and I sit at the base of the tree, watching as the people explore their new home.

On the opposite side of the pine, Jo sits with a far larger—and happier—crowd of children than I've ever seen at the puppeteer's stage. "So, the little frog did not listen to his mother. He wandered away and was caught in the first storm of winter."

Jovi, Ari, and I snicker at all the "Oh nos!" and gasps from the children.

"What a stupid rana," Gabi says.

"Yes, es trágico," Jo says somberly. "And it is worse! The little ice rana was frozen alive!"

Andrew squeals out: "Then what happened?"

"Well, his mother searched and searched," Jo says. "But she and her other children had to hop south for a warmer river."

"Is that the end?" another child asks.

"Oh, no," Jo says. "His mother did not give up hope. She returned in the spring and asked the Creators to return her son to her." He claps his hands together. "And the Creators sent the sun and its rays to thaw the ground, and the naughty little ice frog came back to life, and never wandered off from his mother again!"

Clapping fills the air.

Gabi sighs. "That still doesn't tell me where the ice rana lived..."

I scan the room and see some of us, like the field guard, repairing ladders and helping others to climb up and find which homes will be theirs. Nathaniel, Lilith, and the one-armed Monger have found rooms next to one another, on the main floor.

Others are playing at the river's edge. Both Pocatelans and Cascabeles laugh as they kick and throw water onto one another.

Ahead, Jovi's abuela shakes her head at our crooked rows of plants. She sits next to one of the wide-leafed plants with yellow flowers and smiles at Jovi. She nods her head as she pulls off dead leaves. I look at the growing rows of plants, so long they disappear in the distance, some of them fruiting already. We will have more than we could ever eat.

Ari and Jovi are watching it all too. Are they thinking what I am?

"You know," I say softly, "La Cuna can't belong only to us."

"What are you saying?" Ari asks. But I think she knows.

I sigh and face them both. "We should at least ask if any want to join us here?"

I can tell the question pains Jovi, as it does me. The image of the fighting and chaos in Pocatel, and the pain of what we've lived through these past few years, feels too recent. To welcome that into La Cuna, feels like a betrayal to whoever created this beautiful place. But I know that soon the disease in Pocatel's papa fields will decrease their food supply even more.

Ari smiles, a little guiltily. "There are other ways to share than just bringing them here, Leandro."

"What do you mean?" Jovi asks.

"Plants, seeds . . . then they can have this in Pocatel."

For a bit we are all silent. Transporting new plants and seeds back to Pocatel will take some planning, but if we do it cautiously. . . . Maybe we can protect what we have here and still help them.

"I think that is the best idea so far," Jovi suddenly speaks much more loudly. "If only we knew of a transport drone who could help us . . ."

I glance up at Ezra, who's still hidden between the branches, keeping watch over Rose's grave. So far he's refused to show me who his Cloak is, but there's only one Pocatelan Cloak left, and he has his jaw clenched so tight it might crack.

Even though I know he can hear us, Ezra won't look down. I ask Jovi and Ari to leave. I climb the tree to join him. Maybe if it's just us, I can explain all that's happened. But as soon as I get close, he flies away into the night sky.

I don't know if he'll return.

A few minutes later, I notice Oso waiting at the bottom of the tree. Oso the human is as gentle and delicate as the squash blossoms . . . like Oso. She doesn't rush me or yell for me to hurry down. Instead, she sits to listen to one of Jo's stories. Eventually, she walks to the other side of the tree and calls up to me: "Tortoise would not leave their eggs."

I smile. "That does not surprise me," I call back.

"I think they are happy where they are," Oso continues. "And they invited me back to visit any time."

"Thank you for that, Oso."

"No," she replies, walking away, without giving me another name. "Thank *you* for introducing me to a new friend."

I think of how Tortoise the Skillful might have a longer, happier life in their burrow than most of us. I'll keep their Spark—and the Sparks of the missing Alebrijes—safe for as long as I live.

I crush the green pine needles between my fingers. High in the tree, I feel free again. I can tell this feeling isn't going anywhere. I stare down at the fields that are now even more full of life, with all the people. From within the vines and the homes hidden in their shade, voices and laughter fill La Cuna. I breathe in air that is not filled with dust. I listen to the roar of water that will bring even more growing things.

I think of the words my mother said so long ago, as we looked in the *World Book* of J. and the picture of the word *juh-uhhh-ngle*:

"When you see even the smallest bit of green, know that someone who has left the world before is sending us a bit of the Old-World back, reminding us we are still loved."

In this place I thought impossible, I am surrounded by more green than I ever thought I'd see.

I close my eyes. Dark hair falls over my mother's shoulders as she holds the water to my lips. I squeeze her fevered hand. "Mama?"

"Drink, Leandro," she says.

When I look at her, this time I finally do see her eyes. They are golden brown, and filled with tears. Dark freckles cover her nose. Her breathing is rattled. I remember. It is her. It is real.

"I think I must go be with your father now." She rubs her hand over one of the scars on her neck.

"Please don't leave me. I'm too young, Mama. I'm too little. How can I take care of Gabi?"

She pulls me in tight. Gabi sleeps at her other side. I nestle my head into her neck. "You may be small, mi Leandro, pero you will do great things if you think with your heart as much your mind."

"Tengo miedo, Mama."

She begins to sing the words quietly:

Acitrón, de un
Fandango zango, zango.

I begin singing softly with her.

Sabaré de la randela
Con su triqui, triqui tran.

She smiles and kisses my face. We start over but sing no faster.

Acitrón, de un
Fandango zango, zango.

I take a breath, and realize she is no longer singing with me.

40

· · · ☾ · · ·

I TIE THE BLINDFOLD OVER GABI'S EYES AND LEAD HER ACROSS the fields. The smell around us is more powerful than that last day at the market. Dark green leaves, close to the ground, flow over two entire rows. Squash, four times the size of potatoes, lie under the vines Charlie and I pollinated less than a month ago. As we walk down a row filled with clusters of small red and orange spheres, I steer Gabi away from the ground fruit, but her foot catches the edge of one and it bursts open. Red juice, soft fruit, and tiny white seeds squish from between her toes.

"Ewwww!" she cries.

I giggle.

"Leandro," she scolds, "if we're marching through a dung heap, and that was a larva, you're going to pay."

In the next field, even the leaves of the root vegetables grow high. The potato leaves are already beginning to wilt, ready to harvest. "No," I say. "Estamos seguros. Only papas."

"Speaking of potatoes," she says. "Do you know why potatoes see double?"

"Por qué?" I ask, confused.

She grins. "Because they have so many eyes."

"Terrible, Gabi," I sigh, but I'm hiding my smile. "Terrible."

The air grows sweet. Ahead, I see them. I point in the other direction to distract Gabi. I lift a large leaf. They are hidden beneath, just like Charlie said they would be.

I lean down and gently pick one off. It's still small, but perfect.

I remove Gabi's blindfold and she stares down at my hand. She gasps.

I take it and place it into her palm.

She lifts it slowly, then stops, looking up at me.

"Está bien," I say. "It belongs to you."

Gabi closes her eyes and lifts it to her mouth. Her chin trembles as she takes a bite of the strawberry.

EPILOGUE

⋅ ∘ ❨ ∘ ⋅

MY KNEES CRACK AS I RISE TO ONE KNEE. I UNDERSTAND
now why Lita always moaned when she stood. "You've come a
long way to see me."

Even in the dim turquoise glow of the cave, I recognize Councilwoman Fu by her strong posture. She links her arm through
mine, pulling me the rest of the way up. "The council didn't want
to disturb you, Petra." She stares around the cave and touches a
glowing cave worm. It skitters away. She scans the room.

My vision has gotten worse, leaving me with barely a pinhole, but I can still see her staring at my unmade bed.

"Your trips here are lasting longer and longer," she says.

I step in front of her to block her view. "What is it I can help you with?"

She takes a deep breath. Then, "Do you know what Alebrijes are?"

I flinch back at the unexpected word. I smile, thinking of the animals here on Sagan. So much like alebrijes: strange, and too bright and colorful to seem real. I snicker. "You came all this way to ask me that? Of course I do. I just haven't heard them mentioned in four hundred and fifty years."

Councilwoman Fu sets a librex on the table. "This came through yesterday." She turns it on.

A hologram of a woman stands in front of me. Her peppery hair falls like a wild waterfall down her long white dress, her skin nearly as dark as Lita's. If I didn't know any better . . .

A tree lies behind the woman. I can't help a small gasp. "Hyperion!" Vines crawl up the inside of the giant room the woman stands in. Green fields lie behind her. A river?

"My name is Gabriela Rivera," the woman in the holograph says. "And I am sending this message from what was once called Eeearth. We did not understand for many years that our settlement, La Cuna, was a ship hidden by time, and that those who concealed it in dirt and stone did so to protect themselves."

I lean against the wall to steady myself. This woman who looks like my Lita—who speaks with a similar accent—is alive and on a place I never thought I'd see again with my own eyes. A home. I take deep breaths. They burn, but I hold in my tears.

"La Cuna allowed us to start over. And if you can hear this, it has also allowed me to share a story with you. Along with the Alebrijes, we have made Eeearth new again with gardens and water. Our people are happy again. If you'd like to come, bienvenidos a todos en La Cuna."

I pause the holograph and lean toward the woman. "Even the most unbelievable stories . . . comienzan con una pisca de verdad." I smile and turn to Councilwoman Fu. "Someone with a story to tell is inviting us back . . ." My words hiccup. I pretend to clear my throat and press the play button once more.

The woman continues, a proud smile covering her face now. She carves her leg in an arc in the ground front of her, rattling her tongue like a rattlesnake. "Tccch, tccch, tccch." Tears fall down her cheeks. Her voice trembles. ". . . corazones puros y espíritus fuertes son quienes heredarán la tierra." She lifts her chin high and smiles proudly. "I would like to tell you how this came to be. This is the story of Leandro the Mighty . . ."

ACKNOWLEDGMENTS

Writing can be solitary. But I have made so many true friends along this journey, I am never lonely. And those friends have become part of an irreplaceable family, and I have many to thank.

First and foremost, within the pages of this book is woven the spirit of its editor, Nick Thomas. Nick never ceases to cleverly ask the questions guiding my words in the most interesting of directions, finding what is truly at the heart of each story. He has been my partner on my writing journey, and I will never find sufficient words to thank him for a sincere friendship, and the care and kindness he's given to both me and my work. I hope we travel many more miles together.

So many thanks to my agent, Allison Remcheck, who is a constant source of encouragement and friendship. I am forever grateful for her support, but for also knowing which stories are ready to be written, and those I need to dream on just a bit more. Thank you for believing in me.

Thank you to my husband, Mark, with whom I get to travel the road of life with dogs and chickens and hilarious children. How lucky am I to get to fall asleep with a fellow writer and pester him just as he's about to doze off with my random story ideas and bizarre plotting questions! They say to surround yourself with those you aspire to be. And for that, I have the funniest human, with the most giving and gentlest of souls, as my partner.

Thanks to the people who give me day-to-day strength: My children who are an unending source of writing material. My best friend, Mai Nguyen, for keeping life real, and being an example of strength in a sometimes tough world. My dad, for spending a bit of each day to visit with me and remind me of where I've come from and who formed me.

To Irene Vázquez., who entered my life so quietly and gracefully with intuitive editorial notes. And it continues . . . I now call them the dearest of friends and a priceless member of my family. I'm so proud of both Irene's professional accomplishments and poetry. They are a wonder!

Many thanks to Antonio Gonzalez Cerna for his support and friendship in life and on the road! A broker of friendships, I can never thank him enough for introducing me to new friends in librarians, teachers, students, and booklovers at events across the country. What a gift you've given me.

Thank you to my publishing house family Levine Querido, held together with a mortar of love and support at its heart, Arthur A. Levine. Thank you, Arthur, for creating the most unique of abodes amongst so many. I am so proud to say I live here.

And to others on Team Querido for their help on *Alebrijes*: Mil gracias to Arely Guzmán for their editorial assistance, and assistance with the Spanish throughout the book. Kerry Taylor for all the behind-the-scene work. And Danielle Maldonado for her last-minute help!

As always, greatest of thanks to my agency family at Stimola Literary Studio: Rosemary Stimola, Peter Ryan, Allison Hellegers, Erica Rand Silverman, Adriana Stimola, and Nick Croce, and of course, my aforementioned agent, Allison Remcheck. What a team! Special thanks to my foreign rights agent, Allison Hellegers, who assists in sending my characters around the world to meet readers abroad and in many languages!

Love and gratitude to my critique group family, The Papercuts: Cindy Roberts, Mark Maciejewski, Maggie Adams, Eli Isenberg, David Colburn, and Jason Hine.

Much gratitude to my newest friend, David Álvarez, for creating a cover that brings to the forefront a spirit to this book I would have never dreamed. His image lures the curious in, inviting readers to join a world of secrets and shadows. With goosebumps, we willingly enter, welcomed by the brilliant imagery David brings to this story.

Thank you to Patrick Collins for helping with the design of this gorgeous cover.

Thank you to Richard Oriolo for the interior design of this book.

To Freesia Blizard, Production at Chronicle, thank you for making this book so beautiful.

Gratitude to Mandi Andrejka for catching errors and fixing details.

Sending the deepest gratitude to my hometown librarian, Harriet Hughes. After so many decades, we were able to reconnect! Mrs. Hughes was the first to put books into the hands of a shy, insecure girl. And when she did, she handed her the books she thought she might like, and maybe a few she needed. In doing so, the small-town librarian created a lover of literature, science fiction, and folklore. So long ago, Harriet Hughes planted the seeds of a future writer. Greatest of thanks to her, and all librarians who give this gift to young readers.

Thank you to the oilfield, agricultural field, and farm workers of Central California and the San Joaquin Valley for whom the characters, the Cascabeles, were inspired; workers I am proud to say I am descended from. You are a brave and hardworking people. In this book, your strength is what I imagined would be within survivors at the end of the world. And the people of the San Joaquin Valley are the spirit and heart of those I hoped would survive. Those who would take hints of the beauty of a complex culture hundreds of years into the future of a desolate world.

Finally, to all the children and students I have met over the past few years, thank you for reading my stories. I have met so many future storytellers, and I am anxious for the day I will be able to read your books.

ABOUT THE AUTHOR

Donna Barba Higuera grew up in Central California and now lives in the Pacific Northwest. She has spent her entire life blending folklore with her experiences into stories that fill her imagination. Donna is the author of *El Cucuy Is Scared, Too!*; *The Yellow Handkerchief*; *Lupe Wong Won't Dance*, winner of a Pura Belpré Honor and a PNBA award; and *The Last Cuentista*.

The Last Cuentista was the winner of the Newbery Medal and the Pura Belpré Medal.

Visit Donna at www.dbhiguera.com.

Some Notes on this Book's Production

Art for the jacket, case, and interiors was drawn by David Álvarez. The text and display were set by Westchester Publishing Services, in Danbury, CT, using Celestia Antiqua, a serif designed by US designer Mark van Bronkhorst, evoking the roughness and irregularity of pre-digital printing. The book was printed on FSC™-certified 98gsm Yunshidai Ivory paper and bound in China.

Production supervised by Freesia Blizard
Book case and endpapers designed by David Álvarez and Patrick Collins
Book interiors designed by Richard Oriolo
Editor: Nick Thomas
Assistant Editor: Irene Vázquez

LQ